ERINN MAXWELL

Of Heather and Thistle

First edition

ISBN: 979-8-218-61638-0

Editing by Emileen Judge
Cover art by Bia Shuja

This book was professionally typeset on Reedsy.
Find out more at reedsy.com

For the wanderers who return home, the dreamers who chase stories, and the romantics who believe in second chances.

What's meant for you won't pass you
by.

Scottish Proverb

Contents

Preface

When I first began writing *Of Heather and Thistle*, I thought I was telling a story about a woman renovating an old Scottish estate and unexpectedly falling in love. But as the words filled the pages, I realized this wasn't just a romance—it was a story about **belonging, healing, and** what it means to **stop running** and finally face the truths we spend our lives avoiding.

At its heart, this is a story about Heather Campbell—a woman who has spent her life trying to outrun grief, convinced that if she keeps moving, she can outrun the weight of her past. She arrives in Scotland believing Glenoran is nothing more than an obligation, a piece of history she's meant to tie up and leave behind. But as she strips back the layers of the house, she's also **stripping back the layers of herself.**

Glenoran is more than just a setting—it's **a reflection of Heather herself.** Like her, it has been abandoned, its walls bearing the marks of time and neglect. And yet, underneath all the dust and decay, something substantial remains. **Something worth saving.**

Flynn Duncan is more than just a love interest. He is the embodiment of **steadiness, patience, and home.** He is the counterweight to Heather's instinct to flee, the man who sees her—not just the version she presents to the world, but the woman underneath. He doesn't **chase** her, doesn't **fix** her. He simply **waits.** And in doing so, he gives her the space to finally realize that staying is a choice she is allowed to make.

And then there's the history—the mystery, the lost stories, the pieces of the past that refuse to be forgotten. Heather doesn't just uncover Glenoran's history—she **reclaims it.** The artifacts, the letters, and the whispered legends of long-lost treasures are all reminders that history isn't just something that happened. It's **something we carry.**

This book is for anyone who has ever felt unmoored or questioned where they belong. It's for those who have spent their lives feeling like they were meant to **be somewhere else,** only to realize that what they were searching for was in front of them all along.

Most of all, this book is for people who, like Heather, finally find the courage to **stop running.**

Because sometimes, the greatest adventure isn't in leaving. It's in **staying.**

For those who have ever felt the pull of a place they've never been, for the dreamers who chase stories, and for the romantics who believe in second chances— this book is for you.

To love, history, and adventure,
Erinn Maxwell

Welcome to *Of Heather and Thistle.*

Acknowledgments

No book is ever written alone, and *Of Heather and Thistle* is no exception. Although this story may have started in my imagination, it was shaped, encouraged, and strengthened by the incredible people around me.

To my **husband**, who has stood by me through every moment of doubt and every excited ramble about characters who feel as real to me as the world itself—thank you for your patience, belief in me, and endless support. I couldn't have done this without you.

To my **uncle**, who was not Charles—who was more than his demons, but carried a weight too heavy to bear. I wish his story had found the healing that Heather's did. This book, in part, is about the courage to stay, to fight for redemption, to choose something beyond the past. He didn't get that chance, but I will always love him, even in the chapters that remain unwritten.

To my editor, **Emileen Judge**, your keen eye and thoughtful insights helped refine parts of this story into something stronger and more true to itself. Thank you for your patience, your guidance, and for asking the hard questions that made all the difference.

To **my big sister**, thank you for listening to me obsess over plot twists, historical details, and the perfect way to describe a Scottish sunrise. Thank you for your enthusiasm and for reminding me why I love storytelling. Your encouragement kept me going through every revision.

To my **readers**, thank you for stepping into this world with me. Stories come alive only when shared, and I am endlessly grateful that you chose to share in this one.

To **Scotland**, a land of stories, history, and undeniable magic—your rolling hills, ancient castles, and whispered legends inspired every page of this book.

And finally, **to anyone** who has ever felt the pull of home, the weight of history, or the hope of second chances, this book is for you.

With gratitude,
Erinn Maxwell

Prologue

The last time Heather saw her mother, the world was still warm.

She remembered the scent of lavender drifting through the air, the way the afternoon light slanted through the kitchen window, painting golden streaks across the floor. Her mother's laughter had filled the space between them, soft and lilting, like a melody only they knew.

And then, nothing.

Grief had no shape at nine years old—not the cold precision of condolences, nor the dull ache of longing would settle into her bones years later. It was a sudden and terrible silence. A house too big without its heartbeat. A father who stumbled more than he stood. A closet that smelled of her mother's perfume long after she was gone.

People came and went, their faces blurred by whispered voices and hushed reassurances. "She's too young to understand." Or "She'll forget in time." But Heather understood enough.

Her mother was gone.

And her father—though still there —was someone else entirely. The man who once lifted her onto his shoulders and made her laugh with silly voices had been swallowed by something dark and unrelenting. Brandy replaced warmth. Words slurred into something sharp, something that cut even when she couldn't understand the meaning. The man who once tucked her in at night now let doors slam and shadows stretch in long shapes against the walls.

She learned to be quiet. To stay out of his way. To flinch before she even knew why.

Then came Ivy. Her best friend. Bright as summer; fierce as a promise. She swept into Heather's life like a breath of fresh air, filling the silence with stories, secrets, laughter, and light. She gave Heather something to hold onto, something to believe in. The kind of friendship that wrapped around her like a shield, keeping the worst of the world at bay.

And for a while, it was enough.

But grief does not fade—it lingers, waiting for the right moment to resurface. And years later, when Heather stood at her father's grave, she realized the past never truly lets go.

Chapter 1

Heather Mackenzie Campbell had spent her entire life surrounded by silence, but none as deafening as the stillness that filled her father's empty house.

She lingered in the middle of the living room, staring at the faded floral wallpaper and sagging furniture, barely aware of the scuff of wheels against the floor behind her. The air smelled of stale beer and dust. But beneath it lingered something colder—sterile. Final.

A murmur of voices. The clipped tones of professionals. The metallic rattle of a stretcher passing through the doorway.

And then, with a quiet click, the door shut.

His funeral was small. A mercy, really.

Charles Campbell wasn't the kind of man people mourned.

He had lived hard, drank harder, and left little more than a trail of unpaid bills and broken promises. Heather had been the dutiful daughter, seeing him through his final days despite everything. And now, at twenty-three, she found herself utterly alone.

She stood apart from the handful of attendees clustered near the gravesite. Her black dress and wool peacoat hugged her frame as the wind tangled her red curls, whipping them against her pale skin in unruly waves. The minister's voice droned on, solemn and steady, but the words barely reached her. Her gaze stayed fixed on the casket—a plain pine box that summed up her father's existence. No flourish. No legacy. Just a hollow vessel lowered into the earth.

A few neighbors had shown up out of obligation rather than grief. Mrs. Dempsey, who lived two doors down, dabbled in casseroles and gossip. Mr. Frawley, who once yelled at her father for tossing beer cans into his yard, stood with his hat in his hands, looking uncomfortable. None of these people had truly known Charles Campbell.

None of them had endured the sharpness of his anger or the weight of his silence as she had.

Heather didn't cry. She hadn't cried in years—not for him.

The cloying scent of white lilies clung to the air, thick and too sweet. Her mother had loved lilies. She had filled vases with them, pressed them between book pages, breathed in their scent like it was part of her soul. It felt wrong for them to be here, resting atop the grave of a man who had done nothing but tarnish every memory of the woman who once loved them.

When the service ended, people shuffled away, murmuring platitudes they probably thought she needed to hear.

"He's at peace now."

"He's in a better place."

Heather only nodded, their words sliding off her like water on stone.

Silence settled over the gravesite. The sky hung low and heavy, promising snow. She exhaled slowly, letting the weight of solitude press in around her.

Then came the sharp sound of footsteps crunching on frozen ground.

"Ms. Campbell?"

Heather turned to see Robert Ellis, her father's lawyer, standing a few feet away. Tall and stately, he had an air of precision about him, dressed impeccably in a dark overcoat and leather gloves. Too composed for the rawness of the day.

"Mr. Ellis," she greeted him, her voice quiet.

"I'm sorry for your loss," he said, inclining his head.

She nodded, unsure how to respond. *Loss* didn't feel like the right word. Her father had been gone long before his heart stopped beating. She had lost him years ago.

"I won't take much of your time," Ellis continued, his tone polite but businesslike. Reaching into his coat pocket, he pulled out a thick, cream-colored envelope. "Your father left this with me some time ago, with instructions to deliver it to you in the event of his passing."

Heather's breath caught.

Her name was scrawled across the front in her father's unmistakable handwriting—slanted, uneven, like everything else about him.

She swallowed hard, shoving her hands deeper into her coat pockets. She didn't reach for it.

She wasn't sure she wanted to know.

"What is it?" she asked, her voice barely above a whisper.

"I'm afraid I don't know," Ellis replied. "He insisted it be given to you directly. I understand it contains something significant, but the details are known only to him—and now, to you."

A hesitation. Then, in a softer tone, he added, "You know, your father and I worked together for years. He was a brilliant lawyer before... everything happened. We started at the same firm. Built our careers side by side. When he lost his way, I tried to help, but he wouldn't let me." His expression shifted, something somber threading into his professionalism. "Handling his affairs now—making sure this reaches you—is my way of honoring what we once had."

Heather hesitated a moment longer, then slowly reached out.

Her gloved fingers brushed against the smooth paper as she took the envelope from him. It felt heavier than it should have, as though it carried more than just words.

Her father had never been the type to leave kind words behind.

What could he possibly have to say to her now?

And why did she suddenly feel like a child again, curious but bracing for disappointment?

"Thank you," she murmured, her voice barely audible.

Ellis nodded. "If you have any questions, you know how to reach me."

Heather barely registered his departure, the sound of his retreating footsteps muffled by the growing wind. She didn't know how long she stood there after he left.

Alone.

The cold crept through her coat. The snow melted against

her cheeks. But she didn't move.

Her name stared back at her from the envelope, haunting and familiar. She slipped it into her bag, her chest tightening as she tried to push away the flood of emotions—resentment, sorrow, the sting of old wounds reopening when she'd spent years trying to forget.

She knelt beside the grave after everyone was gone, the bitter chill of the ground through her wool tights.

The words engraved on the headstone were plain, to the point:

Charles Malcolm Campbell
Beloved Father and Husband.

Beloved.

She almost laughed.

"You weren't much of that, were you?" she whispered.

The wind whipped through the cemetery, pulling at her curls. Her fingers traced the rough letters of his name, grounding her.

She didn't know why she stayed. Maybe out of duty. Maybe out of habit.

Or maybe because this was the only goodbye she had to give.

"You made things so hard," she said softly, her voice trembling under the weight of years she had kept bottled up. "You could've... You could've tried, Dad. For me. For Mom. But you didn't."

Her voice broke.

She pressed her hand to her mouth, willing herself to stay composed. If she let go now, she wasn't sure she'd be able to pull herself back together. For years, no matter how far she ran, a part of her had still been tied to him.

But now?

That thread had finally snapped.

And she wasn't sure if she felt free or just lost.

She stood, brushing the dirt from her knees. The sky was gray, the clouds heavy with snow—a perfect match for the heaviness in her chest.

As she turned to leave, she hesitated, glancing back one last time. She wasn't sure if she was mourning her father, or the wounds he left behind.

Maybe both.

Maybe that was the cruelest thing—grief and anger living side by side, neither willing to let her go.

"Goodbye, Dad," she murmured. "I hope you find whatever peace you couldn't here."

A strange mixture of relief and guilt settled over her as she walked away.

She wasn't sure what came next.

But for the first time in her life, it was hers to decide.

Chapter 2

Heather unlocked the door to her apartment and stepped inside, the scent of fresh coffee and laundry detergent wrapping around her like a familiar embrace. It was a stark contrast to the drafty, stale house she'd grown up in—a house that had never really felt like home.

Her apartment wasn't much—a small one-bedroom tucked into the second floor of an older building—but it was hers. She had picked every piece of furniture and every mug in the cupboard, carving out a safe space for herself, for the first time in her life.

Byrdie was waiting for her, perched on the back of the sofa like a tiny sentinel. The tortoiseshell cat blinked at her with wide, curious eyes before hopping down with a chirp, weaving through Heather's legs.

"Hey, Byrdie," she murmured, crouching to scratch behind the cat's ears. Byrdie purred, pressing into her touch, her warmth a welcome comfort against the lingering chill Heather still felt from standing at the gravesite.

Heather shrugged off her coat, draping it over the arm of the couch, and moved into the kitchen. The heels of her boots clicked softly against the hardwood as she filled Byrdie's bowl. The kitchen was quiet except for the faint hum of the refrigerator and the soft crunch of kibble.

She sank onto the couch, exhaustion settling into her bones. For a moment, she simply sat there, letting the silence stretch. Then, with slow, deliberate movements, she pulled the envelope from her bag and set it on the table. She ran her fingers over the heavy paper, tracing the uneven slant of her father's handwriting.

She could open it. Read whatever parting words he had left for her. But if she did, it would become real.

Heather inhaled sharply, then let out a slow, measured breath.

"Not tonight," she whispered, setting the envelope aside.

Instead, she grabbed the fleece blanket draped over the back of the couch and curled into it. A moment later, Byrdie hopped up beside her, pressing into her side with a contented sigh. Heather closed her eyes and let herself breathe, let herself feel the quiet comfort of her cat's warmth, let herself be still.

Tomorrow. Tomorrow, she would face whatever was inside that envelope.

Tonight, she just needed to rest.

Morning arrived too soon.

Heather woke to soft light filtering through the curtains and Byrdie's insistent meows at the foot of the bed. Her body felt heavy—like the weight of yesterday had followed her into sleep. She stared at the ceiling for a long moment, feeling unmoored. The funeral was over. Her father was gone. And yet, the envelope still sat on the kitchen table, unanswered.

Byrdie let out an impatient chirp before hopping onto the bed, nudging her head against Heather's arm.

"Alright, alright. I'm up," Heather grumbled, raking a hand through her tangled curls as she swung her legs over the side of the bed.

She shuffled into the kitchen, Byrdie trotting close behind, her tail flicking with purpose. After feeding her, Heather turned to the kettle, filling it without thinking. It was a small ritual she had developed—always filling it the night before, so mornings were just a little easier.

The water began to warm, the soft hum filling the silence. The whistle eventually curled steam into the air, but Heather barely heard it. Her gaze had locked onto the envelope.

Still unopened. Still waiting.

She hesitated, fingers hovering just above it.

She could do it now. Tear it open. Face whatever was inside.

But her hand faltered.

Not yet.

Instead, she grabbed her coat. If she stayed here, alone with her thoughts, they would suffocate her. If anyone could pull her out of her head, it was Ivy.

The city was still waking up when Heather stepped outside, the crisp morning air biting at her cheeks. She tucked her scarf tighter around her neck and started down the quiet, tree-lined street toward the bus stop.

A few minutes later, she climbed aboard and settled into her usual seat by the window. The ride was short, the city passing by in a blur of weathered brownstones, quiet storefronts, and coffee shops flicking on their lights. The green-and-white sign of *The Roasted Bean* waited for her—just like it always did.

Inside, the smell of espresso and cinnamon wrapped around her like a warm embrace.

Ivy was already there, tucked into their usual corner, hands wrapped around a steaming latte. Her golden-blonde hair was mostly hidden beneath a knit beanie, but a few loose strands framed her face, catching the light. She looked effortlessly put-together, as always, her oversized scarf draped perfectly around her delicate frame. Ivy had the kind of beauty that turned heads without trying.

She spotted Heather and waved, her turquoise eyes bright with warmth.

"Hey, you!" Ivy greeted as Heather slid into the chair across from her. "I was starting to think you were going to bail and leave me to awkwardly flirt with the barista for entertainment."

Heather smirked. "Trust me, I debated it. But pacing my apartment like a crazy person wasn't a better option."

Ivy unwrapped her scarf and shook out her golden waves, the movement easy, practiced. Attention always followed her, like moths to light. And Heather had never minded standing in the glow.

Ivy arched a brow. "So, rough morning?"

"Rough week," Heather corrected.

Ivy hummed knowingly. "Yeah, sounds about right. Funerals are kind of the Olympics of awkwardness. Did you at least make it through without anyone cornering you with unsolicited life advice?"

Heather exhaled a short laugh. "No unsolicited advice. But my dad's lawyer gave me an envelope with my name on it. He said it's important, but I haven't opened it."

Ivy's brows shot up. "Oh? Mystery mail? Are we talking heartfelt letter, surprise will, or a long-lost family scandal?"

Heather sighed, shaking her head. "I don't know. I'm too nervous to open it. What if it's something bad? It's not like it's going to change anything. He's gone."

Ivy tilted her head, studying her. "But what if it's not bad? What if it's something you need to see, even if it's hard?"

Heather's grip tightened around her coffee cup, her stomach twisting. Her father had never ended a conversation with kindness. What were the odds that his final words to her would be any different?

She exhaled slowly, looking up to find Ivy watching her. Steady. Unwavering.

Ivy had always believed in her—so deeply, so unquestionably—that it should have been reassuring. But sometimes, it felt like too much. Like Ivy wasn't just expecting her to succeed—she was expecting her to need her.

Heather wasn't sure how to include Ivy in this.

Silence stretched between them, the only sound the quiet hum of the coffee shop and the snow falling softly outside.

Then Ivy set her mug down with purpose. "No matter

what's in there, it doesn't change who you are. You're Heather *freaking* Campbell, and you figure it out. You always do!"

Heather let out a soft laugh. "You make me sound a lot cooler than I actually am."

"No, I just see you for who you really are." Ivy winked, draining the last sip of her coffee before stretching lazily. "Alright, I've gotta run—I'm meeting Theo for lunch. Not sure if it's a date, but hey, free food."

Heather nodded. "Yeah. I think I just need some time to think."

Ivy nudged Heather's coffee cup. "Just don't think too hard." Then, with another wink, she was gone.

Heather watched the snow drift outside, the weight of the envelope pressing against the edges of her thoughts.

She wasn't ready to go home—not yet.

So instead, she kept walking.

Chapter 3

When she reached the corner where she usually turned toward her apartment, she made a split-second decision and kept walking.

Her therapist's office was only a few blocks away, tucked into the second floor of an old brownstone building. Dr. Lily Andrews had been her therapist for the past year, ever since Heather had finally admitted to herself that she needed help untangling her past. At first, she'd resisted opening up, hesitant to expose the parts of herself she'd spent years hiding. But Lily had been patient, calm and steady, never pushing too hard.

Heather paused at the door, brushing snowflakes from her coat. She hadn't made an appointment, but Lily had always told her to stop by if needed. After a brief hesitation, she stepped inside.

The waiting room was quiet and warm, with the scent of vanilla lingering in the air. A small lamp cast a soft glow, and the receptionist, Brenda, looked up with a welcoming smile.

"Heather! I didn't see you on the schedule today," Brenda said warmly.

"Yeah, I—I don't have an appointment," Heather admitted, unwrapping her scarf. "I just... I was in the neighborhood and thought I'd see if Dr. Andrews had time today."

Brenda nodded, her smile never faltering. "Let me check." She tapped a few keys on her keyboard and then looked up. "You're in luck—her next session just canceled. She can see you in about ten minutes if that works?"

Heather nodded quickly, relief washing over her. "That's perfect. Thank you."

She sat on the plush couch in the waiting room, her hands folded tightly in her lap. Her thoughts buzzed as she tried to figure out where even to begin.

Brenda called her back ten minutes later, and Heather entered the familiar office. Lily stood near the window, watering a small plant on her desk. She turned and smiled warmly when she saw Heather.

"Heather," Lily said, setting the watering can aside. "What a nice surprise. Come in, have a seat."

She sat in the chair across from Lily, her coat still clutched in her hands. The office was as cozy as ever, with its soft lighting, shelves full of books, and a faintly humming space heater in the corner.

Lily sat cross-legged in her plush armchair, notebook resting in her lap. "I can tell something's on your mind," she said gently. "Want to talk about it?"

Heather hesitated, staring down at the fabric of her coat. She wasn't sure why she was nervous—Lily already knew most of it. She knew about her father, about the drinking, about the tangled mess of emotions she still hadn't fully processed.

"My dad's lawyer gave me an envelope after the funeral," she said slowly. "It has my name on it, and it's supposed to be important. But I haven't opened it yet. I can't."

Lily nodded, her expression calm and encouraging. "That makes sense. You've spent so long trying to distance your-self from your father's shadow—anything left unfinished between you is bound to feel overwhelming."

Heather let out a breath she hadn't realized she was holding. "Yeah," she admitted. "That's exactly it. I'm scared of what it might say—what it might mean. I've already got his stack of unpaid bills and his disaster of a house. What if this is just one more burden I have to carry?"

Lily tilted her head slightly. "That's a valid fear. But what do you think is in the envelope? What's the worst-case scenario your mind keeps circling back to?"

Heather exhaled, leaning back against the chair as she stared at the framed watercolor on the wall—a soft, abstract swirl of greens and blues. She often stared at it when words felt hard to form, as though the image might give her clarity.

"I don't know," she admitted, her voice barely above a whisper. "But it feels... final. Like the last thing tying me to him."

"You've been carrying the weight of your father's anger and grief for so long. Are you afraid it'll pull you back into the same old pattern—walking on eggshells, trying to keep everyone else from falling apart?"

Heather swallowed, her throat tightening. "Maybe. Proba-bly." She paused, her voice trembling slightly as she contin-ued. "I spent years taking care of him, you know? Cleaning up his messes, getting him to bed when he drank too much, making sure he ate. And I thought—when I finally moved out—that I'd feel free. But instead, I just feel guilty, even now — like I abandoned him in his addiction."

Lily leaned forward slightly, her expression warm and understanding. "That guilt has been with you a long time. Would opening that envelope help you let go of some of it?"

She hesitated. "I don't know."

Lily gave her a small smile. "Then let's reframe it. What if this envelope isn't about him? What if it's about you?"

Heather frowned slightly, the idea catching her off guard. "I've never thought of it like that."

Lily nodded. "You've been trying to move forward, to separate yourself from the pain of your past. Maybe this is one more step toward doing that. And if it feels too big to face alone, you have people who care about you: Ivy and me. You're not in this alone."

Heather nodded slowly, the weight of the envelope in her mind beginning to shift. She wasn't ready to open it yet, but Lily's words planted a seed of hope for healing that she hadn't felt before.

By the time she left the office, the cold air outside felt bracing rather than oppressive, but the snow had turned to icy slush that seeped through her boots. She climbed the stairs, a deep weariness still clinging to her limbs, but lighter somehow—like she was no longer carrying quite as much on her shoulders.

She unlocked the door as Byrdie greeted her on the welcome mat with an impatient meow, winding around her legs in protest, as if scolding her for being gone so long. Heather sighed, bending down to scratch behind her ears. "I know, I know—I took too long," she murmured. "You act like I abandoned you for weeks."

Byrdie flicked her tail dramatically, lifting her chin with an air of feline indignation. But the act didn't last long. As soon as Heather ran her fingers down her spine, Byrdie let out a throaty purr, her body arching into the touch. She gave Heather's ankle one last headbutt before trotting ahead, her fluffy tail swaying like a victory banner as she led the way inside.

Heather stepped through the doorway. The warmth of their comfortable apartment enveloped her as she slipped off her wet coat and hung it on the hook by the door. Her boots left tiny puddles of melted snowflakes on the worn, oak floor as she trudged toward her bedroom. She peeled off her soaked black dress in the quiet of her room, tossing it over the back of a chair. The thick, woolen tights clung to her damp legs as she peeled them off, revealing faint red ridges where the knit pattern had pressed into her skin.

Standing in her underwear, she turned toward the mirror on her closet door. She rarely looked at herself for too long—it always felt like more of a chore than a self-appreciation exercise—but today, the reflection seemed unavoidable. Her fiery curls were a tangled mess from the snow, the deep auburn strands damp and clinging to her face. She reached up, running her fingers through the knots, wincing as she hit a particularly stubborn tangle. Her hair was one of the things she'd always disliked about herself, though it had been one of her mother's most striking features.

Heather's mother, Eilidh Campbell, had a beauty that went far beyond her appearance. Her wild, strawberry-blonde curls framed a round, freckled face, and her deep green eyes sparkled with mischief. Her smile could brighten the gloomiest day—and when she laughed, it wasn't just sound; it was music.

She looked delicate, but her embrace had a quiet strength that made you feel invincible. Her joy was contagious, her presence radiant. Even now, Heather could close her eyes and see her—barefoot in the garden, humming a Celtic tune, her curls bouncing with every step like she was made of sunlight and song.

Her mother was a force of nature, a wildflower blooming where others couldn't. She was born under the open Scottish skies and carried the enchantment of the Highlands within her. She named her daughter Heather—to pass on the luck and beauty of the heather-covered hills of Inverness-shire that she'd grown up loving. Her lilting Scottish accent had been a song for Heather as a child—soothing and full of warmth. Their time together was far too short; every moment with her was infused with joy, wonder, and love. She saw beauty in everything—the sunlight filtering through trees, the tiniest insects, and the rain that most people tried to avoid.

Their little home was in the heart of Chicago, a far cry from the misty hills and rolling peaks her mother had once roamed. Though she loved the wild beauty of the mountains, life had led her here instead—to a city of towering skylines and bustling streets, where she built a different kind of home— one where she found new ways to stay connected to nature.

She filled their apartment with potted ferns and trailing ivy, tended a small herb garden on the windowsill, and never let a day go by without stepping outside to feel the sun on her skin. But it was never quite enough. So she and Heather's father took every opportunity to escape the concrete and glass, driving out to the woods whenever they could— camping in the cool, pine-scented air of the Wisconsin Northwoods or hiking through rugged trails in the Appalachians on longer trips. Those weekends away felt like stolen pockets of magic, where the hum of the city faded into rustling leaves and birdsong, and her mother could breathe deeply with her bare feet sinking into the earth like she belonged to it.

Heather spent her early summers running wild through the trees, pretending she was the queen of the fae or some fearless woodland adventurer. One of her most vivid memories of her mother was when Heather was seven years old. A warm spring day had suddenly turned into a sunshower, and Heather found her dancing in the front yard, twirling in her favorite green sundress and laughing with her father as if they were teenagers again. Heather had always called that green dress her mom's "fairy dress" because it was so light and airy. Made of soft chiffon, it skimmed her frame and billowed with every step, the fabric whispering against her skin. When Heather was little, she'd run her fingers over it, the cool, delicate material slipping between her hands.

She remembered another afternoon in the backyard, golden light filtering through the trees as her mother twirled barefoot in the grass, the dress fanning out around her like delicate, glowing gossamer wings. Heather had been six, convinced that if she looked closely enough, she'd see real fairy dust trailing in her wake. Her mother's laughter had been warm and lilting, her emerald eyes crinkling at the edges as she reached for Heather's hands, pulling her into the dance.

Heather had giggled, stumbling over her tiny feet, but her mother only held her tighter, guiding her into a world where the ground barely mattered. Where the sky stretched wide, and anything felt possible.

Her skin was soft as wildflower petals, her rose-gold curls sun-kissed and free. She smelled of lavender and earth—real and rooted, yet impossibly light. In those moments, she was more than just Heather's mother.

She was *magic*.

Her dress spun with her, scattering drops of water like loose diamonds, her hair clinging to her face as she laughed. Heather's dad had stood there beside his wife, his eyes full of love, catching her hand as she twirled. When she finally stopped, breathless and glowing, he pulled her into a deep dip, kissing her as if no one else existed. Heather had run to them and her dad had scooped her up, wrapping them all in one big, wet hug. The smell of rain, grass, and earth had surrounded them, and for a moment, the world had felt perfect—wrapped in the love only they could create.

When her mom died, everything changed. It was sudden—a car accident on a rainy night—and in an instant, the vibrant, joyful world she had built for them had come crashing down.

For a while, Heather's dad tried. He did. He held it together long enough to get through the funeral and to assure everyone that they'd be okay. But they weren't. He wasn't okay. Without her, the house felt lifeless, as if the air had been sucked out of it. The garden she'd once filled with flowers grew wild and untamed, and the laughter that used to echo through the halls was replaced by silence. It wasn't long before the silence turned into something worse. Her dad started drinking—not just the occasional beer after work, but bottle after bottle of liquor.

At first, he'd drink quietly, sitting in his chair and staring at the television, the flickering light casting shadows across his face, but never really seeing it. He quickly turned into a man who was angry, bitter, and unpredictable at all times. The man who used to sweep her mom off her feet in the rain turned into someone Heather didn't recognize. He snapped at little things, his voice sharp and cutting. When the liquor took hold, he would yell—at Heather, at the world, at nothing in particular. There were nights when she'd lie awake in her room, afraid to make a sound, listening to him rant in the living room. Other nights, he'd collapse into tears, mumbling apologies to no one, and she'd feel a confusing mixture of pity and resentment.

Heather tried to fill the void her Mom left behind, though she was only a child. She cleaned the house, cooked simple meals, and kept things as normal as possible. But nothing she did was ever enough to fix him. The more Heather tried, the more invisible she felt.

By her teens, she spent most of her time at Ivy's house, where the noise and warmth were a different world. Ivy's parents welcomed her. Her siblings teased her like she belonged. And Ivy... Ivy became her rock. A soft place to land. A way to feel like herself again.

But no matter how far Heather ran, the weight of her father's grief and anger always found her. The house, once so full of love, became a place she dreaded—a constant reminder of the mother she had lost and the father she could no longer reach. Her childhood ended the day her mom died, and in the years that followed, she learned to survive in the shadows of her father's pain. Her father hated that she looked like her mother. He never said so outright, but Heather could feel it in the way his eyes would linger too long on her hair or the soft lines of her face. He'd never been able to hide the bitterness in his voice when he said her name as if she were some cruel reminder of what he had lost.

She was ten the first time she truly *felt* his anger.

She had been spinning in front of the mirror, draped in her mother's old shawl. It smelled of lavender and something earthy she couldn't name. For a moment, she imagined her mother walking through the door, laughing at her clumsy twirling.

But instead, her father stormed in—red-faced, unsteady from drink.

"What the hell are you doing?" he had barked, snatching the shawl from her shoulders. Heather had frozen, her tiny body trembling under the weight of his fury.

"I was just—"

"Don't." He had snapped at her, his words sharp enough to cut.

"Don't you ever touch her things again."

He threw the shawl into the corner, its delicate fabric crumpling into a heap. Then he just stared at her. Too long. Too hard.

From then on, her resemblance became a wound he couldn't stop poking.

"*Fix that mess,*" he'd snap if her hair was loose.

"*Don't smile like that,*" he'd mutter. "*You look too much like her.*"

Her laugh grated on him, and he would snap at her to quiet down. The worst came when he was drunk. His words turned cruel—slurred insults for things she couldn't change. *"You think you're so special, looking like her,"* he'd sneer. *"But you're not. You're nothing like her."*

He never hit her—not in the way people expected.

His punishments were quieter. Meaner.

He took away everything that reminded her of her mother: a scarf, a photo, even the stories she told herself to remember.

Piece by piece, he erased her—until she felt like a stranger in her own skin.

As Heather stood in front of the mirror, her emerald eyes swept over her reflection, again landing on her fiery red curls that framed her freckled cheeks. Her hair was a wild reminder of her mother, untamed and vibrant, though Heather often felt it only made her stand out in ways she didn't want. Her fingers traced the curve of her jaw, then dropped to her shoulders. Lower still. She took in the rest of her figure with a familiar mix of frustration and resignation. Her body always felt like a contradiction—average in build but impossible to ignore.

Her full hips and softer belly made her feel conspicuous, her freckled cheeks flushed with irritation as she tugged at her waistband. She wished she could make herself even smaller— less noticeable, less her.

With a sigh, she turned away from the mirror, her curls bouncing as she moved. Pulling open her dresser, she grabbed a pair of loose sweatpants and an oversized sweater, their worn fabric offering a small, familiar comfort. She slipped them on quickly, the baggy clothes swallowing her figure, wrapping her in a cocoon where she could feel less exposed, less critical of the person staring back at her.

By the time she padded back into the living room, Byrdie

was curled up on the couch, her tail curled lazily around her legs. Heather sat beside Byrdie and pulled the blanket over her legs. Her eyes fell on the envelope, still sitting on the table like it was watching her.

"Just open it," she whispered, reaching for it before she could talk herself out of it.

Her fingers trembled as she unfolded the thick, worn paper. The handwriting was instantly familiar—jagged and uneven, like he'd been angry even while writing it:

Heather,

I don't know how to say this, and I'm not good with words, so I'll get to it. I screwed up. A lot. It's more than I ever want to admit, but I can't ignore it anymore. I know I wasn't the father you needed, and I'm sorry for that. I'm sorry for all of it. The yelling, the silences, the way I blamed you for things that were never your fault. You didn't deserve any of it, and I hate myself for the way I treated you.

You looked so much like her. That wasn't your fault, but it tore me apart every time I saw you because it felt like the universe was mocking me. She was gone, and you were still here, with her hair and her eyes and her laugh. I couldn't handle it. And instead of dealing with my grief like a man should, I took it out on you. I wish I could take that back, but I can't.

You're stronger than me, you know. You always were. You put up with me when I didn't deserve it. You stayed when you could've walked away, and when you finally left, I hated you for it—not because you were wrong to go, but because I knew I deserved it.

I was angry and sad and scared of being alone, but none of that was your fault. I didn't know how to say it.

There's something I should've told you a long time ago, but I didn't have the guts to contact you after you left. Your mother wanted you to have this. I couldn't bring myself to give it to you before you left, but it's yours now. It's what she wanted for you, and I hope it brings you the peace I never could.

I don't expect you to forgive me, Heather. I wouldn't blame you if you didn't. But for whatever it's worth, I loved you. I still do, even if I had a lousy way of showing it. I hope this makes up for a little of the damage I did.

Take care of yourself.
*   Dad*

Her mother left something for her? Heather's pulse kicked up. Was it supposed to be included with the letter? Had something been lost? She reread the words, her grip tightening on the page. Heather's hands trembled as she set the letter on the coffee table, her father's rough scrawl blurring in her vision as tears welled up. She blinked them away angrily, frustrated with herself for crying over words she hadn't even been sure he was capable of writing. She pressed her hands to her face, breathing deep, trying to steady herself. But the words kept echoing in her mind:
You didn't deserve any of it.
You're stronger than me.
I'm sorry.
It felt surreal. Her father had spent her entire life locked in

anger, grief, and bitterness—a man who had rarely, if ever, taken responsibility for his actions. He'd yelled at her for leaving, lashed out when she failed to meet his impossible standards, and punished her for looking like the woman he had loved and lost. The idea of him sitting down to write something so raw and vulnerable was incomprehensible. It didn't fit the man she had known. She didn't know what to feel: Anger? Sadness? Relief? All three twisted inside her like a storm.

She was angry that he'd only said these things now—when he was gone, when it was too late to matter. She thought of all the nights she cried alone as a child, begging silently for him to see her, not just the ghost of her mother.

And now, here it was: a too-late apology written on crumpled paper. He couldn't say it to her face. He couldn't apologize when it might have mattered; when it might have meant something. And yet... he had said it.

The sadness seeped in slowly, catching her off guard. For all his faults—and there were so many—he had been human. Broken. He had loved her mother so fiercely that her death had shattered him in ways he didn't know how to handle. That wasn't an excuse, and it didn't erase what he had done, but it made her wonder, what had it been like for him?

She had spent so much of her life hating him, but now she realized that perhaps he had hated himself even more. And then there was the tiniest thread of something else, something that scared her because it felt like love. His words, as jagged and imperfect as they were, felt... genuine. She could almost hear his voice in them—gruff, uneven, apologetic, but still stubborn in its own way. He hadn't written this to manipulate or redeem himself in her eyes. He had written it because, for once, he wanted her to know the truth. He was admitting his failure. And he was letting her go.

She reached for Byrdie, stroking her soft fur as her mind raced. Could she forgive him? Could she ever let go of the resentment and anger she had carried for so long? She didn't know.

Her eyes fell on a second envelope tucked inside the first. Carefully, reverently, she set her father's letter aside and pulled out the smaller envelope. It had something impeccably penned on the front: *The Estate of Eilidh Mackenzie Campbell.* Her heart lurched—her mother's name.

Her thumb traced the edge as she stared, her stomach twisting with equal parts anticipation and dread. Whatever was inside had been waiting for her for years—an entire lifetime, it seemed. She opened it slowly, her breath catching as she unfolded the contents and a key fell into her lap. Confused, she scanned the pages, her eyes snagging on specific phrases:

"Eilidh Mackenzie Campbell Trust..."

"Estate located in Inverness-shire, Scotland..."

"Sole heir..."

Her fingers trembled as she pulled out the photograph tucked between the pages—a grand stone house draped in ivy, perched on a rugged Highland hillside, and weathered stone walls softened by the rolling mist. Her mother stood beaming in front of the grand wooden door, no older than thirteen, a squirming puppy in her arms. Heather jolted. The wild curls. The freckled cheeks. Her mother looked like *her.*

On the back, written in her mother's elegant handwriting, were the words: *Glenoran House, 1986.* Heather's breath caught in her throat. Her mother had lived there, walked those halls, looked out over those hills. And now, somehow, it belonged to Heather, and it looked like something out of a dream—or a storybook— with its ivy-covered stone walls and misty Highland backdrop. It didn't feel real. It couldn't be real.

But her mother's familiar, looping handwriting on the back of the photograph was undeniable. Heather ran her fingers over the photo's edges as if touching it would somehow reconnect her with her mother—young and full of life before tragedy had taken her away. She took a deep breath and returned to the documents in her lap.

The papers blurred together—property descriptions, estate valuations, lists of holdings from the furniture to the art. Then came the trust: a bank account in her mother's name, untouched for over a decade. And it held more money than Heather could comprehend.

It was too much. Too much to process, too much to take in. She set the papers down, leaned back against the couch, and closed her eyes as she tried to steady her thoughts.

Her mother had never mentioned Glenoran House. She'd spoken of Scotland in passing—of glens, lochs, and morning mist that made everything feel enchanted—but never of a grand estate or family legacy.

It had been a mystery, locked away in her mother's past, hidden even after her death. And now, suddenly, it was Heather's.

What was she supposed to do with all of this? She couldn't just pack up her life and move to Scotland. But her eyes drifted back to the photograph. Glenoran House wasn't just a property or a trust fund. It was her mother's legacy—a piece of her life that she had left behind for Heather, hidden away until now. Heather thought of her father's letter, his apology, and the guilt he had carried to his grave.

She stood abruptly, the photograph still clutched in her hand. Byrdie let out a startled meow from the couch, her tail flicking as she watched Heather pace.

"Sorry, Byrdie," Heather muttered. "What am I supposed to do?"

Byrdie answered with a questioning meow, but Heather barely heard her. She exhaled, glancing at the photograph again until her gaze drifted to the glass of a photo of her and Ivy on the wall. Her own reflection stared back at her, and for a fleeting moment, she saw her mother instead.

She had spent so much of her life hating her features because of how her father resented them, but now, looking at the photo, she felt connection—to her mother, her roots, and the life her mother had dreamed of leaving her. This felt like an anchor. This felt like a chance for her mother to tell her where she came from and who she was meant to be.

The weight of it all pressed against her chest. Needing space, she wandered into her bedroom and sank onto the edge of the bed, still clutching the photograph of Glenoran House. Her fingers traced the edge of the image again. She felt a brave flicker of excitement.

She'd scrimped and saved for so long, budgeting every paycheck to keep her modest apartment and afford little luxuries like coffee with Ivy. And now, a Scottish estate, an inherited fortune, another world—just waiting for her across the Atlantic.

Heather had just been given a gift. A legacy. She needed to embrace the past.

For her mother.

For herself.

Chapter 4

The following day, Heather sat at her usual table in the corner of the coffee shop, staring at the photograph of Glenoran House on the table.

Ivy sat across from her, stirring sugar into her latte with exaggerated focus, even for her.

"You're serious," Ivy said finally, glancing up, her perfectly arched brow lifting in disbelief. "This is real? An estate in Scotland? A trust fund? You're not messing with me?"

Heather smiled faintly, a mix of nerves and excitement bubbling under the surface. "It's real," she said, sliding the photograph across the table toward her. "This is the house. It belonged to my mom's family. Apparently, it's been waiting for me all this time."

Ivy picked up the photo and studied it, her lips parting in awe. "Oh my God," she said dramatically. "This is... Heather, this is like something out of a movie. Look at this place! It's a freaking castle!"

"It's not a castle," Heather said, though she couldn't help

but feel a flicker of pride at Ivy's reaction. "It's a historic estate. And it's falling apart, probably. Who knows what kind of shape it's in after all these years."

"Who cares?" Ivy shot back, her dark eyes sparkling as she returned the photo. "It's gorgeous. And it's yours. Do you even realize what this means? You're, like, secretly royalty or something."

Heather laughed, shaking her head. "Hardly. I'm still me— just... me, with a house in another country that I didn't know existed."

Ivy leaned forward, resting her chin on her hand and giving Heather an appraising look. "So, what are you going to do? You're not seriously just going to sit on this, are you?"

Heather hesitated, the weight of the question settling over her. "I don't know," she admitted. "I mean, I want to go. I need to see it and figure out what's there. But... it feels huge, you know? Like, I'm not the kind of person who picks up and flies across the world to claim some mysterious family estate."

Ivy rolled her eyes. "Heather, you've spent your whole life thinking you're not the kind of person who does big, exciting things. Maybe it's time to prove yourself wrong. Or at least—" she smirked, "—prove to me that you're not the one standing in your own way."

"You make it sound so simple."

"Because it is simple," Ivy said, tilting her head. "Unless you make it complicated. Like you always do."

She sighed, then continued as she picked up the photo and showed it to Heather.

"Don't you think this is what your mom would've wanted?"

Heather swallowed hard, her gaze dropping to the photograph.

"Yeah," she said softly. "I think she would."

She gently took the photograph from Ivy's hands, her fingers curled around it like it might slip right through them. An entire estate was hers? It should have felt thrilling, but a quiet panic lodged in her ribs. She had a steady job at the bookstore and a best friend who felt like family. She'd spent so much of her life craving stability—was she really about to upend everything?

An hour later, Heather walked into Evergreen Books, the cozy bookstore where she worked. The bell above the door jingled softly as she stepped inside, and the familiar scent of old paper and rich wood greeted her. Her work routine offered comfort, a reprieve from the chaos in her mind.

She grabbed the books by their spines and reached to shelve them as her coworker, Mark, carried them to her from a new box behind the counter. The titles in the stack sparked a slight sense of stability—*Wuthering Heights, The Catcher in the Rye, A Tale of Two Cities*—familiar, reliable stories.

Mark had been one of the first people Heather had met when she and Ivy moved to Millhaven after college. Leaving the city had been one of the hardest things she'd ever done when she walked away from the only life she'd known, from the grip of her father's expectations.

On Heather's first day at work, Mark had been behind the counter, sorting through a mountain of returns, pushing up the sleeves of his well-worn cardigan. His thick, chestnut-brown hair, always styled *just so* had slipped into his eyes, and he had huffed dramatically, shoving it back with an exaggerated flair. She'd been too shy to say much at first, but Mark wasn't the kind of person who let awkward silence linger. He'd cracked some self-deprecating joke about his inability to alphabetize under pressure, and she'd laughed, despite herself.

Over time, they'd become more than just coworkers. Mark had a way of quietly stepping into her corner—much like Ivy—though his approach was softer, less sharp-edged. He had a dry sense of humor and an easy smile. He was the kind of person who could coax her out of her head without pushing too hard.

It didn't take long for Heather to see Mark and Ivy click instantly. Ivy had shown up at the bookstore one day, with her blonde hair and her magnetic energy filling the space as she loudly declared her love for the smell of books. Unfazed, Mark matched her wit-for-wit, and before Heather knew it, the two of them were bantering like old friends.

The three of them had fallen into an easy rhythm—Heather: the quiet observer, Ivy: the whirlwind, and Mark: the calm in the storm.

As she sorted through the stack of books, Mark leaned against the counter, watching her with a knowing smile.

"You didn't sleep, did you?" he said, gentle but matter-of-fact, like he already knew the answer.

Heather sighed, pressing her hands against the stack of books to steady herself.

"Not really," she said.

Mark didn't ask why—he didn't need to. Instead, he just

nodded, his voice light but full of quiet understanding.

"Well, if you need a distraction, I can always read poetry dramatically until you laugh."

Heather snorted softly, shaking her head. "Thanks, *Marky.* I'll keep that in mind."

Mark rolled his eyes but grinned. "You're never letting that go, are you?"

"Not a chance," she said, smirking.

Ivy had jokingly called him Marky-Mark after one too many margaritas a few months ago, and Heather had shortened it out of pure laziness. He pretended to hate it, but she knew better. He secretly loved a nickname, even a ridiculous one. For now, just being here with the books and the quiet hum of the store and a friend who didn't need her to explain everything was enough.

She gave him a small smile. "Nothing like shelving classics to ground you, huh?"

He chuckled, wiping his hands on his apron. "Exactly. Customers may come and go, and trends rise and fall, but these books? They're always here. Comforting, don't you think?"

Heather nodded as he handed her an armful and said, "These go in fiction." Balancing the stack carefully, she walked to the fiction section alone. This was what she needed right now. The quiet hum of the shop. The musty smell of old pages. The rhythmic routine of shelving. All of it felt like a balm for her frayed nerves.

As she worked, her mind wandered. It wasn't lost on her how much she relied on her routines: bantering with Mark, chatting with Ivy, curling up with Byrdie, and knowing what to expect each day. These were the constants that kept her steady through moments of chaos. And now, with Glenoran House waiting for her decision, everything felt... precarious.

Unless you make it complicated. Like you always do.

Ivy's words surfaced again, unshakable. Heather exhaled sharply, pushing them down, but the panic clung to her ribs again, unwanted and heavy as she scowled. Was that what she did? Made things harder than they needed to be? Maybe Ivy was right.

She pulled a book off the shelf at random, running her fingers over the embossed title and fighting back tears. The words blurred for a moment before coming into focus—*Sense and Sensibility.* She almost laughed at the title. Maybe she really was over-complicating things.

"Hey, Heth?" Mark's voice broke through her thoughts.

She turned to see him leaning over the counter, a bemused look on his face. "You've got company."

Heather didn't bother looking up as she re-shelved the books. Her lunch hour neared, her mind already halfway out the door. She was distracted by thoughts of Glenoran House and the decisions she had to make.

"...Heather?"

The voice sent a jolt through her chest before she could place it. Deep, warm, familiar. She turned, her fingers tightening around the stack of books she was holding. Sam Ashford. Her stomach dropped at the sound of that deep, smooth baritone with just enough warmth to make her chest tighten. Slowly, she turned to see Sam standing near the front counter, his smile as easy and confident as ever.

Sam Ashford was, without a doubt, the most attractive man Heather had ever seen. Tall and broad-shouldered with perpetually perfectly-tousled brown hair and hazel eyes that seemed to glint with mischief, he turned heads wherever he went. He was also a regular at the bookstore - a fact Heather was painfully aware of.

"Oh, hey...," she said, her voice coming out more breathless than she intended. She fumbled with the books in her hands, trying to appear casual but failing miserably. Sam's grin widened as he watched her. "Are you hiding back there all day, or will you come to say hi?"

Heather flushed and quickly set the books down on the nearest shelf. She walked toward him, smoothing her apron nervously. "Sorry. I was just putting some new books on the shelf. What brings you in today?"

He held up a book—a worn copy of The Great Gatsby. "Needed a replacement. My old one's fallen apart from too many rereads. I figured I'd come here instead of ordering it online. Support local business and all that."

"Very noble of you," she said, smiling as she rang him up.

"What can I say? I'm a man of principle."

He leaned forward slightly, resting his forearms on the counter.

"So, how've you been? I came by a few days ago, and when I saw you weren't here, I left."

Heather's heart raced in her chest. Was he paying that much attention to her?

"Oh, um, yeah...," she said, fumbling for the right words. "Just... life stuff, you know. It's been a weird couple of weeks."

Sam studied her for a moment, his expression softening. "Yeah? Anything you want to talk about?"

Heather shook her head quickly. "No, nothing serious. Just... busy."

From behind the counter, there was a sudden *thud*—then

a cascade of *thunks* as a whole stack of books hit the floor. Heather turned just in time to see Mark standing there, frozen, hands half-raised like he'd been caught mid-eavesdrop.

"Sorry," he blurted, bending down to scoop up the fallen books. "Slipped."

Heather narrowed her eyes, but Mark refused to meet them, his entire focus locked on restacking the books at *record speed.* Heather let out a slow breath before turning back to Sam, pretending like *that* hadn't just happened.

Sam arched a brow, glancing between them with clear amusement. "You good over there, Mark?"

"Peachy," Mark muttered, shoving the last book into place. "Please, continue."

Sam bit back a smirk but refocused on Heather, his voice easy but his gaze steady. "Well, maybe you could use a break from all that. I was thinking... this new Italian place just opened up downtown. How about dinner? My treat."

Heather blinked, sure she'd misheard him. "Dinner?" she echoed, startled.

"Yeah," he said, his grin turning slightly teasing.

"The thing where two people sit down, eat food, and have a conversation?" she asked.

"You've heard of it right?" he questioned.

"Right... No, yeah... I mean... I know what dinner is..." She winced at herself and thought, *Oh my God, did I really just clarify the definition of dinner for him?*

Sam chuckled, sliding his card across the counter.

"Good to know."

She let out a nervous laugh, her cheeks burning.

"I... yeah, of course. I didn't think—"

She stopped herself, realizing that she was about to say

something self-deprecating.

"I mean, that sounds... nice."

"*Nice?*" he repeated, raising an eyebrow. "I was going for unforgettable, but I'll take *nice* for now."

Heather couldn't help but smile, her nerves settling just a little under his easy charm. "Okay," she said, feeling a rush of courage she hadn't expected. "Dinner sounds great."

Sam straightened, his grin widening. "Great. Tomorrow night, then? I'll pick you up at seven?"

She nodded, her pulse racing. "Seven works."

"Perfect." He slid the book off the counter and tucked it under his arm. "Looking forward to it."

With one last dazzling smile, he turned and walked out, leaving Heather standing behind the counter, her heart hammering in her chest and a stupid grin on her face.

The door jingled behind him.

She stood frozen, cheeks flushed and heart hammering, like she might float right off the ground. And then she heard it— a very distinct throat-clearing noise.

She turned slowly to see Mark peeking out from behind a shelf of mystery novels, his arms crossed and an enormous grin plastered across his face.

"So...," he said, drawing out the word like a seasoned interrogator, "Italian food, huh? Fancy."

Heather groaned, covering her face with her hands. "Mark! Seriously?"

"I mean, I was just over here trying to alphabetize Agatha Christie, but the conversation was... impossible to ignore. Riveting, really."

He leaned casually against the shelf, adopting a mock-serious tone.

"Did I hear correctly that *Sam Ashford... Sam Ashford!* ...asked you on a date? ...At an Italian restaurant? ...Is he bringing roses, too, or will he be arriving on horseback?"

Heather glared at him, though the corners of her mouth twitched and she started to smile. "I hate you."

"No, you don't!" he sighed dramatically, clutching an imaginary bouquet to his chest.

Then, with an exaggerated gasp, his eyes widened.

"Wait! Does this make you Elizabeth Bennet? Because *he* is absolutely giving broody-but-besotted *Mr. Darcy* right now."

"That's the last time I let you watch *Pride and Prejudice* with Ivy."

"Oh, please," Mark scoffed. "Like I needed *Ivy* to educate me on the finer points of regency romance. Now tell me: will you be staring wistfully across the rain-soaked moors before declaring your undying love, or should I lower my expectations?"

"Mark!" Heather hissed, glancing nervously toward the door. "Keep your voice down! What if he hears you?"

He raised an eyebrow, unbothered.

"What, through the soundproof windows? Relax, Heather. Your dignity is safe—well...

Relatively."

He shrugged.

She rolled her eyes but couldn't help the nervous laugh that bubbled up.

"You're insufferable, you know that?"

Mark grinned. "Of course! But now I've got front-row seats to what's shaping up to be the most interesting thing that's happened in this bookstore in years. Don't keep me waiting for updates, okay? I want a full play-by-play by Monday."

Heather shook her head, grabbing the nearest book and smacking him lightly on the arm.

"You're impossible."

"And you are going to have the time of your life," he said, pointing a finger at her as he retreated to the counter. "Don't mess this up, Heather. The fate of my entertainment depends on it!"

Heather groaned, but as she turned back to her work, she couldn't stop the small, giddy smile on her face.

Chapter 5

Heather was back at work the next day, trying to focus on organizing a display table of historical fiction novels, but her thoughts kept drifting. It wasn't just the date tonight—although that was enough to keep her nerves in a twist—it was also the envelope sitting on her coffee table at home. Inside it was the key to a house in Scotland. Her house. A place she hadn't even known existed until now. Every time she thought about it, her stomach flipped.

The bell over the door jingled, and Heather glanced up, expecting a customer. Instead, Ivy strolled in like a storm in heels, her scarf trailing dramatically and her expression locked in determination.

"Oh, no," Heather muttered, already bracing herself.

"There she is!" Ivy announced loudly, striding straight toward the counter. She slapped both hands down as if presenting an official proclamation. "Heather Mackenzie Campbell, how dare you not tell me you have a date with Sam-

freaking-Ashford!"

Heather froze mid-step, her stomach twisting. "It's not a date!" she said quickly. "And I didn't tell you because I knew you'd make a big deal out of it."

Ivy gasped, pressing a hand to her chest like she'd been personally wounded. "Me? Make a big deal? Please."

Heather shot her a knowing look.

Ivy huffed. "Fine, maybe. But still! You should have told me. I mean, Sam Ashford?" She leaned in conspiratorially. "I didn't even know he *spoke* to people. He's certainly never spoken to *me*."

Heather hesitated for half a second. Ivy had never spoken to Sam? Then... how did she even hear about it?

Heather froze, her cheeks flushing. "Ivy, keep your voice down!"

"Don't 'keep your voice down' me," Ivy said, wagging a finger in her face. "*Marky*, here, spilled the beans."

"What? ...I didn't spill!" Mark called from the counter, popping his head up from behind a stack of books he was sorting. "I casually mentioned it when Ivy came in and interrogated me when you were on your lunch yesterday!"

Ivy spun around to give him an approving thumbs-up. "And you did the right thing, Mark. You're a man of the people."

"I try," he said, grinning.

Heather groaned in mock exasperation. "Mark, I trusted you!"

He shrugged, completely unbothered. "You didn't say it was a secret. Besides, it's Sam. You can't expect me to keep that kind of information to myself."

Ivy turned back to Heather, her hands on her hips. "How could you not tell me? I thought we were best friends! You're withholding critical information from my entertainment pipeline!"

"I was going to tell you," Heather muttered, her face a shade of deep crimson. "I just... haven't had a chance."

"Well, lucky for you, I'm here now, and we have a crisis to address," Ivy declared, her voice full of mock seriousness.

Mark wandered over, crossing his arms. "Crisis? Is this about the fact that Heather called this date 'nice'? Because if so, I agree. That was an outrage."

Heather shot him a glare. "Are you two seriously teaming up right now?"

Of course," Mark said, completely deadpan. "This is a team effort. We need to get you prepped, polished, and ready to make Mr. Darcy over there fall at your feet."

Heather groaned, covering her face with her hands. "This is mortifying."

"It's a public service," Ivy said, pulling Heather's hands down. "Look, Sam is this town's Holy Grail of eligible men. And somehow, by some *miracle*, he asked you out. We can't afford to let this opportunity go to waste."

Mark nodded sagely. "I second that. You've got the potential for a fairy tale evening, Heather, but you're going to need some backup. Lucky for you, you've got the dream team."

Heather raised an eyebrow. "The dream team?"

"Ivy and me," Mark said, gesturing between himself and Ivy. "She'll handle the hair, makeup, and wardrobe. I'll take care of moral support and witty one-liners. You're in good hands."

Ivy grinned. "After work, you're going straight to my place. I've got the perfect dress for you. Trust me, you're going to look incredible."

Heather hesitated, biting her lip. "I don't know, Ivy. Maybe I should just—"

"Nope!" Ivy cut her off, grabbing her shoulders. "You're not talking your way out of this. You deserve to feel confident, gorgeous, and unstoppable tonight. Let me do this for you. Besides, you need a win, Heather. Between... everything," she gestured vaguely, "and now inheriting some big fancy Scottish castle—you need to feel good about yourself for once."

Mark smirked. "And honestly, who inherits a castle? You're like a Disney princess—just with significantly fewer talking animals and a lot more renovation costs."

Heather's gaze darted wide-eyed between them as Ivy started laughing. "Marky's right. You're a Disney princess now, and tonight is your ball. Don't mess it up." Heather wanted to argue, but then Ivy's infectious excitement started to chip away at her nerves. Maybe this actually was a chance to feel good about herself and about life in general so that she could forget, even for one night, about all the chaos swirling around her.

Heather glanced at Mark, who gave her an encouraging nod. "Yeah, Sam isn't just walking into the bookstore and asking random people out. He picked you, Heather. Own it."

Heather felt overwhelmed, but then Ivy squeezed her shoulders and repeated, "Own it," with a grin so earnest that Heather couldn't help but feel a flicker of excitement.

"Fine," she huffed. "But if you come near me with false lashes or glitter, I'm out."

"Deal," Ivy said, clapping her hands. "Now, Marky, make sure she doesn't chicken out before her shift ends."

"On it!" he agreed, mock-saluting as Ivy disappeared into the romance section, muttering plans for Heather's transformation under her breath. As Heather returned to work, she couldn't stop the mix of anxiety and warmth bubbling inside her. She wasn't sure how the date with Sam would go, but with Ivy and Mark in her corner, what could go wrong?

Heather found herself standing in Ivy's tiny, impossibly chic apartment that evening, surrounded by an intimidating array of makeup palettes, curling irons, and racks of clothes that Ivy had hauled out just for the occasion. The makeover mission had commenced.

Ivy, with her energy at an all-time high, whirled around like a general preparing for battle.

"Okay, Heather, tonight we're going for jaw-dropping. I don't want Sam Ashford just to notice you—I want him to forget his own name."

Heather winced, perched on the edge of Ivy's vanity chair.

"Can't we aim for something more... subtle? Like... 'pleasantly surprised' instead of 'speechless from shock'?"

"Nope!" Ivy grinned, her hands on her hips like this was a matter of national importance. "Tonight, subtlety is canceled. Besides, when have I ever steered you wrong?"

Mark, who was lounging on Ivy's plush white couch with a Diet Coke and a smirk, chimed in: "You did give her bangs that one time."

Ivy shot him a withering look. "That was an experiment, Mark, and sometimes experiments go wrong. Tonight, however, I am fully in control of my craft."

Heather groaned, already regretting agreeing to this. "This feels like overkill for a casual date."

"Casual date?" Ivy gasped, offended. "Heather, this is Sam-*freaking*-Ashford. His parents own like half the town. He doesn't do casual, and neither will you."

She whipped out a black garment bag from her closet, holding it up with a flourish. "Behold, your secret weapon."

Heather eyed it warily. "It's a dress, not a weapon."

"You're wrong—it's both," Ivy countered, unzipping the bag to reveal a rich, scarlet satin dress. The fabric draped like liquid, smooth and impossibly soft, the cowl neckline dipping just enough to tease without being too much. The fitted silhouette would hug her curves, stopping just at the knee. It was sleek, and sultry, but undeniably classy. Under the apartment light, the deep red gleamed like a glass of expensive wine. Bold. Unapologetic.

Heather swallowed. "That's... a lot of dress."

Ivy smirked. "No, darling. That's *the* dress."

Heather hesitated. "I don't know, Ivy. I don't think—"

"—Exactly," Ivy cut in smoothly. "You think too much. That's the problem. Just trust me for once, okay? This will knock his socks off. And his shirt." She raised her eyebrows. "...Maybe more."

Mark nearly spit out his drink. "Geez, Ivy! Let the poor girl breathe."

"Breathe later, seduce now," Ivy retorted.

Heather stared at the dress like it might bite her. "I'm going to look ridiculous."

Mark, still lounging on the couch, must have noticed her hesitation because his expression softened. "Hey," he said, giving her an easy grin. "It's just a dress. If you hate it, you can change. No pressure."

Heather exhaled, shoulders easing slightly. "Thanks, Marky."

Ivy groaned. "Mark! Stop coddling her!"

Heather hesitated, then sighed in defeat, taking the dress. "Fine, I'll wear it. But if I trip in these heels and face plant, I'm blaming both of you."

Ivy squealed with delight. "Deal! I swear, if it were up to you, you'd show up in jeans!"

Heather frowned, opening her mouth to argue, but Mark shot her a look, shaking his head slightly. *Let it go.*

So, for the next hour, Heather endured Ivy's transformation process, which involved everything from taming her curls into smooth, glossy waves to applying makeup that felt far more glamorous than she was used to. Mark stayed in the background, offering commentary now and then.

"That eyeliner's a bit dramatic, don't you think?" he quipped.

"It's called 'cat-eye,' Mark," Ivy snapped without looking up. "And unless you're volunteering to be a model, stay out of it."

Heather, meanwhile, was trying not to panic. "This is too much," she murmured as Ivy applied a final sweep of lipstick—a deep berry shade that perfectly matched the dress.

"It's exactly enough," Ivy said, admiring her work. "Now, let's get you into that dress." With Ivy's insistence and Mark's quips in the background, Heather slipped into the burgundy gown. When she stepped out, the room fell silent.

Ivy gasped, hands on her hips. "I told you! You've been hiding that body under oversized sweaters for way too long."

Heather flushed. "Gee, thanks."

"No, really," Ivy insisted, adjusting the neckline slightly. "It's criminal, Heather. You could look like this all the time if you just put in a little effort."

Mark set down his drink, staring at her with wide eyes. "Well, damn... If *Mr. Darcy* doesn't fall for this, he might actually be blind."

Heather looked at herself in Ivy's full-length mirror and barely recognized the woman staring back. The dress hugged her in all the right places, the silky red fabric draping over her curves like it had been made for her. The cowl neckline, which she'd feared would be too revealing, somehow looked effortless—just the right mix of sultry and sophisticated. And the makeup and hair—well, Ivy had worked actual magic.

"I... I don't know what to say," Heather murmured, her cheeks flushing.

"You say, 'Thank you, Ivy,' and then you walk into that restaurant like you own the place," Ivy said, practically bouncing with excitement.

Mark raised a finger like he was making a royal decree. "One condition."

Heather sighed. "What?"

"You must text me the instant he sees you," he said. "I simply must know if he reacts like a man in a Regency novel—clutching his chest and whispering *"You cannot expect a mere mortal to withstand such beauty!"*

Heather laughed despite herself, the tension in her chest easing slightly. "Thanks, guys. Really."

"Don't thank us yet," Ivy said, handing her a pair of heels

that matched the dress. "You've got a date to win."

She hovered nearby, adjusting the strap of Heather's dress with her usual confidence as Heather nervously smoothed the fabric over her hips.

"Stop fussing," Ivy said with a smirk, giving Heather's curls a final tousle. "You look perfect. Sam's jaw is gonna hit the floor when he sees you."

Heather rolled her emerald eyes but couldn't fight the small smile tugging at her freckled cheeks. "It's just dinner."

"It's not just dinner," Ivy shot back, crossing her arms. "It's you, finally going after what you deserve. And for the record, if he doesn't treat you like a queen tonight, I'll throw my coffee at him next time he walks into the shop."

The sound of a car horn outside cut through their banter. Ivy glanced out the window and let out a low whistle.

"Your chariot awaits. Go knock him dead, babe."

Heather grabbed her small clutch, giving Ivy a grateful smile.

"Thanks... for everything," she said.

Ivy gave one last approving nod, a proud smirk on her lips.

"Look at you. My greatest work yet."

Heather huffed. "I'm not a project, Ivy."

"No, you're a masterpiece!" Ivy corrected, winking as she ushered her toward the door of her apartment, to navigate down to the lobby on her own.

Heather descended Ivy's narrow staircase, the sound of her

heels echoing against the worn wood. Stepping out into the cool night air, she spotted Sam's car idling by the curb. He leaned casually against the driver's side, his broad frame illuminated by the soft glow of the streetlight.

When he saw her, his expression shifted—his dark eyes widening slightly before a slow smile spread. He straightened, opening the passenger door for her as she approached.

"Wow, Heather," he said, his voice low, his gaze trailing over her. "You look... incredible."

God... he said her name as if he'd tasted it first.

She forced herself to stay calm, even as warmth bloomed in her chest. "Thanks. You clean up pretty well yourself."

He chuckled, shutting her car door and stepping to the driver's side. "Pretty well? I'm wounded, truly."

She smiled, the nerves in her stomach easing just slightly. He smelled faintly of something woodsy and warm, and as he settled into his seat, her eyes trailed him without permission.

The city lights of Millhaven flickered past as Sam guided the car down the winding streets toward downtown. The rhythmic sound of the tires on the road filled the silence until Sam glanced over at her, a small smile tugging at his lips.

"So," he said, his voice warm and casual. "I've been looking forward to this all day."

Heather glanced at him, her fingers playing nervously with the hem of her dress. She tried to keep her tone light, but her pulse betrayed her, quickening at his words. "Have you now?"

"I have. Though, full disclosure, Mark might've let it slip that you've had some big news this week. Something about an estate... in Scotland?" He grinned, that easy, self-assured smile that always seemed to throw her off balance.

Heather blinked, momentarily stunned. "Mark has a big mouth."

Sam laughed, the sound rich and infectious. "He does, but I like him for it. So, tell me—what's the story? A whole estate? That's not something you hear every day."

She hesitated, her hands clasping in her lap as she gathered her thoughts. "It's my mom's," she said, her voice quieter now. "Or... it was. She passed away when I was a kid, and it's complicated. I just found out about it and, honestly, I'm still trying to wrap my head around it. It feels... overwhelming."

Sam's gaze softened as they pulled up in front of the restaurant, the warm glow of string lights spilling onto the street. He parked and turned to her, his expression sincere. "That's a lot to take in," he said, his voice low and steady. "But, Heather..." He paused, his dark eyes meeting hers. "That's incredible. Your mom must have been an amazing woman to leave you something meaningful."

Her breath caught at the unexpected weight of his words. She felt the familiar tightness in her throat, the swirl of emotions threatening to rise.

"She was," she murmured, the words barely above a whisper.

Sam stepped out of the car and quickly rounded to her side, opening the door for her before she could even move. He extended his hand to help her, and she just looked at it— strong, steady, unwavering.

"Ready?" he asked, his smile softening into something just for her.

She nodded, slipping her hand into his and letting him guide her toward the restaurant's entrance.

The warm, golden glow of the chandeliers spilled across the

restaurant, casting soft light on the polished wood floors and crisp white tablecloths. The murmur of quiet conversation mixed with the faint strains of classical music, creating an atmosphere of understated elegance. Heather walked beside Sam as the hostess led them to a corner table near the window. The flickering candlelight reflected off the glass, giving the space a cozy, intimate feel.

Heather slid into her seat, smoothing the skirt of her dress nervously.

Sam sat across from her, his mocha-colored eyes scanning the room before landing on her.

"This place is something else," he said, his voice low and smooth. "Have you been here before?"

She shook her head, still taking in her surroundings.

"No. I've always walked by and thought it looked too fancy for me."

Sam smirked, resting his elbows on the table and leaning forward slightly. "Well, tonight, it's just right. Besides, you deserve a little fancy."

His comment sent a self-conscious rush of heat to her cheeks, and she quickly glanced at the menu, pretending to study it. The rich aromas of tomato-basil sauce and fresh bread wafted through the air, making her stomach growl quietly.

A waiter appeared, pouring water into their glasses and offering a practiced smile.

"Can I get you started with some wine?"

Sam glanced at her, his brows lifting in question: "Red or white?"

"Red," Heather answered, her voice more confident than she expected. "Something dry."

Sam nodded at the waiter. "A bottle of Chianti, please."

As the waiter disappeared, Heather looked around again at the leather banquettes, the ornate mirrors, the couples leaning close over their meals. It felt like a different world, far removed from the bookstore and her quiet life in Millhaven.

"So," Sam said, breaking the silence. "Tell me something I don't know about you."

Heather raised an eyebrow. "That's a vague request."

He leaned back, his grin playful. "Okay, fine. Let's narrow it down. What's something you love that you're embarrassed to admit?"

She thought about it, a small smile tugging at her lips. "Fine. I have a thing for those cheesy fantasy romance novels. You know, the ones with the overly-dramatic titles and shirtless men on the cover?"

Sam's laughter was warm and unrestrained, drawing a nearby couple's attention from the next table over.

"That's not embarrassing," he said, shaking his head. "I mean, it's hilarious but not embarrassing. Let me guess: you're secretly hoping to be swept off your feet by a brooding warrior prince?"

Heather rolled her eyes but couldn't stop the smile from spreading. "Maybe! Who wouldn't want that?"

Their wine arrived, and Sam poured it for them before raising his glass. "To brooding warrior princes," he teased, his dark eyes twinkling.

Heather clinked her glass against his, unable to suppress a laugh.

"And to people who don't judge cheesy books."

As the evening unfolded, Heather relaxed, the initial nervousness fading away. The conversation flowed easily from there, Sam's charm and wit disarming her at every turn. She laughed more than she had in weeks, her shoulders relaxing as he told her stories about his travels to Paris and his disastrous attempts at making coq au vin.

They shared plates of bruschetta and perfectly cooked pasta, trading stories about childhood mischief and awkward moments from college. Sam had a way of pulling her out of her shell—his wit and charm balancing out her quieter nature.

By the time dessert arrived, a shared tiramisu served on a delicate glass plate, she realized she hadn't thought about her father, the letter, or the estate for the entire evening.

Sam caught her staring at him as he took a bite of the dessert, his fork pausing midair. "What?"

"Nothing," she said quickly, looking away.

"No, seriously," he pressed, his tone teasing but soft. "What were you thinking?"

Heather hesitated, then decided to take a chance. "I was just thinking... this is the first time in a while that I've felt like myself."

Sam's expression softened, and he set down his fork, leaning across the table slightly. "Well, for what it's worth, I like you. The real you, no matter what that looks like."

Her chest tightened at his words, and she didn't know what to say momentarily. So she just smiled, lifting her glass in silent acknowledgment.

As they stepped out into the brisk night, the cool air kissed her flushed cheeks, but it did little to calm the warmth simmering beneath her skin. The gentle buzz of the city surrounded them—the soft roar of distant cars and the occasional conversations of passersby. But Heather was hyper-aware of the man walking beside her. The heat of his presence beside her, the casual brush of his arm against hers, sent a quiet thrill through her as they walked to the car.

Sam glanced at her, his chocolate-brown eyes gleaming under the soft glow of the street lamps. "You're quiet. You okay?"

Heather tucked a strand of curly red hair behind her ear, her freckled cheeks burning under his gaze as they walked.

"Just... thinking," she said, her voice soft.

"Thinking?" he repeated, his grin tilting into something mischievous. "About how charming I am, or how much you regret letting me order the wine?"

A laugh escaped her, light and breathy. "You're dangerously confident, you know that?"

"Confidence isn't dangerous unless you're resisting it," he teased, stepping closer.

Heather rolled her eyes but couldn't stop her lips from curling into a smile. "You didn't have to pay for dinner," she said, her tone teasing but soft.

"Consider it an investment," he replied smoothly, his hands slipping casually into his pockets.

Investment?

The word barely registered before he continued. His gaze was steady, unwavering, as if she were the only person on the street.

"Besides, it gives me a reason to see you again."

She huffed a quiet laugh. "An investment, huh? Sounds like a business transaction."

Sam smirked. "And what exactly am I investing in?"

Heather tilted her head. "Depends. Is this business or pleasure?"

His brow flicked, his gaze dark and unreadable. "Why can't

it be both?"

The warmth in his voice curled around her, sinking under her skin like whiskey on a cold night. She should have said something clever, something to keep the upper hand. But right now, she didn't want to win.

She just wanted to stay.

His voice dropped slightly, rich and warm as molten honey. "Unless this was a one-time deal?"

Heather looked up at him as they stopped beside the car door, her shining emerald eyes meeting his. How he held her gaze — like he was reading all her unspoken thoughts — sent a shiver down her spine.

"I don't think it is," she whispered, the words leaving her lips before she could second-guess them.

"Good," Sam breathed, stepping closer, his body just a single breath away from hers. He dipped his head slightly, his gaze flickering to her lips before returning to her eyes. "Because I've already decided I like seeing you."

The heat in his voice, the deliberate way he leaned closer, made Heather's pulse race. Her heart thudded against her ribs, her stomach coiling with nerves and excitement.

"I think I like that too," she said softly, her words barely audible over her heartbeat.

Sam's smile was slow, wicked, and impossibly charming.

"Careful, Heather..." His voice was low and smooth, his breath brushing against her skin. "You're making me think I've met my match."

The air between them thickened, his proximity intoxicating. But then he stepped back, his hand brushing hers briefly before retreating. Sam opened the passenger door of his sleek black sedan for her, his fingers barely grazing the small of her back as he guided her in.

Heather's heart pounded. She had expected to head back to Ivy's apartment, recounting every detail over a pint of Ben & Jerry's, when he'd casually asked, *"Do you want to come over for a nightcap?"*

She hadn't even hesitated. Something about him—something magnetic—made her want to throw caution to the wind. As he slid into the driver's seat, the glow of the dashboard lights cast sharp angles across his profile. He glanced at her, that easy, confident smile tugging at his lips.

"...'sure about this?"

Heather exhaled with a mix of nerves and excitement buzzing under her skin.

"Yeah. I am.

The drive to his house was quiet but comfortable, the tension between them simmering just below the surface. Heather's fingers played absently with the hem of her dress, her mind racing with a mix of excitement and uncertainty. Sam seemed so effortless, so sure of himself. She couldn't believe she was sitting beside him, heading to his house.

When they arrived, Sam pulled into the driveway of a modern townhouse, sleek and understated, much like him. He parked and turned to her, his gaze soft but intense. "Welcome to my humble abode," he said, a teasing lilt in his voice.

Heather smiled, trying to steady her breathing as she exited the car. The air was crisp, and she wrapped her arms around herself as he unlocked the front door and gestured her inside.

The interior was warm and inviting, with dark wood floors, leather furniture, and shelves lined with books and records. A low fire crackled in the living room, casting a golden glow.

"Wow," she said, slipping off her heels and looking around. "I wasn't expecting this."

Sam raised an eyebrow as he hung up his coat. "What were you expecting? Beer cans and a beanbag chair?"

Heather laughed. "No, I mean, I knew you had good taste. I couldn't picture it."

He smirked, stepping closer. "I'll take that as a compliment. Make yourself comfortable—I'll grab us something to drink."

She wandered into the living room, her fingers grazing the spines of the books on his shelf. It felt strange to be here, in his space, surrounded by pieces of his life. When he returned, holding two glasses of sweet port wine, she sat on the couch, her legs tucked beneath her.

"Here you go," he said, handing her a glass before sitting beside her, close enough that their knees brushed.

"Thanks," she said, taking a sip. The smooth undertones of sweet summer berries and richly-dark chocolate coated her tongue, warming her from the inside out.

Sam leaned back, his arm draped casually over the back of the couch, his easy confidence drawing her in. He gave her an amused smile, tilting his head.

"So... what's your favorite book? I'd imagine a girl who spends her life surrounded by stories has to have one she's devoted to. Let me guess—Brontë? Austen? Maybe a little Dickens? Or one of those grocery store romances you like so much?" He gestured toward his bookshelf, the teasing lilt in his voice unmistakable.

Heather chuckled softly, shaking her head. "Honestly, I wouldn't say I'm devoted to literature. I enjoy it, sure. But I don't think I'm really devoted to anything."

Sam's grin faltered slightly, replaced by something more curious, almost tender. "Nothing? Not even one thing?"

She hesitated, her fingers brushing the stem of her wineglass. "It's not that I don't care about things—I do. It's just..." She paused, searching for the right words. "... devotion requires freedom—time... space... room to breathe. And for so long, my life has been about survival. Knowing when to step back, when to keep my head down, when to let things go. You learn quickly not to hold on too tightly when leaving is easier than being left behind. I've never had the luxury of giving myself over to something completely."

Sam's gaze didn't waver, his expression thoughtful as he studied her.

"That sounds like a heavy way to live."

Heather offered a slight, self-conscious shrug.

"It's all I've ever known, really. But now, with this whole Scotland thing..." Her voice trailed off, and she shook her head, brushing away the thought. "...maybe things are changing. I don't know."

Sam leaned forward slightly, resting his elbow on his knee. "If you could pick one thing to devote yourself to—one thing that's just for you—what would it be?"

Heather blinked at the profound question, caught off guard.

"I... I'm not sure. I've never thought about it."

She glanced down, a faint smile tugging at her lips to pull the conversation somewhere lighter. "But if we're talking books, Anne of Green Gables is probably the closest thing I have to a favorite."

Sam's eyebrows rose. "Anne of Green Gables? That's not what I expected."

She laughed, the sound lighter than she felt.

"I read it when I was a kid. I think I fell in love with Anne because she saw the world differently, you know? She made things brighter, even when they were hard. She wasn't afraid to dream."

Sam smiled, his voice softer now. "Sounds like she left an impression."

Heather shrugged, her cheeks warming at the intimacy of the moment. "I think I wanted to be like her. Brave, hopeful... open to life, even when it doesn't make sense."

"You're more like her than you think," Sam said, his tone genuine.

Heather's eyes widened slightly. "I don't know about that."

"I do," he said, holding her gaze.

Her breath caught, the sincerity in his eyes disarming her. She couldn't speak, couldn't even think. And maybe, just maybe, he was right. Maybe there was more of Anne in her than she gave herself credit for.

"Anyway," Sam said, leaning back with a grin, the tension breaking as quickly as it had built, "I have to say, I'm impressed. Anne Shirley is a solid choice. But now I'm picturing you roaming the Scottish Highlands in puffed sleeves and talking to trees."

Heather snorted a laugh, grateful for the sudden levity. "Hey, don't knock puffed sleeves. Anne made them iconic."

Sam grinned, his voice dropping to a playful tone. "Noted. I'll make sure to keep an eye out for puffed sleeves next time I see you."

Her heart fluttered at how he said it and the promise laced

in his words. For the first time in forever, she let herself imagine what it might feel like to be open to something new. Let someone like Sam see the world through her eyes—and maybe help her see herself differently.

His gaze was steady, thoughtful. "You deserve something good, Heather. Something that's just for you."

She looked at him, her heart skipping at the sincerity in his voice. "Thank you. That means a lot."

The room fell quiet, the only sound the crackling of the fire. Then Sam shifted, his fingers brushing hers lightly where they rested on the cushion between them.

"You've been on my mind for a while, you know," he said, his voice low, his eyes never leaving hers.

Heather's breath hitched. "I have?"

He nodded, leaning in slightly. "Yeah. You're smart, funny, and beautiful… and I couldn't stop thinking about you. So when I saw you yesterday at Evergreen, I figured, why wait?"

Her heart raced as his words settled over her. "I… I'm glad you didn't."

He smiled, his hand slipping over hers, his thumb grazing her knuckles. "Good."

The space between them disappeared as he leaned in, his lips brushing hers softly, testing before deepening the kiss. His hand cupped her jaw, tilting her face to him as his other hand rested lightly on her waist.

Heather melted into him, her fingers curling into the fabric of his shirt as the kiss grew more heated. The warmth of the fire seemed to wrap around them, her thoughts spinning as his touch sent sparks through her.

When they finally broke apart, his forehead rested against hers, his breath warm against her lips. "Stay," he murmured, his voice rough, almost a plea.

Heather hesitated for only a moment before nodding, her pulse thrumming. "Okay."

Sam smiled, brushing a wayward auburn curl from her face before pulling her into another kiss, and Heather let herself get lost in him: in that moment—in the feeling that, for once, she didn't have to hold herself back.

Heather's pulse raced. His forehead rested against hers, breath warm and steady.

Then—

He laughed.

Low. Awkward. Wrong.

And everything cracked.

Heather pulled back slightly, her brows furrowing in confusion. "What's so funny?"

Sam shook his head, the ghost of a smirk tugging at his lips. "It's nothing," he said, but the hesitation in his voice betrayed him.

The taste of him was still on her lips.

Her breath was uneven, her body still thrumming from the way his hands had just gripped her waist, the way he had pressed into her like he *needed* her. And now—now he was acting ... *off*.

Sam shook his head, a smirk tugging at his lips, but something in his eyes flickered—like he was already bracing for impact. "It's not a big deal." His voice was too casual, too dismissive.

Heather let out a breathy laugh, still catching up to the moment. "You're really going to say that after *that?*"

His smirk faltered. "I just don't think we need to do this." A slow wave of unease crept over her skin. "Do *what?*"

Sam sighed, running a hand through his hair. *"Heather—"* He leaned in again, his lips hovering just above hers, his breath warm against her skin.

"No," she cut in, the remnants of warmth still clinging to her skin now turning cold. "Don't *Heather* me. Just say it."

His jaw tightened. "It's not what you think."

Her stomach twisted. "Then *what is it?*"

Sam let out a short, humorless laugh. "You're overreacting."

Heather's eyes flashed. *He* was the one acting weird, *he* was the one hedging, but *she* was the dramatic one?

"I wouldn't have to ask if you'd just tell me what's going on instead of dancing around it," she snapped.

Tension crackled between them like a live wire. Just minutes ago, this space between them had been *electric*, pulling them together like a force she couldn't fight. Now it felt suffocating.

She sat back, crossing her arms tightly over her chest, grounding herself. *Steady.*

"Tell me the truth."

Sam hesitated. And then—

He *snapped.*

"You wanna know? *Fine!*" His voice sliced through the quiet. "Ivy and I were talking the other day, and she *suggested—*"

Her stomach dropped.

The air turned cold.

"Ivy suggested?" she repeated, her voice like broken glass.

The room spun—memory slamming into place. Ivy, rolling her eyes: *"He's never spoken to me."*

But he had.

She lied.

Heather felt her breath lock in her throat, her skin turning to ice. Sam reached for her then—maybe to reassure her, maybe to soften the blow, maybe just out of habit. But the second his fingers brushed her arm, she *flinched.* Sam went still. Heather forced herself to look at him, even as her vision blurred at the edges, even as the truth ripped through her like a knife.

"Ivy suggested?" she repeated, her voice barely above a whisper, dangerously quiet. Sam didn't speak. Not right away. And that was enough. Heather swallowed hard, her pulse roaring in her ears. Heather shook her head, her breath coming in shallow bursts. "So this wasn't even *your* idea?"

Sam exhaled sharply, rubbing his temples like she was the one exhausting him. "You're twisting this."

Heather let out a bitter laugh. "Oh, I'm *twisting* this? You just admitted my *best friend* pimped me out like some social experiment, and *I'm* the one twisting it?"

His jaw clenched, his frustration slipping through the cracks. "It's not like that."

"Then what is it, Sam?"

He raked a hand through his hair, his voice sharper now: "Damn it, Heather, you act like I *hated* the idea. Like I had to be *forced* to take you out."

The words landed like a slap. Heather's chest tightened, her breath hitching.

"*Wow.*" She pushed to her feet, putting space between them.

Sam must have realized what he just said, because his eyes flickered with instant regret.

"Heather, I didn't mean—"

"No, you did... That's the thing, Sam... You *did* mean it."

His hands flexed, tension rippling through him as he leaned

forward, settling on the edge of the couch. He gripped his hips like he was barely holding himself together.

"I—Shit, Heather! ...Yeah, Ivy suggested it. ...Yeah, I said yes. ...But I didn't do it *out of pity!* I did it because I thought—" He cut himself off, exhaling harshly with his gaze snapping up to hers. .

Heather stepped closer, her voice quieter but razor-sharp.

"Because you thought *what*, Sam?"

His eyes met hers, something raw and conflicted flickering in them before he scoffed, shaking his head.

"It doesn't matter."

Her heart cracked, her pulse roaring in her ears.

"It *does* matter."

Sam's expression hardened, but guilt still tugged at the edges.

"I *liked* you, Heather." His voice was rough, like the words cost him something. "...not just because Ivy told me to. ...not *just* because of her." He let out a dry, humorless laugh. "Hell... if I had a brain, I would've realized she was *using* me just as much as I was using you."

Heather swallowed, her throat tight. She suddenly felt like a stranger in her own skin—dressed in Ivy's clothes, painted in Ivy's colors, like she had stepped into a role she hadn't even auditioned for. The realization curled in her stomach.

"But you didn't have a brain."

Sam shook his head.

"No. I didn't."

His eyes searched hers, desperate now.

"But then I got to *know* you, and I—"

Heather flinched back as if he'd touched her, holding up a hand.

"Don't."

His mouth clamped shut.

Heather let out a shaky breath, anger and heartbreak swirling together into something unbearable. The last time she had felt like this, she was standing over her father's grave, realizing closure would never come. Looking in the mirror, wearing Ivy's choices instead of her own. Always playing a role, always adjusting to keep people happy.

"You don't get to *find* something real in this and expect that to undo what you did, Sam. You don't get to pretend this was a *mistake* that just... happened."

Sam's face twisted, frustration and regret warring in his expression.

"It wasn't—"

"—Yes, it was." Heather's voice cracked, but she didn't care. "You used me. She used you. And I'm the only one who didn't know I was playing a game."

Sam took a step toward her, but she held her ground.

She crossed her arms, her voice trembling as she pressed him.

"So, what is this really, Sam? Yours and Ivy's idea of a joke? A charity case? Or—"

Her stomach twisted as the worst possibility came to mind. Sam's jaw tensed, his gaze darting away from hers.

That split-second of hesitation was all she needed to know the truth.

Heather's breath hitched, her voice barely above a whisper. "*Oh my God.*"

He exhaled sharply, pinching the bridge of his nose.

"Look, it's not like that. Ivy thought—"

"—Don't you dare say that she thought I needed help,"

Heather cut him off with her voice rising. "Because of this? This is worse than help! It's humiliation!"

Sam stepped back, his hands raised as if to calm her.

"Ivy just wanted to give you a push. She thought maybe if you went out and had a little fun..."

Heather's laugh was bitterly sharp.

"Stop sugarcoating it. What was the deal? ...you'd take me out... play nice... and then—what? Get a gold star for effort?"

Sam flinched at her words, but after a moment of silence, he blurted out, "You want the truth? Ivy said if I took you out..."

He hesitated.

"She'd sleep with me."

The silence snapped. And so did she.

Heather stood frozen, her pulse roaring in her ears. The warmth of Sam's home, the soft flicker of the fire, the way he picked up the expensive tab—it all felt like a cruel joke now.

She thought she might be sick. Ivy had betrayed her. Her gaze flickered over Sam. Searching. Desperate to find something—anything—that wasn't a lie. But there was nothing. Merely hesitation. Only regret. It was just... too late to fix it.

She let out a shaky breath, stepping back.

"Wow..." she murmured. Her voice was hollow, the word empty—devoid of the anger clawing at her chest. The sick feeling threatened to pull her under, the same way it always had. The same way it had every time she bit her tongue, swallowed the hurt, let someone else decide who she was. But not this time. This time, the weight didn't sink her—it ignited her.

Her jaw tightened, breath quickening as the fire roared to

life. She thought: ***You know what? No! —Fuck this.***

She lifted her chin with dignity and in a voice that was no longer hollow—no longer small— she shouted:

"So is this some trade-off, Sam? ...take out pathetic Heather and get rewarded with Ivy? ...did you even *plan* on following through, or was I just a box to check off your to-do list before you get to have Ivy?"

Sam's jaw tightened, his eyes flashing—not with cruelty, but with frustration, like he wanted to deny it and couldn't.

"It's not like that," he said quickly, his tone almost pleading.

He closed his eyes briefly as though trying to summon the courage to respond. "Ivy might've promised me that, but Heather, I swear—after tonight, after being with you—"

"—Stop," she cut him off, her voice breaking. "Just stop! Don't try to turn this into some epiphany! You didn't ask me out because you like me; you did it because you were chasing her. And now, I'm supposed to believe you suddenly care?"

Sam's face crumpled with regret.

"Heather, I messed up, okay? I didn't think it through. But tonight... tonight was real for me."

Heather shook her head and took another step back, her voice quieter. "No, Sam. It was just convenient for you."

Sam reached out to her once more.

"Don't!" she said sharply, her voice cracking again as the betrayal and humiliation bubbled over. "You know the worst part? For a second, I actually believed you! I thought maybe— just maybe—you were different... but in the end, you were just another guy waiting for Ivy to pick you."

Sam flinched.

Good. Let it sting.

"Enjoy your gold star." She turned her back before he could answer.

"Heather—!"

She didn't stop for him...

Didn't look back.

She did not break...

...not here.

...not in front of him.

So she walked out.

The cold night air burned her lungs, but she barely felt it. Her hands curled into fists at her sides, her breath coming fast, uneven. She kept moving, kept pushing forward, until the first tear slid down her cheek. Then another.

She wiped at them furiously, swallowing hard, but it was too late; the dam had cracked. She didn't know where she was going. She just knew she couldn't stop. Not until she found somewhere safe to fall apart.

Not yet.

Chapter 6

Heather swiped her cheeks with trembling fingers as she walked briskly down the busy street. The cold air bit at her skin, but she barely noticed because her mind was a swirling mess of anger, humiliation, and heartbreak. She just needed to get home and crawl into bed. She'd figure out how to be strong again tomorrow.

Up ahead, a faint neon sign buzzed above a small 24-hour café, its warm glow spilling onto the icy sidewalk. She slowed as a cab idled near the curb in front of it, its driver scrolling through a phone. Heather didn't hesitate. She raised her arm, waving the cab down as she approached. The driver glanced up at her movement, meeting her eyes and nodding, so Heather climbed into the back seat, closing the door behind her with a heavy thud.

"Where to?" the driver asked, his voice gruff but not unkind.

Heather gave him her apartment address, her voice quiet and unsteady. She leaned back against the seat, clutching her bag to her chest as she stared out the window. The streetlights blurred into yellow and white streaks; her tears clouded her vision again.

She let out a shaky breath as the cab pulled away from the curb. The night's chaos clung to her like a second skin, but now, at least, she was moving away from it. By the time the cab reached her apartment, the raw ache in her chest had dulled into a heavy, hollow weight. She paid the driver, mumbled a thank you, and stepped out into the night. Her apartment building loomed ahead, and she walked toward it with slow, deliberate steps, barely walking into her apartment before her phone buzzed.

Ivy.

Her stomach twisted as she stared at the screen. Her hands were still shaking. Her breath was still unsteady. She almost let it go to voicemail. Almost. Instead, she swiped to answer, putting it on speaker but saying nothing.

Ivy's voice came through, bright and expectant, completely oblivious to the storm she was about to walk into. "Okay, spill! Where *are* you? I thought you were coming back here! You're totally ghosting me, aren't you? Ugh! —that means it was *good... W*ait, was it *really* good?!" Ivy giggled. "Do I need to get the ice cream ready, or should we be blocking his number?!"

Heather stayed silent and then Ivy's laugh faltered. "... Heather?"

Heather finally spoke, her voice like ice: **"You tell me."**

There was a beat of silence, then Ivy let out a nervous chuckle: "Uh... what?"

Heather's grip tightened on the phone. "You said you'd never spoken to him, Ivy."

The words dropped like a stone.

Another pause.

Then, Ivy let out a forced laugh, breezy and dismissive: "Wait, what? ...Who?"

Heather's jaw clenched. "Sam."

Dead silence.

Ivy recovered too quickly: "Oh my God— ...*is that* what this is about? ...Heather, come on... —what— ...you think I had some *secret meeting* with him or something?"

Heather stayed quiet.

Ivy's voice pitched higher, her laugh sharper: "Oh my God— *wait...* Did he say something weird to you? ...Ugh, I *knew* he was kinda awkward. Bookish guys always are... What did he say? ...Because if he made you uncomfortable, I swear I'll—"

"—Stop." Heather cut her off.

Another beat of silence.

Heather exhaled— a humorless, exhausted laugh escaping her lips. "You're actually going to lie to my face right now."

Now Ivy panicked: "Heather, no—hold on—what are you even *talking* about? Where *is* this coming from?!"

Heather's pulse roared in her ears. "I *talked* to him, Ivy. ...I *know!*"

A dramatic silence stretched out between them that felt like the death of their friendship.

Then Ivy did the *inevitable*—she tried to spin it. "Heather, babe, I don't know what he told you, but you seriously need to consider the source."

Heather closed her eyes, forcing herself to breathe before she snapped.

"I'm supposed to believe *you* over *him*?"

Ivy latched onto it immediately. "Exactly!" She let out a

breathy, almost relieved laugh, like she still thought she could salvage this. "He's obviously twisting things, babe. He likes you—I mean... duh... why wouldn't he? ...But guys do this all the time, you know? They make it seem like the girl was all over them just to look cool. It's honestly pathetic."

Heather shook her head slowly. "...Ivy..."

"...What?!" Ivy's voice was getting tighter, *more desperate now.* "...Girl, you *know* I'd never do anything to hurt you! Why are you letting some random guy mess with your head?!"

Heather inhaled sharply through her nose. "You said you'd *never spoken* to him."

Ivy huffed. "I hadn't!"

Heather's voice dropped. "Then how did you know to suggest I go out with him?"

Checkmate.

Ivy's breath hitched. Caught. Heather could *hear* her scrambling, trying to grasp for *any* excuse, but she had *nothing.*

Finally, Ivy let out a forced, nervous laugh. "Okay, wait—*hold on.* This is totally out of context."

Heather felt something *crack* inside her. *Out of context!* Like this was some *miscommunication.*

Her voice came out hollow: "...So it's true."

And now Ivy snapped: "OH MY GOD, HEATHER, WHY ARE YOU ACTING LIKE THIS IS SOME *BETRAYAL?* ...IT WAS JUST A DATE*!*"

Heather inhaled sharply. "Just a date?"

"YES!" Ivy's voice was laced with frustration now, anger replacing her panic. "You're acting like I *sold you off*! ...I was trying to *help*! ...I knew you wouldn't put yourself out there, so yeah—I gave him a little *push.*"

Heather let out a sharp, bitter laugh. "A *push*?"

Ivy scoffed. "Oh, come *on!* If I hadn't said anything, you never would've gone out with him."

Heather's stomach twisted. "So what did you say, Ivy?"

Silence.

Heather pushed. "You promised him something, didn't you?"

More silence. And then—another sharp inhale. "Heather, you're being ridiculous."

Heather's chest burned. "Say it."

Ivy exploded: "FINE! ...Yeah! —I promised him something—*So what!*"

Heather's pulse pounded.

Ivy let out an exasperated breath.

"It wasn't even a big deal, Heather! I told him if he took you out, I'd—" She stopped and let the silence hang between them, then her voice dropped low. Defensive. Biting. "—You know what? Screw this! —I'm done. You wanna be mad at me? Fine... But don't pretend like I *forced* him to like you. He could've said no. But guess what? He didn't."

Heather's vision blurred. Ivy *wasn't even sorry.*

"You know the worst part?" she asked.

Ivy huffed. "Oh, let me guess—I'm a terrible friend."

Heather exhaled, her voice calm now. "I actually believed you cared about me."

That shut Ivy up.

Heather let the words settle; let Ivy *feel* them.

Then she exhaled. "For years, I thought I needed you—" Her voice cracked, but she didn't stop. "Turns out—you needed me... You needed to feel better than me."

And then there was silence. Absolute silence.

Heather swallowed, her throat tight.

"Good luck, Ivy. You're going to need it."

And then Heather hung up.

Heather tossed her phone onto the couch and stood there in shock with her fists clenched at her sides. Her chest rose and fell with ragged, uneven breaths.

The silence in her apartment pressed against her, thick and suffocating. She could hear the faint bustle of the city outside, distant and unbothered.

Meanwhile, her entire world had just cracked open.

Her whole body was shaking with anger, with hurt, with the sheer force of holding herself back for years.

*Ivy? ...**Ivy!** ...*She had spent years thinking Ivy was the one who truly knew her, the one who had chosen her and stood beside her when no one else had.

Had it all been a fucking lie?

Heather let out a shaky breath, dragging her hands through her curls, gripping at the spiraled strands like she could physically hold herself together. Her throat felt too tight. She squeezed her eyes shut, but it didn't stop the tears from burning their way down her face. It wasn't just Ivy. It wasn't just Sam. It was... all of it.

...It was her father.

Heather let out a sharp breath, pressing her palms into her eyes and thought:

*You're supposed to grieve your dad when he dies. You're supposed to feel loss—not this sick, tangled mess of **a**nger and resentment and relief and guilt.*

She didn't miss him. Not really.

She missed the version of him that never existed.

She missed the father who should have been there. The

one who should've picked her up from school without being half-drunk and furious at the world. The one who should've looked at her and seen a daughter, not the ghost of the woman he'd lost.

But he hadn't been that man—not for a long, long time. And now he never would be.

Heather let out a choked, ragged sob as the weight of it all crashed over her.

She sank down onto the couch, curling in on herself, her body folding like it was trying to disappear. The tears slipped hot and fast down her cheeks, her breath catching on every shaky exhale.

Byrdie, curled up in her usual spot on the windowsill, lifted her head. The cat blinked at her slowly, then hopped down, landing lightly on the armrest.

Heather barely registered it until Byrdie climbed onto her side, pressing her small, warm weight against Heather's ribs.

Right against the ache.

Heather let out a shuddering breath, the pressure grounding her and crushing her all at once.

Byrdie didn't purr, didn't knead or nuzzle—just settled there, steady and silent.

Like she knew.

Heather exhaled sharply, one hand buried in Byrdie's fur, the other clamped over her mouth as she tried to quiet the grief swallowing her whole.

Heather swallowed back another sob. The movement made Byrdie snuggle tighter with her back legs on either side of Heather's waist and her front paws and chin on Heather's chest.

It had all been a lie. Her friendships... her family... her entire damn life.

Ivy had taken what she wanted; Sam had made his choice. And her father had left her behind long before the grave had made it final. They had all done whatever the hell they wanted.

They'd taken enough from her already. Her future wasn't theirs to claim.

But why was *she* the one falling apart?

An hour had passed.

The ache in her chest calcified into something else. Something sharp... something cold. She wasn't going to sit here alone, drowning in everyone else's damage, one second longer.

She inhaled deeply, her fingers curling into Byrdie's fur.

She was going to Scotland.

Chapter 7

On Wednesday, Heather woke up to the sharp buzz of her phone vibrating on the nightstand. She groaned, rolling over, her body aching with the weight of last night's revelations. She had barely slept. Not from crying—she'd done enough of that. But from the **r**age still simmering under her skin, from the betrayal thrumming in her bones, from the sheer, exhausting weight of realizing that the two people she was supposed to trust most—Ivy and her father—had never really seen her at all. She squinted at the screen, blinking against the pale morning light. Ivy's name flashed across the notifications, one after the other, relentlessly:

"Heather, are you seriously ignoring me?"

"You're really blowing this out of proportion. Can we talk?"

"Fine. Be mad. I don't care."

Heather stared at the messages, her thumb hovering over the screen, and for a second—just one second—her chest tightened. Because this was Ivy. Her best friend since childhood. The girl who had woven herself into every part of

Heather's life, who had made herself so essential that it felt impossible to untangle where Ivy ended and Heather began.

But now? Now she saw it for what it was. Ivy was panicking. Not because she regretted what she did, but because she got caught. No, if she was sorry, then the messages would have looked different.

Heather exhaled sharply with a sigh and turned her phone over, face down. She wasn't dealing with that. Not today. Not now.

She grabbed it again a second later, firing off a quick text to Mark. *"Not coming in today. Can you cover for me?"*

A moment later, the dots appeared. *"You okay?"*

Heather hesitated, then typed back. *"Just need a day."*

His reply was immediate. *"Got it. I'll tell Irene something came up. Let me know if you need anything."*

Another pause. Then another text popped up. *"Like a hitman. Or a churro. Your call."*

Heather huffed out a breath—almost a laugh. Almost. *"Just a day, Marky. Not a crime spree."*

"Fine. But the churro offer stands."

She sighed, tension slipping from her shoulders. Mark didn't ask questions—he just had her back. Even when she didn't have the words, he knew how to make space for her.

Heather tossed the phone onto the bed next to her and let her eyes drift shut again. Just five more minutes. Then she'd get up. Then she'd start figuring out how to put her life back together.

Byrdie, who was curled at the foot of the bed, flicked her tail once.

Heather sighed. "I know, I know. I'll move in a sec."

Byrdie didn't bother looking at her—not fully, anyway.

Instead, she cracked one eye open, just enough to say, *'Sure you will.'*

Heather groaned. "Traitor."

Byrdie exhaled slowly and rested her head back on her paws, unimpressed but still waiting.

Heather forced her eyes open, pressing her palms against her face. She flipped her phone to silent and forced herself to move.

She threw herself into mindless tasks—rearranging bookshelves, reorganizing drawers, scrubbing the sink until her knuckles ached. Even cleaning out Byrdie's litter box, because at least cat shit was easier to deal with than the tangled mess her life had become. But no matter how much she distracted herself, her gaze flickered to the envelope on the counter. The Glenoran paperwork—her inheritance—her mother's past; Heather's future.

She hadn't let herself dwell on it, not with everything else unraveling around her. But now, as she scrubbed the sink with more force than necessary, she realized she wasn't avoiding the decision to go to Scotland anymore—she'd decided that last night. What she was avoiding was what came next regarding her father's house.

She sighed again, tossing her kitchen sponge into the sink. There was no easing into this, no careful planning. Scotland wasn't just an idea anymore—it was happening.

Her eyes drifted toward her mother's estate documents and, this time, she didn't hesitate in reading over it to learn more.

By nightfall, after cleaning the entire apartment twice and reorganizing a cabinet that didn't need it, Heather sat at her kitchen table, laptop open, staring at the email draft she'd been working on for an hour.

Subject: *Decision Regarding Sale of the Property.*

It was her father's house: the place she grew up— the place she spent years suffocating in neglect.

She could still smell the brandy that had soaked into the carpet. Could still see the cracked walls, the broken cabinets, the stacks of unpaid bills. The real estate agent had suggested she visit his house before finalizing the sale to take inventory, to see if anything was worth keeping.

Heather's fingers hovered over the keyboard. She could go back to see the house one last time. Maybe she owed it to him. Maybe...

No.

She didn't owe it to him.

The last time she stood in that house, the stale scent of liquor hung in the air, and his silence pressed against her like a weight. The last time she stood in that house, they were wheeling his body out the front door. Heather swallowed hard, her vision blurring. It wasn't that she didn't care; it was that she couldn't. She had spent enough of her life drowning there. She refused to sink into it again. Her hands trembled as she forced herself to type:

> *I've decided to move forward with selling the house as-*
> *is. Please proceed with the listing. I won't be visiting*
> *the property, so feel free to coordinate with the cleanup*

crew for access.

She hesitated for only a second before she hit send then stared at the email with her fingers frozen over the keyboard. The words were there; the decision was made. So then why did her chest still ache? Not because she wanted to keep the house—not even close. But because this—this moment right here—was the last time she would ever have to think about it. Wasn't this the last thread connecting her to the man who was supposed to be her father? It was the house where she spent years tiptoeing around his drinking and temperamental indifference.

Her throat tightened as an uninvited memory surfaced, cutting through her like a blade:

She was nine, standing in the doorway of the kitchen. Her dad was at the table with a half-empty bottle in front of him and his head in his hands. She had worked up the courage to say it that night: to tell him that she missed Mom. That she was scared. That she just wanted him to look at her and actually see her—not a shadow of the woman he lost.

"Dad?"

He lifted his head too slowly. His eyes were glassy, unfocused. She had opened her mouth to speak more, but before she could say anything, he let out a sharp humorless laugh.

"Shit, Heather, you still standing there?"

She froze.

"What do you want from me, huh?" he muttered, rubbing a hand down his face. "You wanna hear some bullshit about how everything's gonna be fine? 'Cause it's not. It's never gonna be fine."

She had flinched, gripping the edge of the doorframe,

willing herself not to cry.

"Go to bed, kid."

And she had.

She had stopped trying that night—stopped hoping he'd comfort her, stopped waiting for him to care. Heather exhaled hard now, wiping her face before any tears could fall. Her father never got to choose a better life because his addiction controlled him, but Heather was done carrying the burdens of her father's alcoholism—done with that house, done with his shadow, done carrying the weight of what he left behind.

It was done.

The decision was made.

And just like that, the email was gone.

Byrdie jumped onto the table, her small paw landing on Heather's arm. Heather scratched behind Byrdie's ears and let out a shaky breath: "I'm doing the right thing, right?" she asked quietly. Byrdie just purred in response and Heather took that as a yes.

Heather was pacing the small living room with her phone clutched tightly in one hand and a notepad in the other. She was researching everything she'd need before flying to Scotland—passport, plane tickets, packing essentials—but every time she tried to focus, the reality of what she was doing hit her hard. Was she really doing this? Was she really going to uproot her entire life and leave everything behind? She kept losing her train of thought, her list half-written, her mind spinning between logistics and the terrifying enormity of it all.

"Okay…" she muttered, tapping the pen against her lips. "…Step one: book a flight. Step two: tell Mark I'll be gone for a while. Step three…" She faltered, glancing at the blank space beneath her neatly numbered points. "…figure out everything else."

Byrdie meowed from the couch as if in encouragement. Heather smiled despite herself, tossing the pen onto the notepad. "You make it sound so easy," she said, scooping the cat into her arms.

Byrdie purred loudly and put her paws on Heather's shoulder so she could nuzzle her on her cheek. And for a moment, the weight in Heather's chest felt lighter.

A thin beam of sunlight streamed through the window, illuminating the ornate cursive writing on the Glenoran House Estate papers that were spread across her small kitchen table as she sat down and placed Byrdie in her lap. She hadn't yet called the law office listed in the packet, despite the instructions to do so. Robert Ellis had only handed it off as a favor—he wasn't the one who could give her the answers she needed.

But now, she knew she couldn't put it off. Taking a deep breath, she dialed the number. The line rang twice before buzzing momentarily then clicked, and a cheerful voice answered on the other end.

"Duncan & Reid Solicitors, this is Isla speaking. How may I help ye today?" The familiar lilting Scottish accent threw Heather off for a second.

She cleared her throat quickly.

"Hi, um, this is Heather Campbell. I'm calling about the

Glenoran Estate." There was a brief pause, followed by the sound of shuffling papers.

"Aye! Miss Campbell, we've been expectin' yer call. Hold on just a wee moment while I pull up yer file." Heather waited, the faint sound of Isla humming a tune in the background giving her a strange sense of comfort.

"Right," Isla said, returning to the line. "Here we are! Glenoran House. ...your late mother's estate, aye? Ye know... Yer mother used to say Glenoran had secrets only the right eyes could see."

"Oh, um... okay," Heather confirmed, her voice faltering slightly. "I... I just got to look at the paperwork, and I'm trying to figure out what comes next. The letter said to call your office for guidance."

"Of course," Isla replied with compassion, her tone warm and reassuring. "It can all seem a bit overwhelmin' at first, I'm sure. But dinnae worry; we'll guide ye through it step by step."

Heather let out a breath she hadn't realized she was holding. "Thank you. ...So, what do I need to do?"

"Well..." Isla began, her voice carrying a blend of professionalism and friendliness, "...the first step will be for one of our solicitors to meet with ye in person. There's a good bit to go over—the deed, the land survey, and the property's current standing with the local council. Ye'll also want to review the estate's financials, especially if ye're considerin' sellin'."

Heather's chest tightened. "Do I have to decide right away? About selling, I mean?"

"Not at all, Miss Campbell," Isla assured her. "These things take time. Ye'll want to explore the house and the grounds, get a feel for what ye have here. It's not every day someone inherits a property like Glenoran, aye? It's a big decision, and we'll not rush ye."

"Okay," Heather said, feeling relieved to have a next step. "When can we set up the meeting?"

"I can get ye in with Mr. Reid himself," Isla said, a note of pride in her voice. "He's handled Glenoran's legal matters for years."

"That works," Heather replied.

"Lovely. Mr. Reid can meet ye here in our Edinburgh office, or if it's more convenient, he can make the trip to Glenoran."

Heather glanced around her tiny kitchen, anxiety looming about the possibility of leaving this place behind. "I think I'd prefer to meet with him at the house..."

"Absolutely," Isla chirped. "I'll let Mr. Reid know so we can make the arrangements. Please do let us know when ye will be arriving to Glenoran. He's a lovely man—patient and kind. Ye'll be in good hands, Miss Campbell."

"Thank you," Heather said, the sincerity in her tone surprising even herself.

After ending the call, Heather leaned back in her chair while her eyes lingered on the papers scattered before her. She half-expected to blink and wake herself up, only to realize that this had all been a strange, elaborate dream because owning an estate in Scotland felt too extraordinary to belong to her otherwise ordinary life.

Her phone vibrated on the desk. Her stomach twisted slightly as she reached for it and braced for another message from Ivy or Mark. But the name on the screen caught her attention— Douglas Reid.

"Already?" she uttered with a flicker of surprise crossing

her face as she unlocked her phone. His message was brief but carried a weight that made her nostalgic:

Miss Campbell,

I look forward to finally meeting you after all these years. Your mother's family has entrusted our firm with affairs since the 18th century. Glenoran House has been a part of the MacKenzie family legacy since its construction in the early 1720s. It is a remarkable property steeped in history, and I understand it holds great sentimental value to your family.

As we meet to discuss your inheritance and its future, I will ensure that all legal and historical matters are handled with the utmost care and respect. Please let me know if there is anything specific you would like to address or prepare ahead of our meeting.

Rest assured, we are here to assist you in any way we can.

Yours sincerely,
  Douglas Reid Esq.
  Duncan & Reid Solicitors

Heather reread his words: *...sentimental value to your family...*
   The phrase lingered in her heart, feeling heavy and unfamiliar, and stirring something she couldn't quite name. She set the phone down and leaned back in her chair again, staring blankly at her window as the rain streaked over it outside.

Glenoran House! It was a relic of the past and untouched for years. But yet, there it stood just waiting for her to return—not just a place with a fancy name, but a piece of her own family's legacy.

What would it be like to stand in those rooms and see the world her mother had left behind? ...What would she find? ...Would it feel like stepping into her own past or someone else's? ...Would it be painful like reopening a wound she'd carefully kept closed for years? ...Or would it be like stepping into a part of her mother's life that Heather had never had the chance to know—a glimpse of the woman behind the fading memories of her childhood?

She exhaled sharply and stood, shaking her head like she could physically shove the thought away. The motion startled Byrdie, who let out a tiny huff before leaping down from the couch.

"Wait... what am I doing, Byrdie?" She ran a hand through her hair, pacing.

"It's just a house. Just some paperwork and old bricks. I'll go, see what's what, and then figure it out. No big decisions. No getting attached."

She bent down, smoothing a hand over Byrdie's fur, like she was trying to believe her own lie.

She tried to dismiss it, but a small persistent voice whispered that Glenoran House might hold more than bricks and history. It might hold pieces of her that she hadn't even realized were missing.

She let out a settling breath as she sank back into the chair and typed a reply:

Thank you. I'll book my flight soon and update you

with my arrival time. I'd appreciate having someone meet me there.

She sent the message and stared out the window at the gray sky. On the one hand, her father's house was waiting to be sold, knowing she'd have to handle more logistics soon—yet that felt like a closed chapter, one she never needed to reopen.

But on the other hand... Glenoran was completely different—it wasn't about letting go of the past. She was about to step into something she didn't quite understand yet, still learning how to step into her future.

Glenoran had been waiting for *her*.

Chapter 8

The bell above the door jingled softly as Heather stepped into Evergreen Books, but to her dismay, it didn't feel comforting. The warm scent of paper should have soothed her, and the creak of the wooden floors should have felt familiar—but instead, her nerves buzzed louder than ever.

She spotted Irene Alcott, her boss and owner of the shop, near the front counter, flipping through a hardcover with practiced ease. Irene looked exactly as a bookstore owner should—soft cardigans, wire-rimmed glasses perched at the tip of her nose, and a collection of cat hairs that clung to every surface of her clothing, no matter how often she brushed them off. Her silvery hair was always twisted into a loose bun, a few wisps escaping like they had better places to be.

She had the presence of a person who had spent her whole life surrounded by stories—patient, unhurried, as if time worked differently in her little world. And she was kind, the sort of kind that wasn't loud or overbearing, but gentle and steady, like a cat curling up beside you just because it knows you need the company.

By the window, Mark stacked new arrivals, his easy posture at odds with the way his gaze snapped to her the second she walked in. Heather inhaled sharply, gripping the strap of her bag. No turning back now. She walked toward Irene, her footsteps almost silent.

Irene glanced up, adjusting her glasses with one finger as she spotted Heather. "Well, look at you, bright and early." Her voice was warm, laced with that ever-present knowing sort of quality, like she already sensed something was coming.

Heather swallowed past the lump in her throat.

"Morning."

She could feel Mark's eyes on her, sharp and unreadable.

"Can we talk for a minute?"

Irene's smile faded just a touch, curiosity flickering behind her expression.

"Of course, dear."

She set her book down with careful deliberation, smoothing one hand over the worn cover before motioning toward the tiny office tucked behind the shelves. "Come on, then. Let's have a chat."

Heather followed, her pulse pounding. Inside, the office looked the same as always. Stacks of invoices, old catalogs, a chipped ceramic mug that was filled with mismatched pens, and at least one stray cat hair. Cozy. Familiar.

Safe.

And yet, it already felt like something she was leaving behind.

Irene lowered herself into her chair with a soft sigh, folding her hands over the desk. "Sit, darling."

Heather shook her head, fidgeting with her bag strap.

Just say it, she thought.

"Irene, I... I need to give my notice."

The words tumbled out before she could overthink them.

Irene blinked, then tilted her head, her sharp eyes scanning Heather's face with quiet questioning: "...your notice?"

Heather nodded quickly. "It's just... something came up. Family stuff. I need to go to Scotland for a while, and I don't know how long I'll be gone."

Irene hummed as she reached for her mug and took a slow sip, like she was weighing her words. "Scotland?" she said softly, then paused before continuing. "...that's quite the journey."

Heather hesitated. "It's complicated."

And that was the truth! Life really was complicated right now. She told herself she wasn't running away—just leaving everything behind. But wasn't that the same thing?

Irene studied her for a long moment, then let out a thoughtful sigh. "You've had that far-off look about you for a while now, you know."

Heather's stomach tightened, but she didn't answer. She didn't need to.

Irene set her mug down, the ceramic clinking gently against the desk. "I'll be sorry to lose you, dear. You've been a steady presence here."

Steady.

She'd spent her whole life being steady. Predictable. Safe. ...but not anymore.

Irene smiled then. It was the kind of smile that crinkled at the edges, soft and understanding. "The world's been pulling at you, hasn't it?"

Heather swallowed. "...maybe...?"

Irene nodded, like that answer was enough. She'd already known it before Heather did. "Well..." she said, tapping a finger against the desk, "...you'll always have a place here when you find your way back."

Heather's throat tightened. "Thank you," she murmured, "... for everything."

Irene gave her a long, thoughtful look before nodding. "Go on, then. Take care of yourself."

Heather barely made it two steps out of the office before Mark appeared in front of her with his arms crossed and an unreadable expression.

"So, you're quitting." It wasn't a question.

Heather sighed, adjusting her bag. "I was going to tell you, I just—"

"—Relax," he cut in, waving a dismissive hand. "I figured it out the second you started looking all *wistful* near the travel section." His voice softened. "It's okay, Heth."

She blinked. "Wait. You're... okay with this?"

Mark leaned against the counter, deceptively casual. "Would I *prefer* that you stay here forever and keep me entertained while Irene passive-aggressively critiques my shelving? Obviously." He exhaled. "But if anyone deserves to take a leap, it's you."

Heather hesitated. "...I thought you'd be mad."

Mark let out a dramatic sigh, then shrugged. "Maybe a little.

Yeah, His expression softened. "but mostly? I'm proud of you."

Something lodged in her throat.

Proud of her.

She'd spent years feeling like she wasn't enough— like she was just Ivy's shadow. Or just her father's afterthought. Or just someone who floated through life, waiting for permission from other people. But now? Now, she was giving permission to herself.

Mark studied her face; his usual smirk had faded into something more thoughtful. "This trip— it's your chance to figure out who you're without all the noise. And honestly? I think you're about to have your *'heroine-discovering-herself-in-a-windswept-landscape'* moment."

Heather's eyes stung with the idea of leaving him behind, but she smiled.

He reached out and didn't just squeeze her shoulder but instead wrapped her into a tight, solid hug that felt like a weighted blanket—strong and steady, knocking the tension right out of her.

Heather stiffened with surprise for a second, caught off guard, but then melted into it. She hadn't realized how much she needed the hug—or how much she'd missed him after just one day away. When he finally pulled back, he gave her a mock-serious look. "Okay, just promise me one thing."

She raised a brow. "What?"

His grin turned sly. "Send me a postcard. Or ten. Preferably something ridiculous—like a sheep in a tiny kilt."

Heather laughed now, wiping at her eyes. "If they don't sell one, I'll make one myself."

She was almost free to go, but then Mark's voice pulled her

back. "Hey... are you going to tell Ivy you're leaving?"

The question hit like a punch to the gut.

Her fingers tightened around the strap of her bag again, her pulse spiking with an immediate visceral response. She exhaled through her nose, dropping her gaze to the counter.

"I don't know." The words came out flat, but something sharp twisted in her chest. "She hurt me so badly, Mark. I don't feel like I can."

He sighed and leaned against the counter again as he crossed his arms. "I get that things are messy between you two right now."

Heather huffed a bitter laugh. Messy didn't even begin to cover it.

"But, Heather," Mark continued, watching her carefully, "you and Ivy have been through a *lot* together. Maybe leaving without saying anything isn't how to go about it."

Her chest tightened—not with guilt, but with something frustrated and raw.

Of course, that was his first thought. Of course, everyone always came back to Ivy.

Heather's throat ached with the weight of everything she hadn't said yet. "Did she ever tell you?" she asked.

Mark's brows knit together. "Tell me what?"

Heather hesitated for half a second, but then thought, "Fuck it." "Ivy bribed Sam to take me out."

Mark's expression froze. Heather pushed forward with her confession, and the words tumbled out before she could choke on them. "She told him that if he went on a date with me, she'd sleep with him after."

Silence.

Mark's arms dropped to his sides. His whole posture

shifted—the casual ease was gone in an instant. "She, *what!*" His voice wasn't teasing anymore—low, sharp. Angry. Heather's chest hollowed out at the sound of it.

"Yeah..." she said bitterly, her voice trembling. "That's how little she thinks of me."

His jaw ticked.

The weight of it all pressed down on Heather. "How do I even begin to have a conversation with her after that?"

Mark let out a slow, controlled breath— one of those deep, calming exhales that meant he was trying *very* hard not to explode.

He ran a hand over his face, then rubbed the back of his neck. "That's... uh, wow." His voice was tight. "I didn't know it was that bad." Heather let out a short, humorless laugh. "Neither did I."

Mark shook his head. "I'm sorry, Heather. That's beyond messed up."

For a second, she thought that was it. That he'd understand now, but then he hesitated, and Heather felt it before he even said it.

"...Even so..."

Heather's stomach dropped. *Here it comes.*

He chose his words too carefully: "...maybe saying something will help *you*. Not her."

Heather's fists curled against the strap of her bag. "Mark—"

"—I'm not saying forgive her." He raised a hand, cutting her off before she could argue. "I'm saying that walking away without saying goodbye could leave more loose ends. And you don't need more of those."

Heather's teeth clenched so tightly that it hurt. She knew

what he meant. But *God, it burned.* Because she could feel it—the old instinct pulling at her like a leash—to be the bigger person. To fix it. To *not* let the story end like this. But why was it *always* on her? Why was she always the one who had to worry about loose ends? Why was she always the one who had to make it right?

Heather let herself be angry. "She made me a joke, Mark." Her voice shook, but her resolve didn't waver.

Mark exhaled slowly, shaking his head. "Heather, listen to me. You were never a joke. You are the kindest, most brilliant person I know. And if she couldn't see that?" His voice softened, but his eyes stayed sharp. "...that's not on you. That's on her."

Heather inhaled deeply, the words settling into something raw, something unshakable in her heart. Her chest ached—not just from the hurt, but from the sheer relief of being seen. Of knowing that maybe she hadn't been the fool Ivy had made her out to be.

Her fingers released the strap of her bag, and both hands curled into fists at her sides, then released as she breathed out a slow breath, a steadying exhale. She met Mark's gaze, not just with exhaustion, but with something closer to believing him.

Finally, she gave a small, reluctant nod. "I'll think about it," she said.

It wasn't just a way to end the conversation with Mark. It was a promise to at least let the thought exist instead of shoving it down. To admit—even just to herself—that she might need to tell Ivy she was leaving—for her own benefit.

Mark reached out, giving her shoulder a firm, reassuring squeeze. "That's all I'm saying. Just think about it."

Heather nodded again. The heaviness in her chest hadn't disappeared, but it shifted. She finally took a deep breath, then stepped forward, wrapping her arms around Mark's neck and holding on tightly. "Thanks, *Marky.* For everything."

Her voice was quiet, but full of meaning. He hugged her back, warm and solid. "You don't have to thank me. This is what friends do."

But she did thank him, because for the first time in a long time, she felt like someone was actually standing in her corner.

Mark pulled back, and his grin returned, lighter this time, teasing, "Now get out of here before Irene starts knitting you a goodbye scarf..." He paused. "...Or worse—a full sweater!"

Heather laughed, the sound breaking through the tension. For once, it didn't feel forced. It felt real. She shook her head, smiling as she half-turned toward the door. "I'll send you pictures," she said. "But don't get too sentimental—I'm just going to check things out. Figure out what's what. Then I'll be back."

"You'd better." Mark leaned against the counter again, forcing a smirk, but it didn't quite reach his eyes this time. They were glassy, like he was blinking back something he wasn't ready to let spill over.

Heather's throat tightened, and something in her chest twisted again—not with pain, but with gratitude so sharp it almost hurt. She let out a breath, a quiet exhale that felt heavier than it should. She hesitated. "I'm not gone for good, you know! Just until I figure out what to do with the house."

Mark gave her a look, one eyebrow raised like he didn't quite believe her. "Sure. That's what they all say." He sniffed, exhaled sharply, and then—because he was Mark—shook his head and muttered, "Geez, Heather. Look what you're doing to me. I don't do feelings before noon."

But his voice cracked just a little, betraying him.

Heather pulled back, smiling. "Thanks, *Marky*."

Mark huffed a small laugh, shaking his head, but there was nothing teasing in it this time—just warmth. Just looking at her like he meant it.

Then, as she turned to go, he added, "Anytime, Heth."

Soft. Certain. Sincere. He was a true friend.

And then, with purpose, Heather stepped out of the bookstore and into the crisp winter air.

As she made her way down the street, her boots clicking against the pavement, her mind wandered to what lay ahead. Scotland still didn't feel real. Her inheritance felt like something from one of the novels she loved—impossible, magical, undeserved. She pulled out her phone and tapped the notes app where she'd started making a list: ...rain boots, sweaters —not the old ones with holes in the sleeves, and a decent coat...

As she neared a row of boutiques she'd always passed by but never entered, she paused. She could afford it now. She could actually buy what she needed—and maybe a little of what she wanted.

She thought back to her meeting at the bank that morning. The financial advisor had been kind and patient, walking her through the account details:

*"Your mother must've set this up with you in mind,"
he'd said warmly. "She wanted you to feel secure, to
have something for moments just like this. It was a
large sum to begin with but has collected substantial
interest in the sixteen years that it has sat untouched."*

Heather had nodded, blinking too quickly, her throat thick. She hadn't even known her mother was planning for her this far ahead. But of course she had. Elidh had always done the hard things quietly, without fanfare. His words lingered with her now, stirring a bittersweet mix of gratitude and longing.

As she approached the boutiques, she let herself believe the truth that it was okay to use this money—not out of guilt or hesitation, but because it was time to step into her own life. This wasn't just about clothes; it was about claiming a future her mother had always wanted for her.

Heather felt strange to be shopping without Ivy by her side. But maybe strange wasn't the right word. It was quieter. Freer. There was no one to critique her choices or gently steer her toward something bolder "because it flattered her figure." No careful calculation to make sure she didn't outshine Ivy in a photo. No second-guessing. Just... her.

There was no Ivy here today. Heather embraced her choices and the quiet thrill of stepping into something new. Without anyone else's presence overshadowing her, she felt a flicker of possibility—a chance to see herself differently.

The first shop was cozy, with racks of wool coats and scarves in muted gray, forest green, and deep burgundy. Heather ran her fingers over the soft fabrics, imagining herself walking through the Scottish countryside with the wind whipping through her hair. She stopped before a full-length mirror, holding a Barbour jacket with classic plaid lining against herself. "This," she murmured to no one in particular. "This feels right."

After a quick chat with the shopkeeper—who promised her that the coat would hold up against even the worst Scottish weather—Heather left the boutique with her first purchase tucked under her arm.

The second store was a little trendier, with a window display full of chunky knits and ankle boots. Heather lingered over the sweaters, picking out a few in earthy tones. She caught herself smiling as she held up a soft cream-colored one with intricate cable knitting. It wasn't her usual style—far more polished than the thrifted hoodies she typically wore—but something about the Celtic pattern felt hopeful, like a slight nod to the new start she was chasing.

By the time she stepped out of the third shop, her arms were full of bags—jeans that actually fit, sturdy boots, and a couple of thick scarves. She was about to head home when she turned a corner and found herself standing in front of a lingerie shop she'd walked past countless times but never dared to enter.

Heather stood outside the boutique, fingers curled around the straps of her shopping bags, hesitating. For years, she believed places like this weren't meant for girls like her.

The mannequins were draped in lace bralettes, silk robes, delicate satin. The kind of things Ivy would have picked without a second thought. But Heather? She had always stuck to the clearance racks at department stores.

She tightened her grip on the bags in her hands that were full of various articles of clothing—cozy sweaters, a sturdy coat, *practical things.*

This wasn't practical.

This was something else—a choice. A breath of uncertainty curled in her chest. Could she do this? Did she deserve to? Heather inhaled sharply. Then stepped inside.

A low, sultry melody drifted through the air as the faint floral scent of the store instantly soothed her nerves. The boutique was small but charming, with its delicate racks of lace, satin, and silk in every shade imaginable—all bathed in soft, flattering light.

She meandered through the store, her fingertips skimming over the intricate embroidery and delicate fabrics. She picked up a lace-trimmed slip, the silk cool against her skin. Each piece was more beautiful than the last. Everything about the space felt intimate and unique. It was like stepping into a secret world. Her eyes landed on a matching set with a silk bralette and lace-trimmed briefs in soft lavender, its lace trim so fine that it looked like fairies had spun it. She paused, brushing the fabric lightly with her fingers and marveling at how something so small could feel so exquisite—a far cry from her department store usuals.

"Can I help you find anything?" a cheerful sales associate asked, her smile friendly and genuine.

Heather smiled back, trying not to feel self conscious. "I'm just... looking for a fresh start. Something that makes me feel pretty, I guess?"

The associate beamed. "I've got just the thing. Follow me." Before long, Heather found herself in a fitting room with a pile of options draped over the bench.

She stood before the mirror with her curly tresses tumbling over her shoulders in unruly waves and her fair skin catching the soft, flattering light. Typically, she wouldn't have lingered in the mirror: the roundness of her hips, the soft lines of her belly, the fullness of her breasts that never seemed to sit quite right in anything she wore. But today... she paused. Something had shifted. There was curiosity instead of criticism.

She slipped into a matching bra and panty set of pale pink satin, the silky fabric skimming over her curves. For once, the mirror didn't feel like an enemy. Next, she tried a classic black lace set that hugged her body in all the right places, making her feel bold in a way she hadn't in years. Lastly, she put on a soft gray bralette with delicate floral embroidery, the gentle support making her feel comfortable and undeniably feminine.

Surprisingly, Heather didn't focus on what she usually picked apart. Each piece made her feel a little more like the woman she wanted to be. Confident. Beautiful.

Sexy.

As Heather made her way to the checkout counter, she saw a display near the back: a long-sleeve white linen two-piece set, understated yet effortlessly chic. The top was light and airy, with a relaxed fit, and the flowy pants featured a high, comfortable waistband. She imagined herself lounging by the fire in her new home, cuddled up in a large leather armchair with a hot cup of tea, wearing the effortlessly-comfy-yet-polished outfit, stepping into the next chapter of her life with quiet confidence.

She picked up the outfit without hesitation, adding it to her growing pile as well as a soft cashmere robe in a dainty blush tone, its fabric thick enough to ward off the Highland chill but still delicate against her skin.

By the time she left the boutique, her arms were full, and her cheeks were flushed—not with embarrassment, but with a new and unfamiliar joy. She'd indulged—not out of necessity, but simply because she wanted to. And it felt liberating.

Heather's fingers hovered over her phone. Ivy's name sat at the top of her messages.

You should tell her you're leaving, Mark had said.

Even after everything, some part of her still felt like she owed Ivy something. A goodbye. An explanation.

But for what?

Ivy had already decided who Heather was—small, convenient, disposable. And maybe Heather had spent too many years believing it.

Tightening her grip on her shopping bags, she huffed in frustration: *No! Not this time.* Then she slipped her phone into her pocket and turned toward the bus stop, knowing that she didn't need Ivy's permission to move forward. And she let herself savor the moment for once.

As she waited for the bus, she glanced at her reflection in the glass of a nearby shop window. Her wild red curls framed her face and her cheeks were pink—both from the cold and the day's excitement. She expected to see the same hesitant girl that she always was—the one who lingered in the background, who let others shine while she faded. But the woman staring back at her looked... different. Lighter. It was as if she had finally stepped into her own space—into her own skin.

Heather didn't avert her eyes from herself. She held her own gaze, the hint of a smile curling at the edges of her lips.

She was beginning to see herself truthfully.

The bus pulled up with a hiss, and she stepped on, settling into a seat by the window. As the boutiques and cafés of Millhaven's shopping district blurred past, Heather thought about what lay ahead—the long flight, Glenoran House. The solicitor. Her mother's legacy... It was daunting, but such a big spark of excitement flowed through her. Would Mom have liked this one?

Elidh had always been a memory—an absence. A ghost in photographs. A laugh Heather barely remembered.

But now, she imagined her mother beside her, watching with quiet pride. Maybe she'd have nudged Heather toward the green sweater. Teased her for overthinking. Squeezed her hand and whispered:

You're ready, sweetheart.

The thought warmed her, even as it ached.

Maybe this—this strength, this peace—was what her mother had dreamed of for her all along.

Heather let herself lean into that new perspective, ready to see where it would take her.

Chapter 9

The next few days passed in a whirlwind of preparation, each task chipping away at Heather's nerves and building anticipation. Her laptop glowed in the dim apartment as she sat at her desk late one evening, staring at a list of flight options. She'd always gone straight to economy—no questions, no extras. Just good enough. But her finger hovered over the screen, hesitating. And then, for once, she didn't settle. She booked first class.

Her mother had always believed in treating life as an adventure, finding little joy even when things were difficult.

"We deserve to make room for comfort, Lammie," she'd said, nudging Heather's shoulder as they wound through the Appalachian hills in a rented RV, their laughter echoing through the trees.

Heather drummed her fingers against the desk, her mother's words echoing in her mind. She pressed confirm. It felt extravagant, almost absurd—but that's what the trust fund was for. A chance to leap into something new. When the confirmation email hit her inbox, a small smile tugged at her lips.

Byrdie padded into the room, her tri-colored tail swishing. She hopped into Heather's lap, purring. Heather stroked her soft fur, heart tightening at the thought she'd been avoiding—should she bring her to Scotland?

The practical answer was no. Long flight. New environment. Too much change. But the emotional one? Unshakable. Byrdie had been her constant, her quietest comfort.

The next day, Heather researched pet travel, made the calls, and picked up a soft-sided carrier from the store. Byrdie was coming. They belonged together—whatever lay ahead.

Between packing and sorting her apartment, Heather paused often to pet her or whisper about their upcoming adventure.

"Glenoran House..." she said softly one afternoon, sitting cross-legged on her bedroom floor with an open suitcase in front of her. Byrdie blinked up at her with green eyes that were calm and steady. "...It sounds like a whole other world, Byrdie. But you and me—we'll figure it out together."

Every day, Heather's apprehension was slowly replaced by her growing sense of purpose. Byrdie would be right there with her, a little piece of home as she stepped into the unknown.

She moved to sit on her bed and Byrdie curled up beside her, purring softly. Her phone rested on her lap with its blank message screen glowing. For days, she'd wrestled with the decision about contacting Ivy; whether to say something or whether to walk away completely.

Ivy had been in her life for so long, woven into her days like a second skin. Unraveling from her felt unnatural.

Painful.

But the truth was, they'd been fraying for a long time. Sam was just the final, unforgivable thread. Heather hadn't spoken to Ivy since that night—not when the apology texts poured in, tangled with excuses. Not when Mark suggested she respond for her own closure. And not when the ache of loss settled in her chest like a second heartbeat.

Because Ivy had made her a joke. A prize to be bartered. She'd laughed while Heather stood there, blindsided and humiliated.

But saying goodbye still felt impossible. Silence had become its own kind of closure—sharp and cold.

And yet, the closer she got to leaving, the heavier those unsent words became.

How long would she be in Scotland?

Days? Weeks? Months?

Despite the betrayal—despite knowing she'd never truly mattered—leaving without a word felt unfinished. It wasn't a story she was ready to slam shut, even if she had no energy left to rewrite it.

Heather bit her lip, fingers hovering over her phone. Ivy had shattered her—but Ivy had also been there through her father's worst nights. She'd held Heather when the grief of losing her mother was too heavy to bear.

She'd been her best friend.

And even if they never spoke again, even if it stayed broken forever... Ivy had been a part of her life for too long to leave behind without saying anything at all.

Heather inhaled sharply, then exhaled slowly. This wasn't a reconciliation. It was closure. Quiet... necessary... *final.*

It was about walking away without looking back and about

letting go so that she could finally step forward in life.

Her hands trembled slightly as she started typing, cautious, deliberate:

Hi, Ivy. I just wanted to let you know I'm leaving for Scotland tomorrow. I don't know how long I'll be gone, but I felt like I should tell you. Things between us are still hard for me to process, but I wanted to say goodbye. Take care.

She read it twice. Then a third time. It wasn't angry. It wasn't hopeful. It wasn't a door left open. It was just... the truth. She pressed send. And let it go.

Her phone buzzed almost instantly. She barely had time to unlock the screen before Ivy's name flashed again. Heather hesitated to look. She knew it wouldn't be a heartfelt goodbye. But still, some part of her needed to see it, so with a deep breath, she opened it.

"Oh, so you finally decided to say something. How thoughtful."

Heather's stomach tightened. ...of course.

A beat later, another text came through—petty, venomous.

"Enjoy your fancy castle life. Try not to get trampled by a cow or sheep or whatever."

Heather exhaled slowly, willing herself to stay calm. Another buzz, another message. This time, it cut deeper.

"And next time you decide to go crying to Mark, maybe remember that not everything is about you. Hope you two are happy gossiping about me."

There it was. Ivy wasn't just mad that she was leaving. Ivy was mad that Mark knew—mad that he'd called her out. Mad that, for once, someone had taken Heather's side.

Her chest ached—not with guilt, but with something sharper. Final. Inevitable. And surprisingly, she didn't feel the need to reply.

It wasn't just the words. It was how fast Ivy responded like she'd been waiting to twist the knife, like the idea of Heather moving on was something she couldn't stand.

An unwanted feeling crept in—that old ache of wanting Ivy's approval, even when Ivy didn't deserve to give it.

For so long, Ivy had been the center of their friendship. The one who shined, who dictated the rules, who decided what mattered and what didn't. And Heather had always been the supporting role. Even now, even after everything, Ivy still thought she had the power to reduce Heather to nothing with a few careless words. Heather's fingers curled tightly around her phone. And then—She laughed.

It was a quiet, bitter, incredulous laugh. Because this was pathetic. Ivy wasn't hurt; Ivy wasn't heartbroken. She was pissed that Heather had the audacity to leave.

Heather set the phone down firmly, flipping it face-down. She wasn't falling into this again. She wasn't letting Ivy's words poison her excitement, her choices, and her future. Because Ivy would never get it. She never had. She never would.

Heather took a deep breath now, pressing her palms against her thighs, grounding herself. Engaging with Ivy would only drag her back into the same exhausting cycle. Ivy didn't think she'd done anything wrong, and she never would. There was no point in a losing battle. Heather had said goodbye. And that was all she needed to do.

Byrdie stretched beside her, her soft purr filling the silence. Heather reached out, scratching behind Byrdie's ears, finding comfort in the steady, unbothered presence of her cat.

"That's enough of that..." she muttered, more to herself than to Byrdie.

Heather didn't even bother checking if Ivy responded again. Instead, she stood, crossing the room to her half-packed suitcase.

Because Scotland was waiting.

And for the first time in a long time, she wasn't waiting on someone else to decide her worth.

She was deciding it for herself.

And that felt better than any apology Ivy could have given.

Heather stood and knelt by her suitcase, smoothing out a soft cable-knit sweater. Morning would come fast, and she still had too much to do. Her packing had been slow, deliberate—each item a quiet act of faith. In comfort. In readiness. In herself.

She folded the new jeans and tucked them beside her Barbour jacket—armor for the Highlands. A few scarves followed, rich greens and deep burgundies that reminded her of autumn in Millhaven.

She paused at the shopping bag from the lingerie boutique. The delicate lace and satin inside felt like more than just indulgence. They were tokens of something new. Of feeling beautiful for herself.

Heather folded the blush satin first, then the timeless black lace, then the embroidered bralette and matching panties— each piece making her feel soft, feminine, *seen*.

She traced the cashmere robe with her fingers, smiling as she imagined slipping it on in a grand old room at Glenoran. A quiet thrill rose in her chest.

These weren't just clothes. They were a promise—to

embrace change, to believe she was worth the effort.

She stood and stretched, then wandered toward the window. Outside, the city moved on as if nothing was changing. But everything was.

Back at her dresser, she added a few essentials—pajamas, plain undergarments, fuzzy socks. She glanced at Byrdie's carrier near the door. She had considered leaving her behind, just until she got settled. But she couldn't. Byrdie had to come.

For a moment, doubt whispered.

What if I'm making a mistake?

What if I don't belong?

What if I regret leaving?

No.

She'd spent too long waiting for permission to live. Doubt would always whisper—but she didn't have to listen anymore.

Scotland was a beginning. And beginnings required a leap.

Her thoughts drifted to Glenoran House—the solicitor, the wild hills, the version of herself waiting somewhere beyond them. The grief didn't feel so sharp anymore. It had softened into something else. Something like hope.

She zipped the suitcase and picked up the trust fund paperwork beside her passport. Her mother's voice echoed in her mind—*History matters. Not just in books, but in the stories we carry.*

She would have loved this, wouldn't she?

The thought settled in Heather's chest—bittersweet, but warm. For the first time, she truly believed her mother would be proud.

"New country, new me, Byrdie." Heather smiled.

The cat let out a soft meow from the bed, as if questioning

her.

"Don't look at me like that," Heather laughed. "You're coming too."

Chapter 10

"Why on earth did I choose such an early flight?" Heather groaned as her alarm blared at 3:30 AM, shrill and relentless.

Her hand fumbled blindly across the nightstand, knocking over an empty water glass before finally finding her phone. The screen glowed too bright, making her squint as she silenced the alarm. A grumpy chirp came from the foot of the bed: Byrdie was curled up in a loaf, her green eyes slitted with disapproval and her tail flicking in irritated protest.

Heather let out a breathless, tired laugh. "Sorry, girly," she croaked with a scratchy voice as she rubbed her eyes. "Believe me, I'm tired too."

But she wasn't just physically exhausted. She was emotionally drained. No Ivy. No Mark. No Evergreen Books. No familiar streets, no quiet café mornings, no steady routine to ground her, no comfort in the familiar.

She'd spent the last few weeks cutting ties, but now that it was time to walk away completely, she felt the ache of it in a way she hadn't prepared for. The weight of leaving pressed against her chest, feeling heavier than she had expected.

She sat up slowly, dragged herself to the bathroom, and splashed cold water on her face. She was really doing this!

Her suitcase waited by the door, neatly packed. Byrdie sat beside it in her carrier, blinking with sleepy disinterest. Heather knelt beside the carrier, rubbing her fingers over the mesh lining. "I hope you're ready for an adventure," she murmured. "Because there's no turning back now."

Byrdie let out a soft meow, blinking at her. Heather swallowed. No turning back. Then why did it still feel like part of her was still looking over her shoulder?

Once her greatest comfort, the apartment now felt like something she was shedding: not a home anymore—just a space she'd passed through.

She exhaled and reached for her coat.

It was time.

"...I think that covers it, don't you, Byrdie-girl?" The cat let out a soft meow as if to agree, and Heather smiled.

Byrdie yawned lazily in response, and Heather couldn't help but huff. "You're going to be the most well-traveled cat in the neighborhood," she said with a soft laugh.

She didn't know if she was running toward something or just away from everything—but either way, she was finally moving. The morning air was cold and unforgiving as she and Byrdie stepped outside, with the mist clinging to the pavement and the streetlights glaring in the pre-dawn quiet. Their taxi idled at the curb with its headlights cutting through the early morning haze.

Heather took one last look at the small apartment building she'd called home for years. It wasn't perfect; it never had been. But it had been hers. She inhaled deeply and then swallowed the lump in her throat as she and Byrdie slid into the backseat. As the taxi pulled away, she watched the familiar streets blur past, disappearing into the dark.

The airport was already alive with movement despite the early hour. Heather felt like she was moving on autopilot, as if her body was going through the motions even as her mind swam with the thought of everything she was leaving behind—check-in, security, navigating through the crowds. But a wave of quiet luxury washed over her when she stepped into the first-class lounge—soothing but unfamiliar.

She'd never flown like this before.

Everything about it felt like it belonged to someone else: someone polished; someone who knew exactly where they were going. And yet... Heather was here. She settled into a chair, with a glass of water in hand and her suitcase tucked beside her.

Her jeans and sweater suddenly felt all wrong—like they still belonged to the girl she was leaving behind. Digging through her suitcase, her fingers brushed over the white linen two-piece set she'd bought days earlier.

The fabric was soft and weightless in her hands: a clean slate. She stepped into the lounge's private restroom to change, and then she barely recognized herself. The linen fabric skirted her edges and softened her silhouette while the top draped over her in a way that felt effortless and unburdened.

Heather stared at her reflection, adjusting the neckline and smoothing her hands over her hips. She looked... *New*. Like someone lighter, freer. Like someone who wasn't just carrying ghosts on her back. he saw the version of herself she wanted to be—the girl who had waited, not the girl who had settled. Not the girl who had swallowed her hurt for the sake of peace.

Someone *else*.

Someone... *more*.

"It's just you and me now," she murmured, pressing her palm gently against the mesh front of the carrier. Byrdie sniffed at her fingers, then rubbed her cheek against them, her soft purr vibrating through the fabric.

Heather exhaled, a little of the tension in her chest easing. "We're going to be okay, right?"

Byrdie purred again, and something tight in Heather's chest loosened. Maybe the healing sound of Byrdie's contentment was all the reassurance she needed. By the time the boarding call echoed through the terminal, Heather's nerves had settled into a quiet acceptance.

She adjusted Byrdie's carrier, stepping onto the jet bridge. Her seat on the plane was spacious and semi-private which was a comfort she'd never known before.

She placed Byrdie's carrier under the seat, settled in, and ran her fingers over the plush leather armrest. Not long after she boarded, a flight attendant offered her champagne. She hesitated with the weight of the past twenty-four hours pressing down on her. But then she gave a smile of gratitude to the flight attendant as she accepted the fluted glass.

Her gaze drifted to the window and the sleepy city lights

blurring beneath the clouds... but then the doubt slithered in again:

...What if I hate it there?...

...What if I don't belong?...

...What if I come back even more lost than before?...

She lifted the champagne glass to her lips again, her decision solidifying for her as the plane left the ground.

She wasn't turning back.

Not this time.

Chapter 11

The flight touched down smoothly, with its wheels kissing the tarmac as the early morning light spilled over the hills surrounding Edinburgh Airport. Heather gaped out the window, her breath catching as the soft gray sky gave way to glimpses of green fields, snow-capped mountains, and distant stone buildings. *Scotland!* She was here.

As Heather followed the signs toward baggage claim, she took a steadying breath to settle the nervousness and anticipation in her chest.

The baggage terminal was clean and modern, yet undeniably Scottish. A *Visit Scotland* poster showcased the Highlands, a whisky advert boasted the '*true taste of Scotland*', and cheerful signs welcomed travelers with a friendly "*Fáilte gu Alba.*"

Welcome to Scotland, indeed.

The crisp air from outside the sliding doors sent a shiver down her spine as she exited the arrivals hall, holding onto

Byrdie's carrier over her shoulder and clutching her suitcase handle with her other hand. As she scanned the crowd for the driver with whom her solicitor had made arrangements, she noticed him near the exit, wearing a black coat and holding a sign that read: *Miss H. Campbell.*

Heather squared her shoulders against the chill and walked toward him, the reality of her new life beginning to take shape with every step.

The man holding the sign gave her a polite smile as she approached. He was tall, but unimposing and built with the quiet sturdiness of a man accustomed to long hours on the road. His salt-and-pepper hair peeked out from under his tartan flat cap, the brim tilted just enough to shade his sharp hazel eyes.

"Miss Campbell?" he asked in a thick Scottish accent, lowering the sign. Heather nodded as she adjusted Byrdie's carrier on her shoulder again. "That's me."

"Welcome to Scotland," he said warmly, reaching to take her suitcase. "Name's Alastair. I'll be drivin' ye to Glenoran House."

"Thank you," she said, handing over the suitcase with a small smile. "I really appreciate it."

Alastair tilted his head toward the exit. "Car's just outside. Let's get ye sorted."

As they exited the terminal, she glanced up at the sky: a patchwork of pale gray clouds shifting lazily overhead.

Alastair led her to a sleek black car parked near the curb and opened the door for her. "Ye'll be comfortable in here. Long ride ahead, but we'll make good time."

Byrdie let out a soft meow as Heather slipped into the backseat. "Almost there, Byrd," she whispered, unzipping the mesh just as Byrdie pressed against her hand and purred loudly, though it was barely audible over the noise of raindrops tapping against the car's windows.

Once on the open road, Heather gazed out the window, taking in the rolling hills and quaint stone cottages that dotted the countryside. The city quickly gave way to sprawling fields, their edges lined with dry-stacked stone walls and clusters of trees that looked ancient and wise.

Scotland's winters were nothing like the ones she'd grown used to in Millhaven. Winter back home was a mere inconvenience with slush-covered streets, gloomy skies, and the rush of people hurrying from one place to another despite the weather. It was brutal in its own way with freezing winds, streets buried under snow, and the kind of cold that stung your skin. But here, in the rugged Scottish countryside, it was different. Winter here felt sharper and less forgiving than the bitter cold of Millhaven. The chill here seeped into everything, damp and inescapable, clinging to stone and earth like a memory that refused to fade.

"Ye've come a long way," Alastair said, breaking the silence.

"I have," Heather replied, her voice soft. "It's... a bit surreal, honestly."

"Aye, I can imagine," he said, glancing at her in the rearview mirror. "First time in Scotland?"

"First time," she confirmed, her fingers idly tracing the edge of Byrdie's carrier. "But it already feels... I don't know...

different… like I've been waiting for this without realizing it."

The storm blurred the road ahead, turning the countryside into shifting shadows and fleeting glimpses of green. It was disorienting—how quickly the world could change with a little rain. Then again, that's how her life had felt lately. One minute, clear skies; the next, everything unrecognizable.

Alastair chuckled. "Well, there's magic in these parts. The kind ye feel in yer bones. Sounds like yer right where ye need to be."

Heather turned to the window, watching the hills grow steeper and the roads narrower. The steady drizzle that had followed them now swelled into a torrential downpour. Rain hammered against the car windows, blurring the landscape into a gray smear. Heather anxiously shifted in her seat and glanced nervously at the storm outside. Byrdie released a tiny, uneasy meow from her carrier on the seat beside her.

"Does it always rain like this here?" Heather asked Alastair, trying to keep her voice light.

"Aye, it can be temperamental," he replied, gripping the wheel tightly. "But this is a proper downpour, even for Scotland."

The car suddenly shuddered, and Heather felt it lurch before slowing to a crawl. Alastair frowned, muttering something in Gaelic under his breath.

"*Ò, chan eil seo math*—"

"What's wrong?" Heather asked, her stomach tightening.

"This isn't good," he said, easing the car to the side of the narrow road. The engine sputtered once, twice, then died completely, leaving them in near silence apart from the relentless rain drumming on the roof. Alastair twisted the key in the ignition, but the car refused to start.

"Bloody typical," he muttered, leaning back in his seat with a sigh.

Heather's heart sank. "Is it... is it serious?"

"Could be the battery, could be the engine," he said, shaking his head. "Either way, we're not goin' anywhere for the time being."

Heather peered out the window, her eyes straining to make out anything through the rain. The landscape blurred into a mess of gray and green, but she remembered passing a small town not long ago. It had been a blink-and-you'd-miss-it place with just a few cottages, a church, and what looked like a pub, but right now, it was the closest thing to safety she could think of.

"Is there any cell service out here?" she asked, reaching for her phone.

Alastair pulled out his phone and frowned. "Not likely. These roads are remote." He sighed, running a hand through his damp hair. "I'll check under the hood and see if I can sort it."

"Okay," Heather said, trying to stay calm. Byrdie let out another distressed meow, and Heather whispered to her, her fingers brushing over the carrier. "It's okay, Byrdie. We'll figure this out."

Alastair climbed out of the car, rain immediately soaking him as he popped the hood. Heather watched him through the windshield, feeling helpless as water streamed down his coat. She looked at her phone again—no signal.

Minutes passed, and Alastair finally returned, dripping wet and shaking his head: "No luck. Looks like the engine's given out completely. We'll need to wait for a tow."

Heather swallowed hard, glancing out at the storm. "And if

we can't call for one?"

"We'll have to flag someone down when the rain eases," he said apologetically as he removed his coat and placed it on the passenger seat. "But that could take a while out here. Sorry about all this, lassie."

Heather leaned back in her seat, closing her eyes. This wasn't how she imagined her first day in Scotland.

She let out a breath. "So much for easing into things."

Alastair chuckled grimly. "Aye, lass. Looks like you're diving intae Scotland headfirst."

Heather held Byrdie's carrier a little tighter as the storm water streaked down the glass. She couldn't shake the thought that her fresh start had just gotten off to a bumpy beginning.

The rain showed no signs of easing, pounding relentlessly against the car as the minutes dragged into an hour.

Alastair tried his phone again and sighed, holding it up as if the extra inch might summon a miracle. "Still no signal. And no cars have come by," he muttered, rubbing the back of his neck.

Heather stared out at the curtain of rain with the small town they'd passed earlier on her mind. "What about the village we drove through? Could we walk back there?"

Alastair studied her, hesitating. "It's a fair distance, especially in this weather. But I dinnae see many other options."

She bit her lip, feeling a pang of guilt. "I'm sorry—this is all such a mess."

"Don't be daft, lassie." Alastair said, reassuring her. "Ye didn't summon the rain or break the car!" He gestured to the window. "Right, then. I'll head to the village and see if anyone can help us."

Heather's stomach twisted. "Are you sure? It's pouring out there."

He gave her a bright, lopsided grin. "I'm from here, lass. A bit of rain cannae kill me. It'll take a lot more than that to take this auld fool down." He reached for his coat, still damp from his earlier attempt under the hood, and shrugged it on again.

"What if no one's there?" she asked, her voice quieter.

"Then I'll keep walking until I find someone," he said matter-of-factly. "Just sit tight, and dinnae fash. Keep the doors locked."

Heather nodded, her throat tight as she watched him step out into the storm. Rain swallowed him almost instantly, his figure quickly fading into the distance.

Left alone, the silence in the car felt overwhelming, broken only by the rhythmic drumming of rain on the roof and Byrdie's soft, restless meows. She unzipped Byrdie's carrier just enough to reach in and stroke her fur again and the warmth of her tiny body grounded Heather's frayed nerves.

"It's okay, Byrdie," she whispered, more for herself than the cat. "Alastair will be back soon. We'll be fine."

The minutes ticked by, each one stretching longer than the last. Heather's thoughts raced, pinging between worry about the car, the rain, and whether Alastair would find help—or even make it back safely. Now and then, she glanced at the dark road behind them, hoping to see headlights or even a glimpse of his silhouette.

Nearly half an hour passed. She shifted in her seat, trying to shake off the rising anxiety. Her fingers tightened around Byrdie's carrier again as she whispered, "This wasn't exactly in the plan, huh?"

Byrdie blinked up at her, her tiny face unbothered. Heather managed a small, wry smile. "At least one of us isn't panicking. I guess you're just wanting to be home?"

But the rain wasn't letting up, and neither was the unease curling in her stomach. Byrdie let out a small, impatient meow, the sound cutting through the steady patter of rain. Heather rubbed her knee, grounding herself. "Yeah, I know, Byrd," she whispered with a shaky voice. "Me too."

Heather checked the clock again, the numbers glowing accusingly back at her. Now it had been almost an hour since Alastair disappeared into the storm. Every minute that passed without sight of him was now gnawing at her, feeding worst-case thoughts. What if he'd gotten lost? What if he'd been swept off the road? What if he'd just... decided she wasn't worth the trouble?

Byrdie let out a plaintive meow, louder this time, her wide green eyes pleading. Heather's heart twisted. She didn't want to leave her—but sitting in the car, waiting for help that might not come, wasn't an option anymore. If she wanted to find Alastair—or at least figure out where the hell she was—she had to move.

She swallowed hard and reached for the door handle. "I promise I'll come back for you, okay? Just stay here, safe and dry. I'll figure something out."

She checked that the carrier was securely fastened, giving Byrdie one last reassuring stroke. "You're braver than I am, you know that?" she murmured.

Then, out of the corner of her eye, she saw it: a flicker of light in the distance.

She sat up straighter, wiping at the condensation on the car window. For a second, it was gone. Then, there—a faint glow.

Her pulse quickened. A house? ...a car? ...someone who could help?

It was better than sitting here, waiting.

Heather took a breath and shoved the door open. The wind hit her like a slap, the rain soaking her within moments. She stepped out, sneakers sinking into the wet ground, and threw one last glance at the car. Byrdie's silhouette was barely visible through the window. With a deep breath, she shut the door with a loud *thud*, sealing her decision, and then she turned toward the light.

The wet grass squelched beneath her sneakers as she trudged forward, muttering to herself to keep her nerves at bay. "You're fine. This is fine. Just... a little rain. Not an ideal start, but it's not the end of the world."

But as she walked, the field stretched on longer than she expected. The wind howled through the open land, and the rain made it impossible to see more than a few feet ahead.

The light flickered again. Still distant.

Heather exhaled sharply. It had looked closer from the road.

Her foot hit something solid.

A fence.

She blinked, rain dripping into her eyes, and hesitated. Had she wandered into someone's property?

Gripping the slick wood, she peered ahead. The light still flickered in the distance, but the storm made it impossible to gauge how far away it was. If she turned back now, she'd be stuck waiting in the car, now soaking wet, with no idea when Alastair would return.

Heather exhaled, steeling herself. Carefully, she climbed over the fence, dropping onto the other side with a soft *plop* in the mud.

A shiver crawled down her spine as she looked around. The darkness shifted, shapes materializing in the storm.

Large. Unmoving. Silent.

The scent of damp earth and something unmistakably... *organic*... filled her nose.

A low, heavy exhale sounded to her left. *"Moooo..."*

Heather turned her head, stomach dropping.

Cows.

A whole field of them.

She was in a pasture.

Oh, shit.

The cows stared at her, eerily still, their hulking forms barely visible through the rain.

Heather swallowed hard. "Okay... no sudden movements."

The wind howled again, nearly knocking her off balance. She turned in a slow circle, panic creeping in.

What if there was no house? What if she had walked in the wrong direction?

She squeezed her eyes shut for a second, forcing herself to focus.

Then... a light.

This time, stronger. Steady. Glowing like a beacon in the distance.

Relief surged through her. She wasn't lost. The house—or whatever it was—was real.

But it was still a long way off.

Heather steadied herself, wrapping her arms tighter around her shivering body. She just had to keep moving.

She took another shaky breath, pushing forward.

What if no one was home? What if it wasn't a house at all—just an abandoned building, or worse— private property? The last thing she needed was to be chased off by some grumpy old farmer with an axe.

But what choice did she have? Sitting in the car, waiting for help that might not come, wasn't an option. And she had already come this far.

Another gust of wind howled through the open field, sending rain straight into her eyes. Heather wiped her face with frozen fingers, her shoes squelching against the soaked earth as she forced herself forward.

Then, through the storm, she saw it clearly.

The cottage.

The light from the windows grew brighter, glowing warm against the storm.

Just as she allowed herself a flicker of hope, her foot landed in something soft and squishy.

Heather froze.

Slowly, she looked down.

Oh, for the love of—

Cow shit. Fantastic.

Another loud moo sounded closer this time, and Heather froze mid-step. A particularly enormous highland cow was staring straight at her, its wet fur plastered to its face and its long, intimidating horns gleaming in the rain.

"Okay," she whispered, hands raised as though negotiating with a hostage taker. "No sudden movements. You're just a big, fluffy cow. Nothing to be scared of."

The cow snorted, a deep, rumbling huff that sounded suspiciously amused, stomping one hoof in the mud.

Heather's stomach dropped. "Oh my God, it's going to charge," she gasped, panic bubbling up.

She darted to the side, misjudged her footing, and her shoe

landed squarely in yet another pile of cow poop.

The cow let out another loud huff, its breath misting in the rain—almost like it was laughing at her.

"Why? Why is this my life?" she questioned loudly, throwing her arms up in exasperation.

Dragging forward in sheer determination, she muttered, "You just had to leave the car, Heather. You just couldn't wait for Alastair. Nooo, you're Miss Independent now. Brilliant idea."

The warm glow of the cottage shimmered like an oasis. Just a little farther.

So, she pushed forward, rain dripping from her hair, the scent of wet earth and livestock clinging to the air. She was almost there—

Her chest collided with something solid.

Another fence.

Heather let out a strangled sound, somewhere between a gasp and a groan. "You've got to be kidding me."

She wiped the rain from her face and squinted. The wooden posts stretched out on either side, vanishing into the mist. It wasn't as tall as the last one, but still enough to be a problem.

Gritting her teeth, she grabbed the top rail and hoisted herself up. The wet wood was slick beneath her frozen fingers, but after a few ungraceful attempts, she threw one leg over, then the other, landing with a heavy squish on the other side.

The... *mud?* ... sucked at her shoes, nearly taking one off her foot as she plodded through it. This was fine. Everything was fine.

She blew a rain-soaked curl out of her face, ready to make a run for the front door—

Then she looked to her right. A gravel road.

Heather froze, blinking against the rain. An actual, proper road leading straight to the cottage. A perfectly walkable, cow-shit-free road.

Her stomach dropped. She had hopped fences, trudged through a muddy pasture, and stepped in *God-knows-what*, all while there had been a clear, easy path the entire time.

She let out a slow, disbelieving breath.

Of course.

Because of course she had to take the hard way.

With one last, exhausted sigh, Heather turned away from the road she *should* have taken and trudged toward the front door, cold, drenched, and thoroughly unimpressed with herself.

She banged on it harder than she intended, her knuckles slick with rain.

"Hello?" she called, shivering as water dripped from her hair into her eyes.

Her soaked linen outfit clung to her like a second skin, and she became painfully aware of just how see-through it had become. Her new black lace bra and matching panties—lovely in the boutique, now mortifying in real life—were on full display, and her freezing-cold nipples were clearly outlined against the fabric.

The door swung open, and a tall, broad-shouldered man stood there, his dark hair damp and curling slightly at the ends. His gray t-shirt clung to his chest, making it hard not to notice how ridiculously fit he was. His stormy blue eyes widened in surprise, and his gaze darted—unsuccessfully—to anywhere but her soaked figure.

"Uh..." He cleared his throat, his Scottish accent thick and startled. "Can I help ye?"

Heather blinked up at him, raindrops clinging to her lashes.

"Hi," she managed, her voice slightly breathless. "My car broke down. It's raining... Obviously." She gestured vaguely to herself and the storm, very aware that she looked like a drowned rat in lingerie.

The man arched an eyebrow, the corners of his mouth twitching like he was fighting a grin. "Aye, I can see that."

"And," she continued, her cheeks burning, "I stepped in cow poop. Twice. So if you could... not judge me right now, and also not actually be a murderer, that'd be great."

That did it—he laughed softly and shook his head. "Come in before ye catch yer death, lass."

Heather hesitated, glancing back toward the field. The cows were still watching her. "Okay, yeah," she said quickly, stepping inside and trying to preserve what little dignity she had left. But as she stepped inside, she immediately regretted it. The cozy warmth of the cottage hit her like a tidal wave, and the combination of cow shit, rain, and wet linen created a genuinely unique, horrifying aroma that she was sure filled the entire room.

The man stepped back, politely wrinkling his nose. "Right, well... that's a smell."

Heather closed her eyes, wishing the floor would swallow her whole. "I know! It's me... I'm the smell. I'm so sorry!"

He crossed his arms, his biceps flexing in a way that was frankly distracting. "Yer also drippin' all over my floor."

"Cool, cool. Add it to the list." She flicked her gaze down, realizing she was standing in a rapidly expanding puddle of water, her sneakers sloshing with ungodly brown liquid with every movement.

"Oh, God. Do you have a towel—or a time machine,

maybe?"

The man bit back a laugh and crossed the room to a wooden cabinet by the window, pulling out a towel. He tossed it to her, and she caught it awkwardly, nearly dropping it in her haste to wipe her face.

"Thank you," she muttered, attempting to pat herself dry but only managing to smear water around.

"I'll put the kettle on," he said, heading toward the kitchen. "Ye look like you could use some tea. Or maybe a dram."

"Tea would be great," Heather called after him.

She caught sight of herself in the mirror above the coat rack and winced. Her makeup was wrecked, her underwear on full display in the light.

Fabulous.

She grabbed the towel again, holding it strategically in front of her, and then let out a breath, shoving her drenched hair out of her face. "Fantastic. I may as well be wearing cling film," she muttered.

The man returned with a steaming mug of tea, his eyes flicking to her before quickly looking away again.

"Here," he said, holding it out to her. "And, uh... if yer needin' somethin' to change into, I might have somethin' that'll fit."

Heather accepted the tea gratefully, the warmth seeping into her frozen fingers. "Thanks. Though, unless you happen to have a full set of dry clothes for a random stranger, I'll probably end up in, like, one of your t-shirts and—"

"—probably... uhh... safer? ...than what ye've got on now," he interrupted, his lips twitching.

Heather groaned, burying her face in the towel. "This is officially the worst day of my life."

The man snorted in amusement, leaning against the counter. "Could've been worse."

"How?" she demanded, peeking out from behind the towel.

He tilted his head, pretending to think.

"The cows could've chased ye."

She stared at him, horrified. "That was an option?"

He grinned now, complete and easy. And despite her embarrassment, Heather felt her heart flip.

"Aye, since ye decided to traipse through the pasture." he said, his accent lilting. "But dinnae fash, lass. Ye survived. And now ye've got a story to tell."

"Yeah, a story about how I showed up half-naked and smelling like shit at some stranger's house," she muttered, taking a sip of tea. "Real inspirational."

"Och, at least I'm a friendly stranger," he said again, winking at her this time.

Heather rolled her eyes but couldn't stop the laugh that bubbled up.

"Lucky me." She shifted awkwardly, glancing toward the door. "So... uh, I kind of left my cat in the car."

The man blinked at her. "Ye left your cat?"

"Yes, my cat," she said defensively. "Her name is Byrdie, and she's in a carrier. I didn't want to bring her out into the rain, but now I'm realizing leaving her in a cold car might not have been the best decision either."

The man raked a hand through his damp, dark hair—evidence of his own trek through the storm—and let out a bemused sigh. "Sounds like ye've had one hell of a day."

"You don't even know the half of it," she muttered, clutching the towel closer.

He nodded toward a hallway. "Loo's just down there. I'll

grab you some dry clothes."

"Really? That would be amazing. Thank you."

As he disappeared into another room, Heather stood awkwardly, dripping water onto the floorboards. A moment later, he returned with a neatly folded bundle of clothes.

"Here," he said, handing her what looked like a pair of sweatpants and a faded flannel shirt. "Not exactly high fashion, but it's dry."

"It's perfect," she said, taking the bundle gratefully.

"The loo's the second door on the left. I'll take the truck and fetch yer cat."

Heather blinked at him. "Wait—you're going out there? ...in this weather?"

He shrugged, already grabbing his keys. "Cannae leave the wee thing out there alone. Besides, I'm not the one soaked through and freezing."

"Are you sure? I can go with you—" He cut her off with a wave of his hand. "Stay here, dry off, and warm up. I'll be back in a bit."

Before she could protest, he was out the door, the sound of the rain swallowing his retreating footsteps. Heather sighed, heading toward the bathroom. She flicked on the light, catching sight of herself in the mirror again. "Oh, good..." she muttered. "I look like a drowned raccoon."

She peeled off her soaked linen outfit, grimacing at the state of it, and draped it over the bathtub's edge. The mud-streaked sneakers, now reeking of rain and cow pasture, were set near the front door—out of the way but impossible to ignore. Slipping into the soft sweatpants and oversized flannel, she inhaled the faint scent of cedar and soap. The clothes hung loosely on her, but after the night she'd had, their warmth felt like a small mercy.

When she emerged, fresh-faced and scrubbed clean, with her damp curls tied back in a loose bun using a rubber band she had found on the bathroom counter, she heard the rumble of a truck pulling back into the driveway. She rushed to the window just in time to see the man step out, Byrdie's carrier in hand.

"Thank God," she whispered, a wave of relief washing over her.

A moment later, he walked back in, dripping-wet but grinning.

"Yer wee beastie's safe and sound," he announced, setting the carrier gently on the floor.

Heather dropped to her knees, peeking into the carrier to find Byrdie blinking up at her, unimpressed but unharmed.

"You're my hero," she said, looking up at him with genuine gratitude.

He shrugged, his grin turning sheepish. "I cannae leave a wee kitty-cat in distress, now can I?"

"Seriously," she said, standing up. "Thank you. I owe you, like, a million favors."

He raised an eyebrow, smirking. "I'll settle for you tellin' me how, exactly, you ended up in the middle of my cow pasture."

"It's a long, embarrassing story," Heather groaned, covering her face with her hands.

Amused, he walked toward the kitchen. "I've got more tea. And I reckon you're not going anywhere in this weather. Start talking, lass."

Despite the chaos of the evening, Heather couldn't help but laugh with him. She launched into the whole tale of her misadventures, starting with Alastair and the broken-down car and ending with her unexpected arrival on his doorstep.

Heather took a deep breath, still feeling slightly ridiculous standing in his shirt and sweatpants, but she mustered a smile. "I'm Heather, by the way. Heather Campbell."

The man leaned casually against the kitchen counter, his arms crossed as he gave her a warm, lopsided grin. "Flynn Duncan. Nice to meet ye, Heather Campbell. Though I'll admit, this isn't exactly how I thought my night would go—soaked underthings and cow shite included."

Heather groaned, her cheeks flushing. "Please don't remind me. That was… not my finest moment."

Flynn chuckled gleefully, his eyes crinkling at the corners. "Och, dinnae fash about it. Happens to the best of us."

God, even his laugh was attractive. Unacceptable.

"Really? You've stepped in cow poop before?" she asked, arching an eyebrow.

He shrugged, smirking. "Aye. It's a rite of passage in these parts. Though I cannae say I've done it while marching through a storm wearing… whatever it was you were wearin'."

Heather laughed despite herself, the tension in her chest easing slightly. "It was supposed to be my stylish-yet-comfortable travel outfit. You know, for my grand new start in Scotland. So much for first impressions."

"Well, I think you've made quite the first impression," Flynn teased, pushing another mug of tea across the counter toward her. "Though I'm not sure it's what ye were goin' for."

Heather rolled her eyes but couldn't help smiling. "Thanks. For everything. Seriously. I don't know what I would've done if you hadn't opened the door."

Flynn straightened, his gaze softening. "Ye'd be surprised what ye can manage when yer desperate. But I'm glad you knocked. Yer safe now, and that's what matters."

She sipped her tea, the warmth spreading as the rain continued pounding against the windows.

"So... Flynn Duncan. Do you always rescue wayward travelers, or is this a one time thing?"

He laughed, a deep, genuine sound that filled the cozy cottage. "Not usually. Most folks know better than to wander into a highland cow pasture in a storm."

Heather shook her head, smiling. "Well, lucky me, then."

"Aye," Flynn said, his grin softening into admiration. "Lucky for both of us, I'd say."

Heather shifted in her borrowed clothes, still damp and clinging uncomfortably, but her focus landed on Flynn. He was tall—easily over six feet—and built like someone who knew the value of hard work. His broad shoulders stretched the fabric of his plain gray shirt, and the damp ends of his dark brown hair curled slightly at his temples from when he'd braved the storm himself. A stubbled beard shadowed his jaw, adding to the rugged, effortless charm. But it was his eyes that caught her most—starkly blue, yet warm, holding her gaze with a quiet attentiveness she wasn't used to. Not assessing, not appraising—just seeing. It threw her off balance in a way she couldn't quite name, like she'd stepped onto unsteady ground. She told herself it was nothing, just a stranger being polite, but the feeling lingered.

He leaned back against the counter again with his arms crossed, the muscles in his forearms flexing just slightly while she looked him over. "So, Heather Campbell," he said, tilting his head, "what exactly brings ye and yer cat to the middle of nowhere Scotland? Besides a run-in with my cows, of course."

Heather flushed, a mixture of embarrassment and awareness bubbling under her skin. "Long story short? I'm on my way to Glenoran House. It's... well, it's a family property. Judging by how my night's gone, I'm beginning to think the universe has other plans."

Flynn raised an eyebrow, a new grin tugging at the corner of his mouth. "Glenoran House? That explains the luggage in the car—and yer determination to trek through a pasture in the middle of a downpour." His voice was deep, his Scottish accent wrapping around the words in a way that quickened Heather's pulse. "...though I have to say, ye dinnae exactly seem like the fixer-upper type."

Heather blinked at him, wiping rainwater from her forehead. "You know the property? Glenoran?"

"Aye," he replied. "It's in Inverness—just the next town over. Big place. Stands out, even around here. People talk about it like it's a landmark or something."

Heather nodded, feeling a tiny flicker of relief. "That's the one. It's my family's estate on my mother's side. I've never been, though. This is... kind of my first trip to Scotland."

Flynn tilted his head, his green eyes studying her thoughtfully. "Yer first time here, and ye landed in the middle of nowhere, soaking wet, dodging cows? You've made quite the entrance."

Heather let out a soft laugh, though her cheeks flushed again with embarrassment. "Not exactly the trip I imagined. I was supposed to get there today, but... well, like I said, things haven't exactly gone to plan."

"They rarely do," Flynn said with a shrug. "But yer closer

than ye think. Inverness isn't far, maybe another half hour or so from here—once yer car's sorted, anyway."

Heather exhaled, relief washing over her. "That's good to hear. I was starting to wonder if I'd made a huge mistake coming here."

"Nah," Flynn said, his voice steady. "Yer just getting yer welcome to the Highlands, that's all. Rain, cows, and a bit of chaos—it's part of the charm." His lips twitched into a smirk. "Next time, maybe skip the pasture. Ye dinnae have the right footwear."

Heather stared at the oversized flannel and loose sweatpants she'd borrowed, then back up at him, her lips curving into a wry smile. "Noted. I'll keep that in mind for future adventures."

Flynn chuckled, the sound warm and easy. "Good. Now, once the rain lets up, we'll get ye back to your car—or at least figure something out. Glenoran's not going anywhere."

Heather's smile faded as she studied the window, where the downpour remained steady against the glass. "Alastair's been gone for ages. He said he'd try to find help, but what if he's stuck somewhere in this weather? I feel terrible just sitting here."

Flynn's brow furrowed slightly. "Alastair—your driver, I assume?"

She nodded. "Yes. The car broke down just after we passed the last town. He decided to walk back when no one passed us on the road, but now it's been so long..."

"If he made it back to the town, he's likely holed up somewhere warm, waiting this out. Most folks around here wouldn't turn a man away in weather like this." His voice was calm and reassuring, but Heather couldn't help the knot of guilt in her stomach.

"I just... I don't like the idea of him out there," she said, fidgeting with the hem of the flannel shirt Flynn had lent her.

Flynn tilted his head again, with a faint smile playing on his lips. "Ye've got a good heart, Campbell. But he's a grown man—he'll manage. Besides, ye've got your own storm to weather." He gestured to her damp hair, still clinging to her neck. "Though I have to say, yer pulling off the drowned-kitten look; it actually looks quite good!"

Heather laughed again despite herself, the tension in her shoulders easing just a little. "Thanks, I'll add that to my list of glowing compliments tonight."

"Hey, it's a rare club!" Flynn teased, his green eyes sparkling with humor. "And for the record, I'd say ye handled the whole thing admirably. Most people wouldn't have made it to the door, let alone knocked on it."

"Admirably is a stretch," Heather said, shaking her head. "I'm pretty sure I looked like a lunatic charging through that field. Honestly, I was about two seconds away from turning around when I stepped in—well, you know..." She grimaced, and Flynn let out a knowing laugh.

"Ye've got grit, lass. I'll give you that," he said, his smile softening. "And I'll admit, it's been a while since I've had company out here. Yer a bit of a surprise tonight."

Heather arched a brow, her lips curving into a playful smile. "Oh, you weren't expecting a soaking wet American to show up at your door in the middle of a storm?"

Flynn pretended to think momentarily, his hand rubbing his stubbly jaw. "Not exactly on my bingo card for the evening, no. But I'd say it's a welcome surprise. Definitely beats spending the night alone with a bottle of whisky and the rain for company."

She laughed, her cheeks warming at his casual charm. "Glad I could spice up your evening. Though, to be fair, Byrdie is technically your guest too. Don't forget her!"

"Ah, yes, how could I forget the infamous Byrdie?" Flynn said with a grin. "I reckon she's more polite than most of the tourists I've met, so she's welcome to stay as long as you like."

From her carrier, Byrdie let out a pointed little *mrrow*—a sound that was distinctly unimpressed. Heather set Byrdie's carrier down near the fireplace, opening the door so she could stretch her legs. 'Sorry, girl, I wasn't exactly prepared for a detour.'

She glanced at Flynn. 'Got a spare dish? She's gonna stage a coup if I don't feed her soon.'"

Byrdie let out another *mrrow*, this time softer—almost like a challenge.

Heather sighed dramatically, shaking her head as she unlatched the carrier door. "Oh, she already expects it. You've just sealed your fate."

Byrdie stepped out hesitantly, stretching her front paws before arching into a long, luxurious stretch. With a flick of her tail, she trotted toward the fireplace, as if claiming the coziest spot in the room as her rightful throne.

Flynn huffed a quiet laugh, shaking his head as he moved toward the kitchen. "Well, as long as she doesnae start demandin' room service..."

Heather smirked, watching Byrdie sniff at the hearth before settling in front of the warmth. "Too late. She already owns the place."

Flynn cast a glance over his shoulder, amusement tugging

at his lips before he tucked into the kitchen. Heather let out a breath she hadn't realized she was holding, her gaze lingering on him for a beat too long. He was rugged in a way she wasn't used to—confident, but without the arrogance that so often came with it. His presence had an easy steadiness, the kind that made everything feel a little less chaotic. And his grin—damn his grin—had a way of making her forget just how much of a mess she was at the moment.

Heather sat down at the small kitchen table, again brushing her still-damp curls away from her face as Flynn turned to check the kettle that was staying warm on the stove.

The rhythmic patter of the rain against the windows filled the space, punctuated by the occasional crackle of the fire in the hearth. Despite the situation, the scent of woodsmoke wrapped around her, the warmth melting into her frozen skin. She should've felt out of place in someone else's home, yet for the first time all night, the shivering in her bones started to ease.

"So..." Flynn said, breaking the silence. "What's the full story with Glenoran House? I don't often meet Americans venturing out here, let alone ones aiming for a place like that."

Heather hesitated, wrapping her hands around the warm mug he'd placed before her. "Well, like I said: it belonged to my family—on my mom's side. But I didn't even know it existed until recently. My mom passed away when I was a kid, and my dad... well, he didn't exactly tell me much about her side of the family. After he passed last month, I found out about the house." She shrugged, her voice soft. "It felt like a sign. A chance to... start over, I guess."

Flynn's expression softened, the teasing glint in his eyes replaced by something gentler. "I'm sorry for yer loss..." He pulled out a chair and sat across from her at the kitchen table, his voice quieter now. "...but picking up and coming all this way? That's brave. Not everyone would take that kind of leap."

"More like running away and hoping for the best." The words slipped out before she could stop them. She blinked, hearing them hang in the air, solid and undeniable. Had she really just said that? Out loud? To *Flynn*? The truth settled in her chest a beat too late—she hadn't admitted it to herself until just now.

"Running away from what?" he asked, his tone curious but not prying.

Heather fixed her gaze into her tea, debating how much to share. "Just... life. It wasn't exactly working out the way I thought it would. And Glenoran House felt like a chance to start fresh."

Flynn nodded, lifting his mug and taking a slow sip of tea. He set it back down on the table in front of him, his fingers resting loosely around it as he studied her.

"Fair enough. I reckon a lot of people feel that way when they come to the Highlands—like it's a reset button. Cannae say I blame you. There's something about this place that makes everything feel a bit simpler."

Heather smiled softly. "That's what I'm hoping for. Though to be honest, this whole night has been anything but simple."

Flynn smirked. "Aye, I'll give ye that. But hey... yer surviving. That counts for something."

She shook her head, laughing despite herself. "Barely. I can't believe I left my driver to deal with the car and ran off into a field full of cows. This is not how I pictured my big adventure starting."

"Well, if it's any consolation," Flynn said, his grin returning, "yer definitely going to have a story to tell about yer first night in Scotland."

Heather raised her mug, the warmth spreading through her hands as she gave him a wry smile, her eyes catching his. "Here's hoping the rest of the trip is a little less... eventful."

Flynn smirked, tilting his head as he watched her. "Something tells me, lass, that with you, it's never going to be boring."

She felt a blush creep up her neck and quickly looked down at her tea while her heart gave an unexpected flutter. Flynn had a way of saying things that made her feel like he saw right through her—but in a good sort of way that she wasn't used to, like he wasn't judging her for the chaos that she had brought with her.

Before Heather could respond, a sharp knock at the door interrupted them. Flynn set down his mug with a quiet thud, pushing back his chair as he stood. With a glance toward her, he strode toward the door and swung it open. Alastair stood there, drenched and disheveled, with the lights of a tow truck illuminating the rain behind him.

"Well, that was a wild goose chase; I couldnae find ye anywhere, lass!" Alastair said, stepping into the doorway and brushing rain off his jacket. His eyes landed on Heather, taking in her oversized flannel. "You've certainly made yourself at home, I see."

Heather crossed her arms, feeling her cheeks heat. "It's not what it looks like. My clothes were soaked, thanks to the rain—and the cows."

Flynn leaned casually against the wall, arms crossed, his

expression amused. "It's true! She showed up looking like she'd gone a few rounds in a Highland mud wrestling match. Couldnae exactly leave her dripping everywhere."

Alastair sighed, shaking his head. "The car's done for the night. The tow truck driver's taking it into town, and he mentioned there's a nice little bed and breakfast in Inverness he can drop ye at."

Heather's eyes widened. "Inverness? That's close to Glenoran House, isn't it?"

Alastair gave a nod. "Aye, but with this storm, no one's getting up that road tonight. Ye'll need to wait it out in town."

Heather exhaled, relief loosening the knot in her chest. "And you're sure the driver doesn't mind taking me there instead?"

The tow truck driver appeared in the doorway, giving a quick nod. "It's no trouble. I have plenty of room in the cab, and I'll ensure ye get there safely."

She hesitated. The fire crackled behind Flynn, its golden light flickering over the room, casting soft shadows along the wooden beams. The warmth of the cottage still clung to her skin, the scent of cedar and tea settling deep in her chest. Outside, the rain seemed to soften slightly, as if the storm itself were hesitating—urging her to linger just a moment longer.

Flynn stood just inside, arms crossed, watching her. There was nothing in his expression that asked her to stay—but something about the way he held her gaze made her hesitate all the same. It was nothing, she told herself. Just a stranger seeing another stranger off.

Still, the moment stretched between them, thick with something unspoken.

Flynn gave a small, knowing smile. "Safe journey, lass."

Heather swallowed, nodding. "And... thanks. For everything." She hesitated, then added, "Oh—my clothes. The ones I left in the bathroom. Just... burn them."

Flynn smirked. "Aye, I'll give them a proper Highland sendoff."

She huffed a quiet laugh, then bent to scoop up Byrdie from her cozy spot near the fireplace. The cat let out a grumpy little *mrrow* as Heather tucked her gently back into the carrier. Nearby, her mud-caked sneakers sat in a defeated heap by the door. She shot Flynn a sheepish look. "I should probably take those, too. Can't leave you with all my baggage. Emotional or otherwise."

Flynn raised a brow. "More's the pity. I was gonna bronze them."

Heather rolled her eyes but grabbed the shoes anyway, holding them at arm's length as she stepped toward the door.

The night air hit her with a biting chill, the steady drizzle creeping beneath her borrowed clothes and raising goosebumps along her skin. She ducked her head against the wind and climbed into the tow truck, her bare feet cold against the worn rubber mat while she cradled Byrdie's carrier on her lap.

Flynn was still there, standing in the doorway, watching her go.

Heather turned back, finding Alastair still standing by Flynn's porch, hands tucked into his coat pockets.

"Hey, Alastair?"

He looked up, the drizzle catching in his salt-and-pepper hair.

Heather offered a small smile. "Thanks... for everything."

Alastair waved. "Just try to stay out of trouble from here on out, aye?"

Heather groaned. "Never living that down, am I?"

"Not a chance." He tipped an imaginary hat. "God go wi' ye, lass."

The tow truck engine rumbled to life, and as Heather reached for the door handle, Alastair's phone buzzed in his pocket. He glanced at the screen and nodded. "That'll be my ride. One of the lads from Inverness is swingin' by."

Relief loosened the last bit of tension in her chest. "Good. I'd hate to be the reason you ended up stranded, too."

"Och, I'd have been fine," he said with a wink. "But I appreciate the concern."

She huffed a quiet laugh and shut the door. As the truck pulled away, she caught one last glimpse of Flynn's cottage, its windows glowing warm against the storm, before both Alastair and Flynn turned and disappeared back inside.

She hoped this wouldn't be the last time she'd see Flynn Duncan.

The drive to Inverness was quiet, save for the truck's steady hum and the rhythmic rain tapping against the windshield. The driver, a middle aged man with a thick, broad Scots accent, kept his eyes on the road. He had a weathered face—the kind that had seen its fair share of long nights and hard work—with deep set eyes that flicked between the road and his passengers. His wiry frame was bundled in a heavy jacket, the collar turned up against the cold, and a short, grizzled beard framed his mouth as he broke the silence.

"Yer headed tae Glenoran House, aye? Ye've got yer work cut out for ye, lassie. Big place like that's bound to need some fixin'-up."

Heather offered a faint smile, though her stomach knotted. "I guess I'll find out soon enough."

He chortled. "Aye, well, ye picked a hell of a night for it. It's pishin' doon out there! Proper Highland welcome, that."

Heather let out a breathy laugh. "Yeah, I got that impression."

"Dinnae fash yerself," he went on. "Inverness folk are friendly. Ye'll have nae trouble findin' someone to help, should ye need it. And if yer lookin' for proper supplies, there's a hardware shop near the town square—good lads there."

"Thanks," she said softly, her thoughts already spiraling into the endless unknowns awaiting her at Glenoran House.

When they reached the bed and breakfast, Heather's eyes were immediately drawn to the charming stone exterior, softened by climbing ivy and framed by neatly trimmed hedges. Warm golden light spilled from the mullioned windows, creating a welcoming glow against the misty night. Smoke curled lazily from a chimney, promising the comfort of a crackling fire inside.

The tow truck driver helped her unload her bags, his expression softening at the sight of Byrdie's carrier tucked under her arm. The faint meows from within earned a chuckle. "Sounds like she's had a rough night too."

Heather offered a tired smile now, glancing toward the wooden door that was adorned with a small brass bell and a cheerful wreath. A hand-painted sign hanging above the door read: *Thistle Haven Inn.* The faint smell of rain-soaked earth was mingled with something daintily floral from the surrounding garden. Despite her exhaustion, a slight sense of relief settled over her. She felt grateful that warmth and shelter were waiting for her inside.

The innkeeper was a cheerful older woman named Claire who welcomed her with open arms. "Och, look at ye, yer hair's drenched! And nae even shoes on yer feet! Come in, come in—I'll get ye a pot of tea and a warm blanket."

Heather felt a lump rise in her throat at the kindness in Claire's voice. "Thank you. Really."

Claire showed her a cozy room with a view of the misty town square. Through the rain-streaked window, Heather could make out the glow of old fashioned street lamps casting golden pools of light on the cobblestone streets. A few late-night stragglers moved between the warmly lit shopfronts— some tucked under umbrellas, others hurrying to escape the downpour. Across the square, the silhouette of a centuries-old stone church stood tall against the night, its spire disappearing into the low-hanging mist.

The bed was covered in a thick patchwork quilt, its fabric worn soft with age, and a small radiator in the corner hummed softly, chasing away the damp chill. A window framed by dainty lace curtains let in the muted glow of the streetlamps outside, the rain tapping gently against the glass. On the walls, a few framed prints of Highland landscapes hung in neat rows—rolling hills, a lone stag standing in the mist, a castle perched on a rugged cliff. The scent of lavender lingered in the air, mixing with the faint warmth of tea leaves from a small tray set beside the bed.

Heather opened Byrdie's carrier and watched as she cautiously stepped out, sniffing the unfamiliar surroundings.

"Well, Byrdie..." she mused, sitting on the edge of the bed, "...we made it through day one."

She pulled out her phone, her thumb hovering over the screen. She considered texting Ivy to let her know she'd arrived safely—but the thought stalled, the weight of their unresolved tension pressing down on her. Reaching out felt both necessary and impossible.

Heather sighed, locking her phone and setting it aside. She wasn't ready to bridge that gap— not yet. Instead, she turned her attention to Byrdie, whose wide eyes scanned the unfamiliar room.

"It's just us now," she murmured as Byrdie stealthily sniffed at the floral-patterned rug before leaping onto the bed and curling into the soft quilt.

Heather let out a small laugh. "At least one of us is settling in nicely."

As the outside wind hushed against the glass, she wandered over to it and rested a hand against the frame, staring out into the mist-covered hills beyond Inverness. Somewhere out there, past the winding roads and darkened countryside, was a house that had belonged to her family for generations. A house she'd never seen—yet it had already set her life on a new course before she'd even stepped foot inside.

She thought of her mother—of the pieces of Eilidh's heart that must still linger in Glenoran's old stone walls. She wondered what it might feel like to stand in those rooms, to walk the same halls her mother once had. Would she find answers there... or just more ghosts?

She inhaled, pressing her forehead lightly against the cold glass.

For months, it had felt like her world was unraveling. But standing here, in the quiet glow of a place that wasn't yet home but held the promise of safety, she felt something new... Not certainty. Not peace. But... possibility.

She exhaled, turning from the window and crossing the room. Scooping Byrdie into her arms, she slipped beneath the heavy quilt. Byrdie's soft purr rumbled against Heather's chest, steady and grounding her after such a long day.

Heather lay back against the pillows, staring at the shadows cast by the low glow of the bedside lamp. The day had taken more turns than she could count— none of them what she expected. But somehow, despite the chaos: the storm, the cow encounter, the near-total embarrassment... She felt... okay... maybe even *good*.

She considered Byrdie, who was now curled into a tiny ball of warmth beside her, blissfully unbothered by the day's events. Maybe that was the trick: taking things as they came, one moment at a time.

Outside, the rain softened against the window; the wind was no longer howling— just whispering.

She wasn't sure what tomorrow would bring, nor the day after that.

But for now... she was here. She had made it to Scotland.

And that was enough.

Chapter 12

Heather barely remembered falling asleep, but the pale morning light streamed through the lace curtains when she woke, painting the room in soft, delicate patterns. Flynn's borrowed flannel and sweatpants hung off her in the least flattering way, yet they were so comfortable she couldn't bring herself to care. She adjusted the collar and caught the faint whiff of cedar and soap that still clung to it, letting the warm, earthy scent ground her.

She slid out of bed, her feet landing on the cozy rug. Pushing aside the delicate curtains, she took in the view—Inverness was everything she'd imagined. Stone cottages with neat chimneys, cobblestone streets damp from last night's rain, and the soft, rolling haze that clung to the rooftops.

Byrdie chirped from her new perch on the windowsill, her tiny nose pressed against the glass as she watched the world outside.

Across the way, a bakery's sign swayed gently in the morning breeze, and the scent of fresh bread and coffee curled into the air. Her stomach growled.

"Alright, breakfast soon," she murmured.

But before tackling anything else, she needed a proper shower. The long day before had left her feeling too grimy to face the world. The hot water washed away the lingering exhaustion and, as she stepped out, the cool bathroom air tingled against her skin. She wrapped herself in a towel, catching her own gaze in the fogged mirror. Yesterday's chaos had left its mark: pale exhaustion, shadows beneath her eyes, the weight of too little sleep. She looked... different? ...or maybe she just felt it. Either way, at least she was starting to feel human again.

She quickly swapped Flynn's clothes for dark jeans, a snug cream sweater, and waterproof Chelsea boots, folding his flannel neatly and placing it in her bag to return later.

"Can't forget this," she said, grabbing her Barbour jacket from the closet. With a teasing glance at Byrdie's carrier, she added, "Definitely don't want another see-through situation like yesterday."

Byrdie meowed in response, and Heather chuckled, feeling just a little lighter than before.

Downstairs, the bed and breakfast's dining room was warm and inviting with the smell of scones and bacon wafting through the air. The hostess, a rosy-cheeked older woman with a singsong Scottish accent, greeted her with a bright smile.

"Good morning, dear. Did ye sleep well?"

Heather smiled back. "Very well, thank you. This place is beautiful."

"Well, let's get ye fed, then," the woman chirped, bustling off to the kitchen.

She sat by the window, sipping a cup of strong coffee as she gazed at the sleepy town. Last night's rain left the streets saturated, tiny rivers of water trickling along the gutters.

Her phone's screen glowed with the directions to Glenoran House. Her chest tightened: *What if she hated it?* She tried to picture it—a grand old house, tucked away in the hills. But all she could see was the uncertainty of it. The weight of history, of responsibility, of a past she didn't even know. She focused on the reality of what awaited her. Would the house feel like home? Or would it feel like stepping into a stranger's life?

Her breakfast arrived—a hearty plate of eggs, bacon, toast, and black pudding. She hadn't expected such a generous spread, and her stomach clenched at the sight of it—equal parts nerves and hunger.

Eat first. Panic later.

As she ate, her thoughts drifted to Ivy. She hadn't heard from her in days. Had Ivy even noticed she was gone? ...or had she been too wrapped up in whatever mess she was making with Sam? Heather swallowed down those thoughts along with a bite of toast. No. She wasn't going to think about Ivy right now.

A glance at the clock sent her pulse stuttering: *8:30 a.m.*

She had exactly thirty minutes to get to Glenoran House to meet Mr. Reid. And no way to get there.

Think, Heather.

She stirred her coffee absently, staring out at the fog rolling over Inverness. The warmth of the bed and breakfast with the soft chatter of other guests and its scent of fresh bread—it all felt safe.

Her thumb hovered over Mr. Reid's number.

What if you don't belong?

The thought gripped her, cold and sharp.

But if she left, if she walked away now... No. That's what her father would have done. A low stone wall curved along the roadside, moss softening its edges. A single sheep stood just beyond it, blinking at the passing car as if none of this mattered. Somehow, the sight grounded her. Life kept moving—even here.

She exhaled sharply and dialed.

"Mr. Reid? ...it's Heather Campbell." She tried to sound calm, but her voice was slightly shakier than intended. "I'm supposed to meet you at Glenoran House this morning. There's just one small problem... I don't have a way to get there."

There was a brief pause on the other end, and Mr. Reid's warm voice came through.

"Ah, I see. Not to worry, Miss Campbell. I'm just gettin' intae Inverness now. I can come pick your up. Where are ye staying'?"

She gave him the address and then released a breath that she didn't realize she'd been holding. After they ended their call, she glanced around the cozy room, taking in the morning's soft, golden light and the scent of freshly brewed coffee lingering in the air.

She quickly checked her watch: *8:45 a.m.*

With only fifteen minutes to spare, she moved into action. She gathered her things and checked once more to ensure she had everything: phone... wallet... jacket... she'd come back for her luggage and Byrdie once she saw exactly what she had inherited.

She hurried out of the room and down the stairs to meet Mr. Reid. As she stepped outside, the brisk air hit her face, making her aware that she hadn't even thought about the chill that had come in with the morning mist. Her jacket was warm enough, but it did little to brace her against the uncertainty curling in her stomach as she waited.

Not long after, a black sedan pulled up to the curb, and she stood straighter, ready to face whatever came next. The door opened, and a well-dressed older man with neatly-combed hair and a friendly smile stepped out.

Heather shook his hand, trying to steady the flutter of nerves in her stomach. She offered a polite smile as she slipped into the passenger seat of the car. "Thank you for coming to pick me up."

"Of course," he said, settling into the driver's seat. "It's my pleasure. I trust yer stay here has been comfortable?"

She nodded, trying to sound nonchalant. "Yes, very much so. The *Thistle Haven* is lovely."

"That's good to hear," Reid replied, adjusting the rear-view mirror before pulling into the quiet street. "The inn's not much, but it has charm, especially with the weather we've been having. But I digress; you're here now for more important matters: Glenoran House awaits!" Reid offered her a small smile, as if sensing her nerves, but kept his eyes on the road.

She felt her pulse quicken at the mention of the house. The weight of the day ahead settled on her shoulders, but she took a deep breath, forcing her mind to focus.

"Yes, I'm looking forward to it. I have to admit: I never expected any of this. It's... a lot to process." She could feel the weight of her own words as they left her lips.

Reid glanced at her briefly, his expression understanding.

"I can only imagine, Miss Campbell. Not every day one learns of a family legacy like this. But yer here now, and we'll take it step by step."

The road stretched ahead as they left town, the steady hum of the car beneath them doing nothing to quiet the anticipation pressing against Heather's ribs.

"The house is a bit off-the-beaten-path..." Reid said. "... one of those places that's tucked away, like something from a storybook. But ye'll see for yerself soon enough."

She offered a faint smile. "I'm sure it's beautiful."

But *was she sure?*

"I've heard a bit about the house," Heather said. "But honestly, I don't know much. My mother never talked about it. At least, I don't think she did."

Reid nodded, gaze still on the road. "Understandable. Families have their reasons for keeping things quiet. Especially when it comes to old estates like Glenoran."

"A burden," she clarified.

Reid glanced at her. "Aye. Ye'll ken what I mean when we get there."

His words made her stomach churn with curiosity and apprehension. "I'm not sure I'm ready for all that."

"Ye'll manage," Reid assured her with another small smile. "Ye don't have a choice now, do ye?"

Heather laughed softly despite herself. "No, I suppose not."

The trees slowly started to thin out, and she caught a glimpse of the house—dark, looming, wrapped in lingering cloud and a dusting of fading snow.

Her stomach twisted. It felt less like she was arriving at a home and more like she was approaching something ancient. Something... waiting.

The car turned onto a winding, narrow road flanked by towering trees, the mist curling away from the treetops as they moved forward—revealing the estate piece by piece. The dark stone. The towering silhouette. The gaping windows.

She had expected something imposing yet beautiful—something out of a story.

But, this? This felt... forgotten.

The veil of clouds clung to the crumbling stone like grasping fingers, reluctant to let go.

The house stood like a sentinel on the horizon, its weathered walls watching her just as much as she was watching it. Something in her chest fluttered—recognition or dread, she couldn't tell.

Something shifted in her chest, a quiet tightening. This was the place her mother had known, had maybe even loved. And yet, it was a stranger to her.

The air felt different here. Thicker. Charged. Not quite ominous, but not welcoming either. Just... expectant. Like the estate itself was waiting to see what she would do next.

"Here we are," Reid said as he slowed the car to a stop in front of the wrought-iron gates that guarded the entrance.

Heather swallowed with her heart beating faster as she stared at the imposing structure. This was it: The House. The Family Legacy. The reason she was here.

The house loomed at the end of the drive, its presence pressing against the haze, against the cold air itself.

It wasn't **just** a house.

Her fingers tightened around the seat belt.

She wasn't ready.

Reid cut the engine and turned to her with a slight, reassuring nod. "It's a lot to take in, but we'll go inside and chat. I'll be here for the whole process."

Heather took a steadying breath and nodded, her fingers tightening around the door handle.

She stepped out, pausing as Glenoran loomed before her. The mist curled around the stones, softening their edges, wrapping the house in an eerie charm. She pressed a hand to her coat, bracing herself against the weight of everything she still didn't know. Today had to bring answers—about her mother, about this place—something to make sense of what came next.

Her footsteps crunched over damp gravel as she approached the entrance.

The heavy door sagged slightly at the hinges, its once-imposing presence worn by time. Chipped stone, creeping ivy, and the slow pull of decay blurred the edges between past and present.

"Miss Campbell?" Reid's voice cut through her thoughts. "You ready?"

She blinked, realizing she'd been staring too long. "I think so."

Reid opened the door with a groan, the sound of old wood creaking as it swung inward. Inside, the entryway was cold, the vaulted ceiling stretching high above, its exposed beams darkened with age. The flickering light from a single lamp cast odd shadows across the flagstone floor, catching the carved details of the wainscoting along the walls.

The grand fireplace, once the heart of the house, stood

empty and cold, its iron grate rusting beneath a thick layer of dust. Cobwebs clung to the substantial wooden banister of the staircase, and the antique furniture, adorned with intricately carved legs and faded upholstery, stood like forgotten relics of a long-lost time. A musty smell filled the air—old wood, mold, and damp stone. Everything felt weighty and forgotten, as if time had passed the house by but left its ghosts behind.

Here, buried beneath the dust and stone, was something almost familiar. A scent. A feeling. Like brushing against the edge of a memory that wasn't hers but had lived in her bones all along.

A man in his mid-fifties stood near the staircase, his suit slightly out of place in the dilapidated surroundings. His hands were clasped behind his back, but it was his eyes that caught her attention— piercing blue, cool and assessing. There was something familiar about them, a nagging sense of recognition she couldn't quite place. Like a face from a half-remembered dream. The way he looked at her was sharp and scrutinizing. It made her feel as though she were being examined under a microscope.

"Mr. Reid." He nodded, then turned to her. "Ye must be Miss Campbell." His voice was professional, but not entirely warm.

She snapped out of her thoughts and stepped forward to shake his hand. "Yes, that's me."

The man took her hand firmly, his grip surprisingly strong. "I'm Charles Duncan. Mr. Reid and I will be the solicitors overseeing yer late mother's estate," he said, his tone formal. "It's a pleasure to meet ye, despite the... conditions of the place. I'll take ye through everything shortly."

She spoke past a lump in her throat at the mention of her

mother. "Thank you for meeting with me," she said quietly, taking in the room as she tried to avoid crying.

Mr. Reid, standing just behind Duncan, gave a polite nod. "Aye, we understand this can be overwhelming. No rush, lass. We'll go through everything step by step." His voice was smoother than Duncan's—measured, reassuring, as if he was the one meant to soften the edges of what was to come.

Duncan motioned for her to follow him into the sitting room. The old floorboards groaned beneath her steps, warped with age and wear. The air was colder than expected, carrying the damp scent of stone and dust. The sitting room was no better than the hallway—furnished with timeworn pieces that had once been elegant but now faded in quiet decay. A tufted settee, its brocade upholstery faded and fraying, faced a stone hearth that hadn't seen fire in years. Dark wooden paneling lined the walls, its carved details dulled by neglect. The curtains, once rich damask, hung massive and motionless, blocking all but the faintest slivers of light. Above, a few oil paintings clung stubbornly to the walls, their gilded frames cracked and splintered, their subjects watching with hollowed, timeworn eyes.

"Please, have a seat." Duncan gestured toward the armchair across from him as he reached for a worn leather folder on the desk, flipping it open with practiced ease. Papers rustled as he sifted through them, pausing briefly to straighten a loose sheet before glancing up. "I'll explain things to ye in a moment."

Heather hesitated but sat down, the chair's springs groaning in protest. Reid remained standing by the fireplace, absently dusting his fingers over the cracked stone mantel, his expression unreadable.

"Aye, best to get comfortable," he added, glancing at her. "There's a fair bit to go over."

She glanced around the room, her eyes settling on the peeling wallpaper and the cracks in the ceiling that all seemed to grow wider the longer she looked at them. The house felt heavier with every breath, its history pressing in on her.

"Glenoran House," Duncan began, flipping through the documents before him, "has been in yer family for generations. It's a fine estate, but as ye can see, it's seen better days." He gestured toward the worn surroundings. "The upkeep has lapsed over the years, and it's no small undertaking to restore it."

She nodded, gripping the armrest of the chair. She already knew that much.

Duncan continued, "As the sole heir, ye have a few choices. Ye can sell the estate outright—though it'd be worth more with renovations. Or ye can restore it, either to keep or to rent. There's historical value, but that comes with its own set of rules."

Heather swallowed. "Rules?"

"Aye." He tapped one of the documents. "Because the house is a heritage property, there are preservation guidelines if ye choose to renovate. Ye'll need approval for major structural changes, but there are grants and resources to help with restoration."

She exhaled, trying to process it all. "And if I sell?"

Duncan exchanged a glance with Reid before answering. "To a developer? Maybe a private investor? Someone who might tear it down, is most likely."

The words hit harder than she expected. "I see."

Reid spoke up, voice gentler than Duncan's. "It's a lot to

take in, lass. No need to rush a decision. But once ye sell, there's no goin' back."

Heather tried to listen—tried to focus—but her chest felt tight. She glanced around the room again, her throat becoming unbearably tight.

The cracks in the ceiling. The sagging wallpaper. The weight of generations pressing down on her.

She needed to breathe.

Just breathe.

But it was crushing her, this place—this history that had waited for her, wrapped in silence.

Focus on the paperwork. Don't think about the dust, the decay, the expectation. "I'll need time to think."

Duncan nodded, sliding the documents toward her. "Of course. Look it over, and when ye're ready, we'll discuss next steps."

Mr. Reid replied, "If ye need anything else, dinnae hesitate to reach out." His tone was gentle but businesslike.

Mr. Duncan nodded in agreement, his expression unreadable. "Aye, we're here if ye need us."

Reid exhaled, adjusting his coat. "It's a lot to take in, lass. But there's no rush."

As the conversation wrapped up, Heather lingered by the door. Mr. Reid was about to step outside when Mr. Duncan spoke up from the corner of the room.

"If yer thinkin' about restoring the place," Duncan said, glancing at her with a thoughtful expression, "my son runs a business specializing in historic homes. Lad's got a knack for it."

Reid huffed, shaking his head. "Aye, and a stubborn streak. But he's good at what he does."

She barely absorbed the name Duncan mentioned, her thoughts still too tangled, but the idea of renovations suddenly felt a little less impossible.

As they stepped outside, Reid hesitated by the door. "If ye'd like, I can take ye back to yer accommodations? No point in wanderin' about in the cold."

She shook her head. "I think I'll stay for a little while. I'd like to take a look around."

Reid's eyebrow quirked, but he nodded. "Very well. Just be careful."

Heather offered a small smile. "I will. Thank you."

She watched him step into the rain, mist curling around him as he hesitated—just for a moment—before glancing back. Something in his gaze made her pulse stutter, as if he could see the questions tangled in her mind. But he only nodded once and walked away, leaving her in the looming shadow of Glenoran House.

The night pressed in, thick with unanswered questions, but beneath her unease, something else stirred. Possibility. Whatever this was, it wasn't over.

She stepped back inside.

One step at a time — for her mother, for herself... and for the history that refused to stay buried.

Chapter 13

As the sound of Mr. Reid and Mr. Duncan's cars faded down the gravel drive, she crossed the threshold and closed the heavy door behind her.

She turned to the window, eyes adjusting to the muted light slipping through warped panes of glass.

Venturing forward, her boots padded over the dust-dulled oak floors. The house wasn't haunted, exactly—but something about it felt like the walls had been holding their breath, waiting for someone to notice.

She stepped into what must have once been the drawing room—a wide, high-ceilinged space where tall mullioned windows framed the rolling green fields beyond. The fireplace was massive, its stone mantel coated in dust. She unlatched a window near the hearth, nudging it open. A Highland breeze curled inside, crisp and tinged with rain, ruffling her curls. Heather's fingers brushed the chipped frame, her gaze drifting to the snow-dusted hills and a grove of trees hugging the horizon. In the distance, a crumbling stone wall marked the estate's edge. Even in ruin, it was beautiful.

She could almost see it—flames crackling, laughter echoing. Now, only silence remained. A faded settee and side table clung to what had been. Sunlight had once danced across these walls, glinting off teacups and warming the air. Heather moved forward, step by step.

Beyond the drawing room, the dining hall's long wooden table sat warped from years of damp. A tarnished chandelier hung above, its crystals scattering faint light. She traced the dust-covered surface. Once, this place had been full of life. Now, it barely had a pulse.

The kitchen was dim, tucked behind the dining hall. A massive hearth took up most of one wall, with a rusted iron stove beneath it. Forgotten firewood lay in a crumbling heap. A worn groove marked the wooden counter—a quiet trace of meals made, hands at work. Someone had tried to modernize it, though the grimy Formica and outdated fixtures only highlighted the loss. Still, it had been more than functional. It had been loved.

She shook the thought away. This was a business decision— it had to be. Anything else was too complicated. It wasn't her home. And yet, it already felt familiar.

As she wandered deeper, her fingers skimmed the cold stone walls. Some rooms were empty; others held furniture draped in white sheets—ghosts of a life long gone.

In one of the downstairs bedrooms, she caught her reflection in the glass and almost didn't recognize herself. Damp curls wild, cheeks flushed, eyes wide with something unnamed—uncertainty? Determination? Maybe both. The mask she wore every day had slipped. She wasn't the guarded girl anymore.

She was just... her.

Outside, the rain had stopped, leaving the world slick and gleaming. She stepped into what had once been a private garden—stone pathways now tangled with weeds, a broken bench tilting against a crumbling fountain. Kneeling, she brushed her fingers over a stubborn patch of lavender that had survived the neglect. The scent hit her: soft, floral, familiar. A memory stirred—a warm lap, a lullaby, her mother's fingers weaving through her hair. Maybe she hadn't lost everything. Maybe, in some small way, her mother was still here.

As the dimming sunlight slipped behind the clouds again, Heather reentered the house and climbed the stairs, curiosity guiding her. A floorboard groaned under her boot—too loud in the stillness. A chill crawled up her spine. For a moment, she felt like an intruder. The silence stretched, thick and expectant, as if the house itself was waiting.

Downstairs had smelled of damp stone and old wood—preserved, museum-like. But this floor felt different. Lived in. The same oak floors creaked beneath her steps, but they were blanketed in once-plush carpet, matted with age. The bedrooms, the heart of daily life, carried faint traces of perfume and dust. Long faded, but not entirely gone.

The walls were papered in soft florals, pastel pink and green, unmistakably 1980s. The doors were painted cream, a contrast to the rich paneling below. Heather ran her fingers along the wallpaper, its colors dulled by time. It made sense—downstairs had been built to impress. Up here, they had lived. The space didn't feel eerie, just... forgotten. Like no one had walked these halls in years. She wasn't sure if that comforted her—or unsettled her more.

Then she saw it—the door at the end of the hall, a sliver of golden light slipping through the crack. Her hand hesitated on the knob, the brass cool and worn smooth. She swallowed, then slowly pushed it open.

Heather stepped inside and froze.

The room hadn't been abandoned.

A twin bed sat neatly made, a quilt in soft blues and pinks smoothed over it. A wooden dresser stood opposite, cluttered with trinkets—porcelain figurines, a jewelry box, a stack of worn books with cracked spines.

"This was hers," she whispered, thick with emotion. Her mother's room. Her childhood sanctuary. The realization hit like a wave. She pressed a trembling hand to the dresser for balance. This wasn't just a property. It was a thread to her mother, a window into a past she'd never fully known. And it had always been waiting.

She crossed the room, fingers grazing a faded photo tucked in the mirror's edge—her mother, young and laughing, so full of life. Did she love it here? Did she ever want to come back?

Heather glanced around: framed pictures on the wall, records stacked beside a dusty turntable, a worn stuffed animal perched on the bed. This wasn't history. This was a life. One she'd never been part of. She sank onto the bed, eyes drifting to the ceiling—cream-colored, smooth and unstained, unlike the rest of the house. The pale yellow walls and faded curtains still held a trace of whimsy.

Everything about this room felt intentional. Not forgotten. Preserved. Like someone had stepped out briefly and might return at any moment.

Her breath caught. The book on the nightstand lay open, its pages splayed like it had been left mid-read, waiting.

This place wasn't just a house.

It was a memory, a heartbeat, a home.

Outside, mist gathered over the garden. The light was fading fast. And for the first time, Heather didn't want to leave. Despite the decay, despite the unknown, something had clicked into place.

She stood and smoothed the blanket, quiet determination settling in her chest. She could walk away. But she wouldn't.

Not yet.

She didn't know if Glenoran was a burden, a calling, or something in between.

But she knew one thing—

For now, she was staying.

Chapter 14

The last rays of daylight faded over the hills, swallowing the house in shadow. Heather stiffened, scanning the room.

It had grown too dark.

Shadows stretched in long shapes across the cracked floors, and the faint creaks of the old beams settling in the cool night air set her nerves on edge. She glanced around the room, clutching her bag a little tighter.

Staying here overnight didn't seem like the wisest choice—at least not yet. She wasn't ready to sleep in a house with questionable electricity, no central heat, and an undeniable sense of abandonment. It wasn't fear—just something she needed to ease into. One more night at the inn wouldn't hurt.

She stepped back into the hallway, carefully locking the door to her mother's childhood bedroom before heading downstairs. As she passed the grand, decaying staircase, her footsteps echoed in the vast space. The air felt thick—like it had been holding its breath for years, unsure what to do with the girl standing in its doorway now. Pausing by the front door, she glanced back into the house one last time, feeling the weight of its silence.

"I'll be back tomorrow," she murmured to herself, as though reassuring the house itself—or maybe her mom's lingering memory.

Heather pulled out her phone, checking the ride service app.

One bar. Barely enough, but she tapped 'Confirm' with relief.

She wrapped her jacket tighter around herself, the day's weight settling into her shoulders. The house loomed behind her, its quiet emptiness pressing down like a sigh.

At last, headlights cut through the dark, bouncing down the uneven dirt road. She felt relieved when a modest sedan rolled to a stop at the gate near the bottom of the drive. The driver, a middle-aged man with short, blonde hair, leaned out the window with a curious expression.

"Are ye Heather Campbell?" he asked in a gruff Scottish accent.

"That's me," Heather replied, heading down the drive with her bag in tow. He popped the trunk as she loaded her bag. "Bit of an odd spot out here. What's a lass like you doing all alone in a place like that?"

Heather hesitated. It was an innocent question, wasn't it? But something in the way the driver asked it—like he already had an answer in mind—made her stomach twist.

Heather hesitated, glancing back at the shadowy silhouette of Glenoran House. "Family property," she said vaguely. "Still figuring it out."

He nodded knowingly as Heather slid into the passenger seat. "Well, if you need a ride back tomorrow, let me know.

Not many cars go this way. Name's Curtis, by the way."

"Thanks, Curtis," Heather said, grateful for the kindness. As the car wound toward Thistle Haven Inn, Heather rested her head against the window, watching the rolling hills disappear into the dark. Her thoughts drifted to Glenoran, her mother, and the daunting task of what came next.

The drive back to the Thistle Haven Inn was quiet, the evening mist softening the Highland landscape.

By the time she arrived, the cozy lights of the inn were glowing warmly through the windows, promising comfort and familiarity.

Heather pushed open the door to the inn and was greeted by the smell of something delicious baking in the kitchen. Claire Kinnaird peeked out from behind the reception desk, her kind face lighting up at the sight of Heather.

"Och, back already?" she asked, smiling warmly. "How was the place, then?" Heather hesitated, giving her a sheepish grin. "It's... *something*..." she admitted. "...needs a lot of work. I thought it might be better to clean some stuff up during the day before committing to an overnight stay."

Claire chuckled knowingly. "Och, that place hasn't had a proper soul in it for decades. Ye'd be braver than me to stay there at night." She motioned toward the stairs. "Yer bed's been made. Go on, make yourself comfortable. Dinner will be ready soon if you're hungry."

Grateful, Heather nodded and made her way up to her room.

Byrdie chirped sleepily from her spot on the bed when she arrived at her room. "Don't worry, girl," she said, stroking her back gently. "We're sticking with creature comforts tonight."

After washing up, Heather settled into bed, the warmth of the inn wrapping around her like a cocoon.

With a sigh, she wrestled with the thought of heading downstairs for a bite to eat.

Nope. Too comfy.

Opting out of dinner was the right move. She thought about the house—her house—and all it represented. It felt overwhelming, a weighty blend of excitement and apprehension. As she drifted off to sleep, she decided that tomorrow would be the start of her new beginning. But tonight, she was content to let herself rest and dream of what Glenoran might become.

The following day, Heather woke with a renewed sense of purpose. After a hearty breakfast of porridge, fresh scones, and tea at *Thistle Haven Inn*, she made a list on a scrap of paper. It felt satisfying to list what she needed: linens, cleaning supplies, groceries—and maybe a few cozy touches to make it feel like home.

She went to the town's car rental office, a modest building just off the main street.

After some paperwork and a friendly chat with the attendant, Heather drove off in a small but sturdy hatchback, its tires crunching along the gravel road as she navigated the countryside.

Her first stop was a local shop that specialized in home goods. Inside, she found shelves lined with colorful bedding, plush towels, and simple kitchenware. She paused in front of a display of quilted duvets, her fingers brushing over the soft fabric before selecting one in a soft cream color. "Something simple," she murmured, adding matching sheets and pillows to her basket.

Next came a quick stop at the grocery store, where she filled her cart with essentials: bread, eggs, milk, coffee, and a few treats for Byrdie. She also picked up a collection of cleaning supplies—bleach, mops, scrub brushes—and then wandered down the candle aisle, where she chose a lavender-scented one for good measure. Her trunk was packed when she returned to the car, and seeing it all made her feel oddly accomplished.

Byrdie, safely nestled at the inn, was next on her list. Heather carefully packed Byrdie's food, dishes, a small blanket, and a litter box when she arrived at Thistle Haven. The cat let out a questioning chirp as she scooped her into his carrier. "I told you I'd take you with me," she said softly, scratching her head through the mesh. "It's time to see your new home for the time being."

The drive back felt lighter—or so she told herself. The sun had broken through the clouds, and the rolling hills seemed less imposing, more welcoming.

As she turned onto the familiar dirt road leading to the estate, Heather glanced in the rear-view mirror at Byrdie. Her green eyes were wide, taking in the sunlight streaming through the car windows.

When they arrived, Heather parked near the front of the

building and began unloading the car.

"Alright," she said, gently setting Byrdie's carrier down on the porch. "Home sweet home."

Inside, the house was still as dusty and dim as she'd left it, but now, with supplies in hand, it felt like she could begin making it her own. She opened all the windows to let in fresh air, her curls whipping in the breeze as she swept cobwebs from the corners and wiped down surfaces. When she finished unpacking the groceries and setting up the bed with new linens, the bedroom upstairs felt almost... welcoming.

Byrdie padded across the floor cautiously, sniffing at the furniture before hopping onto the bed and curling up in a sunbeam. Heather leaned against the door frame, her arms crossed as she took in the sight. "What do you think, Byrdie?" she asked softly. "It's not perfect, but it's ours."

The cat purred in response, her contentment echoing her tentative optimism.

Hair in a messy bun, sleeves rolled, she surveyed the task ahead. Dust motes danced through the open windows, and every surface seemed coated in a thick layer of grime. It was daunting, but Heather was determined to reclaim the space, room by room. She started in the kitchen, scrubbing the countertops until they gleamed beneath years of neglect. Byrdie perched on the windowsill, watching her wide eyed as she attacked the ancient sink with a sponge and some elbow grease. She unearthed a small stack of old tea towels in one of the cabinets and smiled, imagining her mom drying dishes in this room as a little girl.

Moving on, she hauled a mop and bucket into the main hall, wrinkling her nose at the musty smell that lingered in the corners. The floors were beautiful underneath all the dirt—a dark wood that, once cleaned, reflected the light pouring in from the tall windows. She worked her way up the staircase, pausing occasionally to catch her breath and marvel at the intricate banister.

"You're starting to look alive again," she muttered to the house, almost feeling a sense of camaraderie with its tired walls. The living room took the longest. The fireplace was clogged with ash, and the furniture was draped in sheets so stained they were beyond saving. She tossed them into a pile by the door and wiped down the worn leather armchairs underneath. There was a small bookshelf in the corner, and as she dusted it off, she found an assortment of faded books, their spines cracked with age.

She picked one up—a collection of Scottish poetry—and set it aside for later. By mid-afternoon, Heather was sweaty, covered in a thin layer of dust, and starving. She took a break in the kitchen, slicing herself some bread and cheese she'd brought from town. Byrdie padded over to sit by her feet, letting out a slight chirp as she bent down to stroke her head.

"Not bad for a day's work, huh?" she said to her, glancing around the room. It wasn't perfect, but it was a start.

After lunch, she tackled the upstairs bedrooms. Most of them were in various states of disrepair, with peeling wallpaper and creaky floorboards. She focused on tidying the ones closest to hers, sweeping out debris, and airing them out. It was hard not to imagine what it must have looked like in its prime—bright and lively, with family bustling in every corner.

The final task of the day was the downstairs bathroom. The clawfoot tub was a masterpiece hidden under layers of grime, and Heather scrubbed at it until her arms ached. When she finally rinsed it clean, she stood back and admired her work, already picturing a hot bath to reward herself later.

Heather collapsed onto the small loveseat in the sitting room as the sun dipped lower in the sky, casting the room in a golden glow. Byrdie hopped beside her, curling into a tight ball against her side. As she dozed off for a quick nap, Heather felt a quiet sense of purpose settle over her.

After the long cleaning day, Heather stood in the bathroom, peering into the streaky mirror. Her face was smudged with dust, and her hair had escaped its messy bun in all directions. She groaned softly, turning on the faucet to wash her hands and splash cool water onto her face. "You look like you've fought the house and barely survived," she muttered to her reflection, giving Byrdie, who sat perched on the side of the tub, a sideways glance. "Time to scrub up."

She hopped in the archaic shower, letting the warm water rinse the sweat, dust, and grime from the day's work. She felt human again when she stepped out, wrapped in a towel. She chose a casual but flattering outfit—dark skinny jeans, a soft navy sweater, and waterproof Chelsea boots. Her hair, still damp, curled naturally around her freckled face. She dabbed on a bit of concealer and mascara, her freckles still visible, and decided it was good enough.

As she grabbed her jacket, she paused to stroke Byrdie's head. "I'll be back soon. Don't wreck the place, alright?" Byrdie let out a small, unimpressed chirp before curling back on the chair she'd claimed. Heather headed downstairs and locked up, the cool evening air hitting her as soon as she stepped outside. The sun was starting to set, painting the sky in hues of pink and orange. She'd noticed a pub in town earlier that day—a cozy looking place with a wooden sign that swung gently in the breeze. It wasn't far, and after a day of sandwiches and scrubbing, the thought of a hearty meal (and maybe a glass of wine) was too tempting to resist.

When she arrived, the pub, The Highland Hearth, was precisely what she'd hoped for: warm, inviting, and filled with the murmur of conversation. The scent of roasted meat and fresh bread greeted her as soon as she entered. She found a small table near the fireplace, the flames crackling cheerfully. As she waited for the bartender to take her order, Heather leaned back in her chair, taking in the surroundings. The pub was quaint and rustic, with mismatched chairs, low beams, and walls lined with old photographs and faded maps of the Highlands. A group of locals played darts in the corner, their laughter echoing through the room. When the bartender finally came over, Heather smiled. "I'll have the steak pie, please. And a glass of red wine." He nodded, jotting down her order. "First time in town?" She nodded. "Just moved here. Sort of."

He raised an eyebrow but didn't pry, disappearing into the kitchen. Heather sighed in relief and pulled out her phone, scrolling absently as she waited for her meal. It wasn't long before the plate arrived, steaming and delicious-looking, and she tucked in, savoring every bite. She couldn't help but feel the day's tension melt away as she ate. The pub's warmth, the delicious food, and the hum of life around her were comforting in a way she hadn't expected. Heather allowed herself to relax for the first time since she arrived in Scotland. As Heather polished off the last bite of her steak pie, she leaned back in her chair, cradling her glass of wine. She let her gaze wander around the room, soaking in the relaxed atmosphere. The fire crackled warmly, and the faint hum of a fiddle playing from the small sound system added to the pub's charm. She couldn't remember the last time she'd felt this grounded, even after such a chaotic start to her new life here. "Not bad for a solo dinner," she murmured with a small smile.

She was about to wave for the check when the bartender came back over. "How was it?" he asked, his accent thick and friendly. "Absolutely perfect," Heather replied, meaning it. "This might become a regular stop for me."

He grinned. "Yer welcome anytime. We don't get too many new faces in town, so you'll be remembered, that's for sure." Heather chuckled softly, but his words reminded her of how small this community likely was. Moving to Glenoran might make her stand out in ways she hadn't fully prepared for.

A voice interrupted her thoughts as she gathered her things and paid her bill. "Excuse me, miss." She turned to see a middle-aged woman with kind eyes and a welcoming smile near her table. "Sorry to bother you, but I couldn't help overhearing you're new around here. Are you staying in town?"

Heather hesitated her instinct to guard her privacy clashing with her desire to meet people. "Sort of," she said with a polite smile. "I recently inherited a property nearby—Glenoran House?"

The woman hesitated for too long, her fingers tightening around the napkin she held. "Aye, well... it's a grand auld place. Full of history."

"You say that like it's a bad thing," Heather tilted her head. "I'm sorry... I didn't catch your name."

The lady's smile didn't quite reach her eyes. "Not bad, just... well, Glenoran's been empty a long time. Some places don't like being left behind— and the name's Eleanor, hen."

Heather smiled politely, but Eleanor's unease lingered. As Heather reached for her glass, she noticed the bartender had gone quiet behind the counter, wiping down an immaculate spot with a bit too much focus. At a nearby table, an older man who had been chatting animatedly only moments ago fell silent, his tankard frozen mid-air. A slow sip, a glance toward her, then away—too fast, like he didn't want to be caught looking. The bartender wiped an already clean spot on the counter, his shoulders a touch too stiff.

The air shifted.

Not much. Just enough for Heather to notice. Heather cleared her throat, forcing a light tone into her voice. "I take it people don't exactly line up to buy the place?"

Eleanor chuckled, but it didn't quite reach her eyes. "No, lass. They don't." She wrung a napkin in her hands, then gave her a nod. "You enjoy your meal now."

Heather watched as Eleanor walked off, her back straight but her pace slightly quicker. She let out a low whistle to herself, swirling the last of her wine in its glass. What the hell was that about? Heather blinked. "What does that mean?"

Eleanor chuckled, shaking her head. "Nothing to worry about, love. Just auld ghost stories. Ye take care out there."

"Thank you," Heather said, a bit confused. "I appreciate that." Eleanor nodded and waved, leaving Heather to collect her things. The wind tousled her curls as Heather entered the crisp evening air, and she pulled her Barbour jacket tighter around her. The streets were quiet, most shops closed, their windows dark. As she walked to her rental car, her thoughts drifted to Eleanor's reaction. It wasn't the first time someone had seemed wary when Glenoran was mentioned.

She slid into the driver's seat, Byrdie's empty carrier still tucked into the back. "Ghost stories," she murmured aloud, repeating Eleanor's word with a smirk. "That's not ominous at all."

The narrow road wound through the hills, the headlights carving brief light tunnels in the darkness. The radio crackled softly, but Heather kept the volume low, preferring the sound of the tires against the gravel. The headlights carved a narrow path through the darkness, illuminating the mist swirling low over the road. Heather adjusted her grip on the wheel, keeping her focus ahead. Then—movement. Just a flicker at the edge of her vision, gone almost before she could process it.

Her heart jumped, her foot easing off the gas as she peered into the rear-view mirror. Nothing but an empty road behind her. She scanned the trees lining the narrow lane, searching for an animal, a stray branch swaying in the wind—anything.

The radio crackled—a sudden burst of static that sent a shiver down her spine.

The movement at the edge of her vision was gone. Nothing but trees and mist.

But for one breathless second, she could have sworn...

No. She shook her head, forcing out a laugh.

Okay, Heather. No creeping yourself out on day two.

She pressed her foot back to the gas and kept driving. Heather drummed her fingers against the steering wheel, Eleanor's words still circling in her head. First Alastair, now Eleanor. Even the bartender had raised an eyebrow when she'd mentioned the place. It wasn't just the repairs that made Glenoran an "ambitious" project. People here had opinions about it. She sighed, pressing the accelerator again as the town lights faded behind her. "Guess I'll find out why soon enough." She exhaled, shaking her head.

Once she arrived, she turned the key in the lock, the heavy wooden door groaning as it settled into place.

Heather lingered momentarily, her fingers resting against the old brass handle. She could walk away—take the money, sell the place, and never look back. That would be the easy thing.

But something in her hesitated.

Maybe it was because her mother had once lived here. Perhaps it was because she wanted answers that she didn't even know how to ask yet. Maybe—just maybe—it was because she wanted something that belonged to her, only.

"It's just a house," she murmured.

She lingered on the threshold, fingers resting against the old brass handle. The estate stood in silence—not empty, but waiting. Steadying herself, she squared her shoulders and stepped inside.

Chapter 15

Heather startled awake, breath catching in her throat.

For a moment, she didn't know where she was. The air was too cold, the silence too thick. Faint embers glowed in the hearth, casting flickering shadows across the stone walls. Early morning light filtered through the dust-coated windows, pale and thin.

She exhaled slowly, dragging a hand over her face. Everything ached—not just from the labor of yesterday, but from another night spent twisting beneath unfamiliar ceilings, sleep always just out of reach.

She'd tried the bedrooms. The first night, she'd climbed into her mother's childhood bed, quilt pulled to her chin, staring at the ceiling. But the walls had felt too close, too full of memory. After ten restless minutes, she'd gathered her blankets and padded downstairs.

For the past three nights, she'd slept by the fire in the sitting room, curling into its quiet glow. And still, the house hadn't quite settled around her. Not yet.

Byrdie was already awake, perched on the windowsill like a sentry, tail twitching in crisp, deliberate flicks. Not lazy—watchful.

Heather sat up and rubbed the sleep from her eyes. "What do you see out there, huh?"

Byrdie chirped in reply but didn't turn. Didn't blink.

Frowning, Heather shuffled over to join her. The fields beyond stretched quiet and still, damp grass gleaming under the hesitant sun. Nothing seemed amiss. But a strange feeling crept into her gut, like she was watching something she wasn't meant to. She shook it off and sighed. "Alright. Another big day. Let's see how much I can get done before I collapse."

First up: plumbing—or what might pass for it. The pipes groaned in protest when she tested the taps, but after some coaxing, a sputter of water came through. Rusty at first, then clearer. It was enough. The upstairs bathroom would need a deep clean, but at least she wouldn't have to haul water from town.

She spent the morning wiping down windowsills, knocking decades of dust and cobwebs loose. Each swipe of the cloth revealed more of the house's story—cracks in the plaster, intricate woodwork, hints of wallpaper faded to near memory.

She paused at the staircase, her hand resting on the banister. Had her mother once stood here, just like this?

Had she run these halls? Laughed in these rooms?

Had she ever imagined her daughter would return, trying to stitch their history back together?

Heather exhaled slowly. *Maybe I'll find out. One way or another.*

By noon, her stomach growled. She made a sandwich and tea, then stepped outside to the back garden while Byrdie took her usual inspection of a single patch of grass, nose buried, tail upright in concentration.

The air was crisp with damp earth and distant woodsmoke. Birds rustled in the hedges. Somewhere beyond the trees, a sheep called out in a bleating yawn.

Peaceful. Unexpected.

Heather glanced at the tangled garden. The stone paths were nearly swallowed by weeds, but beneath the mess, she could see what it might become again—if she was willing to try.

A vision bloomed: lavender lining the walkway, wildflowers spilling over the edges, a weathered bench tucked beneath the old willow at the property's edge.

The idea settled in her chest—warm, steady.

One thing at a time, she reminded herself, draining the last of her tea.

After lunch, she turned her attention to the attic.

The stairs groaned underfoot as she climbed, dust rising in lazy spirals. The attic door was swollen with age, reluctant to give way, but after a few firm shoves, it opened with a long, splintering creak.

The space stretched wide and quiet. Sloped ceilings met at timber beams that looked older than the house itself. The air was heavy with dust, the scent of old paper and something faintly sweet—like forgotten flowers pressed between pages.

She stepped carefully across the worn floorboards, each one whispering beneath her boots. Trunks and boxes loomed in uneven stacks, draped with sheets faded to the color of ghosts. Stray shafts of sunlight slipped through cracks in the shutters, catching the dust midair—stars suspended in stillness.

She tugged the sheet from the nearest trunk. A puff of dust rose like a breath released, making her cough as she waved it away. Kneeling, she unlatched the brass clasp and lifted the lid with a soft groan of hinges.

Inside: neatly folded linens, a few moth-eaten sweaters, and—beneath it all—a bundle of letters tied with a fraying ribbon.

Heather froze.

She hadn't expected to find anything of value, much less anything personal. But the paper was fragile beneath her fingers, the ink faded but still legible.

And then she saw the name.

The top letter was addressed in looping script to Elidh Mackenzie.

Her mother.

Department of Archaeology & Historical Studies

University of Illinois at Chicago
Office of Admissions
August 14, 1990
Dear Miss Eilidh Mackenzie,

It is with great pleasure that we inform you of your acceptance into the **Master's Program in Archaeology & Historical Studies** at the **University of Illinois at Chicago** for the Fall 1990 term. Your passion for historical preservation and your academic achievements in Scottish history and anthropology have made you an exceptional candidate.

Our faculty was particularly impressed by your research on **Jacobite artifacts and cultural memory in the Scottish**

Highlands. Your work demonstrates intellectual depth and an innovative approach to historical investigation. We believe you will be a valuable addition to our program, contributing both scholarship and insight.

Please find enclosed details regarding enrollment, orientation, and housing options for international students. If you require assistance with visas or financial aid, our administrative office is available to guide you through the process.

We look forward to welcoming you to campus and supporting your continued exploration of history's untold stories.

Warmest congratulations, and we hope to see you in Chicago soon.

Sincerely,

Dr. Aaron Allenson
Dean of Admissions
Department of Archaeology & Historical Studies
University of Illinois at Chicago

Heather ran her fingers over the aged paper, its edges softened by time but still crisp beneath her touch. The University of Illinois logo was stamped at the top—a seal of a life-changing moment. One she'd heard about dozens of times, always told with a spark in her mother's eye.

She smiled faintly, reading through words she already knew by heart. This was how it all started. Her mother had been accepted into a master's program in archaeology. She'd packed her bags, left Scotland behind, and chased history across the ocean. Heather could still hear her voice telling the story, equal parts excitement and wistful amusement.

"I thought I'd be unearthing ancient treasures—maybe even discovering something no one had ever found. Instead, I met your Da... and, well..." Eilidh would laugh, shaking her head. "You were my greatest discovery."

Heather had rolled her eyes every time she said it, but now—sitting in the dim light of Glenoran—she wished she could hear it again.

Her fingers traced the phrase *Jacobite artifacts and cultural memory in the Scottish Highlands.* Of course that's what her mother had studied. It was in her blood. Eilidh had spent her life drawn to the past—to stories etched into stone, buried beneath wild earth and silence.

And then she'd come to Chicago. And met Charles Campbell.

Heather sighed, leaning back against the worn velvet chair. Her parents had been opposites—her mother, passionate and curious, always chasing mystery; her father, practical and grounded, more interested in answers than questions. And yet, for a time, they had worked.

Eilidh had always spoken about Chicago with fondness, painting it in sepia tones—crisp autumns by the lake, the thrill of new beginnings. She used to describe the university library, the smell of old books, the sense that she was exactly where she was meant to be.

"And then, of course," she'd say with a teasing grin, "your father walked in, looking so serious and impatient, trying to check out the same book I'd already claimed."

Heather chuckled under her breath. That had been their beginning—a fight over a book about Scottish history.

"I let him have it, eventually," Eilidh would say. "He was cute. And I like to keep things interesting."

Heather's smile faded as her gaze dropped to the letter in her lap.

She had never doubted her mother's love. But here, in Glenoran—the place Eilidh had left behind—it struck her just how intentionally her mother had chosen a different life. She hadn't run from something. She had run *toward* it.

Adventure. Discovery. A new world she built with her own two hands.

And yet, she had never really let go of Glenoran. Somehow, she'd anchored herself to this place—as if she always knew Heather would need to find it one day.

Eilidh hadn't been stuck here. She had left because she wanted to.

Because there was a whole world waiting. And still... she had made sure Glenoran would come back to her daughter.

A lump formed in Heather's throat, but it wasn't grief. Not exactly.

It was gratitude.

"I hope you get to have an adventure too, *mo leanbh*," her mother had once whispered, brushing a curl behind her ear. "It doesn't have to be like mine. But promise me—you won't let the world stay small."

Heather swallowed hard, thumb brushing over her mother's name at the top of the page.

"I promise, Mom."

Carefully, she folded the letter and tucked it back into the box.

She hadn't expected an old acceptance letter to make her feel so close to her mother. But it did. It was a reminder that Eilidh had once been young, too—a dreamer. A girl ready to take on the world.

Heather glanced at the darkened staircase, the upper floors cloaked in quiet shadows. She still wasn't ready to sleep up there. Not yet.

Instead, she pulled a thick blanket from her things and settled on the couch in the sitting room, letting the last embers of the fire warm the space. Byrdie curled at her feet, purring softly, and for a brief moment, Heather allowed herself to feel safe.

The house creaked as wind stirred outside, a low groan passing through its bones. She pulled the blanket tighter, adjusting it over her shoulders.

"Alright, house," she murmured to the empty room. "We'll figure this out together."

The words hung in the silence, but somehow... they made her feel less alone.

Tomorrow, she'd begin.

One room at a time.

One step at a time.

And for now, she let her eyes drift shut—finally surrendering to sleep.

Chapter 16

Heather jerked awake, the cold clinging like a second skin—settling deep into her bones. The scent of dust and old wood filled her nose. It took her a moment to place the heavy quiet around her, the kind that only existed in places long forgotten.

Glenoran.

She groaned, rolling onto her back; the thin blankets she'd purchased barely warded off the chill that had seeped into the makeshift sleeping areas she had thrown together in the sitting room. The grand, ornate fireplace was dark now, nothing but cold embers and lingering smoke curling through the air.

"This was a terrible idea," she muttered, staring at the ceiling. The house didn't feel empty. It felt aware. She shook the thought off, but couldn't deny the eerie feeling that wouldn't budge.

The wind whistled through the cracks in the stone, rattling the windowpanes. A creak echoed from somewhere upstairs.

Heather froze, every nerve in her body going rigid. "It's just an old house, Byrdie." She whispered under her breath. "Old houses make noises."

Byrdie, unbothered, released an exasperated mew as she stretched and rolled over, exposing her soft belly.

Every squeak and sigh of the walls made her jump, and she spent far too long staring into the dark, trying to convince herself it was just the house settling. Still, it felt like the house was watching her. The distant rain and wind against the windows didn't help her sleep, either. With a groan, she dragged herself out of bed, rubbing her eyes as she made her way to the kitchen.

She immediately froze when her feet hit something cold and wet on the floor. Looking down, she saw the water—clear, but a puddle nonetheless. A leak. Fantastic. She glanced up toward the ceiling, realizing the rain from the previous night had done more damage than she'd anticipated. Heather stared at the puddle, her hands clenched at her sides. It wasn't just about the leak—it was about everything. The peeling wallpaper, the eerie quiet, the way the house felt like it belonged to someone else's past rather than her future.

She had come looking for a fresh start. All she had was a soggy towel, a leak she didn't know how to fix, and the creeping suspicion that she was in way over her head. What a joke. The only fresh thing about this place was the smell of damp wood and regret. Was she out of her depth? Was this house going to fight her every step of the way?

"Well, this is just great," she muttered, kneeling to inspect the puddle. She could already feel the frustration rising. Her mind immediately began ticking off everything else she would need to deal with—the roof, the plumbing, the fact that she hadn't even had time to tackle unpacking yet.

She grabbed a towel and mopped up the water, the sound of it soaking into the fabric echoing in the empty room. Heather knew this place needed work, but seeing it firsthand—the leaks, the dust, the old furniture left behind—made the weight of it all sink in. There was no turning back now. This was her responsibility. She had to make it work, no matter how overwhelming it felt. After mopping up the last puddle, Heather took a deep breath and pulled out her phone.

The leak was just the beginning, and if she was going to tackle the repairs on this place, she needed professional help. She remembered Mr. Duncan mentioning his son had a business restoring historic homes. This was her chance to get some advice, at the very least. She dialed Mr. Duncan's number, pacing the room while waiting for him to pick up. After a few rings, his familiar voice came through.

"Good morning, Miss Campbell," Mr. Duncan said, sounding cheery. "I trust you've survived the night in the house?"

Heather let out a small chuckle despite the frustration building up. "I've survived, but it's a challenge. I was hoping you could help me out with something." She hesitated before continuing. "You mentioned your son runs a business restoring historic homes. I was wondering if he could help with some repairs here. I'm starting to see just how much work this place needs."

There was a slight pause on the other end before Mr. Duncan responded. "Aye, that he does. He's got a company in Inverness that specializes in these kinds of projects. The office is in Inverness. Duncan Restorations. I'll send ye the address."

"Thank you, Mr. Duncan. I appreciate it," Heather said,

feeling a glimmer of hope.

He replied, "I'll text ye the details now. Best to pop in and speak with them directly. They can give ye a good idea of what's needed."

She felt a bit lighter after the conversation and was starting to see a path forward, even if it was still hazy. The house wasn't going to fix itself, and while she didn't know exactly how much needed to be done, she was confident she couldn't take on such a vast project alone."Thanks again, Mr. Duncan. I'll head over soon."

"Aye, take care now." With that, Heather ended the call, quickly pulling up her messages to find the text from Mr. Duncan. Sure enough, he had sent the address for Duncan Restorations in Inverness. She glanced at the clock—mid-morning already. Maybe it was time to make a trip into town. The house had enough work to keep her busy, but she needed a professional opinion. It would also allow her to explore the city more and get a feel for things.

Heather's car hummed steadily as she drove down the winding road toward Inverness, her thoughts still swirling around the house. The rain had stopped, leaving the air fresh and crisp, with the scent of wet earth clinging to the ground. The town was only a short drive away, and she felt a slight sense of relief at the thought of a change of scenery. The roads leading into Inverness were lined with tall trees and scattered cottages, giving way to the quaint, cobbled streets as she approached the heart of the town. It felt like a mix of modern life and old world charm, with its small shops and cafes nestled between towering stone buildings. She found a place to park near a bustling square. She took a moment to appreciate the town's vibrancy—people walking along the sidewalks, a market setting up in the corner, and the faint sounds of music spilling out from the pub she visited the night before.

As she walked down the street, she passed by a few stores, her attention briefly caught by the mix of antiques and local wares. The town had a certain warmth, a welcoming quality that contrasted with her isolation when she first arrived at the estate. It reminded her of the cozy little bookstore she used to manage back home, with the smell of fresh paper and a sense of familiarity.

Duncan Restorations was located just a few blocks down, a modest office nestled between two more significant buildings. The name on the door was simple and understated, but Heather felt a jolt of hope seeing it. Heather pushed open the door to Duncan Restorations, her thoughts already spinning with the possibilities of restoring Glenoran House. The bell above the door chimed softly as she stepped inside, the scent of wood and freshly printed plans filling the air. Her eyes scanned the office, filled with framed blueprints and historical photographs of buildings. She hadn't expected much—but what she saw was beyond anything she imagined. The room was a perfect blend of professionalism and comfort. But what honestly threw her off was the man sitting behind the desk.

Flynn.

Her heart stuttered. What the hell was *he* doing here?

He looked just as surprised to see her as she felt, his eyebrows raising in genuine astonishment. "Well, if it isn't Miss Campbell," Flynn said, his voice warm with surprise.

Heather blinked, completely thrown off. "Flynn? What are you doing here?"

Heather's brain felt like it had short-circuited. The man who had seen her in transparent pants was now supposed to fix her house? A grin tugged at the corner of his mouth, though something about how he looked at her told her he was trying to mask a more profound recognition.

He straightened, offering her a slight bow as he leaned against the desk. "I work here," he said casually, a soft chuckle escaping him as he spoke. "I own the company."

Heather stared at Flynn, her brain momentarily freezing as she tried to process the information. Flynn—the guy who'd rescued her from the rain-soaked, cow poop fiasco—was running Duncan Restorations? Her mind finally caught up, and the realization clicked.

Flynn Duncan.

"Wait," she blurted, pointing at him. "Your dad—Charles Duncan—is the one who sent me here?"

Flynn gave a lopsided smirk, amusement flickering in his blue eyes. "Aye. He mentioned someone would be coming by, but he didnae say it was *you*, the woman who made the most dramatic entrance into Scotland I've ever seen." He let out a low chuckle. "I'd have rolled out the red carpet if I'd known."

Heather huffed a laugh, shaking her head as the full picture settled in. Of course, Flynn was Mr. Duncan's son. She should've put that together sooner. It wasn't exactly a common last name. And yet, looking at him now—yeah, she could see it. The resemblance was there. Same sharp jawline. Same assessing gaze.

Heather raised an eyebrow. "Would it have changed any-thing?"

His grin turned a shade cockier. "Might've had the lads tidy up a bit. Or at least prepared a speech about why I'm the best man for the job." Flynn leaned back in his chair with a grin that could've come straight out of a rom-com, his eyes glinting with mischief. "I'm full of surprises," he said, giving her a wink. "You'd be surprised to hear I do more than muck about with cows and rescue damsels in distress."

Heather raised an eyebrow, crossing her arms. "Ah, a humble brag. So, it turns out men across the pond share that particular trait, too. Good to know."

Flynn laughed, clearly enjoying her sass. And God help her, she was enjoying it too. She was here to fix a house, not develop a ridiculous appreciation for the way a man smirked like he had all the time in the world. "If it helps, I usually need rescuing—mostly from my own bad decisions."

She chuckled, the initial shock of the situation melting into something a little more comfortable. "Well, that makes two of us. First, I get lost in the middle of nowhere. Then, I wreck my new shoes stepping in cow shit. Oh, and let's not forget the wardrobe malfunction."

Flynn's grin widened. "Ah, yes. The legendary transparent pants incident. I'll admit, that's a first for me. But at least you didn't get *stuck* in the cow pen. That could've been a whole different level of embarrassing."

Heather groaned, rolling her eyes. "Please, don't give me any ideas. I'm already traumatized enough."

Flynn's grin grew wider. "Well, I must admit, I've never had someone make such a memorable first impression. The pants incident alone could be a story for the ages."

Heather rolled her eyes but couldn't suppress a smile. "I'm glad I could entertain you. Maybe I'll throw in a herd of sheep for extra flair next time."

He raised an eyebrow and muttered under his breath, *"Mo*

chreach! Now that I'd pay to see. "

Heather winced. "Let's not tempt fate. I'm not sure my dignity could handle any more wildlife-related disasters."

Flynn chuckled, leaning forward. "I'll be sure to keep the wildlife—and your dignity—at a safe distance from now on."

She smothered a smile, but when she looked up, Flynn was watching her—amused, but with something unreadable flickering behind that lazy grin.

For a brief second, her stomach did that stupid, traitorous flip. Nope. Not going there. She had a house to fix, not time to entertain ridiculous thoughts about attractive Scottish contractors. She crossed her arms, shifting her weight. Flynn was still watching her, head tilted slightly, that infuriating smirk tugging at his lips—like he knew exactly where her mind had just gone.

Flynn nodded towards her. "You can keep the flannel, by the way. Suits you."

Heather scoffed. "And the sweatpants?"

He sighed, all faux regret. "Aye, those too. A great loss."

Heather huffed a laugh. "Tragic."

Flynn grinned. "Och, a noble sacrifice, nonetheless..."

Heather gave a mock glare, then took a deep breath, shifting gears back to business. "Alright, well, in all seriousness, I'm really going to need some help with Glenoran House. It's a mess. There are leaks, and the floors are squeaky—actually, the whole place is just begging for some TLC... I'm not sure where to start, but I know it's going to be a huge project." She hesitated for a moment, rubbing the back of her neck. "And I've never had to take on anything like this before, so if you know anyone who can help me get started..."

Flynn's expression softened, the teasing grin fading into

something more thoughtful. "Well, that's right up my alley. Duncan Restorations specializes in historic properties, after all. If you're serious about restoring it, I can help you figure out where to begin. And no, it won't involve any cows, I promise."

Heather looked at him, her brows raised in surprise. "You really think it's possible to restore it? It's been in such bad shape for so long."

He gave a reassuring nod. "Absolutely. It'll take time and money, but with the right approach, you can bring it back. And if you need help with the heavy lifting, we've got the crew for that, too."

Some of the weight she'd been carrying seemed to lift. "Well, I guess it's a good thing I found you then."

Flynn raised an eyebrow, a playful smirk tugging at his lips. "So, just to be clear—are you here for the house, or have I won you over already?"

His grin was smug, and she really wished it wasn't attractive. He leaned back in his chair, his gaze lingering on her with just enough intensity to make her heart skip a beat. "Either way, I'm happy to help. You're in good hands."

Heather scoffed, shaking her head. "Right, because nothing's more appealing than a crumbling estate and an overwhelming to-do list."

Flynn let out a bemused huff. "Could've fooled me. You still walked into *my* office."

Heather gave an exasperated huff. "Desperation makes people do crazy things."

He leaned in slightly, voice dipping just enough to make her breath catch. "Aye, well, not every day a woman strides into my office asking for a miracle. Makes a man wonder if it's fate."

Heather swallowed, forcing herself to hold his gaze. She refused to fidget, refused to react—but *God*, did he make it difficult. "Well, I do like to keep things interesting," she said, aiming for light and teasing—but her voice came out softer than she intended.

Flynn's smirk deepened—he'd caught it.

She cleared her throat, shifting her stance. "But seriously, I appreciate the offer. I just... don't know where to start. If you're willing to help, I'm all in."

"Of course, I'm in," Flynn said, his grin tipping just enough to be dangerous. "This place has potential. And let's be honest, if I can survive another run in with your four-legged fan club, I think I'll have earned a medal."

Heather huffed a laugh. "Oh, so now you're looking for hero status?"

Flynn's eyes twinkled as he leaned in. "Lass, I'm just trying to keep you in one piece."

Heather groaned, scrubbing a hand over her face. "I will never live that down, will I?"

He tilted his head, eyes glinting. "Not a chance."

She shot him a dry look, but couldn't bite back a smile. "Fine. I'll do my best to avoid any more near-death—or near-naked—experiences."

"Good. Wouldn't want the cows thinking you're easy prey," Flynn teased, his grin pure mischief.

Heather shook her head, biting back a laugh. "Alright, alright. But I'm not making any promises."

She crossed her arms, tilting her head. "So? When do we start?"

Flynn raised an eyebrow, mischief glinting in his blue eyes.

"Eager, are we?" He leaned back in his chair, arms crossing over his chest. "Well, first things first—I need to see Glenoran up close. If we're going to make that place livable, we'll need a plan."

Heather nodded, excitement buzzing beneath her nerves. "Sounds like a plan. Lead the way, Mr. Duncan."

He beamed, "Flynn," he corrected smoothly. "Let's stick with Flynn." His voice dipped just enough to feel personal, like he wasn't just talking about names.

Heather grinned. "Alright, *Flynn.* Lead the way."

He stood, pushing his chair back effortlessly, his gaze lingering on her for half a second longer than necessary before he turned toward the door. "Right this way, then."

They stepped out of the office, the Inverness air still crisp from the morning chill. Heather inhaled deeply, already feeling the weight of what lay ahead. But beneath it, something else stirred—excitement. A new chapter. A fresh start. And maybe, just maybe, a little help from a very attractive contractor.

Flynn fell into step beside her, his stride easy, effortless. "So, tell me about Glenoran. You said it's been in your family for generations—what's your vision for it? Restoration? Modernization?"

Heather hesitated, rolling his question over in her mind. She hadn't thought much past survival—patching leaks, fixing the most urgent repairs, keeping the roof from caving in.

"A bit of both, I guess," she admitted. "I don't want to strip away the character, but it needs a lot of work. The roof leaks, the windows groan, and don't even get me started on the floors."

Flynn let out a low chuckle. "Sounds like a dream."

Heather huffed. "Sounds like a headache." She hesitated, then added, "I haven't decided if I'm keeping it. At first, I thought I'd fix it up and leave. But now…" She exhaled, shaking her head. "I don't know. Maybe it's not worth the effort."

Flynn nodded thoughtfully. "It's a lot to take on, especially when you're still figuring things out. But from what I've seen, the house has potential. Sometimes, it just takes someone to see that vision."

He glanced at her. "I'm guessing you want to keep some of the charm—modern amenities without sacrificing history. Not an easy balance, but it can be done."

Heather studied him, surprised. "Exactly. You're good."

Flynn smirked. "Well, I do know my way around a restoration project or two."

They reached her car, and Heather hesitated for a beat, fingers grazing the door handle. Anticipation hummed beneath her nerves. This was it—the real start of something new. Maybe even an adventure.

Flynn leaned against his truck, arms crossed, watching her with a knowing glint in his eye. "I'll follow you to the house."

"Great," Heather said, flashing him a quick grin as she slid into the driver's seat. Her fingers tightened around the wheel, nerves humming beneath the surface.

She wasn't sure what she expected when she came here—maybe some answers, maybe just a chance to close a door she never meant to open. But instead, she found herself at the start of something that felt bigger than her.

The engine rumbled to life, and as she pulled onto the road, Flynn's truck stayed close behind. This was happening.

Glenoran, the renovations, all of it. She let out a slow breath. Sink or swim, she was in it now. Glenoran. Flynn. All of it.

And she had enough to deal with without getting distracted by a smug Scottish contractor and his stupidly charming smirk.

Chapter 17

Heather kept her eyes on the road, hands tight on the wheel, but her thoughts drifted—to Flynn, to Glenoran, to the whirlwind of the past few days. Everything was happening so fast, and she wasn't sure how she felt about *any* of it.

Flynn's presence had been an unexpected constant, a quiet camaraderie settling between them. She hadn't expected that—any of this.

As she turned onto the long gravel drive, the sight of Glenoran sent a ripple of nerves through her chest. Anticipation. Uncertainty. The weight of a decision not yet made.

It was hers—technically. But could she really handle it? Or was she walking into something far bigger than she was ready for?

She parked beside Flynn's truck but stayed in the seat, gripping the wheel with white knuckles, eyes locked on the house. Glenoran stood before her—weathered, waiting. Hers.

A minute later, she opened the door and sighed, "Well... here we are."

Flynn didn't reply right away. He climbed out of his truck, shutting the door with a quiet thud. He stood, taking in the house, the land, the sheer weight of it all.

Heather hesitated before finally pushing her door open. "It's mine," she said, stepping out onto the gravel. "But I don't know if I'm ready for it."

Flynn glanced at her, then back at the house, his expression unreadable. "Nobody's ever ready for something like this." He leaned against the side of his truck, arms crossed. "But you're here. That's the part that matters."

Heather huffed a quiet laugh, shaking her head. "Guess we'll find out if that's enough."

A flicker of amusement passed over his face. "Aye. I guess we will."

Flynn pushed off the truck, ambling toward her with that easy confidence, nodding toward the house. "You know, Campbell, this place isn't just a house. It's a bloody time capsule."

Heather arched a brow. "A time capsule?"

He smirked. "Aye. Built in 1725. It's stood through rebellions, betrayals, maybe even hid a few fugitives. If these walls could talk, they'd have stories older than most countries." His gaze drifted over the weathered stone, something thoughtful flickering behind his eyes. "It's stood through it all—fights, losses, the rise and fall of names long forgotten."

Heather looked back at the house, a new weight settling over her. "And now it's mine."

Flynn glanced at her, lips twitching. "Aye. No pressure."

She stared at the house, her mind racing to comprehend the magnitude of what Flynn was saying. It wasn't just an old house. It had been a silent observer of one of the most significant periods in Scottish history. The weight of it settled in her chest like a stone.

How many lives had passed through these halls? How many secrets had these walls swallowed whole? The idea that her family—her blood—had been part of something so monumental made her feel both deeply connected and impossibly small. "I had no idea. That's... incredible."

Flynn chuckled, shaking his head. "It's more than just stone and timber, you know." His voice dipped slightly, a quiet reverence threading through it. "Places like this... they don't just stand through history. They carry it. Every wall, every beam—it's a reminder of a time when people risked everything for what they believed in."

His gaze flicked back to her, steady. "If you bring this place back, you're not just fixing up an old house, Campbell. You're keeping a piece of Scotland's past alive."

Heather shifted, smoothing her hands over her hips, her gaze climbing the stone walls with something like awe. It was strange—how something so old, so deeply rooted in the past, could suddenly feel like it was reaching for her. She thought of her mother. Had she known about this? Had she ever walked through these halls and felt the weight of history pressing down as Heather did now? She wished she could ask."I didn't expect it to be... so important. So much bigger than I thought."

Flynn glanced back at her, his smile easy, steady. "History's like that—heavy... But yer not in this alone, Campbell. You'll have help."

Heather took a slow breath, her gaze tracing the worn stone, the weathered windows. It wasn't just an old house—it was a story waiting to be uncovered. She exhaled, glancing at Flynn. "If I'm doing this... I'm glad I don't have to do it alone."

Flynn's grin widened. "Ye won't be. Not while I'm around."

Heather's fingers curled slightly at her sides. The words shouldn't have meant as much as they did. But standing here, in front of this house—her house—she felt the weight of them settle deep, steady, and certain.

Together, they walked toward the house, the weight of its history—and the weight of the future—looming over them, but there was a quiet understanding between them. Whatever the challenge, they'd face it together. As they approached the front door, Flynn looked over the house, his gaze sweeping over the crumbling facade and the overgrown yard.

He tilted his head, hands in his pockets, his brow furrowing slightly as he assessed the damage. "This place has potential, no doubt about it," he said thoughtfully, running a hand through his hair. "But it'll need a lot of work. Let's start with the roof and foundation—can't have the auld place collapsing before ye unpack yer suitcase."

Heather swallowed, taking in the enormity of what he was saying. What if she failed? What if she poured herself into this place, only to find it would never feel like home? Or worse— what if she started to care too much, only to lose it? She'd known the place was a mess. But hearing it laid out so plainly still made her stomach twist.

Still, she must admit, Flynn knew what he was talking about. He glanced back at her, a slight grin tugging at the corners of his lips. "Don't worry. We'll get it sorted. It's just a matter of time and effort."

Heather nodded, trying to keep her anxiety in check. "Right. Time and effort. Sounds... doable, right?"

"Absolutely," Flynn said with confidence. "Once we start on the basics, it'll be like piecing together a puzzle. One step at a time."

He walked along the side of the house, inspecting the aging siding and the overgrown ivy that had claimed one of the walls. Heather followed, her mind racing with everything that needed doing.

"How long do you think it'll take to get it livable?" she asked, her voice filled with uncertainty.

"Depends on how much you're willing to throw at it," Flynn replied, his voice turning businesslike. "But I'd say a solid six months to a year, depending on the scope of work. It's not a quick fix, but it's definitely doable."

Heather sighed, her mind racing. Six months to a year—longer than she'd planned, assuming she'd ever had a plan in the first place. What would she do about her life back in Millhaven? Her apartment was in limbo, subleased to Mark's friend for now, but that arrangement couldn't last forever. And her dad's house... She still hadn't made any real progress towards selling it. It just sat there, waiting, much like everything else in her life that felt unresolved.

Flynn studied her momentarily, his expression shifting—not teasing, not playful, but something closer to understanding. "Ye don't have to decide everything today, you know," he said, his voice softer. "It's alright to take yer time."

Heather blinked, caught off guard. Was she that obvious? She forced a smile. "That obvious, huh?"

Flynn shrugged, his grin easy but knowing. "I've seen that look before. People standing at the edge of something big—usually just before they jump."

The weight of it all pressed on her chest as she glanced

around the grand but crumbling Glenoran. Was she ready to take on something this big? Or was she running from the life she'd left behind?

"I'll be honest, Campbell," Flynn said, turning toward her with a rare note of gravity. "This place is a right beast—but it's worth it. The history in these walls is something special. If you're really serious about restoring it, I can give ye a hand—my company handles this kind of work all the time."

"You'd help me?" The question slipped out before she could stop it.

Flynn shrugged, but there was something deliberate about the way he looked at her. "I wouldnae offer if I didn't think it mattered. Besides, we're old friends now, right?" His tone was light and teasing, but his voice had an underlying sincerity. "I'll give you a discount for the work. Let's say you're getting the 'old friend' special. Ye'll still be broke, but at least ye'll feel better about it."

Heather let out a breathy laugh, shaking her head. "Well, I guess that's a win." But underneath the humor, there was something else. Relief. She hated admitting it, even to herself, but knowing she wasn't in this alone made something in her chest loosen. She had spent so much time carrying things on her own—her father's death, the bookstore, the house in the city. And now, here was Flynn, casually offering to take some of the weight off. She didn't know what to do with that.

It was a relief. And—if she let herself admit it—maybe even a temptation. She wasn't sure what kind of friends they were becoming, but restoring the house with his help suddenly seemed less daunting. "Well, in that case, I might just take you up on that," she said with a half-smile. "It sounds like I'll need all the help I can get."

Flynn's grin widened, and for a moment, Heather could've sworn she saw something flicker in his eyes—something warmer than just professional concern. "Glad to hear it. We'll get started soon. I'll get the team out here next week and start with the most urgent stuff. If we're going to do this, we'll do it right."

Heather looked at the house again, feeling more specific and hopeful. Maybe this wasn't the disaster she had imagined. Maybe, just maybe, this was the beginning of something bigger. She'd arrived in Scotland expecting to clean up a house and move on. Now, she wasn't so sure she even wanted to leave.

"Thanks, Flynn," she said, her voice softer now, touched by gratitude.

"Dinnae mention it," he joked, "Just doing my civic duty to ensure Scotland remains a no-transparent-pants zone."

Heather laughed, a thread of tension loosening in her shoulders as she glanced at the house. "I'll take that as a promise."

Their hands met in a firm shake, and Heather felt a jolt of something unexpected—warmth that traveled straight up her arm from his palm. His grip was steady, his skin slightly rough, and it felt like an anchor, grounding her amid her swirling doubts, and the gesture lingered just a second too long—long enough for her to notice. Long enough for her to wonder if he did, too. Her breath hitched, and Flynn's smile softened, his hand holding hers just a beat longer before he released her.

"That's settled, then," he said, his voice low and sure. "Welcome to the chaos."

Heather tried to play it cool, even as her heart thudded.

"Chaos might be putting it lightly. This place is practically falling apart."

"Aye," Flynn said, a teasing glint in his eye, "but it's yer chaos now. And lucky for ye, I have a soft spot for fixing disasters."

Heather raised an eyebrow, crossing her arms with a bemused grin, "Are you calling me a disaster?"

"Not you, Glenoran," he shot back with a wink. "You, Miss Campbell, are more of a... challenge."

"Glad to know I'm keeping you on your toes," she said, unable to stop smiling back.

"Always," Flynn replied, his tone light but with just a hint of something else that made her stomach flutter. He stepped back, his gaze sweeping over the house with fondness and determination. "Right, then. Let's get to it! I'll come back tomorrow to go over the priority repairs and draw up a proper plan."

Heather glanced up at the house, its weathered facade and sagging roof still daunting but somehow less overwhelming with Flynn standing beside her. "Right," she murmured.

"Ye've got time," he said with a small smile, his voice steady and reassuring. "We'll get there."

As Flynn headed toward his truck, he paused, turning back to her with a grin. "Oh, and Campbell?"

"Yeah?"

"Try to avoid wandering off in the rain while I'm gone, eh?" He winked, his grin widening as he climbed into the truck.

Heather laughed despite herself, shaking her head as she watched him drive away. The sound of his engine faded into the distance, leaving her alone once more in front of Glenoran House. But this time, the solitude didn't feel quite so overwhelming. She turned back toward the house, wrapping her arms around herself as the wind carried the scent of damp earth and old stone. A distant crow called through the trees, echoing like a memory.

The enormity of it all pressed in around her—the repairs, the history, the uncertainty of what came next—but something was different now. She wasn't entirely alone in this. For the first time since arriving in Scotland, that thought felt like something she could hold onto. She took one last look at the road where Flynn had disappeared, then turned back to Glenoran.

It was broken. Haunted. Heavy with history.

But so was she.

And maybe—just maybe—if she could fix it, she could fix something in herself, too.

Chapter 18

The last light of day slipped through the old windows as Heather sat in her mother's childhood bedroom, wrapped in silence. Only the creak of old beams and the soft patter of rain broke the silence. Byrdie lay curled on the bed, her tiny body rising and falling as she dozed.

Heather ran her fingers along the walls, pausing at the delicate color that had probably once been vibrant. This room had been her mother's world once, long before Heather existed. It was a strange, bittersweet connection to someone she'd lost so long ago.

She opened the small wardrobe in the corner, its hinges squealing in protest. Inside, a few forgotten items hung like ghosts of another time: a faded blue dress with a lace collar and a plaid scarf neatly folded on the shelf. Heather carefully pulled out the blue dress, the fabric soft and worn from age. She held it up, imagining her mother as a girl twirling in this very room. The thought sent a pang through her chest—grief and connection tangled too tightly to bear. On the shelf above, her fingers brushed over an old wooden box. Curious, she pulled it down and carried it to the bed, sitting cross-legged as Byrdie stretched and yawned. The box was small but sturdy, with a delicate carving of thistles etched into the lid.

She opened it slowly, the hinges groaning with a brittle creak. Inside, she found a collection of little treasures: a stack of photographs, black-and-white and slightly yellowed with age, of a smiling young woman she recognized as her mother. A handwritten letter caught her eye, folded neatly and addressed to Eilidh MacKenzie in elegant script. Heather carefully unfolded the letter, her hands trembling slightly. The paper felt fragile, as though it might crumble at any moment.

Dearest Eilidh,

I hope this letter finds you well and that you are dreaming big, as you always do. Someday, this house will be yours, and I know you'll make it something extraordinary. Never let anyone tell you your dreams are too big.

Heather exhaled shakily, her fingers tightening around the fragile paper. *Someday, this house will be yours.*

She read them again. They didn't change.

Her mother was supposed to inherit Glenoran. She was supposed to make it extraordinary. But she never did. Her pulse quickened. Had her mother ever wanted to come back? Had she stood in this very room, hands trembling over this same letter, wondering if Glenoran was her future? But something had kept her away. Something had changed. Heather's throat tightened. Why? What had stopped her?

For a moment, the weight of it all was too much. Heather

clutched the letter to her chest, eyes squeezed shut against the sting of tears. The scent of old paper and faded lavender clung to the box, stirring something wordless and familiar inside her. A memory she could almost grasp—but not quite.

The letter was signed simply *Aunt Margaret*—a name her mother had only mentioned once or twice. Beneath it were trinkets: a pressed flower in glass, a silver locket, a tiny porcelain Highland cow. Heather smiled. Even then, the cows had been part of this place. Somehow, in this house full of ghosts, she felt closer to her mother than she had in years. Overwhelming—but unexpectedly comforting. Almost like... belonging.

Byrdie meowed softly, nudging her arm. Heather stroked her absentmindedly.

"What am I supposed to do with all this, Mom?" she whispered.

Byrdie chirped and climbed into her lap, curling against her stomach. Heather let out a watery laugh. "You always know, don't you?" The cat purred in answer.

It didn't matter that no one could respond. Being surrounded by her mother's past made Heather feel a step closer to her own. Byrdie's weight in her lap grounded her. She exhaled slowly, wiped a tear from her cheek, and placed the letter back in the box, tucking it under the bed.

"I'll figure it out," she said, steadier now. "I have to."

It wasn't just a project anymore. It was a chance to rebuild, to rediscover, to begin again. The wind rattled softly outside, drawing her gaze to the window. The house felt old, yes—but alive. And now, it was part of her story.

"I can do this," Heather murmured.

Byrdie stretched and hopped down, padding across the

wooden floor. She stopped at the door, tail twitching.

"What is it?" Heather asked, still smiling.

Byrdie let out an insistent meow, then pawed at the crack beneath the door. With a sigh, Heather stood and opened it, expecting her to dart out—but Byrdie only stared into the hallway, still and alert. The hairs at the back of her neck rose.

"You're being dramatic," she teased, though her voice was quiet.

Byrdie turned to look at her with bright, knowing eyes. She chirped—decisive and smug—and trotted back to bed like she'd solved something only she could understand. Heather chuckled and slid beneath the covers as Byrdie curled into a neat ball.

"You little weirdo." She smoothed a hand over her soft fur. Byrdie purred, loud and steady in the silence.

Maybe Glenoran was still too big. Still too much.

But if Byrdie had already made it home...

Maybe she could too.

Chapter 19

As dawn's pale light crept across the room, Heather stirred beneath her blankets, the chill seeping through the thin fabric. She opened her eyes slowly, her breath visible in the frosty air.

The house was still, but not silent. Wood groaned softly, expanding in the cool morning air, while the patter of rain on the window added a quiet rhythm. She rubbed her eyes and sat up, curls tumbling over her shoulders. The fireplace had burned out hours ago, leaving only a trace of smoke curling faintly in the draft.

The stone walls felt cold and heavy, but as she inhaled deeply, a faint floral note—lavender?—lingered in the air. It was subtle, barely there, but it made her pause. Maybe it was her imagination, or maybe the house was offering a quiet reminder of her mother.

Byrdie lay curled in a tight ball at the foot of the bed, and Heather smiled, stroking her fur. She stretched luxuriously, her contented purr rumbling beneath her fingertips.

"Good morning, Byrdie," she murmured.

She chirped, blissfully unconcerned with the day ahead.

Heather swung her legs over the edge of the makeshift bed, her feet meeting the cold floor with a soft thud. The chill bit at her skin, urging her to move quickly. She glanced around, taking in the peeling wallpaper and the faded floral curtains framing the frosted glass.

The house was alive—breathing, groaning, whispering its stories.

It urged her to listen. To pay attention.

But she also felt the weight of uncertainty pressing in. Yesterday had been a whirlwind of revelations, and now, in the quiet morning light, she couldn't outrun her thoughts.

This wasn't just a renovation project.

It was her mother's memory. A legacy of family history. And a future she wasn't sure she was ready to claim.

She shook off the thought and pulled a sweater over her head before padding into the kitchen. The rough, uneven floor beneath her socks was a reminder of the work still waiting. As she stood at the sink, filling the kettle, her gaze drifted to the window.

The rain had softened to a mist, clinging to the rolling hills and skeletal trees. A landscape both foreign and deeply familiar.

Tea in hand, she returned to the sitting room. Byrdie followed, hopping onto a windowsill, her tail swishing lazily as she peered outside. Heather leaned against the doorway, watching her—Heather's little shadow, just as curious about this place as she was.

She chirped softly, as if urging her forward.

And so she did.

Not just into the day, but into the house's story—her story.

She didn't have all the answers, but in the morning light, the house didn't feel as daunting. It was a challenge, yes, but also possibility.

Her fingers itched to uncover what had been hidden.

She knelt beside Byrdie, stroking her fur as she looked out at the misty hills.

"Alright," she murmured. "Let's see what this day brings."

By the time she finished breakfast, Flynn was already at Glenoran, a toolbox in hand.

Heather spotted him through the sitting room window, moving across the gravel drive, his breath curling in the cold morning air. His jacket was unzipped, his work boots kicking up bits of frost-dusted dirt as he approached.

She wrapped her hands around her mug, watching him a moment longer than she probably should have.

There was something steady about him. The way he moved with purpose, his focus already locked on the task ahead.

She wasn't sure what to make of him—but she'd have plenty of time to find out.

Stepping outside, she crossed the gravel path to meet him. Flynn was already assessing the front porch, his broad shoulders shifting easily as he inspected the wooden beams.

"Morning," Heather called, her voice still hoarse from sleep.

Flynn turned, his smile breaking across his face.

"Morning," he replied, his eyes lighting up. "You're up early. Ready to get your hands dirty?"

Heather smiled, though she felt a little out of place. "I didn't expect to be... involved just yet."

Flynn chuckled, a rich sound that sent an unexpected flutter through her stomach.

"It's a big place. If we're going to make progress, we might need more than just me working on it. I can show you how to help with the smaller stuff—fixing up windows, maybe some clean-up."

Heather hesitated, glancing down at her boots. They were sturdy, but she had no intention of getting them covered in paint or dirt.

"I... I'm not sure I'm cut out for this kind of work."

Flynn stepped closer, warmth radiating from him despite the brisk morning air.

He flashed her a playful grin. "You've already survived haunted creaks and leaky ceilings. A little DIY? That's child's play."

Heather groaned at the reminder, but she couldn't help laughing.

"You really have no mercy, do you?"

"None whatsoever. I call it like I see it," Flynn said, his eyes glinting with mischief. "But if you need moral support, I can always supervise. Maybe hold the flashlight dramatically while you hammer something?"

Heather exhaled in mock exasperation, glancing at the tools scattered around the porch. Part of her was reluctant, but another part...

Another part was intrigued.

And, if she was honest, the idea of working alongside him was more than a little tempting.

"Okay, fine," she said, rolling her eyes. "But don't get used to me doing the heavy lifting."

Flynn winked, crouching down to grab a set of old tools.

"Alright, while you watch me work, feel free to criticize my technique."

"Don't tempt me," Heather said with a teasing grin. "I've seen enough DIY shows to know what not to do."

"Oh, now I'm worried," Flynn teased, laughter in his voice. "You'll be giving me tips before the day's out."

Heather shook her head, laughing. "Only if you're aiming for a 'before' photo on a renovation disaster blog."

Flynn straightened, brushing dust from his jeans. "I'll take my chances. But if you change your mind, feel free to jump in. You might surprise yourself."

Heather nodded, unsure whether to observe or help. As much as she wanted to contribute, something about the work—and the man doing it—felt a little intimidating.

Flynn moved with focus, skill, and an ease that made it all look effortless. His hands were sure, his movements deliberate, yet his easy grin and playful remarks kept the air light.

Heather lingered near the doorframe, watching. There was something captivating about the way he handled the house—like he cared about it. Not just the physical labor, but the patience, the precision, the way he treated every worn, neglected piece like it was worth restoring.

Her gaze drifted to the flex of his arms as he measured and adjusted the old wooden beam, strength and skill working in tandem. It struck her how natural he seemed in this space, how at home he was in the challenge of bringing something back to life.

She wrapped her arms around herself, but not from the chill. It wasn't just admiration—it was something else...something warmer. Closer.

And then there was the way he looked at her.

Not always. Not obviously. But sometimes—fleeting glances that lingered just a second too long.

Her heart did a ridiculous little flip, a sensation she hadn't felt in a long time. She shook her head, willing it away.

This wasn't the time for... whatever that was.

She had a house to restore. A life to figure out.

Flynn was just someone who knew what he was doing—someone helping her through the chaos.

And yet, as he bent to pick up another tool, sunlight catching the dark strands of his hair, she couldn't quite convince herself that was all there was to it.

Flynn didn't look up, but his grin was unmistakable.

Her stomach dropped straight to the floor.

"If you keep looking at me like that, Campbell, I might start thinking you like what you see."

Heather choked. Actually choked.

She barely covered it with a scoff, shifting her weight and desperately trying to mask the heat crawling up her neck. "Oh, please," she shot back, folding her arms across her chest. "I was just wondering how many more things you plan to mansplain today."

Flynn chuckled, clearly amused. Clearly not fooled. "Och, you wound me," he said, pressing a hand over his chest in mock injury. "But dinnae fash, lass... I'll let you take the lead next time. Wouldnae want to bruise your pride."

Heather needed a new planet to live on immediately.

She mustered an indignant, "Are you actually suggesting that I help?"

"Only if you dinnae mind getting your hands dirty," Flynn said, nodding toward a loose piece of molding. "I could use a second pair of hands to hold that in place while I secure it.

Unless, of course, ye'd rather stick to 'observing.'"

Heather hesitated, but the glint of challenge in his eyes made her straighten her shoulders.

"Fine," she said, stepping into the room. "But don't blame me if I break something."

Flynn smirked, handing her a mallet. Their fingers brushed, just a quick, fleeting touch, but Heather felt the heat of it like a spark jumping from skin to skin.

Flynn didn't react. Didn't flinch. He just nodded toward the wooden molding, like nothing had happened. Like he hadn't just sent a jolt up her arm that made her grip tighten around the handle.

Heather swallowed. *Focus.* She was holding a tool, not his hand. Get a grip.

"Here, hold this steady while I nail it back in," he said, voice easy, professional.

"Right," Heather murmured, positioning the board. She could do this. She wasn't thinking about his hands. She wasn't thinking about how solid his grip looked as he steadied the hammer.

But as they worked side by side, the air between them felt... different. Warmer. Charged.

Flynn caught himself glancing at her from the corner of his eye. She was concentrating, brows knitted in determination, biting her lip as she steadied the board.

He smirked. Cute. Too damn cute.

She wasn't like his usual clients—older couples restoring vacation homes, business owners flipping properties. Heather cared about this place. And, if he was being honest, she was also dangerously adorable when she pretended to know what she was doing.

He cleared his throat and smirked. "Careful now, Campbell. If you get too good at this, I might have to put you on payroll."

Heather raised an eyebrow. "Don't get used to this. I'm not planning on becoming your full time assistant."

Flynn chuckled. "Too bad. You're better company than most of the lads on my crew."

Heather laughed, the tension in her chest easing. "Glad I could meet your high standards."

"Well, you're setting them now," Flynn said with a lopsided grin. "And for the record, you're welcome to stare—uh, observe—anytime."

Heather groaned, rolling her eyes, but she couldn't stop the smile tugging at her lips.

Flynn was trouble—the best kind of trouble.

Usually, being around someone this confident, this capable, would have set her nerves on edge. But with Flynn? It felt effortless.

He had a way of putting her at ease with a grin, a playful comment, making her feel lighter, steadier.

She wasn't used to it.

And that realization caught her off guard.

She paused, watching as Flynn adjusted a beam, his movements steady and sure.

What would Ivy think of him?

Heather could almost hear her voice—mocking, not teasing. She would point out how ruggedly handsome Flynn was, how Heather should stop second-guessing and enjoy the attention while it lasted.

Heather chuckled dryly, shaking her head.

If Ivy were here, she'd try to turn her charm on Flynn, just to prove she could. She always did. Beautiful, confident, and unapologetic, Ivy never hesitated to take what she wanted, no matter the cost.

Heather could almost hear her now:

"Oh, Heather, he's too delicious to ignore. If you're not going to make a move, someone has to."

But Flynn wasn't like the guys in Millhaven. He wasn't the kind of man who saw Ivy first.

His gaze always landed on Heather—steady, lingering, like he was actually seeing her.

Not as an extension of someone else.

Just her.

And if he didn't?

Well, maybe it was time she stopped measuring her worth by whether or not she caught someone's attention.

She rolled her eyes at the imagined scenario... Ivy would try it. Flash that grin. Flynn wouldn't know what hit him. But Heather... didn't want to fade this time.

And as much as Heather hated to admit it, part of her wondered if he'd even notice her standing in Ivy's shadow.

That old pang of insecurity flickered in her chest.

"Not this time," she murmured, more to herself than anyone else.

For once, she didn't want to fade into the background.

Flynn didn't seem like the type to be easily swayed by Ivy's theatrics, but even if he was, Heather was done competing with a ghost of who Ivy used to be.

This was her story—her chance to figure out what she wanted. Not just for the house, but for herself.

And Flynn?

Well, he was complicating things in the best way possible.

The thought lingered as she watched him from the corner

of her eye. Kneeling by the base of a broken door frame, his brows furrowed in concentration, he worked with a quiet confidence that set her at ease.

She wasn't used to feeling this way around someone she barely knew—comfortable, playful, like she didn't have to measure every word before speaking.

Flynn had a way of making her feel like she belonged, as if being here wasn't just some random twist of fate, but exactly where she was meant to be.

Would Ivy see that, too? Probably.

But Ivy, for all her dazzling charisma, wasn't the one sanding floors, climbing ladders, and figuring out how to turn this crumbling house into a home.

Ivy hadn't stood in her mother's childhood bedroom, holding onto pieces of the past while trying to figure out what to do with her future.

Heather glanced at Flynn again, watching how the afternoon sunlight caught in his dark hair as he leaned back to inspect his work. He wiped a hand across his forehead, smearing a streak of sawdust across his skin.

"Okay," he said, standing with a crooked grin. "That doorframe might not win any beauty contests, but at least it won't collapse on you."

Heather smiled back, a familiar flutter in her stomach. "Looks like you've got a real gift there."

Flynn raised an eyebrow, his grin widening. "Careful with the compliments—I might start charging extra."

She gasped, pressing a hand to her chest. "Shouldn't I get some sort of loyalty bonus?"

He laughed, shaking his head as he wiped his hands on a nearby cloth. "You drive a hard bargain, Campbell."

As he stepped closer, Heather caught herself wondering—what would it be like to just... what? Run her fingers through his hair? Kiss him?

The thought sent warmth rushing to her cheeks. She shook it away.

Flynn didn't notice her inner turmoil, which was both a relief and a disappointment. Instead, he was focused on cleaning up the remnants of his work, his voice casual. "Ye alright there, lass?" Heather cleared her throat, forcing herself to act normal. "Oh, I'm fine. Just, uh... taking it all in."

"Taking in my superior craftsmanship, you mean," Flynn teased, flashing his disarming grin. "It's alright. Most people are speechless in the presence of genius." Heather snorted, rolling her eyes. "Right. Genius-level door frame repair. You'll be in all the architecture magazines next month, I'm sure."

"Hey," Flynn said, feigning offense. "I'll have you know, I've worked on some of the finest estates in the Highlands. Glenoran might be a bit of a fixer-upper, but this place has good bones. And you've got me, so you're in excellent hands." The teasing edge to his voice made her smile despite herself. "Modesty really isn't your strong suit, is it?"

"Not when it comes to my work," Flynn replied with a wink. Then, with a clap of his hands, he straightened up. "Alright, back to it. Let's see if you're brave enough to tackle the paintbrush. You up for the challenge?" Heather laughed, shaking off the sudden weight of emotion. "I don't know, Flynn. Paintbrushes are pretty advanced. Are you sure I'm ready?"

"Oh, you'll be fine," he said, grabbing a can of primer and

handing it to her. "Just don't get it all over yourself. Or your wee beastie over there."

He nodded toward the foyer as Byrdie strode in, oblivious to what she'd just walked into.

Heather took the can, raising an eyebrow. "I make no promises."

As they worked side by side, the steady rhythm of the task—and Flynn's constant banter—kept her grounded. There was something easy about being around him, like she didn't have to overthink everything.

Maybe, just maybe, that was precisely what she needed.

Flynn moved to reattach a loose banister, his hands steady and precise. Heather watched for a moment, marveling at how effortless he made it seem.

Once it was secure, he dusted off his hands and smirked. "There—no more wobbly stairs. You won't have to worry about breaking your neck on your midnight trips to the kitchen."

"Good to know," Heather said with a smirk. "Though I'm starting to think you're just trying to eliminate all the ways I could embarrass myself."

Flynn grinned. "Call it preventative care. You're a magnet for trouble, Campbell."

He moved to the fireplace, crouching to clear out debris and check the flue. "This'll need a proper sweep before you light anything, but it's not as bad as I thought." Standing, he wiped his hands on a rag. "With a bit of TLC, this place will start feeling like a home again."

Heather felt a little lighter at his words. "It already feels more manageable with you here."

"Well, don't get too comfortable. The roof's another

story," Flynn said, more serious now. "There are a couple of leaks that need patching immediately. I'll bring my crew out tomorrow to get started. That's priority number one—keeping this place dry."

"Sounds good," Heather replied, appreciating his take-charge attitude.

She lingered in the doorway before finally speaking again. "There's a room upstairs I'd like to keep as close to how it is now as possible."

Flynn studied her, then nodded. "Alright." He wiped his hands on his jeans and motioned for her to lead the way.

Heather hesitated, fingers curling against her palm before stepping toward the staircase. The old wood creaked beneath her steps, the sound strangely comforting in the silence.

She felt Flynn just behind her—quiet, solid.

The door to the room was slightly ajar.

Soft yellow walls. Faded floral curtains. A twin bed draped in a pastel quilt.

A life preserved in stillness.

Heather stepped inside, her fingers ghosting over the chipped paint of the dresser. "This was my mom's room when she was a little girl."

Her voice was quieter now, as if speaking too loudly might disturb the space that had remained untouched for so long.

Flynn didn't respond right away. He just took it in.

She was noticing this about him—he looked first, listened first. He didn't fill silence with meaningless words.

Finally, he exhaled. "It's in good shape, considering how long it's been left alone." He ran a hand along the bedpost, testing its strength. "You want to keep it just like this?"

Heather nodded. "As close as possible. Fresh paint in the

same shade. The bed stays. If the curtains can't be salvaged, I'd like to replace them with something similar."

Flynn studied the fabric, rubbing the edge between his fingers. "Aye, they're fragile, but I know a place that can match the pattern close enough."

Heather let out a breath she hadn't realized she was holding.

He turned his attention back to the walls. "I can patch the cracks and repaint without losing the texture. Might take some time to get the right match, but I'll get it there."

She glanced at him, surprised by the shift in his tone—how carefully he spoke to her now, how much attention he was giving this room, and what it meant.

"Thank you," she said softly.

Flynn met her gaze, holding it just long enough that something shifted between them.

"Some things are worth keeping the way they were."

Heather swallowed hard and turned back to the room. She cleared her throat, suddenly feeling exposed under Flynn's steady gaze.

"Anyway," she said, waving a hand toward the peeling wallpaper in the hallway. "Let's talk about something really tragic—this wallpaper situation. Did they even have color palettes in the seventies, or did they just throw random pastels at the wall and hope for the best?"

Flynn huffed a quiet laugh, crossing his arms. "Campbell, you're dodging."

"I have no idea what you're talking about," she said, already moving toward the door. "This is serious design trauma, Flynn. The people need answers."

"Aye, well, the people need better taste." He smirked, following her out. "Dinnae worry, Campbell. We'll fix your tragic wallpaper crisis first thing.”

“Oh, good. That’s obviously the most pressing issue in the entire house,” she tossed back.

Flynn scoffed. “While we’re working on that, you’ve got a job, too.”

“Oh? Are you about to hand me a hard hat?” she teased.

“Not quite,” he said with a chuckle. “This house is full of... well, history. You’ve got old furniture, boxes of who-knows-what, and probably some hidden treasures in the mix. You’ll need to go through it all and decide what stays, what goes, and what’s worth restoring.”

Heather’s gaze drifted to the shelves filled with dusty books and forgotten trinkets.

“That sounds like a full time job.”

“It probably is,” Flynn admitted. “But it’s your chance to put your stamp on the place. And hey, if you find any skeletons in the closet—literal or figurative—you know who to call.”

“Flynn Duncan, professional ghostbuster?” she said with a grin.

“Among other things,” he replied, winking.

Then he grabbed his tool bag and slung it over his shoulder. “I’ll be back first thing tomorrow with the crew. You’ll probably hear us stomping around on the roof before you’ve had your morning coffee.”

Heather nodded, feeling slightly less daunted now that a plan was in place.

“Thanks, Flynn. For everything.”

He paused by the door, his smile warm.

“Anytime, Campbell. Don’t work too hard going through all that stuff. And remember—no lighting any more fires until I give you the all clear.”

"Oh, and Heather." He glanced at her, something softer in his expression. "Just so you know.' he said as if it were an afterthought. "I'll take care of that room. Exactly the way you want it."

Heather swallowed again, but this time, she managed a small smile. "Yeah. I know you will."

And that was the problem.

With that, he headed out, leaving Heather in the middle of the room. She looked around at the overwhelming amount of things to sort through, but finally, it didn't feel so impossible. Heather took a deep breath, turning in a slow circle as she surveyed the room. The enormity of the task ahead loomed, but Flynn's presence earlier had left her feeling more grounded, even a little energized. One step at a time, she told herself.

She grabbed a pair of gloves she'd found in a drawer earlier and started with a corner of the sitting room, where a large wooden trunk sat beneath a dusty throw blanket. Pulling the blanket off sent a cloud of dust into the air, making her cough. "Lovely," she muttered before flipping open the lid.

Inside, she found stacks of yellowed letters bound with twine, their edges brittle with age. Faded photographs. A few antique-looking jewelry boxes. A wooden crate full of books. And an old tartan shawl.

Heather unfolded it carefully, running her fingers over the worn wool, frayed slightly at the edges. Had her mother wrapped herself in this on cold nights, standing by this very window, dreaming of places beyond Glenoran? Had she pressed it to her nose, breathing in the same faint scent of peat smoke and lavender that lingered now?

Heather stilled, her hands brushing over the fragile fabric.

A scent clung to it—faint, familiar, something she couldn't quite place. Age, memory, maybe time itself. But it made her think of open fields and hearth smoke.

She closed her eyes, picturing her mother here, fingers curled around this very shawl.

A whisper from the past—a reminder that her mother had once been a daughter, a dreamer. Someone who had walked these halls as a child, maybe pulling this same shawl tight around her shoulders on a cold Highland morning.

It was a side of her mother Heather had never known—a side erased by years and the version of herself she had become in America. The mother Heather remembered was busy, reserved. Distant. But this room held echoes of someone different.

The hush pressed in as Heather sat back on her heels, the shawl still cradled in her hands. For a fleeting second, she swore she could hear laughter—faint, far away—as though the walls had stored the voices of those who had come before her.

Her mother's voice—younger, lighter—drifted through her mind, carrying an accent softer than the one she'd brought to the States. Had she once twirled in this room as a girl, laughing at nothing, dreaming of the world beyond these walls?

Heather's chest tightened. There was no way to be sure.

Her mother had never spoken much about her life here. A few offhand comments—names of relatives Heather couldn't remember, stories that had felt distant, foreign, to a child growing up in the Midwest. But standing here now, holding this shawl, taking in the faint scent of old wool and memory, it felt different.

It felt real.

It felt personal.

Beneath the shawl, a bundle of letters waited, tied in fading twine. She traced her finger over the delicate handwriting, the ink faded but still legible.

She hesitated.

Opening them might shatter the fragile connection she had just found. But a part of her ached to know more—to uncover the pieces of her mother's story that had been tucked away.

Still, she held back. Not now. Not tonight.

Instead, she tucked the shawl back into the box and placed the lid on top.

Even after all these years, her mother's room still held so much.

It wasn't just furniture and trinkets.

It was a piece of her mother's soul.

A piece she hadn't known was missing.

Heather ran her fingers along the spines of the old books stacked inside the worn wooden crate. Most were familiar—dusty history texts, a few classic novels—but one stood out.

It was smaller than the others, its deep green cover worn at the edges, the gold lettering on the spine faded with time. When she pulled it free, the binding creaked in protest.

She turned it over in her hands. *Anam agus Cuimhne.*

Heather swallowed. She didn't need a translation to feel the weight of those words. *Soul and Memory.*

Her stomach twisted. She knew some of the language, or at least pieces of it. Enough to understand. Enough to feel the meaning settle in her bones.

She hesitated, thumb resting on the edge, before flipping it open.

The text inside was old-fashioned, the letters flowing in a script that felt impossibly foreign—and yet, not entirely unfamiliar.

'Chan eil'... *Not something.*

'Mo chridhe' ... *My heart.*

A prickle ran down her spine. She knew that phrase.

Chan eil seo ceart.

It's not right.

The words slipped out before she could stop them, halting, uncertain. But the moment they left her lips, her chest clenched, because she knew them.

A memory flickered, clear as day—her mother's voice, soft yet insistent, correcting her pronunciation at the kitchen table.

"Again, a ghràidh. Chan eil seo ceart."

Heather sucked in a breath. She hadn't thought about that moment in years. She had been—what? Five? Six? Barely old enough to string the words together, twisting her tongue around the unfamiliar sounds while her mother guided her through them. But at some point, the lessons had stopped. At some point, English had swallowed everything else.

She snapped the book shut like she had burned herself.

For a long moment, she just sat there, staring down at it, feeling the weight of something she couldn't quite name settle in her chest.

Had her mother read this? Had she run her fingers over the very same pages?

Had she whispered these words to herself, the same way Heather just had?

She exhaled sharply and shoved the book back into the crate.

She wasn't here to get lost in nostalgia.

She was here to pack up a past that didn't belong to her.

Heather turned to the letters. The handwriting was elegant, the ink slightly faded, but the words were still evident. Most were addressed to her great-grandmother, Fiona MacKenzie. Heather traced the name with her fingertip, a quiet awe settling over her. How many women in this family had stood where she was standing? Had they felt the exact weight of history pressing down on them? Had they wondered if they were strong enough to carry it forward? She spent the next hour lost in the letters, reading snippets of her family's life from decades past. There were mentions of celebrations at the house, notes of hardship during the world war, and tender exchanges between Fiona and her husband, Callum, her great-grandfather. It was a window into a life she never knew, making her feel oddly connected to the place.

The afternoon sun dipped lower in the sky when she pulled herself away from the trunk. Byrdie padded into the room, meowing in protest, and Heather smiled. "Alright, alright. Dinner time."

She fed Byrdie, then pieced together a quick meal from her limited groceries. Her thoughts wandered back to Flynn as she ate at the ragged kitchen table. How he'd worked so effortlessly, been both professional and charming, and made her feel more at ease in just a few hours than she'd felt in weeks. It wasn't just his looks—though those certainly didn't hurt. It was his warmth, his humor, and how he genuinely cared about her and the house. Her thoughts drifted again. What would Ivy think of him?

Heather snorted softly at the thought. Ivy would probably try to sweep him off his feet the moment she laid eyes on him. But would Flynn be charmed by Ivy's larger-than-life charisma? Or was he the kind of man who noticed quieter things? She shook her head, pushing the thought away. Flynn was here to work on the house, and she was here to figure out her life—not to get distracted by a man, no matter how much he smiled at her or teased her in a way that made her stomach flip. Still, as she cleaned up her plate and headed upstairs to her room, she couldn't help but glance at her reflection in the mirror. She tucked a curl behind her ear, then caught herself. What was she even doing?

It wasn't like Flynn was looking at her that way. Not really. Sure, he was charming. Sure, he teased her like it was his full time job. But that didn't mean anything.

Did it?

She leaned closer to the mirror, studying herself: the freckles she never quite liked, the sharp angles of her cheekbones, the way her curls never seemed to behave.

The thought slipped in uninvited, and Heather hated it instantly.

Ivy wouldn't stand here second-guessing whether a man found her interesting. She'd just know.

Heather shook her head to clear the thought. She wasn't here to be noticed. She was here to rebuild something—her life, her future, her family's home.

And if Flynn noticed her along the way? Well, that was his problem, not hers.

Chapter 20

That night, Heather sank into bed with an unusual sense of calm.

Despite the occasional creak of the old house settling and the groan of wind against the windows, she felt... safe. Maybe it was the progress she'd made sorting through her family's things. Or maybe it was knowing she wasn't tackling this massive project alone.

Either way, she drifted off more quickly than she had in days, with Byrdie curled contentedly at her feet.

Heather woke to sunlight streaming through the thin curtains. She sat up, blinking at the sky—a bright, cloudless blue.

Dew glistened on the grass and Glenoran looked vibrant. Alive.

It was, as Flynn might say, a braw day.

She stretched, feeling surprisingly refreshed, then dressed, tied her hair back, and headed downstairs. The house felt lighter, as if it, too, had woken up with a new sense of purpose.

After feeding Byrdie and grabbing a quick breakfast, she stepped outside, savoring the crisp air and the sun's warmth.

Flynn's truck rumbled up just as she finished her coffee. Grinning, he hopped out and shielded his eyes from the light.

"Morning, sunshine," he called. "Not a cloud in sight. Perfect day to get started on that roof."

Heather laughed, walking toward him. "I was just thinking the same thing. Did you order this weather, or is Scotland finally playing nice?"

"Pulled a few strings," Flynn teased, leaning casually against the truck. "Had to make sure you didn't get scared off by another torrential downpour."

As he spoke, two more vehicles pulled in behind him, and a small crew piled out, greeting them warmly. Flynn wasted no time getting them organized. "We'll start by stripping off the damaged slates and checking the structure," he explained. "If it's solid—great. If not, we'll reinforce it before laying down the new materials. It'll be a long day, but with this weather, we'll make good progress."

Heather nodded, taking it all in. "Sounds like you've got it under control."

Flynn smirked. "I like to think so. But don't think you're getting off easy. There's still plenty for you to do inside."

"Right," she said, rolling her eyes. "My glamorous job of sorting through decades of dusty treasures and junk."

Flynn chuckled. "Hey, you might uncover something good. A priceless artifact, maybe. Or at least something that doesn't smell like mildew."

"Fingers crossed," she replied, but she couldn't help smiling. As the crew got to work, Heather returned inside, diving back into the mountain of furniture, books, and trinkets.

Some things felt worth saving. Others... not so much.

She started with a stack of old books—some with her mother's name scrawled inside— the classic loops a familiar balm to her frayed nerves.

She kept going, sorting through old portraits and forgotten knickknacks, though her attention often strayed to the window.

Flynn was out there, working alongside his crew with practiced ease. He'd ditched his jacket hours ago, leaving him in just a fitted t-shirt, dusted with remnants of old slate and sawdust. His forearms, tan and dust-streaked, flexed as he hammered. Years of work had left him strong—and completely unfair to look at.

Heather swallowed, heat creeping up her neck. It should be illegal to make roofing look that attractive.

She tore her gaze away, shaking her head at herself. You are here to restore a house, not to ogle your contractor.

Not that it stopped her from stealing another glance or two.

By midday, she stepped outside for some air. The steady rhythm of hammering filled the air, mingling with laughter from the crew.

Flynn caught her eye and gave a quick wave. After a beat, Heather lifted her hand and waved back.

There was something solid about him. Reliable. The kind of person who made things happen.

She turned her gaze to the house, taking it in.

Maybe I can do this, she thought. Maybe I can turn this place around.

And maybe, along the way, I'll figure out what to do with my life.

By sunset, the roof had taken shape, and Heather had made

a real dent inside. A few minutes later, Flynn appeared in the doorway, looking tired but still wearing that easygoing smile.

"How's the inside going?"

Heather gestured to the piles around her. "I think I made a dent—barely. The house is still full of stuff."

Flynn scanned the room, taking in the cleared surfaces and neatly stacked keepsakes.

"Ye've done more than I expected," he admitted, a note of appreciation in his voice.

Heather scoffed lightly. "Did you think I'd be napping all day?"

Flynn smirked. "Wouldn't have blamed you."

Heather shook her head, laughing softly as she leaned back against the chair.

The house still had a long way to go.

But still, it felt like progress. Heather rolled her eyes, but she felt the warmth in his words—and in how he saw her effort. She was surprised at how much she'd accomplished. "Better than I thought. I've started going through some things—books, pictures, and the like."

"Good," Flynn said, leaning against the doorframe with a thoughtful look. "So how exactly did you come upon this property? The house has been empty for years. I've heard of a few people trying to buy it, but nothing ever came of it. Always been a dream of mine to restore it."

Heather hesitated, her fingers absently tracing the edge of the door.

How much should she share?

It felt personal—too personal—to spill everything right now.

"It's... complicated," she said slowly. "I didn't know about the house until recently. My mom passed away a long time ago, and my dad never talked about her. Not once. I only found out about Glenoran after he passed a couple of months ago—when I got the deed from his lawyer. That's when everything started falling into place."

Flynn watched her closely, sensing her hesitation.

He didn't push. He just waited.

"It's a lot to take in," Heather added, trying for casual, though she wasn't entirely sure she believed it herself. "But I'm here now, trying to make sense of it all."

Flynn nodded, giving her space to breathe. "I get it. You don't have to explain everything right away. You're doing fine."

His voice was softer now, steady in a way that made her feel a little more at ease.

Heather exhaled, offering a small, grateful smile.

She stepped into the room, brushing her fingers over the old wood of the window frame. "I guess part of me wonders if I'm doing the right thing. The house is... a lot. And it's a big responsibility. But I can't shake the feeling that maybe it's meant to be. Like there's something I'm supposed to do here."

Flynn followed, his gaze thoughtful but never intrusive.

"Sometimes, the right thing isn't the easiest," he said. "But that doesn't mean you're on the wrong path. You don't have to have all the answers yet. You're here. That's a good start."

Heather's chest tightened at his quiet reassurance.

Uncomfortable with how easily he saw her, she shifted gears. "So, what's next?"

Flynn paused, glancing around the room before straightening. "Let's start with what's in front of us. The roof's still the biggest priority, but once that's sorted, we can focus on the interior."

He adjusted the straps on his work gloves. "We've ordered more materials, but they won't arrive for a few days. In the meantime, we'll tarp the roof, but it won't be fully waterproof."

His gaze flicked to her, careful now.

"I'd suggest heading back to the Thistle Haven Inn for now. Just until we get it sealed up properly."

The house still smelled like dust—but also of her. Her shampoo. Her coffee. It was starting to feel like hers. Like it remembered her.

Her fingers curled around the edge of the windowsill, reluctant. She had only just begun to settle in—to carve out a space for herself in this house and history. But Flynn was right. The roof needed work. The house wouldn't be livable for a bit longer. Still, the thought of sleeping somewhere else, even just a few nights, left an odd pang in her chest. "We'll take care of what we can for you," Flynn continued, noticing her shift in mood. Heather raised an eyebrow. "What about the rest of the stuff? The things I'm not sure about yet?"

"Good point," Flynn said with a nod. "With roof work starting and everything else going on, we should think about moving the furniture and anything worth keeping out of the way." Heather frowned, glancing around the dusty parlor, where old furniture sat beneath white sheets, untouched for years. "You mean moving everything out of the house?"

"Not everything," Flynn clarified. "But some of this stuff could get damaged with all the work happening. Dust, debris, and possible leaks aren't exactly ideal for keeping heirlooms in good shape. I was thinking of renting a storage unit in town.

Just temporary, until we get through the worst of it."

Heather hesitated, crossing her arms instinctively.

It made sense, of course. The house wasn't livable, and renovation wasn't exactly gentle. If she left everything where it was, the furniture could be ruined beyond repair, the books warped with moisture, the curtains coated in dust and plaster.

But the thought of packing up her family's things and locking them away off the estate made her stomach twist.

"I don't want to lose track of anything," she said finally.

Flynn's gaze was steady. "Then help us go through it. Decide what stays, what gets stored, and what's beyond saving."

Heather bit the inside of her cheek, glancing at the furniture, the old trunks stacked in the corner, and the dusty bookshelves.

"Once things leave this house, it feels like more of it slips away."

Flynn was quiet for a few breaths, then exhaled softly.

"I get that." His voice was gentler now, less pragmatic. "But I'd rather move things for a little while than watch them get ruined for good."

Heather sighed, rubbing a hand over her temple. "Alright... but I get the final say on what goes."

Flynn nodded. "Fair enough."

She narrowed her eyes at him. "And if you throw anything out without asking me first—"

His mouth quirked up. "You'll kill me. Got it."

Heather rolled her eyes, but the tension inside her loosened a little.

She could fight this all she wanted, but the truth was, Flynn was right.

If she wanted to save the parts of Glenoran that mattered, she had to accept that change—temporarily or not—was inevitable.

Flynn must have noticed the shift in her expression because he clapped his hands together. "Good. That's settled, then. We'll handle the heavy lifting. You should get some rest."

Heather scoffed. "You make it sound like I've done nothing all day."

Flynn's smirk was pure mischief. "Oh, you've done plenty—keeping me on my toes takes real effort."

Heather huffed. "Oh, I'm sorry, am I exhausting you?"

Flynn leaned in slightly, his voice dropping just enough to make her pulse jump. "Wouldn't call it exhausting, exactly."

Heather blinked. There was something in his voice, not quite teasing, not quite serious, but it sent a shiver straight down her spine. She opened her mouth to retort, but nothing clever came out. Instead, Flynn just smirked, his gaze lingering for a second too long before he turned back to the furniture.

Heather exhaled sharply, heart stuttering in her chest. That was new.

She shook her head again, choosing not to argue. Maybe stepping back—just for now—wasn't the worst idea. She turned toward the hallway, tossing her curls over her shoulder. "I'll be back before you can mess anything up."

Flynn chuckled, already moving toward the first piece of furniture. "Aye, lass. I figured as much."

With one last glance around the house, Heather felt a wave of gratitude, tinged with apprehension. It was a lot to handle, but having Flynn and his crew on her side made it feel possible.

And for the first time since she'd stepped foot in Glenoran

House, she felt like things might actually work out.

Heather gathered Byrdie's things, ensuring she packed everything for the night. Byrdie didn't seem to mind the change of location, happily purring as Heather carefully placed her into the travel carrier.

A few hours later, settled in her borrowed room at Thistle Haven, Heather sat by the window, Byrdie purring softly in her lap. The day had been long—exhausting, even—but it felt like something was finally moving in the right direction.

Flynn and his crew had tackled the roof with an ease she envied—confident, capable, like he belonged here.

And wasn't that the difference?

He was sure of his place. She wasn't.

While she'd spent the day sorting through old books and furniture, she couldn't help but watch Flynn work. He moved quickly, chatting with his team and laughing, his sleeves rolled up to his elbows as he hammered—all golden skin and sawdust—like he'd been ripped from the pages of a very specific fantasy novel that Heather refused to admit she'd had.

He moved like a man who knew exactly what he was doing— and exactly what it looked like. Sleeves rolled up, sweat at his temples, forearms roped with muscle. Honestly, it felt like a personal attack.

She felt ridiculous gawking at him while he hammered shingles and climbed ladders. She'd come to reconnect with her family's past—yet here she was, ankle deep in dust and indecision, wondering if she could restore more than just the house.

But Flynn's confidence was contagious.

She thought of his smile—that warm, easy grin that made

the entire project seem less daunting.

Maybe that was his gift.

Making people feel like they weren't alone.

Heather's gaze drifted to Byrdie, who was stretching luxuriously across the quilt. "You've got it all figured out, don't you?" she muttered. Byrdie responded with a lazy chirp, and Heather found herself smiling.

Still, her thoughts kept circling back to Glenoran.

The roof repairs were coming along, but that was just the beginning. Every creak and groan of the house felt like a challenge, daring her to see this through.

She'd uncovered her mother's old room—untouched, filled with small, precious memories. It brought her closer to the woman she'd lost, but it also made her feel the weight of all the unfinished stories this house held.

And then there was Flynn.

He made her feel... unsteady. Like the ground beneath her feet wasn't as solid as she thought.

Not in a bad way. Just... different.

As the evening stretched on, she promised herself she'd stay focused. Glenoran needed her attention, her effort.

She had to stop thinking about Flynn—his laugh, his quiet reverence for Glenoran, the way he'd looked at her like she mattered. From the way he had looked at her when he promised to take care of her mother's room like she wasn't completely lost—the way he had looked at her when he promised to take care of her mother's room.

And as sleep finally pulled her under, she let herself wonder, just for a second, what it would feel like to let that warmth pull her in completely.

Chapter 21

Heather woke before sunrise, yesterday's weight pressing down like a boulder. She had slept, but not rested. The safety she'd felt the night before—that fragile sense of forward motion—already felt like mist dissolving in the morning light. Soon, she'd set off to the storage unit, leaving Byrdie behind at the inn. The cat had settled in nicely at the bed and breakfast, and Heather wasn't sure she could manage the storage trip with her curious feline companion in tow.

As she pulled up to the unit, Heather was taken aback. Flynn's crew had already moved so much of the furniture out that the place looked emptier than when she'd left it the day before. She could hear the buzz of their voices as they worked and the sound of furniture being shifted around. They were clearly on a tight schedule and moving faster than she expected.

Heather stood with her hands on her hips, eyeing the overstuffed storage unit Flynn had secured in town. Boxes stacked haphazardly, furniture wedged into every available space—one particularly rebellious trunk looked one sneeze away from toppling.

"This is your idea of organization?" she asked, eyeing the stack like it might explode.

Flynn, standing beside her, crossed his arms. "It's all there, isn't it?"

"Yeah, and I'm guessing if I pull the wrong box, the whole thing's coming down like Jenga on a tilt."

"You wound me, lass," he said dryly. "That's quality stacking there." Heather snorted, stepping carefully inside—like one wrong move might trigger an avalanche of ancestral regrets and dusty secrets.

She ran a hand over the dust-covered edge of an old wooden cabinet—something about it felt faintly familiar. "Well, I hope you're proud of yourself, Flynn. You've single-handedly turned multiple lifetimes of family history into a really sketchy game of hide-and-seek."

He smirked, leaning against the frame of the roll-up door. "You're just mad I got it done before you could supervise."

Heather turned to face him, narrowing her eyes. "I will find something to yell at you about. Just give me a minute."

"Take yer time, Campbell," he said. "But if ye actually want to find anything, we might need to do this my way." Heather arched a brow.

"And what may I ask is that?"

Flynn grinned, stepping forward and reaching past her to a box marked 'fragile' near the bottom of the stack. "Trial and error." Before she could protest, he yanked the box free.

The boxes moaned under the sudden shift, a creak of pure betrayal. Heather took one step back. "Amazing. You broke physics."

Flynn barely had time to react before an entire stack of boxes wobbled and started to fall. Heather jumped back as an old framed portrait tilted forward and smacked Flynn square in the chest. He caught it instinctively, stumbling back slightly as dust exploded into the air.

Silence.

Heather pressed her lips together, watching him blink through two-hundred-year-old dust, the painting still clutched against his chest. Finally, she crossed her arms. "So, just for clarification—this is your way?"

Flynn batted dust from his shirt like it had personally insulted him. "Aye. Controlled chaos."

Heather fought back a laugh. "Sure. Very controlled."

She wasn't sure when it started—this sharp, unfiltered banter with Flynn—but it unsettled her how natural it felt. She had spent most of her life learning how to be agreeable, smooth over rough edges, and blend in instead of standing out. With her father, silence had been survival. With Ivy, deference had been a habit. With past boyfriends, she had been soft, accommodating, and never the one to push back.

But with Flynn, something cracked open.

She quipped back without thinking, meeting his sarcasm with her own. It was unnerving, thrilling, and addictive. She should've felt off balance around him—but instead, she felt awake, sharp, like someone had finally spoken her language. Like some long-buried version of herself had been waiting for someone who could keep up. And Flynn kept up.

The strangest part? He didn't seem surprised by it. Almost as if he had seen that side of her before she had even realized it existed. She remembered once trying to tell her father she was afraid.

She was ten—old enough to recognize grief, too young to survive it alone. The TV was flickering in the dark and a liquor bottle was tipped on its side.

"Dad?" she'd said, barely above a whisper. "Can we talk?"

He didn't even look at her. Just muttered, "About what?"

She'd wanted to say, *I'm scared.* To ask, *Why does everything feel wrong?* But the words never came. They caught in her throat like splinters.

Instead, she just shook her head. "Never mind."

He never looked back.

She had spent so much of her life swallowing words, silencing herself before anyone else could. She'd learned early that quiet was safer than risk being dismissed.

With Flynn, she didn't hesitate. Didn't second-guess. She spoke before she thought—pushed without fear of being pushed away. And that scared her more than she wanted to admit. Heather spent hours in the storage unit, the dust and silence of the place wrapping around her like a blanket. She worked methodically, sorting through the piles of boxes, some packed to the brim and others barely taped shut. Each item felt like a thread from her mother's past—and with each passing hour, the weight of it pulled heavier.

She started with the old photographs—images of her mother as a young girl in Scotland, smiling with friends at what looked like a birthday party from the '70s. There were pictures of her at the beach, the hills, and family gatherings. The vibrant, sunlit photos starkly contrasted Heather's foggy memories of her mother, so distant in some ways but present in others. It was strange to see her mother as a child, as a person who had a life before she ever became Heather's mom.

She found a stack of old birthday cards tucked inside one of the boxes, the handwriting instantly recognizable—curvy, neat, undeniably her mother's. There were sweet, often funny notes written to family members and friends. She flipped through them slowly, pausing to read a few, her heart-tugging as she imagined her mother writing them in a time and place that seemed so foreign now. There were also trinkets from her mother's teenage years—small gifts, a handkerchief embroidered with delicate stitching, and a few items foreign to Heather—things from a life she'd never truly understood. Her mother had left Scotland for the United States to attend university, where she met Heather's father. All Heather had ever known was the version of her mother, who was already firmly planted in American life, married and raising her. It was hard to imagine her mother ever being this young woman with a life in another world—a life that Heather had never been a part of.

As she sifted through more boxes, Heather came across a few more personal items—books, letters, even some old records her mother had kept, with handwritten labels on the sleeves. They all felt like pieces of a puzzle Heather couldn't fully see. The more she uncovered, the more it felt like peeking into a life she'd never been invited to—a version of her mother she could never truly meet.

A few of the items seemed unnecessary, relics from a past that was long gone, but the deeper she went, the more attached she became to the memories embedded in each item. She couldn't throw everything away. But she also knew that not everything should be kept either. Hours passed, the task feeling endless, but with each item, Heather began to understand her mother in new ways. It was a strange and bittersweet experience, seeing her mother not just as the woman who had raised her but as the woman who had lived her own entire, vibrant life before—the life Heather had never really understood—until now.

Heather carefully opened a wooden box tucked at the bottom of the trunk. The box was worn with age, its edges rough and chipped, but it had been carefully preserved. As she lifted the lid, she was met with a faint, musty smell—a mix of old wood and forgotten time.

Inside, she found a folded bundle of fabric. Her hands trembled slightly as she unwrapped it, revealing an ancient Scottish flag. The material was faded, its once vibrant colors now muted by age. Frayed at the edges, but unmistakable— the white saltire stretched across faded blue. Time had worn it down, but the history still clung to it. She couldn't help but be struck by how... important it felt.

Next to the flag was a piece of parchment, yellowed and brittle, almost disintegrating as she unfolded it carefully. The writing was hard to read, the ink faded with age. But when Heather's fingers brushed over the parchment, one date stood out.

April 16th.

The date tugged at her memory; important, familiar— but just out of reach. She stared at it momentarily, the numbers lingering in her mind, but no particular memory or explanation came to her. The pieces of the past she was uncovering felt like they were about to fall into place, yet the weight of this particular date left her with an unsettling feeling of mystery.

Then, beneath the parchment, she found something else: a tattered piece of Mackenzie tartan. The fabric was frayed and torn, but Heather could still make out the green, blue, and black pattern. Her heart raced as she realized what this was. Her mother's family had roots in the Highland clans, but the tartan... wasn't just a family connection. It was a piece of history, a reminder of the past her mother had left behind. Heather swallowed hard, holding the items carefully in her hands. A part of her felt like she had uncovered something monumental.

Flynn had been standing nearby, watching her sort through the boxes, and stepped closer when he noticed the items in her hands. "What have ye got there?" he asked, his voice low with curiosity. Heather held the flag up, gently unfolding the fabric further. "I... I'm unsure, but I think this is an old Scottish flag. And this parchment— And this"—she gestured to the piece of tartan—"this looks like Mackenzie tartan. It has to be..." Heather's fingers brushed over the parchment, and her breath hitched.

The ink was faint, the numbers ghostlike—but something about it slid cold down her spine. It felt... important. Familiar, almost. Like a word on the tip of her tongue that she couldn't quite say. She glanced at Flynn. "Does this date mean anything to you?" Flynn's brow furrowed as he leaned in. "April 16... that's the day of the Battle of Culloden." Heather's pulse quickened. She knew little about Scottish history, but she knew that name. Culloden. The battle that had crushed the Jacobite uprising.

And now, somehow, it was tied to her family.

Flynn's eyes widened as he examined the items in her hands. He reached out to touch the fabric of the flag with reverence. "This is something special, Campbell. The date, the tartan... this could be from the time of the Jacobite uprising in 1745.

These flags were battle standards. Ye don't just find them lying about."

She whispered, "But why was it in the house? Shouldn't this be in a museum or something?"

"I'm not sure," Flynn said thoughtfully, rubbing his chin. "But I'd guess it's tied to yer family history. The Mackenzies were deeply involved in the Jacobite cause. This flag might have belonged to someone who fought in that rebellion or supported it." Her mind raced as she absorbed Flynn's words. It felt almost surreal to think that this small piece of fabric, this relic from the past, was somehow connected to her bloodline. Her mother had never mentioned anything about this part of their heritage. The only knowledge Heather had of Scottish history came from her high school World History class, and it barely scratched the surface. The weight of the discovery felt both exhilarating and overwhelming. How had she never known?

Flynn noticed her pensive expression and smiled gently. "If ye want to know more, I'd suggest talking to Dr. Morrow in town. He's a historian who specializes in the Jacobite period. He could tell ye more about the flag and its significance." Heather nodded, still holding the items with a newfound reverence. She had no idea what she'd just uncovered, but it was clear that her connection to the past ran deeper than she had realized.

As she carefully placed everything back in the box, her thoughts shifted, momentarily pulled back to the present. The ping of her phone startled her out of her reverie. She pulled it out and saw a message from the realtor:

Your father's house outside Millhaven has sold. Congratulations. The new owners are excited to move in.

The words didn't register at first. Just a blur of black text against a glowing screen. Your father's house outside Millhaven has sold. Heather blinked. Read it again.

Then—impact. A gut punch. Sharp. Breath-stealing. It was the last piece of her mom she still had. The house had held her voice. The scent of her baking still clung to the old curtains, the bookshelves still carried the dust of her hands. And now? It belonged to strangers. People who would repaint the walls, change the floors, erase every piece of her mom until there was nothing left. Her mother had filled that house with warmth and care. But after Eilidh died, it was like someone had flipped a switch. The light went out. The warmth evaporated, replaced by the coldness of her father's bitterness. The man who had once been a loving husband had turned into someone unrecognizable—angry, volatile, consumed by alcohol. And Heather, still a child, had borne the brunt of it.

There had been nights when she had hidden in her room, afraid to come out. Her father's yelling would echo down the halls, and she would shrink into herself, wishing to disappear. He would take his anger out on everything around him, sometimes on her. She remembered the sting of the words he'd hurled at her, the silence that followed the chaos, and the hollow feeling that lingered long after. And yet, somewhere in that house, there were memories of love— small, quiet moments when her mother would sit beside her, brush her hair, and tell stories of faraway places. When the world outside felt like it was falling apart, her mother had been the one constant, the one person who made Heather feel like she was enough. Those memories had been her lifeline through the years of her father's abuse. They were the good parts of the house, which Heather tried to hold on to even after her mom was gone. But now, those memories felt like they belonged to someone else.

The words hit her harder than she expected. The house had sold. The house where she had lived through so many difficult years, the place she had spent so much of her childhood and young adulthood, was no longer hers. It felt like an ending, a door closing on something she hadn't fully processed. There was a finality to it, an unspoken acknowledgment that the weight of that house, of everything it symbolized, was no longer her burden to carry. But there was also relief, a sense of release. The house had been under constant stress and uncertainty for a long time. Now, it was gone—no more worrying about repairs, no more wondering whether she should keep or sell it, no more reminders of the man her father had become. It wasn't a simple relief, though. It was bittersweet, tinged with grief for the mother she had lost, for the little girl she used to be in that house, and for all the parts of her past she wasn't sure she could ever truly let go of. She looked up, lost in thought when Flynn's voice gently broke through her trance. "You okay?" His gaze was soft, his concern evident as he noticed the shift in her expression.

Heather swallowed hard, feeling a lump in her throat. She nodded slowly. "Yeah, just... a lot going on. My father's house sold. It's done. It feels... final." Flynn's gaze softened, and Heather could feel the weight of his understanding pressing down on her. She appreciated his concern, but something about his kindness and closeness made her chest tighten. She didn't want to be vulnerable, not with him now. She couldn't afford to be. With a quick, forced smile, Heather stepped back, clutching the old box tighter in her hands. She could feel herself retreating into the familiar walls she'd built around her heart. "I should get going; it's getting late," she said, her voice a little too sharp. "I'll pay Dr. Morrow a visit later." Flynn's jaw tensed briefly—so quickly that Heather almost missed it. Almost. But she did see it. The flicker of something in his eyes. Not just confusion. Not just frustration. Something closer to... disappointment.

It was subtle. A tightening of his shoulders, a beat too long before he nodded. But it was there. Like he already knew she was slipping away. The flicker of something behind his eyes, something close to frustration, but not quite. He wanted to say something—but she'd already shut the door. Then, just as quickly, it was gone. He nodded, stepping back. "Alright," he said lightly. "I'll check in later."

He turned toward the crew, but Heather felt the shift. The moment where Flynn stopped reaching. She had seen him leaning in all this time, effortlessly closing the distance she never knew she had let exist. But now? He wasn't leaning in. He wasn't trying to understand. Because she had shut the door before he even had the chance to ask what was wrong. She barely remembered the walk to the car, the cool air brushing against her skin as she set the box down in the passenger seat. Her mind was a whirl of emotions, and the tightness in her chest wouldn't loosen.

When she reached the Thistle Haven Inn, she didn't even bother to check in with Ms. Kinnaird. She went straight to her room, locking the door before collapsing onto the bed. Her breath was uneven, her thoughts scattered. The house had sold. She had thought she was ready for it, but she wasn't. And Flynn had been kind and understanding, but that made it worse. She wasn't sure how to handle someone like him, who seemed so steady—while she felt as though she could barely keep it together.

Heather sat up slowly, picking at the edge of the box, her thoughts drifting to the items inside. Her mother's life was there, the past she had never fully known. But now, with the house gone, what did that even mean? What was left for her to hold onto?

She sat there for a long moment, staring at the box in her lap—the room's stillness pressing around her. The items inside were so small, so insignificant on their own—tattered pieces of fabric, old parchment, a flag—but they held so much weight. She clung to memories she wasn't sure she could face. Her phone buzzed on the bedside table, breaking the silence. She glanced at it but didn't move to pick it up. She already knew who it was. Flynn. He was probably checking in, making sure she was okay, wanting to ensure she didn't shut him out. But that was the problem. She didn't know how to let him in either.

She sighed, sinking back into the pillows. The house was gone. Her father's house was no longer hers. She hadn't realized how much of *her* still lived in that house. As painful as it had been, it was still a part of her story, and now that chapter had closed. It felt like losing another piece of her mother, another piece of her childhood that she wasn't ready to let go of.

But it wasn't just the house that was hard to let go of—it was the guilt—that corrosive ache that she hadn't been enough to fix him—couldn't save him from the demons that had slowly consumed him. And now, all of that was gone. The house, the memories, and the weight of responsibility that had followed her for so long were all just... gone.

The tears threatened, but she blinked them back—too stubborn to let grief win. She had already cried enough in her life. She wasn't doing it again.

She looked at the box again, her fingers brushing the items' edges. The tartan, the old flag, the parchment—things that meant nothing to her, yet everything. She had to figure it out. She owed that much—to her mother's memory, and to the girl still learning how to live without her.

But not today.

Today, she was done with decisions. She was done with heavy emotions that threatened to drown her. Today, she needed peace, something simple. Pulling the box closer to her, Heather tucked it away on the shelf, promising that tomorrow, she'd take another step forward. But not tonight. Tonight, she just needed a break—a quiet moment to breathe without the weight of her past on her shoulders.

She climbed beneath the quilt like armor and silence, pulling it tight around the frayed edges of herself. She allowed herself a final glance at the window before closing her eyes.

Tomorrow.

Tomorrow, she'd rebuild the walls.

But tonight, she let herself disappear.

Chapter 22

The next day, Heather walked to Dr. Morrow's office—the historian Flynn had recommended. She clutched the old wooden box, her fingers digging into the grain. It felt heavier today. Yesterday, it was just a curiosity. Today, it carried the full weight of her mother's absence, her father's silence, and a history she'd never been allowed to claim. She had left Byrdie at the inn, knowing she needed the time and space to focus on what she was doing.

The house had been hell, but also where her mother's laughter once echoed. Selling it meant letting go of both. The relief of the sale unearthed everything she'd tried to bury. Pain she'd spent years boxing up was now spilling out of the seams.

By the time she reached Dr. Morrow's office, her grip on the box had tightened. The building was old, its weathered stone cloaked in ivy—much like the man who occupied it: an eccentric, scholarly type—part of the town as much as the ivy and stone around him.

Dr. Morrow greeted her at the door with a broad smile, his round glasses perched slightly askew on the bridge of his nose. "Ah, good morning to you, lass! Come in, come in!"

His voice was warm and full of energy. He looked exactly like you'd expect a historian to look—snow-white hair in a wild halo, like he'd run his fingers through it a hundred times mid-thought. His tweed jacket was a size too big, its elbows patched with darker suede, and his plaid tie was loosely knotted, dangling just off-center like a shrug. A chain dangled from his pocket, presumably attached to an old pocket watch, and a pair of scuffed leather loafers completed his look.

Despite his slightly disheveled appearance, his pale blue eyes had an undeniable sharpness. They sparkled with curiosity and enthusiasm only someone deeply passionate about their work could possess. His movements were quick and nimble for his age, as though fueled by an unending excitement for discovery.

"Ye must be Miss Campbell," he said, clasping her hand briefly in his. His hands were calloused and warm, with faint ink stains along his fingertips, remnants of countless hours spent poring over old texts and documents. "Welcome, welcome! Let's have a look at what ye've brought me, shall we? Oh, I do love a good mystery!" Heather blinked, caught off guard. "Wait... do I know you?"

Dr. Morrow gave a hearty chuckle, his blue eyes twinkling with amusement. "Ah, Mr. Duncan gave me a ring. Said to expect a bonnie redhead from America with a mystery box and no patience for nonsense."

"Flynn called you?" She frowned. "I didn't tell him I was coming." The older man grinned, shrugging as he motioned her inside. "He thought I might be able to lend a hand with whatever mystery you're trying to solve. He's sent me plenty of historic pieces over the years." He gestured toward the box in her hands. "And from the sound of it, he was right to send you my way."

She hadn't told Flynn—but of course he'd called ahead. Always one step ahead. It should've reassured her. Instead, it felt like being nudged down a path she hadn't chosen. Still... she wouldn't pretend it didn't make things easier. She exhaled through her nose. "I didn't realize he'd called ahead, but... I'm here now, so let's see what you think."

Heather placed the box gently on his desk, suddenly feeling self-conscious. "I found these in storage. I think they might be connected to my family's history, but I'm unsure what to make of them." Dr. Morrow leaned in, his hands resting on the desk as he examined the box like a treasure chest. "Ah, this looks promising!" He opened the lid with care, and his eyes widened when he saw the tattered flag and the piece of tartan. "By Saint Andrew! Do ye know what you've brought me here, lass?"

She shook her head, overwhelmed. Dr. Morrow's fingers trembled as he turned the fabric, but his excitement barely registered. His words blurred at the edges of her consciousness—something about rarity, rebellion, and erasure. She nodded along, but it felt like she was watching the moment happen from outside herself.

Like *she* was the artifact.

"After Culloden, the British burned most of them to erase any trace of rebellion."

The air wooshed out of her lungs. "So, this survived when others didn't?"

He nodded, his voice reverent. "These flags weren't just

symbols—they were resistance. People risked everything to keep them. And the tartan—it wasn't just a fashion choice. After 1746, wearing Highland dress was outlawed for nearly 40 years. This could have belonged to someone who defied that law, who held onto their identity despite the cost. And this"—he carefully unfolded the piece of Mackenzie tartan—"this is unmistakably from your clan. What a find! What a marvelous find!" He turned his attention to the parchment, squinting at the faded text as he held it up to the light.

"April 16th... yes, yes, the date of the Battle of Culloden! This is extraordinary. A relic like this, connected to the battle... it's a piece of history, lass. A piece of your history."

Her throat went dry.

His excitement was palpable, his words tumbling out in rapid succession. Heather felt a mix of awe and discomfort as she watched him. She couldn't help but feel the weight of the objects in a way she hadn't before as if they were more than just old items—they were part of something far bigger than herself. Dr. Morrow finally looked up, his face glowing with enthusiasm. "My dear, ye've brought me something truly extraordinary. These pieces—this flag, the tartan, the parchment—may hold stories lost to time. Ye've stumbled upon a treasure that connects the past to the present in ways we rarely see."

He gestured to the parchment, his voice rising with excitement. "This faded writing is a puzzle begging to be solved. The date, April 16th, is a powerful clue tied to such a pivotal historical moment. If you're comfortable with it, I'd suggest sending these to my colleague at the University of Edinburgh. She has access to advanced imaging technology that can help us uncover what's written here—technology far beyond my means. Together, we can unravel this mystery, piece by piece!"

His eyes sparkled as he leaned forward. "Ye've brought me something remarkable, Miss Campbell. It would be my honor to help uncover its secrets." Heather ran her fingers over the box's splintered edges. It felt like handing over the last thread connecting her to her mother. Like sealing something shut before she could even read the ending.

What if it got lost? What if it never came back? What if she was giving away the only chance she had to understand? Her throat tightened. But she forced herself to nod. "Okay. If you think your colleague can help, then... let's do it."

Dr. Morrow's face lit up, his excitement practically radiating from him. "Excellent decision! Professor Henderson at the University of Edinburgh is brilliant—an expert in her field. If anyone can unlock the story behind these items, it's her. I'll make the arrangements straight away."

Heather managed a small smile, feeling lighter now that she'd made the choice. "Alright," she said quietly. "What happens now?"

"Well," Dr. Morrow said, carefully placing the items back into the box as though they were precious jewels, "I'll write to her immediately, explain what we've found, and arrange for secure transport of the artifacts. Of course, she'll need a little time, but I promise ye'll be the first to know as soon as we have any updates."

She nodded, the weight on her shoulders easing. "Thank you. It's exciting to think that we might learn something so significant."

Dr. Morrow smiled warmly. "My dear, ye've already done the hardest part—finding these treasures and recognizing their value. The rest is simply a matter of patience."

"Thanks," she said, her voice steady. "I'm looking forward to seeing what they uncover."

Dr. Morrow handed her a card with his contact information. "If ye have any questions—or if ye happen to find more treasures tucked away somewhere—don't hesitate to call."

Heather tucked the card into her pocket and shook his head. "I appreciate it. And I will."

She stepped into the crisp air, breath fogging in the quiet. This wasn't a loss, she told herself. It was a beginning. That giving the artifacts away was a beginning, not an ending. But it still felt like something had slipped through her fingers. She stood on the sidewalk, the weight of the past pressing against her spine. She'd planned to head back to storage. To keep sorting. Keep pushing. But the thought of another hour surrounded by ghosts—literal or not—was too much. She turned toward the city instead. Away from Glenoran. Away from Flynn. He was steady. Too steady. The kind of man you could believe in. And that was the problem—because she couldn't afford to believe in anyone

Neither of them was supposed to pull her in. She just needed to breathe—to exist without the ache of the past or the pull of what might come next.

Chapter 23

The streets of Inverness pulsed with quiet energy—locals weaving through routine, tourists pausing to check maps or snap photos. Heather had never walked these streets before. Never traced the edges of her family's history with her fingertips.

The city should have stirred something in her—roots, memory, connection. Instead, she drifted like a ghost, untethered.

She meandered toward the River Ness, watching the water rush past in a steady, endless current. It reminded her of the burn that cut through Glenoran's land, the way the water permanently moved, even when everything else felt still. She leaned against the bridge's stone railing, the city's hum flowing around her. Would her mother have brought her here? To this very bridge? Would she have pointed out the best spots for tea, woven stories from the stones beneath their feet, made this foreign place feel like home?

Heather swallowed the thought and kept going. She let herself move without a plan, following the river's curve, cutting through narrow streets lined with historic buildings. The stonework, the history—it made her think of Glenoran. She wondered if Flynn had worked on any of these buildings too—if his hands had shaped more than just her family's estate. She wandered past historic stonework, the scent of pastries in the air, and ducked into a quiet bookshop. The hush of paper and wood wrapped around her like balm.

She ran her fingers along the spines of books she couldn't quite justify buying—she had nowhere to put them—but she still lingered.

A few streets over, she spotted a display of wool scarves and sweaters, tartan patterns neatly folded behind the glass. She hesitated, fingers brushing against the soft fabric of a shawl. It was deep green, edged with delicate weaving, lighter than she expected but warm to the touch. Would it feel like home—or like a borrowed costume from a history she wasn't sure she had a right to wear?

Everything about her life lately felt borrowed. The house, the land, the history. Even her name felt like something she wasn't sure belonged to her anymore. She had never worn her family's tartan before—never even thought about it. But standing here, with the fabric soft under her fingertips, she wondered if it would feel more like belonging than pretending.

Eventually, she found herself at a small café and nursed a cup of tea by the window. No Glenoran. No Flynn. Just warmth and steam and a rare hush inside her chest.

Outside the window, the world moved on without her—

locals with familiar paths, visitors with camera straps and wide eyes. People who belonged. People just passing through.She'd always seen herself as the latter. Just passing through. But Glenoran was still in her mind, an unfinished thought, a question she wasn't ready to answer. She told herself Glenoran was temporary. A stop, a project, a place to finish what had been left undone so she could move on.

And yet.

The artifacts came to mind—the flag held by someone who had stood in this country centuries before her, and the letter written by hands that had long since turned to dust. She thought about the quiet ache in her chest when she walked through Glenoran's halls, the way she couldn't seem to distance herself from it, no matter how much she tried.

And she thought of Flynn. How he treated Glenoran like it mattered, like the land had a pulse. How he looked at her like she belonged there, even when she wasn't sure she did. She let out a slow breath and took another sip of tea. Maybe she wasn't just passing through.

Maybe it wasn't that she didn't belong.

Maybe she just hadn't found home—yet.

Heather lingered at the cafe for a while, nursing the last of her tea, watching the world pass by outside. The city had been a welcome distraction, a much-needed reprieve from the weight of Glenoran, but she couldn't shake the feeling that she was drifting toward something she wasn't ready to name. Heather wanted to shut herself off. To stop feeling. Stop thinking.

But that's the thing about spiraling—once it starts, you don't get to decide when it stops. With a sigh, she pushed back from the table, grabbed her bag, and returned to where she parked outside Dr. Morrow's office. The drive back to the Thistle Haven Inn was quiet—green hills rolling past as the sky shifted into the dusky hues of early evening. When she pulled into the small gravel lot of the inn, the air had turned crisp, the scent of damp earth and distant wood smoke curling around her as she stepped out of the car.

The inn's warmth wrapped around her the moment she stepped inside. The soft clink of dishes from the dining room, the low hum of conversation—comforting in contrast to the cold unraveling of her afternoon. She went straight to her room, shrugged off her coat, and collapsed onto the bed with a heavy sigh.

For the first time all day, she let herself feel it—the exhaustion creeping into her limbs, pressing into her bones. She closed her eyes and let the weight settle. And then, her phone buzzed. Heather frowned, pulling it from her pocket and glancing at the screen.

Hey. Can we talk? Call me if you're free. —Ivy.

Her stomach clenched. She should ignore it. She should set the phone down, roll over, and let it ring out. But old habits don't die. They just settle deeper, like a weight you learn to carry. And Ivy's voice had always been the only thing that made the weight bearable. Maybe it was the way the afternoon left her feeling adrift, or perhaps the realization she'd had by the river—that no matter how much she tried to distance herself from the past, it always found a way back.

Moments later, her phone lit up with Ivy's name. Steadying herself, Heather answered.

"Hey," Heather said softly.

"Hey..." Ivy countered.

Heather took a deep breath and listened to Ivy's voice on

the other end of the line. Her heart ached with the weight of everything unspoken between them. She had wanted this conversation, but now that it was here, she didn't know how to process the emotions it stirred up.

"I know I messed up, Heather." Her voice was quiet. Soft. But not her usual kind of soft—the kind that drew people in, made them feel chosen. This was different. A calculated softness. Heather knew the difference. And still, she listened.

"I've been thinking about it a lot, and I realize how much I've been trying to fix things for you, to take control and make decisions for you. I should've just let you figure things out on your own."

There was a long pause, and Heather could practically feel Ivy gathering the courage to keep going. "I slept with Sam." Heather's throat closed. Ivy exhaled shakily. "I don't know why I do it."

Heather stilled. She hadn't expected that level of honesty. Ivy never said things like this—not without an angle.

The words trembled, laced with something fragile. "Why I always think my body is the only thing I have to trade. Why I think it's the only way people will give me what I need."

Heather's fingers curled around the blanket. Her throat burned. Her heart hated how familiar this all was—the pivot. The moment Ivy turned her mistake into a wound.

"I thought if I just promised him what he wanted, he'd take you out—get you to open up, move on. I thought I could control the situation. But I see now how wrong that was. I thought I could make things better by controlling what others did, by using what I had to get what I wanted."

Heather felt a sharp pang in her chest, the memory of that night coming back in waves. She had felt cheap, like a pawn, like her best friend had treated her like a project rather than a person. Ivy's actions had made her feel as though she wasn't enough—like she needed to be fixed and that the solution was always someone else's choice.

"I've always done that, Heather," Ivy continued, her voice cracking. "Used my body, used my appearance, to get things, to manipulate people into giving me what I want. I've never known how to get people to care about me any other way. But I see now that I've been doing the same thing to you. I thought if I could control the people around you, I could make you better, make you happy. But it wasn't about you; it was about me feeling like I was doing something for you, even if it meant crossing boundaries."

She stared at the window, breath misting against the glass. She *should* be furious. But Ivy's voice still wrapped around her like a lullaby—gentle, dangerous, and far too easy to believe. She wanted to reach through the phone and tell Ivy she wasn't broken, that she wasn't alone, that she was more than just her looks. But hadn't she done that before? A thousand times? And hadn't Ivy always taken it, always nodded and thanked her, and then done it all over again?

She had wanted this and wished Ivy to understand what she'd done. But hearing it aloud—hearing the regret—made her chest twist. It made it real. She was angry. But she was also tired. And tired hearts forgive too easily.

"I don't know if I can trust you yet," Heather said, voice smaller than she meant it to be. "You've made a lot of decisions *for* me." Heather swallowed hard, her heart heavy. She knew something wasn't right with how Ivy orchestrated everything with Sam, but hearing Ivy say it so openly and honestly made it real.

Ivy was admitting, in a way she never had before, that her attempts to "fix" Heather had been selfishly motivated.

"I don't know what's wrong with me," Ivy whispered, ashamed of her confession. "I thought fixing you would fix me. That if I controlled the people around you, it would make me feel needed. But it wasn't about you—it was about me."

There was a long, heavy silence between them as if both were absorbing the weight of Ivy's words. "I don't know how to fix this, babe," Ivy added quietly. "But I want to try. I want to respect you and your choices from now on, and I won't try to control things anymore. I see now that I've hurt you in ways I never meant to, and I'm so sorry."

Heather's throat tightened, her mind still grappling with Ivy's vulnerability. It was difficult to reconcile the Ivy she had known—the one who always seemed so self-assured and dominant—with the one she was hearing now, the one who was finally confronting her insecurities and weaknesses.

"I just don't know if I can trust you right now," Heather admitted, her voice quiet. "And I don't know how to move past it."

"I know," Ivy said softly. "I understand. And I'm not asking you to forgive me right away. I just wanted you to know that I see my mistakes and want to make them right. Whatever you need, whenever you're ready, I'll be here. ... please know that I'm sorry for everything. I didn't mean to hurt you."

Heather exhaled slowly, her chest tight. "I'll need time, Ivy. But... I'm glad you're finally being honest with me. It's a start."

"Yeah," Ivy agreed, her voice still carrying a note of uncertainty but also hope. "It's a start."

Heather took a deep breath, her fingers tracing the edge of

the window frame as she gazed out at the street below. "I'm not sure what comes next, Ivy. But I'm willing to try...to move forward, I guess. One step at a time."

"I'm sorry," Ivy's voice was softer now, raw in a way Heather hadn't heard before. "But I promise." Heather closed her eyes. "I'll be better," Ivy whispered. "For you, Heather. For us."

Us.

That one word shattered whatever wall Heather had been trying to build. Heather's chest tightened. She hadn't expected Ivy to be so vulnerable, which caught her off guard. She closed her eyes, the weight of everything—her father's house, the artifacts, the distant echoes of her past—pressing down on her. She knew they had a long road ahead, but maybe, just maybe, they could start again.

"I believe you," Heather said quietly. There was a long pause before Ivy's voice, lighter this time, came through.

"Thanks, Heather. I'm here, okay? Whenever you're ready."

"Yeah," Heather replied, her heart feeling slightly less heavy. "I'll reach out." As they said their goodbyes, something shifted. Not big, but real. Like a door cracking open to let in the faintest light. Heather set the phone down.

She felt... uneasy.

Or maybe just empty. It was probably a mistake—Ivy asking for forgiveness and Heather giving it too easily. But for tonight? She wanted to believe it. She needed a break, a little distraction to let her thoughts settle. So she stood, brushed herself off, and headed down to The Highland Hearth.

She needed something simple. Something warm. Something that wasn't Ivy.

The familiar warmth of the pub wrapped around her the moment she stepped inside, the low hum of conversation blending with the lively strum of folk music that made Heather's foot tap along with the rhythm. The atmosphere was cheerful and welcoming, and peace settled into her bones for the first time in days. She ordered a hearty plate of bangers and mash at the bar, then found a cozy seat near the window to watch the world go by.

The bartender—a tall man with kind eyes and a gentle grin—caught her smile and leaned in. "Enjoyin' the tunes, are ye? Hope you're free come Beltane—we're throwin' a ceilidh."

Heather looked up, curious. "A *ceilidh*?"

"Aye, that's right," he said, wiping the counter. "Music, dancing, good fun."

She'd never been much of a dancer, but something about a ceilidh felt different. Like it belonged to the story she hadn't meant to walk into. "I'll think about it," she replied. "Sounds fun."

The bartender gave her a wink. "Ye won't regret it. Ye'll fit right in. I'll save you a seat if ye decide on comin'."

The thought of letting go—even for a night—made her heart lift. Something spontaneous. Maybe even something healing. She took another sip of her drink, the music's rhythm filling her with a quiet sense of belonging. As the night went on, Heather felt lighter, the music and the pub's warmth washing away some of the heaviness that had lingered for so long. Maybe the ceilidh was exactly what she needed. Not to forget—but to remember who she was, outside the ache.

Chapter 24

Heather didn't mean to ignore the storage unit. Not really. But winter had melted into spring, and still, she hadn't returned. It wasn't intentional—at least, that's what she told herself. There had always been something else to do. The renovation work took priority—the walls needed reinforcing, the roof repairs were ongoing, and the never-ending logistical headaches of permits, budgets, and the crew's schedules had kept her hands full.

And then there was Flynn.

She wasn't sure if he was a part of the distraction or just another thing she didn't want to examine too closely. Between early morning check-ins and late evening progress reports, between the effortless teasing and the unexpected moments of quiet understanding, she spent more time in Glenoran's present than its past. Maybe it was easier to fix walls than feelings. It was more straightforward to ignore the storage unit altogether than to stand in front of it and feel the weight of everything inside—the things that had been packed away, waiting for her to deal with them.

And so she didn't.

Not on the rainy days when she could've easily driven into town. Not on the bright, crisp mornings where she had nothing but time. Not even when Flynn offhandedly mentioned that they should go through it soon.

"Whenever yer ready, Campbell." That's all he said. No push, no expectation. It's just a simple statement, easy to brush aside. And she had. Because if she never went, then nothing inside had to change. Nothing had to be sorted, thrown out, or questioned. Most of all, nothing had to be remembered.

So she let spring settle over Glenoran, the trees bursting into fresh green, the scent of earth and new beginnings curling through the open windows. And still, the storage unit waited. Heather had gotten really good at avoiding things. The storage unit. The past, and for the last two days, Flynn.

She hadn't planned on ignoring him completely, but after his last text: "Still breathing, lass?"

She didn't owe him anything, but silence didn't feel as satisfying as she'd hoped, so she tossed it onto the bedside table, refusing to engage.

She dropped her head back against the pillow and exasperatedly flipped her phone over, staring at the blank screen... waiting. As if he'd text again. As if she wanted him to.

She didn't. Obviously.

She exhaled through her nose, shut the phone off, and tossed it onto the nightstand. It didn't matter. He didn't matter.

At least, that's what she kept telling herself every time she nearly picked up the phone.

She spent the last few days holed up in her room, doing nothing productive. No renovations. No storage unit sorting. No thinking about why, despite her best efforts, she kept feeling like Glenoran was pulling her back in. She told herself she needed space, but it hadn't helped her.

Mostly, it had left her staring at the ceiling, contemplating every lousy decision she had made in the last few months—including but not limited to getting involved with a crumbling estate and a contractor who was entirely too steady for her liking. She stretched out on the bed, flipping her phone in her hands, debating whether to turn it back on. It wasn't like she owed Flynn a response. But also.... she did.

She wasn't sure how many hours had passed, only that the sky outside her window had darkened, and the hum of the inn had shifted into the lively buzz of the evening. A knock at the door made both her and Byrdie jump—Heather nearly dropped her phone on her face, which sent Byrdie scrambling under the bed with a dramatic thud of protest. She frowned, pushing up onto her elbows. No one ever knocked. She considered ignoring it, but then a voice, cheerful, too chipper for this late in the evening, called out:

"Heather! Are ye in there?"

Heather groaned, rolling onto her stomach and pressing her face into the pillow for a second before dragging herself up.

Claire.

Slipping off the bed, she opened the door just enough to glare at the woman on the other side. Claire Kinnaird, the owner of the Thistle Haven Inn, stood there with her arms crossed, wearing the patient but unyielding expression of someone who had dealt with far too many difficult guests before.

"Yes?" Heather asked flatly.

Claire arched her brow. "Ye coming down to the ceilidh, or hiding up here with yer wee cat till the walls cave in?"

Heather's breath escaped in a slow rush. "Not in the mood, Claire."

Claire hummed like she'd bet money on that exact response. "Aye, well, that's a right shame. Didn't strike me as the type to ghost a good party, hen."

Heather stiffened. "I never said I was going."

"No, but ye havenae left the inn in days, and quite frankly, ye look miserable." Claire gave her a once-over before nodding toward the hallway. "Get dressed, mo ghràidh. You could use a drink and a dance."

Heather wanted to argue and tell her to mind her own business, but instead, she stared at Claire in silence. She could stay here. Keep avoiding everything. Keep pretending she didn't feel anything at all. Or...

Heather sighed, rubbing a hand over her face. "Fine. One drink."

Claire smirked as she walked away. "That's the spirit."

She'd planned on sulking. Not dancing. But now, standing in front of the small dresser in her room, she found herself combing through her red curls, smoothing out the tangles with careful fingers. It had been a while since she put effort into her appearance. Since arriving in Scotland, most days had been filled with dust-covered clothes, practical sweaters, and her hair thrown into a messy bun without a second thought. But tonight... after Claire's pestering, she decided it might be better to feel like herself again.

She reached for her small makeup bag, dusting a light layer

of powder over her freckled cheek and adding a hint of soft blush and mascara. Nothing too dramatic—just enough to make her more alive. And finally, she pulled out the dress. Dark green, elegant, but effortless, the fabric hugged her soft curves in all the right places. She had packed it just in case, though she hadn't been entirely sure what "just in case" meant. Maybe now she did.

It had a fitted bodice that cinched at the waist before flowing into a soft, sweeping knee-length skirt. The kind that would move beautifully while dancing. The neckline dipped into a tasteful V, showing just enough of her cleavage to be flattering but not over the top.

Heather hesitated as she studied herself in the mirror, her eyes drifting to the curve of her chest. Her large breasts had always made her self-conscious, like their very presence needed an apology. She had spent years hiding them under loose shirts, crossing her arms, avoiding anything that drew attention.

But tonight, she didn't feel exposed or uncomfortable. She looked... good. Feminine. Confident. Sexy, even. Her mother had been the same—soft with feminine curves, vibrant, a woman who had never shrunk herself to make others comfortable. Her beauty rivaled those of classic Hollywood starlets. Even *Marilyn* would've blinked twice. Heather traced her fingers over the fabric, swallowing against the tightness in her throat. She looked like her mother tonight. Like the kind of woman who didn't apologize for taking up space.

And somehow, that softened her mood.

Claire had insisted that a ceilidh was something everyone should experience at least once. Heather had been reluctant at first, but the more she thought about it, the more she realized she had spent too much time alone and stuck in her head. So tonight, she would go. Not for Glenoran. Not for the past. Not for anyone else.

Just for herself.

With a slow, steadying breath, she grabbed her coat and purse and glanced in the mirror before heading out the door. She didn't know what the night would bring. The unknown used to terrify her. Tonight, it felt like an open door.

Chapter 25

When Heather stepped inside the pub, she realized she had vastly underestimated the energy of a ceilidh.

She hadn't meant to come. Not really. Claire had dragged her out with promises of "just one drink," but Heather had planned to slip in, have a quick cider, and ghost before anyone expected her to enjoy herself. The pub was alive—too alive. Music swelled. Voices crashed. Boots stomped. And for a moment, she just stood in the doorway, feeling the heat of the crowd press in on her. She wasn't ready for this. It was too loud, too bright, too... *real*.

Her fingers curled around the strap of her purse, nails pressing into her palm. Maybe she could just turn around. Pretend she hadn't seen any of it. The air was thick with the scent of whisky and warm cider, the low hum of conversation punctuated by bursts of joyful shouts and stomping feet as couples spun across the wooden floor. A lively tune pulsed through the space, fiddle and accordion, weaving together in a rhythm that was impossible to ignore.

People clapped along, their faces flushed from dancing and drinking. She slipped through the crowd, maneuvering toward the edge of the room where she could take it all in. he hadn't been in a space this bustling—this full of life—in longer than she cared to admit. It was comforting in a way she hadn't expected—chaotic, warm, and inviting. She was about to head to the bar for a drink, but then—

Her eyes found *him*.

Heather's breath hitched.

Flynn leaned against the bar, laughing at something, whisky glass loose in his grip. His white shirt was rolled up at the sleeves, showing the forged strength of his forearms, and his usual work-worn look had been replaced by something relaxed yet effortlessly put together. The dim glow of the pub lights cast a warm hue over his stubbled jawline, the deep blue of his eyes, and the way his hair had fallen into an unruly mess that looked entirely too good for someone who clearly hadn't tried. Relaxed, easy, comfortable in a way that made her stomach twist.

Because *she* wasn't.

She was coming apart at the seams, and he was here, looking like some kind of damn safe haven. And then he looked up. And saw her.

Oh, hell.

Flynn just stared. Not in surprise. Not in casual recognition. But in knowing. Like he'd been waiting. Like he'd known she'd come. The crowd dissolved. The ceilidh buzzed on, but Heather was caught in the pull of his gaze, like a thread had been tied between them and tightened. Then— The smirk. Heather braced herself. Too late. Flynn excused himself from the group, set his drink down, and walked straight toward her. Heather's brain screamed: *Go!*

Her body stayed.

"Campbell."

Heather sighed dramatically. "Oh, you again." Flynn chuckled, tilting his head at her. "Didnae think ceilidhs were yer thing." Heather forced a wry smirk, like she wasn't seconds from turning into static. "They're not. I made an exception."

"Lucky me."

God, the way he said that.

She rolled her eyes, desperate for something sharp, detached, easy. "Don't flatter yourself. I didn't know you'd be here."

His smirk deepened. "And yet, here we are." Heather exhaled through her nose. The bar was too close. The music was too loud. The air was too warm. And Flynn was everywhere. He tilted his head toward the dance floor. "So?"

She frowned. "So, what?"

His eyes sparked. "Are you going to keep pretending yer just here to spectate, or are you actually going to dance?"

Heather snorted. "Oh, absolutely not."

He leaned in, nearly whispering in her ear. "Why not?"

Her pulse jumped at how close he was to her, feeling his breath on the shell of her ear. "I... I don't know the steps." She hated how weak it sounded. She glanced at the dance floor where people were spinning and weaving through the lively Dashing White Sergeant.

Flynn grinned and offered his hand. "Neither do half the people out there. But that's the fun, aye?"

Heather arched a brow. "Are you about to ask me?"

He stepped closer, tilting his head slightly. "Aye, I am." His voice was low, smooth, and confident. Heather swallowed.

Well. Damn.

Heather blinked, startled by the question. "I don't think that's a good idea."

"Why not?" he asked, tilting his head. "Go on, lass. Ye came all this way to Scotland, didn't you? Might as well get the full experience. And what's the worst that could happen?"

Heather hesitated.

This was a terrible idea.

But also—

Maybe that's why she reached for his hand.

The Dashing White Sergeant was a whirlwind of movement and energy, and Heather was entirely out of her depth. Flynn guided her through the steps, his hand steady at her back, his laughter infectious every time she stumbled. "Ye're doing great," he said, catching her arm as she nearly missed a turn.

"I feel like a baby giraffe on ice," she shot back, her nerves starting to melt away. The music surged, and Heather felt everywhere at once. The dance was a whirl of motion; she wasn't thinking—not about Glenoran, not about the storage unit, and not about how she had spent weeks shutting herself off from everything that felt too much.

But Flynn's hands were warm, his grip steady. The floor tilted beneath her, but he never let her fall. She laughed. Out loud. The sound felt foreign in her mouth. And Flynn? He was watching her—really watching her. Like he had just caught her doing something she hadn't meant to do. Heather hadn't expected to like this.

She had told herself she wouldn't. But Flynn made it impossible not to. And suddenly, she felt it. The way he was pulling her in without trying. The way this moment felt bigger than just a dance. The realization hit her like a punch.

Oh. Oh no.

She was in trouble.

"Better than a baby giraffe not trying at all," he teased, spinning her around with surprising grace. By the end of the dance, Heather was breathless and exhilarated, her cheeks flushed from the exertion. As the music slowed, Flynn didn't let go.

The pub buzzed around them, but in this moment, it felt silent. Flynn leaned in slightly, his breath warm at her ear. "Still thinking about running out the door?"

Heather's pulse spiked.

She glanced up at him, half-dizzy, half-terrified. Of him. Of herself. Of whatever this was. Maybe. Flynn tilted his head, studying her. Like he already knew. Like he was waiting. Heather exhaled slowly. And for once, she didn't run.

She glanced up at him, her pulse racing. "Maybe," she said, but a faint smile tugged at her lips.

"Well, if you do, you're going to miss the next dance," he said, lingering at her waist.

Heather hesitated momentarily, her heart thudding as she weighed the choice. Maybe it was the warmth of the whisky or the energy of the music calling to her, but doubt tried to creep in for a fleeting moment. What if this was too soon? What if she wasn't ready? But then she looked up—really looked at him. The way his blue eyes softened, waiting for her decision. The way he held himself still, not pushing, just... hoping. And suddenly, the fear wasn't as loud as she wanted.

Flynn took her hand as The rhythm built, urgent and bright again, guiding her back onto the dance floor. The energy of the ceilidh wrapped around them, the rhythm of the dance infectious. Initially nervous, her feet unsure, but Flynn's confidence grounded her. He moved with ease, his hand warm around hers, his steps light and assured.

"Dinnae fash, lass. I'll lead," Flynn said with a playful grin, his blue eyes twinkling. Heather's breath hitched a little, her pulse quickening.

She nodded, her chest tightening. "I'm not... fashed," she lied, trying to focus on the steps and not noticing how his presence seemed to fill all the space between them.

The dancers swirled around them, the energy contagious, the quick steps and lively tunes pulling her in. With each step, Flynn's hand guided hers, his movements smooth but not rushed. They fell into a rhythm, and she felt herself getting lost in it. She couldn't help but laugh at how they twirled and spun, the action making her feel lighter.

"You make it look easy," she said, breathless.

"That's the trick," Flynn replied with a grin, his voice low and teasing. "Make it look effortless, even if ye're thinking about tripping over yer own feet." Heather chuckled, but it was hard to ignore how the back-and-forth banter had an undeniable effect on her—how the heat of his hand against hers and how he caught her gaze made her heart beat faster.

As the music swirled to a new, faster tune, Flynn gave her a quick wink, his smile turning a little mischievous. "Ready for the next spin?" he asked, his voice low, sending a little shiver down her spine. "Absolutely," she replied, her words more confident than she felt. He pulled her into another spin, and it felt like the world faded away. The music, the people, the noise—it all blurred, leaving just the two of them moving in sync, the space between them charged with something unspoken.

Her heart was racing now; the dance was no longer just about the steps. She looked up at him, meeting his eyes, and suddenly, it was all too clear—how easy it was to be with him, how natural the connection felt. She smiled, breathless but exhilarated, a soft laugh escaping her lips. "See?" Flynn winked, voice warm but teasing. "Told ye you'd be great." As the dance ended, he didn't let go of her immediately. He looked at her, his blue eyes searching hers, a flicker of something there she couldn't quite name. For a breath, the world around them seemed to pause.

"Ye're good at this," he said, voice low. "I don't know about that," Heather replied, still catching her breath, her cheeks flushed. "But it's fun." There was an intensity in his gaze, something quiet and serious beneath the teasing. "It's not just the dancing, though, is it?" Flynn asked, his voice soft. The banter had been easy, but this—this felt different. She could feel the weight of his words lingering between them, a question neither had entirely answered. Flynn's grin flickered.

His hand, firm at her waist, tightened just slightly. Heather barely had time to process it before he spun her, and— She slipped. Not literally. Emotionally. Just for a second. Long enough for her gaze to catch on his mouth. And Flynn noticed. His grip flexed. His blue eyes darkened. It wasn't just a dance. It wasn't just a ceilidh. It was something else—something she couldn't name but felt in her heart, warm and dangerous.

She should step away. Right now. Right this second. Before it became something she couldn't take back. Before she lost herself to it. Before—Heather sucked in a breath.

Oh, hell. Oh no.

And he saw it. The precise moment her guard slipped. The moment her body betrayed her. The music swelled, the dance pulled them closer, and for one terrifying second, she thought—

He's going to kiss me.

Flynn didn't ask. He just read the moment. One second, she was spinning. The next—his fingers skimmed her jaw, tilting her face up. His lips brushed hers, a whisper of heat. Soft. Questioning. She could still pull away. But she didn't.

Heather broke.

The kiss deepened. Heat flooded her veins, her fingers curling into the fabric of his shirt. Flynn groaned against her mouth. And suddenly, the rest of the world ceased to exist. There was only this: his mouth, her breath, and the fire between them.

Flynn, solid and steady. Heather, coming apart at the seams. She needed this. She needed him. And that scared the hell out of her. When they finally pulled apart, Flynn stayed close, their foreheads rested together as Heather's chest heaved. Her brain short-circuited and heart slammed against her ribs. She had to stop this. Had to shut it down. Had to— Flynn was still looking at her, forehead resting against hers, breathing just as hard.

Oh. Oh, she was so *screwed.*

She wanted more. And that was a problem. Because this wasn't just a kiss. It was a free-fall. And Heather wasn't sure she knew how to land. Flynn's voice was low, husky, dangerous. "So... do I get another dance?"

Heather laughed, feeling some tension she hadn't even realized was there to melt away. She shook her head, her chest still fluttering. "You are persistent, aren't you?" He raised an eyebrow. "Wouldn't be much of a Scot if I wasn't." She paused, her heart racing before a grin tugged at her lips. "Alright, alright. I guess one more dance won't hurt."

Flynn's eyes lit up at her words, and he stepped closer, his hand brushing against hers as he took it. "That's the spirit," he said, the flirtation still simmering between them, but there was something genuine in his gaze too. They moved back into the center of the dance floor, and this time, Heather was more relaxed, a little more willing to let herself enjoy the moment.

Flynn led her effortlessly, his hand warm on her back, syncing their steps with ease. This time, they fell into rhythm—steps syncing like they'd danced together for years. "Ye know, you're actually not as bad as ye were a few minutes ago," Flynn teased as they twirled around.

Heather couldn't help but laugh. "Says the guy who nearly tripped over his own feet two seconds ago."

"Hey, I was just testing the waters," he replied with a grin. "Ye can't have too much finesse all at once, right?"

Heather rolled her eyes, but their warmth made her laugh again. She found herself leaning in a little closer to him, their connection deepening with every shared glance and every playful retort. It felt like it was just the two of them, lost in the music and the laughter. "I thought I'd be stepping on your toes all night."

"You're a quick learner," Flynn replied with a wink, his hand resting lightly on her waist. "I'll give you that."

As they danced, the world around them seemed to disappear, the pub noise fading into the background. It was just the two of them, spinning and laughing, caught up in something that felt like both the beginning and the end of something entirely new. As the final notes of the ceilidh faded and the crowd began to thin, Flynn and Heather stepped off the dance floor, the night buzz still humming between them. The connection was undeniable now, even if neither had said much about it. Always so easygoing, Flynn seemed to take the lead, slipping his jacket on before offering her a warm smile.

"You ready to head back to the inn?" he asked, his voice low, almost intimate in the quiet moment they shared. Heather nodded, her heart still fluttering from their last dance, kiss, everything. His hands were steady, but she suddenly wasn't. Not just from the kiss. From the way he felt against her—warm, solid, strong. From the way her body reacted, instinctual and dangerous. From the way she wondered—just for a second—what it would feel like if he didn't stop at just this. Heat curled low in her belly, unfamiliar and unwelcome, because it meant one thing—she didn't just **want** Flynn. She wanted him in a way that scared the hell out of her.

The cool air hit her skin as they walked out into the crisp Inverness night, but it didn't cool the fire she felt inside. She couldn't stop thinking about the kiss—the way he pulled her close, the way it lit her up from the inside out.

She'd wanted it. More than she should. More than she could admit—even to herself.

Chapter 26

They walked side by side, and the only sounds heard were their footsteps on the cobblestone path and the occasional car passing by. The Thistle Haven Inn was just down the street, but Heather wasn't in a hurry to get there. She wasn't ready to break this moment yet, to break the ease that had finally settled between them.

Heather swallowed hard, her breath still uneven from the kiss, from the warmth of his hands on her waist, from the way he'd looked at her like she was something worth savoring. Her fingers twitched at her sides, the ghost of his touch still warm on her skin. This wasn't supposed to happen.

She wasn't supposed to feel like this— untethered, unraveling. For weeks, she had been numb. Floating through Glenoran, avoiding the storage unit, avoiding Flynn. It had been easier not to feel anything at all. And now? Now her entire body was alive with it. With him.

Her stomach twisted violently, her pulse too wild, her skin too hot. This was the exact thing she had been running from.

The exact reason she had kept her distance. Because what if she let herself want this? What if she let herself have it? And what if it was just another thing that would slip through her fingers in the end? Flynn's voice broke through her spiraling thoughts.

"So..." Flynn started, a mischievous glint in his eye, "did ye enjoy yerself, lass?" Heather smiled, the tension in her chest easing with his teasing tone. She was still reeling from the intensity of their last moments together, but she wanted more. She couldn't remember the last time she'd felt so alive, so carefree.

"Definitely," she replied, her voice more confident than she felt. He chuckled, his arm brushing lightly against hers.

"I'm glad to hear it. You make a fine dance partner." The compliment sent a small thrill down her spine. They walked in comfortable silence for a few moments before Heather spoke again, her thoughts suddenly more pressing than she realized.

"You know..." She hesitated for a second, then pushed on, her words tumbling out before she could stop them. "That kiss... it wasn't just because of the dancing, was it?"

Flynn stopped walking, turning toward her with a serious look, his eyes scanning her face as if looking for something. "No, it wasn't," he said quietly, his voice sincere. Heather felt a lump form in her throat. Her heart was racing again, her pulse quickening at the thought of what she was supposed to say. She didn't want to complicate things, but couldn't deny her feelings.

As they reached the inn, Flynn paused outside the door, looking down at her with a soft smile. "Well, this is me," she said, voice still low, the night wrapping around them. Heather's fingers tightened around the strap of her purse, her heart hammering wildly. She needed to walk inside. To end this here. But her feet wouldn't move.

Flynn stood there, watching her, waiting—not pressing, not pushing, just letting her decide. And that was the problem, wasn't it? That he was giving her the space to walk away. That if she said goodnight, he wouldn't argue, wouldn't try to convince her otherwise. Because he wasn't like the others—wasn't danger wrapped in charm. He was steady. Safe. And that scared her more than anything. Heather's throat was dry. She should say goodnight. Turn around. End this here. But her fingers flexed at her sides. Because what if she let herself have this? Just once. Just for tonight. Her pulse was a steady drum against her ribs, the weight of his gaze heavy on her skin.

It had been so long since she had let someone get this close—too close. And she was so, so tired of pushing him away. Before she could stop herself, before she could think too hard about what she was about to do—"Do you want to... do you want to walk me up? To my room, I mean." The words were out before she could stop them. Her heart slammed into her ribs, her breath catching—*oh God*, had she really just said that?

Flynn's expression flickered—surprise, then understanding, then something deeper, darker. "Are you sure?" He let the question hang in the air—no pressure, just the space for her to choose. He wasn't pushing her, just standing there, allowing her to figure it out alone. Heather hesitated. Just for a second. Just long enough for that final chance to run—

But she didn't take it.

She lifted her chin, exhaling a slow, measured breath. "I think so."

Heather stood there momentarily, looking up at him, feeling the pull of their chemistry, the undeniable spark between them. She could feel the uncertainty swirling inside her—was this just a fling? A distraction? Or something more?

Her mind raced, thoughts of her past, of the pain she'd carried, all swirling together. She didn't want to rush this; she didn't want to jump into something only to be hurt again. But then again, how long could she keep running from the things that felt good and made her feel alive?

"Alright then." Flynn's voice was gentle now, his teasing tone replaced with something quieter, almost reverent. He stepped back, offering her his arm with an exaggerated little bow. "Lead the way." Heather rolled her eyes at the gesture—but linked her arm through his anyway. Together, they walked into the Thistle Haven Inn, the cozy warmth wrapping around them as they crossed the threshold. Byrdie, perched on the windowsill in the small lobby, glanced at them before curling back up into her patch of moonlight, unimpressed.

"Well," Flynn murmured, a slow, teasing smile curving his lips, "I didn't see this evening coming. Though, I cannae say I'm complaining."

Heather's lips twitched despite herself. "Don't get too cocky," she said, though her voice wavered slightly, betraying the storm still swirling beneath her calm.

"Too late for that," Flynn replied, his grin widening, though something earnest in his gaze softened the banter. "You've officially ruined me now, lass. I might never recover."

She rolled her eyes, ignoring how her heart fluttered at his words. "You'll manage."

They climbed the creaky staircase in silence, but it wasn't uncomfortable. Flynn let her set the pace, his hand brushing against hers occasionally, his presence solid and reassuring. The hallway was too quiet. When they reached her door, she hesitated, her hand resting on the doorknob. She turned to face him, and the look in his eyes made her breath catch. There was no pressure or expectation—just warmth, patience, and infuriating, irresistible charm.

"Thank you," she said softly.

"For what?"

"For... I don't know." She huffed a laugh, shaking her head. "For being here, I guess."

Flynn smiled, the corners of his eyes crinkling. "Anytime, lass." The space between them shrank. Heather didn't even know who moved first, but suddenly, Flynn was right there—close enough for her to feel his warmth and his breath brush against her lips. She should stop this. She knew that. But she didn't step back. Didn't move away. Instead, her breath came shallow, her pulse unsteady as Flynn's fingers skimmed her jaw, tracing fire where he touched. Her body tilted forward before she could stop it, before she could remind herself that letting this happen meant letting him in.

And then—

His gaze dropped to her lips.

Heather sucked in a sharp breath, and he felt it. His fingers curled at her waist, his grip tightening. He had seen it. The exact moment she wanted him. And she knew—knew—he wasn't going to let it slip past them this time.

He lifted a hand, cupping her jaw with aching tenderness, his thumb tracing the curve of her cheek. It was a question, an offering. She answered by closing the gap between them.

Heather was falling. And she didn't care if she hit the ground. His hands tangled in her hair, his breath rough against her lips, the heat of his body pressing against hers, and oh—

Oh, she was *gone.*

Flynn groaned into her mouth.

One hand slid to her waist, the other drifting down her spine, anchoring her to him until there was no space left—no breath, no thought, only heat.

Heather whimpered, the sound tearing something loose in him. His teeth caught her bottom lip. His hips pressed into hers. And—God—she needed more. She needed *all* of him.

This was reckless. Dangerous.

And she was already too far gone.

She melted into him, her body yielding like it had been waiting for this—for him—all along.

He was solid and warm, steady as stone, but this? This felt like freefall.

When he finally eased back, Flynn rested his forehead to hers. They were both breathless, caught in the hush between decisions.

She could still end this. Pretend it hadn't happened.

But she didn't want to.

Heather swallowed, her voice barely a breath.

"Do you... want to come inside?"

Flynn exhaled slowly, like it took everything in him not to say yes too fast.

His fingers traced the small of her back, feather-light, patient. Heather's heart hammered against her ribs as he watched her, his blue eyes searching hers like they held the answer.

"You sure?" he murmured.

Her lips parted. Her breath caught.

"Yes."

The moment the word left her mouth, everything shifted.

His restraint unraveled.

Heat. Motion. The press of his chest. The sharp inhale against her lips.

She barely had time to brace before he kissed her—hard, hungry, *certain.*

She wasn't standing at the edge anymore.

She had jumped.

And there was no going back.

Heather shut the door behind them, but neither of them moved. The only sounds were the quiet crackle of the fireplace and the soft rhythm of their breath—hers shaky, his steady. Her pulse pounded in her ears like a warning or a dare.

She turned slowly, spine pressing to the door. Flynn stood across the room, watching her—still, silent, unreadable. His blue eyes shimmered in the dim firelight, heavy-lidded but calm. He was still giving her an out. Still letting *her* decide.

Heather's hands trembled. She wanted to say something—to confess that she didn't know how to do this without destroying it. That she was scared of wanting something real. Scared of *him.* Scared of what it might mean.

But nothing came out.

Flynn's gaze flicked to her lips. Just for a breath. Just long enough.

Heather inhaled sharply.

And then—

He reached for her.

A single touch—his fingers grazed her jaw, trailed lightly down the side of her throat. Heather's knees nearly buckled. Flynn paused, as if sensing her unraveling, his thumb brushing the skin just beneath her ear. A question. A tether. A final moment to turn back.

She didn't take it.

Heather's mind spun, thoughts racing and colliding, none of them louder than the ache between them. Flynn stepped closer—close enough that his warmth kissed her skin, his breath feathered across her mouth.

His hand lifted, cupping her jaw with reverence. His thumb traced the arc of her cheekbone like she was something fragile and holy.

Then his hands slid—shoulders to arms to waist—drawing her into him as his lips found hers.

The kiss was soft at first, tentative. Then deeper. Hotter. Desperate.

Like a dam breaking.

Heather whimpered into his mouth, and that sound snapped something in him. His hand found her waist. His hips pressed forward. His mouth devoured hers like she was something to be claimed.

Her hands roamed his chest, feeling the heat under her palms, the strength of him. He was solid, immovable— and yet something about this felt wild and uncertain, like uncharted land neither of them had dared explore until now.

When he pulled back, he pressed his forehead to hers. Both of them breathless, trembling.

His lips trailed down her neck, his stubble grazing fire over her skin. Her fingers fisted in his shirt. She wanted him closer. Deeper. Everywhere.

Flynn's hands found the zipper at her side. He hesitated, breath ragged at her ear.

"We can stop," he murmured, voice low and aching. "Say the word, and I'll walk out that door."

Heather's hands covered his. Steady. Certain.

"I don't want to stop," she whispered.

Flynn exhaled hard—like she'd just given him permission to breathe.

And then—everything else disappeared.

She barely registered the sound of her dress sliding from her shoulders. Only the heat of his hands, the weight of his body, the way his mouth claimed hers like she was the only thing he'd ever wanted.

He lifted her with ease, carrying her to the bed. Heather's arms curled around his neck, a smile brushing his lips as she whispered his name.

Tonight, she wasn't running.

She was his—completely, irrevocably his.

Flynn set her down gently, her feet still brushing the floor. But he didn't pull back.

His hands stayed at her hips, thumbs circling slowly, like she was something to be unwrapped with patience and awe.

His gaze raked over her—hungry, reverent.

"I've wanted ye since the moment ye walked into my cottage," he murmured, mouth brushing her jaw, her neck.

"I tried to be a gentleman... but ye ken, I saw every inch of you in that soaking wet outfit. "

Heather moaned at his bold admission, arching into his touch.

"That lacy little thing ye wore that day…" Flynn's voice dropped to a low rasp, thick with heat. "I've thought about it more times than I care to admit. How easy it would've been to slide it down… to see what ye were hidin' beneath it. To touch. To taste."

His words sent a fresh wave of heat curling through her. She could picture it—his hands, rough and reverent, slipping the straps down her shoulders. The way his breath would hitch, how his pupils would dilate with need as her skin was slowly revealed. He'd stare at her like she was a revelation. Like she was something holy.

"I want that too," she whispered, her fingers fisting the fabric of his shirt. "I want you to touch me, Flynn."

Flynn let out a guttural sound, something between a groan and a growl. His hips pressed against hers, his restraint fraying at the edges.

"Ye dinnae ken how much I want that," he murmured, his voice trembling with need. "To feel your skin under my hands. To taste every inch of you. I burn for it, mo chridhe."

Heather tugged him closer, mouth crashing into his in a searing, hungry kiss.

Their tongues tangled, breath hitching, hearts racing.

Every touch, every gasp, every press of their bodies was a spark thrown onto a growing fire.

And neither of them wanted to put it out.

Flynn's hands roamed her body like a man starved, mapping every dip, every curve, with aching reverence. He cupped her breasts through the delicate lace of her bralette, his thumbs circling her nipples until they strained beneath the sheer fabric, drawing a soft gasp from her lips.

His movements were slow, deliberate, as he reached behind

her for the clasp. His fingers grazed her skin, sending a shiver down her spine. The air between them was charged—thick with tension, anticipation, hunger.

Finally, the straps slid from her shoulders, the lace slipping free.

Heather didn't look away. Her cheeks were flushed, her chest rising and falling as she held his gaze. There was no fear in her now—just desire, and something rawer beneath it. Vulnerability. Trust.

Flynn exhaled sharply as her bralette fell to the floor. His eyes swept over her, dark and wide, reverent and wrecked.

"Christ," he breathed. "Ye're even more breathtaking than I imagined."

His voice was hoarse, thick with awe. "Bloody hell, lass… you're exquisite."

Heather's cheeks flushed, heat rising beneath his stare. No one had ever called her that—not really. The words lit something inside her, wild and unfamiliar.

For a split second, her old doubts tried to claw their way back in. Would he see the flaws? Would he change his mind?

But then she looked at him—really looked.

He wasn't seeing imperfections.

He was seeing her.

And he looked at her like she was something rare.

Like he'd found a miracle and was afraid to breathe too hard in case it vanished.

She took a breath and chose boldness.

No second-guessing. No hiding.

Her skin buzzed with anticipation, every nerve alive beneath his gaze. She wanted his hands on her. Wanted to feel something that didn't ache.

"Please, Flynn," she whispered, voice low and wrecked. She didn't know if she wanted more or just wanted him. Maybe both.

He placed his finger to his lips, "Shh, patience, *mo chridhe*." His fingers skimmed along the edge of her underwear, an agonizingly slow, deliberate touch. He held her gaze as he eased the lacy fabric down, tracing the path with his hands, leaving a trail of warmth in their wake. Every moment was unhurried, reverent—like he was memorizing her, piece by piece.

She was trembling now, every nerve on edge, her body aching—starving—for more.

"You like to take your time, don't you?" she murmured, a slow smile curving her lips. "I can't tell if you're savoring this... or just testing how long I can take it." She arched into his touch, her voice a low purr.

"Can't it be both?" He murmured, his lips brushing just beneath her ear. "I like to do things properly, lass. Wouldn't want to rush into something worth savoring."

Her breath caught as his hands moved slowly.

Deliberately tracing fire across her skin.

Each touch curled heat low in her belly, winding tighter with every pass.

He didn't rush. Didn't fumble. He moved like a man with time to memorize her.

She should've felt exposed. Vulnerable. But with him?

She just felt *wanted.*

"Flynn," She whispered, as he lifted his head, his blue eyes dark with something unreadable. He didn't rush. He just looked at her, like he was letting himself take in every inch of her, every sound she made, every way she responded to him.

"Yes?' he murmured, his voice low, rough with restraint.

She swallowed, her fingers curling into his shirt, pulling him closer. "Just kiss me already."

Something in him snapped—patience burned off like mist in the sun.

His mouth claimed hers, and suddenly there was no space left to breathe, only heat, only hands, only the way she came undone beneath him.

And this time? She didn't hold back.

She met him with everything she had—want, wonder, *yes*.

He cupped her breasts, thumbs brushing over the stiff peaks, drawing a gasp from Heather's lips. Leaning down, he took one into his mouth, suckling and teasing until she was writhing against him.

"Yes," Heather hissed, fisting her hands in his hair to hold him closer. "More..."

Flynn obliged eagerly, lavishing attention on each sensitive peak until Heather was nearly mindless with pleasure. His hands continued their exploration, trailing down her sides to grip her hips, pressing her more firmly against his straining erection.

Her hands slipped between them, urgency sparking in every movement as she fumbled with his buttons.

She had to feel him—warm, solid, real beneath her palms.

When she finally peeled the shirt from his shoulders, it hit the floor with a soft thud, forgotten.

"Well, damn," she murmured, her fingers tracing the firm ridges of his abdomen. "You've been holding out on me."

Flynn captured her lips again, swallowing her moan as she caressed him. In one swift movement, he lifted her, laid her on the bed before them, and sat up to take her in—his eyes roving over every bare inch of her, exhaling appreciatively.

"Christ, ye're so beautiful," His hands and mouth explored her with aching patience, unraveling her piece by piece until she was lost to him completely. "What am I to do with you?"

Flynn looked up at her mischievously, sliding his index finger down the center of her arousal. "Ye're so ready for me," he growled against her. "You want this as badly as I do."

"Yes," Heather panted, bucking into his touch. "I need you, Flynn. Now."

He complied immediately, pulling back just long enough to shed his pants and boxers, allowing himself to spring free before covering her body with his own once more. The feel of his hot skin against her made Heather shudder with pleasure. She could feel every chiseled muscle pressed against her soft curves.

With a deep groan, he gave her exactly what she needed. Heather cried out at the sudden intrusion, inner muscles clenching around him greedily. He began to move within her, deep and unhurried, each thrust sending sparks along her spine, "Yes," Heather moaned, nails scoring down his back. "Flynn, please."

The hard press of Flynn's desire lingered at her entrance as his voice dropped to a rough whisper. "You're mine, Heather. Say it."

"I'm yours, only yours." Heather agreed quickly.

"Good girl." Flynn exhaled, rewarding her with a deep, claiming kiss as he thrust into her. They both gasped at the delicious sensation, pausing to savor the feeling of being so perfectly joined. Then Flynn began to move, setting a slow, sensual rhythm that had them both seeing stars.

They moved together with a perfect rhythm, each touch a

silent confession of need. Heather met Flynn's every thrust with an upward roll of her hips, pulling him deeper, harder. She grazed his back with soothing strokes as she urged him on, lost to everything but the feel of him moving inside her.

Flynn could feel his release building, winding tighter with every stroke of their joined bodies. He slipped a hand between them, caressing her apex in slow, deliberate circles, determined to bring her with him. "Let go for me, mo chridhe. Let me feel ye come undone."

His words, spoken in that deep, honeyed tone, were all it took. Heather flew apart with a keening cry, inner muscles rippling around him like a vise as she came. The sound of her pleasure pushed Flynn over the edge, and he followed her into bliss, spilling himself deep inside her with a hoarse shout of her name.

He rolled off of her, breathless and sated, his body still humming with the lingering aftershocks of their shared ecstasy. As he lay beside her, his dark blue eyes—softened by firelight—held her in their gaze, drinking her in.

Flushed, she traced the line of his stubbled jaw with a fingertip, her own body still trembling from the intensity of their passion. A soft sigh escaped her lips as she studied him, her gaze lingering on the faint blush that stained his skin.

Flynn reached out, cupping her face gently, his touch as tender as a feather.

"You," he whispered, his voice husky with emotion, "you are everything I've ever dreamed of."

A slow, lingering smile played on Heather's lips, a silent affirmation of the truth in his words. They laid tangled in the hush that followed, breath soft against skin, the heat between them still humming like an aftershock.

His arm slipped around her waist like it belonged there. She exhaled softly against his chest, fingers brushing his skin—still warm from everything they'd shared.

He let his hand drift along her hip, lingering at the curve of her breast. A quiet smile tugged at his mouth as he closed his eyes, holding on to the way she felt right then. The rise and fall of her breath matched his own, steady and slow beneath the hush of night.

Heather's eyes fluttered shut, Flynn's warmth anchoring her as she melted into his arms. His body curved around hers, steady and sure. The night sounds faded—the hush of wind through trees, the distant chirp of crickets—like the world itself had gone quiet just for them.

He dreamed of her laughter, the fire in her eyes, the way she challenged him without flinching. No woman had ever disarmed him like this—tender and sharp all at once. He didn't just want her now. He wanted *every version of her*, in every moment still to come.

She dreamed of his arms, of lips that knew every inch of her, of the way he held her like she wasn't breakable—but precious.

Not just his touch.

The *feeling* of him.

Safe.

Seen.

Wanted.

Like she was someone worth staying for.

And she knew she wouldn't survive it when it all fell apart.

Chapter 27

Heather stirred, the sheets cool beside her. Her fingers brushed the empty space where Flynn had been, and her stomach clenched. A slow, sinking weight settled in her chest—cold and unwelcome. The bed was too big, too empty. Her fingers curled into the sheets, searching for lingering warmth, but there was none.

Of course it was empty.

She sat up so quickly, blankets tangling around her legs, her pulse hammering in her ears. What had she expected? That he'd stay? That last night had meant something more than a moment stolen from reality? She should've known better.

A floorboard creaked downstairs, followed by the soft thump of a door closing. Heather froze, her breath catching in her throat. Footsteps climbed the stairs, slow and unhurried. A second later, the door pushed open, and there he was.

Flynn.

His dark hair was mussed like he'd run a hand through it a dozen times on his way back. He had a brown paper bag tucked under his arm and a takeaway coffee cup in each hand. His blue eyes softened the moment they met hers.

"Mornin', mo chridhe," he murmured, his voice deep and smooth like honey.

Her composure shattered.

"I thought you might still be sleeping," he said softly, stepping inside. "I didn't mean to wake ye."

He lifted the bag. "I got you a coffee and a pastry. I figured you might be hungry."

She stared at him, her throat tightening. It was too much—too kind, too thoughtful, too easy. She didn't know what to do with it. She didn't know how to hold onto something that didn't already feel like it was slipping through her fingers.

Flynn frowned, setting the coffee on the nightstand before sitting at the edge of the bed. "Did ye think I left?"

Heather swallowed, her fingers tightening in the sheets. She should say something—anything—but her throat tightened around the words.

Finally, she forced a hollow laugh. "Wouldn't blame you if you did."

His jaw ticked. "Aye. Well, I didn't."

She exhaled slowly, staring at the wall instead of him. The weight of his presence and last night's warmth still lingering between them was too much. Her heart hammered. For a split second, she almost let herself believe it.

But hope was dangerous.

Because if it hadn't been a mistake, then it meant something.

And that was worse.

She shook her head, her voice quieter this time. "This... this was a mistake, Flynn."

His body went still. A long beat of silence stretched between them, thick and heavy.

"No," he said, voice low and steady. "It wasn't."

Heather's chest ached. The way he looked at her, the quiet certainty in his voice—it made something splinter inside her.

So she did what she always did. She pulled away.

"It didn't mean anything."

Something flickered in his eyes. Something quiet. Something hurt.

He exhaled sharply, nodding once. "If that's what you need to tell yourself."

She swallowed hard. Her fingers curled tighter in the sheets. "I think you should go."

Flynn hesitated, just for a second. Then he stepped toward the door, jaw tight.

At the threshold, he glanced back. "I meant what I said, Heather." His voice was quiet, but sure.

Heather gripped the sheet tighter, her nails pressing into the fabric.

The words were right there on her tongue.

Wait.

Stay.

But she swallowed them down, locking her jaw.

Then he was gone, leaving behind the scent of coffee—and the taste of regret.

Heather sat frozen, Flynn's words still hanging in the air long after the door closed behind him.

I meant what I said, Heather.

Her heart.

She pressed a hand to her chest as if she could steady the uneven rhythm of her heart. As if she could force herself to ignore the way those words had cracked something open inside her. This was precisely why she couldn't do this.

Flynn Duncan was... good. The kind of good that made her chest feel tight and made her want to believe in things she had no business believing in. The type of man who brought pastries and coffee after a night tangled in the sheets instead of slipping out before dawn. And that terrified her.

She swung her legs over the side of the bed, her bare feet hitting the worn wooden floor. The room felt too small. The air was too thick. She needed to move—before the weight of it crushed her.

She pulled on the shirt from the floor, jamming her arms through the sleeves with more force than necessary. The scent of sawdust and something unmistakably him clung to her skin, only making it worse.

She stood there for a long time, staring at the closed door. Hoping. But he wouldn't walk through it again. Her throat was tight, a dull ache spreading through her chest, but she pushed it down.

This is what you wanted.

It had to be.

She forced herself to move, shoving back the covers and yanking on her jeans with quick, jerky movements. The room smelled like him—sawdust, soap, and something warmer. Something she couldn't name.

She hated how much she liked it.

Catching her reflection in the mirror, she barely recognized the woman staring back. Her hair was tangled, her lips kiss-swollen, and a bloom of color still lingered low on her throat. A stranger. Someone who had let herself be wanted.

She traced her lips with unsteady fingers.

Proof of him.

Tearing her gaze away, she slung her bag over her shoulder, ignoring the untouched coffee and pastry on the nightstand. She couldn't touch it. Not when it made her feel... wanted. She wouldn't think about how thoughtful it was. How easy kindness seemed to come to him.

Downstairs, the inn was quiet, the breakfast rush long over. The scent of coffee and toast still hung in the air. She slipped past, head down, avoiding Claire's friendly smile at the front desk.

She needed to move—to outrun the restless energy clawing at her ribs.

The storage unit. *Yes.*

That's why she was here. To sort through her mother's things. To close the book on a history that had never included her. Not to get tangled up in a man who made her want to stay.

Outside, the morning air was crisp, and the overcast sky stretched low over the town. A sharp breeze bit at her cheeks as she walked briskly down the cobblestone streets, locking down her thoughts.

It didn't matter that Flynn had been sweet. It didn't matter that she'd woken up expecting—wanting—him to be there.

Because he was gone.

And maybe that was for the best.

She just had to convince herself to believe it.

Chapter 28

By the time summer had swept into the Highlands, Heather had made more progress than she had ever expected. The storage unit—once an overwhelming cavern of dusty boxes and forgotten heirlooms—was nearly empty. Sorting, cataloging, and deciding what to keep or let go had become methodical.

She'd unearthed old family letters, some written in careful, slanted handwriting that she suspected belonged to her mother's grandmother. There had been faded photographs, sepia-toned, of people who looked like strangers but shared the same high cheekbones and unruly curls. A delicate silver locket with a thistle engraved on the front, tucked away in a box of moth-eaten tartan fabric.

Some things she kept, others she carefully packed into donation bins or arranged for historical preservation. But with every box she emptied, the weight in her heart grew heavier because clearing out the storage unit meant that soon, there would be nothing left tying her there.

Nothing but Glenoran.

She had spoken to Flynn a handful of times since then, but only when necessary. It was strictly business: updates on the restoration, material approvals, and brief logistical check-ins. She kept every call clipped and every email impersonal, refusing to engage beyond what was necessary.

And he let her.

Never pushed. Never called her *mo chridhe* again. And maybe that was what hurt the most—that he'd believed her when she said it didn't mean anything.

Now, with the storage unit nearly cleared, she had one last thing to do—find a buyer for Glenoran. Because the longer she stayed, the more it felt like Glenoran was trying to convince her to stay, too. And she couldn't afford to listen to ghosts.

She'd already started looking into distant relatives—anyone from her mother's side who might have more of a connection to the place than she did. The last thing she wanted was to see it go to a developer or left to decay. It needed someone who would care for it and see it for what it was. Because that someone wasn't her. Couldn't be. Even if, late at night, when she closed her eyes, she still dreamed of Glenoran's stone walls and the scent of sawdust and rain. Even if, no matter how much distance she put between them, she still thought about Flynn.

Heather stood at the entrance of the nearly empty storage unit, dust motes swirling in the golden evening light. The final boxes were stacked neatly by the door, ready for donation or shipping, and all that remained was a battered old trunk that she hadn't yet brought herself to open. She exhaled, pressing her palms to her thighs. Almost done.

The thought should've brought relief, but it didn't. Instead, it left her feeling... untethered. For months, this task had given her something to focus on. It had given her a reason to stay long enough to sort through the past without getting lost. But once this was over, once the house had sold, there would be nothing left for her here. She brushed her hands off on her jeans and grabbed her phone from her bag, scrolling to the latest email from Mr. Reid she had contacted about her distant relatives.

"There is a potential family connection on your mother's side—a cousin twice removed, still living in Scotland. I've reached out and will follow up when I have more information."

Heather clutched her phone tighter, her chest tightening with something that felt a lot like regret. This was the right thing to do. Glenoran deserved someone who would stay and tend to it like her mother's family once had. Not someone who had spent her whole life running.

Her phone buzzed in her hand. Flynn.

She hesitated, staring at his name on her screen, before pressing accept.

"Campbell," he greeted her, his voice as steady and familiar as ever.

Campbell. Not mo chridhe.

Not even Heather.

It was like he had drawn a line between them, and she had no one to blame but herself.

She ignored the sting of it.

"Mr. Duncan," she said, keeping her tone even. "What's the update?"

There was a beat of silence before he exhaled. "The new roof is nearly done. The new windows are in, and the stonework has been reinforced where needed. It should be all wrapped up next month."

She nodded to herself, even though he couldn't see her. "Good. That's good."

Another silence, heavier this time.

Finally, he spoke again, voice measured. "You've thought about what you're doin' next?"

Heather swallowed. "I have."

"Yer selling it?"

Her grip on the phone tightened, fingers curling around the edge like it was the only thing tethering her to solid ground. The words were right there:

I don't know yet.

But they felt too dangerous. Too real.

She glanced at the old trunk beside her, the faded initials carved into the lid. Her mother's, maybe. Or someone before her. The past always left traces—whispering reminders of things she didn't understand.

Flynn's silence stretched on the other end of the line. Waiting.

Heather exhaled sharply, forcing steel into her spine. "Yes."

Flynn was quiet for so long she thought the call had dropped. Then—finally, a quiet, resigned, "Aye. Figures." His voice was quiet, but it scraped something raw inside her. She didn't know what she expected—understanding? Disappointment? A fight?

Heather squeezed her eyes shut. "It's the right choice."

"For who?"

The words slammed into her like a punch, knocking the air from her lungs. *For who?*

Heather's heart stuttered.

Her nails bit into her palm, but she barely felt it. The answer should have been easy. It was logical, practical, the right choice.

Then why did it feel like a lie?

Her throat worked, but she shoved it down, smothering the flicker of doubt before it could grow into something she couldn't control.

"For Glenoran," she said, forcing the words out before she could take them back. "It needs someone who wants to be here."

A beat. Then another.

"Right," Flynn said finally, his voice unreadable again. "I'll keep ye updated on the final work."

She nodded again, uselessly. "Thanks... Flynn."

He hesitated for half a second. Then, just before the call disconnected, she thought she heard him murmur something in Gaelic—low, rough, like the words had been torn from his throat.

Heather's breath caught. It was quiet—barely more than a whisper—but she heard it.

"Chan eil seo ceart."

This isn't right.

Her chest tightened, a sharp, painful squeeze. She almost—almost—said something. But then the line went dead.

Heather stood there, still holding the phone to her ear like an idiot, as if she could pull back time, as if she could make him say it again.

She pressed her lips together, swallowing the ache threatening to spill over.

It didn't matter.

It *couldn't* matter.

And yet, long after she set her phone down, long after she turned away—those words still echoed in her bones.

This isn't right.

And yet, she walked away.

Chapter 29

Summer was coming to a close, wrapping the Highlands in a golden haze. The days stretched long, the sky a brilliant blue that melted into soft hues of pink and purple come evening.

The air smelled of sun-warmed earth, wild heather, and the distant brine of the sea, carried inland by the shifting breeze. Even the rain, when it came, was different—warmer now, gentler. The kind that misted over the hills instead of lashing against them. Heather had never seen anything like it.

When she arrived, winter clung to the land, the skies perpetually gray, the wind biting her skin. The damp cold had seeped into her bones, making everything feel heavier—like the past she had come to sort through. But now, the world felt alive. The fields near Glenoran were bursting with color—heather and thistle swaying lazily in the breeze, their purples and greens painting the hills like watercolors.

The lochs shimmered under the sunlight, and the forests hummed with birdsong, the deep green of the trees richer than she had ever imagined. It was beautiful. And yet, the more beautiful it became, the more it *hurt* to look at. Every wild bloom and polished stone felt like a thread tightening around her heart—tugging her closer to something she couldn't let herself want.

She had spent the last few months trying not to notice. Trying not to let it sink in. Because soon, she'd be leaving. Heather pushed aside the thought as she walked into her room at the inn, dropping her bag on the floor. She'd finished going through storage and was nearly done with the last few loose ends tying her here. All she needed was confirmation from Mr. Reid about her mother's relatives, and she could move forward with selling Glenoran. Then, she could go back to Millhaven, back to the life she spent so much time building for herself. She told herself that life was still waiting for her. A career. A clean slate. A city where no one expected anything. But the truth was, Millhaven didn't feel like hers anymore. Not really. Not like this place did.

And that terrified her.

Her phone buzzed in her pocket, pulling her from her thoughts. She reached for it absently, but her pulse stuttered when she saw the name on the screen.

Flynn Duncan.

Swallowing, she swiped the message open.

'The House is done. All's left is furniture and final touches. You should come to see it.'

Heather inhaled again slowly, the warmth of the summer air pressing against the windowpanes. It was time. And she wasn't ready. Her fingers hovered over the keyboard. The logical response would be a simple thank you, maybe a promise to stop by soon. Something detached, professional.

Instead, she typed, *"I'll be there this afternoon."*

The moment she hit send, her stomach clenched. Returning to Glenoran felt like stepping into a story that wasn't hers to finish. And worse, stepping into a place that had started to feel like home, even when she fought against it. Even when she fought against him.

Heather pulled up to the house, her fingers gripping the steering wheel tighter than necessary. The sight of Glenoran, fully restored, sent a sharp pang through her chest. The crumbling edges had been smoothed, the windows gleamed in the soft summer light, and the once-weathered wood of the doors now stood strong, rich with new stain. It looked like it had been waiting—like it had been brought back to life. And Flynn had done it.

She inhaled deeply before stepping out of the car. The air smelled like rain and freshly cut wood, like earth warmed by the highland sun. She wasn't ready for this. But she walked up the steps anyway, pushing open the heavy door without knocking. She stepped inside Glenoran, the scent of sawdust and polish lingering in the air. The house was warm, golden afternoon light spilling through the tall windows, illuminating the restored stone walls and rich wood beams. Footsteps echoed through the kitchen.

"Thought I heard you pull up."

Heather turned to find Flynn leaning against the banister, arms crossed over his chest. His shirt was dusty, his jeans stained from work, but he looked the same—steady, solid, like the kind of man who didn't waver. Like the kind of man who didn't leave.

She exhaled, pushing down the strange swirl of emotions. "You finished it."

His blue eyes flickered to her, searching her face. "Aye. Come see."

She followed him down the hall, the sound of their footsteps softened on the refinished floors. The sitting room was first—cozy and elegant, with the grand fireplace at its heart. The original stone had been carefully cleaned, and the old wooden mantel was restored to its former richness. The furniture hadn't arrived yet, but she could already picture it: tufted armchairs by the fire, a whisky decanter on the side table. Heather ran her fingers along the windowsill, nodding. "It looks...right."

Flynn hummed. "That was the idea. Keep the first floor true to what it was, just—" he gestured around, "—Usable."

She followed him into the library next. The built-in shelves stretched floor to ceiling, freshly oiled and waiting to be filled. The large windows framed the lush greenery outside, and in the center of the room, a heavy wooden desk sat, its surface smooth and inviting. Her mother would have loved this.

Heather swallowed. "It's perfect."

Flynn glanced at her, but she quickly turned, moving to the next room before he could look too closely. The dining room was grand, the long wooden table refinished and polished, and the chandelier above it was carefully restored. The room was steeped in history, yet it felt alive again.

He watched her. "You approve, then?"

She forced a light tone. "For someone who spent months

covered in dust and arguing with suppliers, you did a decent job."

His lips twitched, but he didn't smile. "C'mon, one more room." He led her into the kitchen, and the second she stepped inside, something inside her stopped. It was stunning. The flagstone floors had been deep cleaned, and the massive hearth was preserved as a focal point. The cabinetry was rich, dark wood, carefully updated for function while still feeling like it belonged to the house.

A farmhouse sink sat beneath a wide window, and the countertops were smooth, cool stone. It was the kind of kitchen that looked lived in, even though it was brand new. Heather trailed her fingers along the edge of the counter. "It's beautiful."

Flynn leaned against the island, arms crossed over his chest. "Aye. She's bonnie."

There was something in his tone that made her turn. His gaze was steady, unreadable. Heather's pulse ticked up. She knew this moment had been coming since the second she walked through the door.

"I'll start reaching out to my relatives soon," she said, bracing herself. "I just need to confirm a few things before I make the offer."

Flynn's jaw tightened. "You're really sellin' it then?"

She exhaled. "Flynn-"

"Just answer the damn question, Heather."

The kitchen suddenly felt too warm, too small. "Yes," she said, forcing the word out even though it felt wrong. "I told you that from the beginning."

Flynn let out a slow breath, rubbing a hand over his stubbled jaw. "Aye, ye did." He shook his head, muttering something in Gaelic under his breath. "And yet, I still believed you might change your mind."

Heather's throat tightened. "Don't do that."

"Do what?" His voice was sharp now, rough around the edges. "Expect you to stop running?"

Heat flared her cheeks. "I'm not running."

Flynn's laugh was humorless. "You've been runnin' since the day you got here." He stepped closer, his broad frame crowding the space between them. "Tell me something—if I hadnae brought you that damn coffee that morning, would you have run then too?"

Heather stiffened, but he wasn't finished.

"Would you have slipped out of that inn before I woke?"

His voice dropped lower, rougher. "Was that the plan, lass? Leave before I could ask you to stay?"

She hadn't planned it exactly but didn't know what else to do. How he had looked at her that morning and had been so kind and uncomplicatedly good had terrified her. And he knew. That was the worst part. Flynn had seen it all and seen her.

"I–"

"Say it," he pushed, stepping closer still. "Say you don't feel it. Say that night meant nothing—" he didn't hesitate. "—say you don't want me!"

She wanted to.

God, she wanted to lie.

To say it didn't matter. That none of it had changed her. But the truth was right there in her chest, thudding so loud it drowned out every excuse.

Her hands curled into fists at her sides. "I can't!"

"But you won't stay." His voice was quieter now; there was

something raw in it. Something unguarded. "Even if I asked you to."

Her chest ached. "Don't."

Flynn exhaled slowly, eyes fixed on hers like she was the only thing anchoring him to this moment. One breath. One beat of silence.

And then—

She moved.

In an instant, his hands were on her, his mouth finding hers in a kiss that burned through every coherent thought. Her mind short-circuited—no logic, no planning, just heat and want and the press of his body against hers.

Flynn's hand slid from her cheek to the back of her neck, cradling her gently as his forehead came to rest against hers. Their breaths mingled, sharp and shallow.

"Tell me what you want, Heather," he murmured, his voice low and urgent. "Tell me what you're afraid of."

Her pulse thundered in her ears, wild and relentless. His grip was steady—grounding—his fingertips hot against her skin, holding her in place when everything else felt like it was unraveling. She could feel the weight of his breath, the heat of his body, the raw emotion burning in his storm-blue eyes. Frustration. Longing. Something deeper and more dangerous.

Heather's fingers fisted in the front of his shirt, clinging to it like it was the only thing keeping her tethered. "Flynn—"

The rest caught in her throat. The words felt too big, too exposed.

Because what could she say? That she was terrified of how easily he fit into the cracks of her? That she'd spent her whole life staying guarded—and he made her want to throw every wall down? That wanting him didn't feel like a choice but a freefall she couldn't stop?

She was afraid of how badly she wanted this.

Afraid of what it would mean if she stayed.

Even more afraid of what it would mean if she left.

Because leaving would be safer. Cleaner. Easier to explain.

But Flynn Duncan didn't make her feel safe.

He made her feel *alive*.

And that—*that* was the scariest part of all.

Because being alive meant feeling everything.

The ache of grief. The risk of hope.

The terrifying possibility that this—whatever this was—might actually be *real*.

"I—"

The word barely escaped before it caught in her throat, tangled in the storm of everything warring inside her. Panic. Longing. Fear.

She shook her head, hands pushing weakly at his chest—but he didn't move.

He *wouldn't*.

Flynn's voice was quiet, almost calm. But something in it cracked around the edges—like holding back was costing him something real.

"You don't get to run from this."

His hand slid lower, slow and deliberate, resting at the curve of her hip. His thumb traced a lazy circle, grounding and possessive.

"You don't get to run from *me*."

Her breath stuttered in her chest. She wanted to fight him. Wanted to hurl words sharp enough to wound.

To rebuild every wall she'd ever lived behind and slam the

door on whatever this was.

But then his mouth found hers again—hungry, aching, devastating—and every single defense she'd ever built crumbled beneath it.

There was no resistance.

Not anymore.

His kiss devoured her hesitation, burned through her fear until there was nothing left but heat and surrender.

Flynn's hands traveled lower, skimming the delicate curve of her back, pausing at the hem of her dress.

His fingers grazed her skin—soft, reverent. A whisper of heat that made her shiver.

Heather gasped, her breath catching as his lips brushed just above the neckline of her dress—light, teasing kisses that made her skin feel too tight. Her back arched instinctively, body straining toward him. Every place he touched lit a fire beneath her skin.

His hand curved around her waist, holding her steady as he pulled back just enough to meet her eyes.

Blue. Blazing. Bare.

"Tell me, *mo chridhe*," he whispered again, his voice barely holding together. "What keeps ye from lettin' go?"

His gaze—searching, searing—cut straight through her.

Every wall she'd built, every instinct to flee, began to crumble beneath the weight of his stare.

She didn't speak. Couldn't.

The words lodged somewhere in her throat, swept away by the rising tide of want and something deeper.

Her body softened against his, no longer rigid with fear but pliant with need—her apprehension unraveling into something far more dangerous: desire laced with vulnerability.

Flynn's fingers traced the line of her hip, then drifted lower, coaxing a tremble from deep within her. Fire bloomed where he touched, bright and consuming.

His mouth skimmed along her jaw, and when he spoke, it was a molten whisper that made her knees weaken.

"Let me teach your mind what your heart already knows."

The words vibrated through her—low, raw, resolute.

One hand slid from her cheek to the nape of her neck, fingers threading into her hair as he drew her closer. The look in his eyes—hungry, reverent, possessive—devoured her whole.

In one fluid motion, Flynn lifted her. Her breath caught as he carried her with startling ease, setting her down atop the cool, smooth surface of the kitchen counter. The quiet thud echoed through the space, punctuated only by the frantic rhythm of her heartbeat.

The moment felt suspended—timeless.

Flynn reached for the hem of her sundress, his movements swift but tender, the fabric bunching easily around her waist.

Her bare legs brushed against his jeans, the heat of his body stark against the chill of the countertop.

His gaze flicked downward for the briefest moment, the sight of her skin undoing something in him. A guttural sound escaped his throat as his hand slid up her thigh—confident, reverent.

He leaned in slowly, the edge of his breath brushing her lips.

His fingers traced down her sides, a slow and deliberate path that left her skin tingling in their wake.

He never broke eye contact.

Never rushed. Never looked away.

Every move was purposeful.

Every touch said *you're mine.*

Heather's heart pounded, each beat echoing in her ears like a drum summoning something ancient. Her skin burned everywhere his hands lingered, every inch of her alive under his touch.

He didn't rush.

Didn't fumble.

Just moved with that same steady, devastating patience that had been undoing her since the moment he first touched her.

His fingers traced along the bare skin of her thighs as he knelt before her, reverent and unhurried. He pressed a kiss just above her knee—soft, lingering.

The scrape of his stubble dragged a gasp from her throat, the contrast of rough and tender sending a shiver racing up her spine.

He reached for the delicate lace of her underwear, fingers hooking beneath the edge of the fabric. And then—he paused.

His gaze lifted, meeting hers with intensity that stole her breath.

A silent question.

A final out.

But Heather didn't flinch.

Didn't move.

Didn't want to.

Instead, she reached for him—her fingers threading through his hair, trembling, but sure. Her chest rose and fell with ragged breaths, but her grip was steady.

That was all the answer he needed.

Flynn eased the lace down her thighs with agonizing slowness, the soft drag of fabric heightening every nerve, every ache. She clenched around nothing, her body coiled so tight she thought she might unravel before he even touched her.

His lips followed the path his hands had taken—kissing her hip, her inner thigh, everywhere but the place that ached for him most.

Feather light. Worshipful.

A torment she never wanted to end.

When he finally settled between her legs, his hands splayed wide over her thighs, grounding her, she let out a soft, broken breath—her head falling back against the cabinets with a quiet *thud.*

It wasn't just sex.

It hadn't been for a long time.

And that terrified her more than anything.

Because this—*this*—was the kind of moment that left echoes. The kind that carved itself into memory and never let go.

Flynn's voice, low and wrecked, broke the silence. Teasing, yes—but laced with something deeper. Something that sounded a lot like love.

"Mo chridhe..."

His lips brushed her skin, soft and sure.

"Let me show you what you mean to me."

He lowered his head slowly, deliberately, his lips brushing the tender skin of her inner thigh. His tongue followed, drawing soft, teasing strokes that made her breath catch and her hips twitch forward, aching for more.

A moan slipped from her lips—quiet, helpless—as he trailed kisses along her thigh, slow and sinfully patient. Every press of his mouth was a promise, every pause a torment.

Her fingers tangled at the back of his neck, nails digging

lightly into his skin as if she could anchor herself there—hold on as the world tilted beneath her.

The tension between them crackled like lightning waiting to strike. Her body was a livewire—every nerve a lit fuse, every breath a plea.

Flynn's mouth hovered, lips brushing maddeningly close but not quite. His voice was a velvet rasp against her skin.

"Aye, that's it, lass," he murmured. "Don't hold back. Tell me what you need."

Heather's voice trembled, breathless with want.

"You, Flynn," she whispered, broken and bare. "I want you."

A groan rumbled low in his throat—dark, wrecked, and so full of hunger it stole the strength from her legs.

"Good girl," he whispered against her skin, the praise like a brand. "That's what I wanted to hear."

He moved closer, his lips finding the soft, flushed heat of her. His tongue danced across the sensitive folds, a delicate caress that quickly became urgent. He lapped and licked. Explored and demanded. Her breath hitched in her throat. He lowered his head further, and the taste of her was pure ecstasy.

Her hips lifted instinctively, seeking him, chasing the wave that crested higher with every wicked stroke of his tongue. He worked her with maddening precision—slow, relentless, devastating—until thought dissolved and only sensation remained.

Each flick, each languid circle, sent tremors through her, coaxing breathless sounds from her lips she hadn't known she could make. Her fingers fisted in his hair, her thighs trembling around his shoulders, her body arching into him—

wordless and desperate.

She was unraveling for him. Coming apart thread by thread.

The air between them crackled with heat, her body trembling as he deepened the rhythm. A low groan rumbled from his chest, vibrating through her core. She arched into him, breath hitching, pleasure winding tight.

Another flick of his tongue—and she shattered, a strangled cry catching in her throat as her body pulsed around the wave that crashed through her.

He didn't stop. His mouth moved with steady reverence, drawing out every last tremor. Her body quaked beneath him, breath stuttering. When he finally looked up, his eyes found hers—dark, hungry, and full of awe.

Time slowed. The kitchen faded, leaving only the hush between them—soft breaths, flushed skin, the echo of everything they'd just shared. Flynn pressed a kiss to her neck, his touch gentler now, grounding her.

Heather leaned back against the counter, fingers still tracing the line of his jaw. He ran a hand through his hair, eyes locked on hers, quiet and steady.

A shiver ran through her—not from pleasure, but something deeper.

"I... I'm afraid," Heather whispered.

Flynn reached for her hand, their fingers intertwining. His touch was gentle now, a stark contrast to the fire they'd just shared.

"What are you afraid of?" he asked softly.

She looked up at him, eyes brimming with fear. "Getting too close. Getting hurt again. This place—Scotland, Glenoran— it's so heavy. My mom, my dad... the grief is suffocating. This house feels like a tomb. I can't breathe."

Flynn's gaze softened. He understood. Glenoran wasn't just stone and timber—it carried echoes of everything lost. Her pain. Her history. Her ghosts.

He squeezed her hand. "I know. It's not easy. Grief lingers—it doesn't ask permission. But you don't have to carry it alone."

He paused, searching her face. "I want to help you heal."

Heather's voice cracked. "But what if I can't? What if I'm too broken?"

Flynn's half-smile was full of memory. "I knew you were the one the second you showed up at my door, soaked to the bone and covered in cow shite," he said with a soft chuckle. "You looked completely out of place—and yet, somehow, stronger than anyone I'd ever seen."

His thumb brushed her cheek. "I didn't plan on you, Heather. But I knew, right then, you were meant to be in my life."

Her heart twisted. Tears stung. "Flynn," she breathed.

He leaned in, his lips grazing hers—not with hunger, but with quiet promise.

"I'll be here," he whispered. "No matter what."

Heather searched his face, desperate for doubt. But there was none—only steady, unshakable certainty.

It scared her. But it also gave her the one thing she hadn't let herself feel in a long time.

Hope.

Her breath caught. The walls she'd built around her heart—stone by stone—were starting to crack. And somehow, with him, that felt okay.

"I... I need to tell you something," Heather said, voice trembling. She gripped Flynn's hand tighter, grounding herself. "I've never really said it out loud. Not to anyone. But you deserve to know. Why I'm like this."

Flynn didn't speak. He just looked at her—open, steady, patient. His presence was a lifeline, the kind she hadn't known she needed.

"My mother died when I was nine," she began, barely above a whisper. "I remember the silence afterward. The way the house felt hollow. Like everything that had been warm in the world was just... gone."

She stared at their joined hands, as if they held the past in their grip.

"My dad didn't know how to grieve. So he drank. And when he drank, he got mean. It wasn't just yelling. It was the way he said things—the things that stuck. I'd come home and never know which version of him I'd find. If I messed up—or even if I didn't—it was always my fault. Everything was my fault."

Flynn's hand tightened in hers, silent and solid.

"He called me worthless. Said I ruined everything. And the worst part? I started to believe him." Her voice cracked. "The words were like chains. They didn't go away just because I got older."

She swallowed hard. "When he got sick, the alcohol had already destroyed him. And when he died... I thought I'd feel relief. Closure. But it just felt like stepping out of a cage and realizing I didn't know how to live outside it. I was free, but I was still numb. Still carrying it."

Her voice went quiet.

"I don't know who I am without that weight. And some-times... I think I'm afraid to find out."

Heather looked up at Flynn, his eyes dark with quiet ache.

He was listening—really listening—but she still felt like she was sinking under the weight of it all. Her chest ached as the next truth clawed its way out.

"And then there was Ivy…"

She hesitated, gripping his hand tighter.

"She was my best friend for years. The loud one. The fearless one. She pulled me out of my shell, made me feel like I wasn't completely broken. But then… she did something I can't forget."

This was different than her father. This wasn't grief.

This was betrayal.

And shame.

Flynn's brows drew together. "What did she do?"

Heather swallowed hard. "There was this guy—Sam. I never told her I liked him, but she knew. And instead of encouraging me, instead of just letting it be… she made a deal with him. She bribed him to ask me out. Promised she'd sleep with him if he pretended to like me for a night."

Flynn's grip tightened, his jaw ticking. "She *what?*"

"She thought she was doing me a favor," Heather said bitterly. "Said it would help me feel confident. But it wasn't about me. It was about control. She always gets what she wants—no matter who it hurts. And I let her. I let her shape how I saw myself."

Her voice cracked.

"After that, I couldn't unsee it. The way she used people. The way she used *me*. I realized I had to get out. I couldn't stay in that life, around those same patterns. So… I ran. I came here. To Glenoran."

Flynn's thumb traced gently over the back of her hand. "To escape?"

She nodded, brushing away a tear. "Yeah. I thought distance would fix it. That if I ran far enough, I'd finally feel free. But I didn't leave the pain behind....

I brought it with me.

All the broken pieces. All the fear. I thought this place could be a fresh start, but..."

Her voice faltered. "Now I don't even know what I want. I don't know who I am without the pain."

Flynn stepped closer, his voice low and steady. "You don't have to know yet. And you don't have to carry it alone. Whatever you decide—wherever you go—I'm here. I'm not going anywhere."

Heather looked up, breath trembling—something fragile and fierce blooming in her chest.

She didn't want to run anymore.

Not from this.

Not from him.

Not anymore.

Chapter 30

Heather sat at the worn wooden table in the kitchen, Flynn's hoodie draped over her shoulders, the sleeves swallowing her hands whole. The warmth of their moment still clung to the air, mixing with woodsmoke and something faintly sweet—tea, maybe. Or the lingering taste of Flynn on her lips.

She'd told him everything. About her mother. About Glenoran. About Ivy. About the tangled mess of grief and longing she'd carried since she was nine years old. And he'd listened—in his quiet, steady way. No empty reassurances. No fixing. Just being there.

As Flynn rinsed their mugs at the sink, she let her head rest against the back of the chair and exhaled. "You're being suspiciously quiet, Duncan,"

"Aye. Because I'm thinkin'," he said, setting the cups aside. He dried his hands on a rag and turned to face her, arms crossed over his chest. "Come with me for a second."

Heather raised a brow. "Where exactly? Because last time I

followed you, things got a bit... involved."

A slow smirk curved his lips. "Not *that* involved... though keep talkin' like that, and we might never leave this kitchen."

A blush crept up her throat, but she rolled her eyes and stood. "Fine. Lead the way."

Flynn took her hand, as if it were the most natural thing in the world, and guided her out of the kitchen, up the stairs, and down the dimly lit hall. When he stopped in front of a door, her breath caught.

Her mother's room.

Heather's chest tightened. She hadn't really stepped inside since arriving—it had felt too raw. Too real. Too empty. Flynn pushed open the door, stepping aside so she could see.

And suddenly, it wasn't empty at all. The furniture was back—all of it. The antique vanity stood by the window, its surface polished to a soft gleam. The iron twin bed frame was dressed in fresh linens, the same delicate cream and blue pattern she remembered from her arrival. And the quilt. Her mom's pastel, handmade quilt lay proudly across the mattress. The armchair, the bookshelves, even the little wooden jewelry box tucked away in storage—all restored, all placed precisely as they had been.

Heather's hands flew to her mouth.

"Flynn," she whispered, stepping inside. Her legs felt unsteady, as if the moment's weight might knock her over. "You—when did you do all this?"

"Finished it yesterday," He said, watching her intently. "I figured you'd want to see it when your heart could handle it."

Her vision blurred. She reached out, trailing her fingers along the vanity and then the edge of the bed. It was as if she were stepping into the past—like walking into a memory she'd never been allowed to keep.

"She used to sit here," she murmured, running a hand over the vanity stool. "Brush her hair..." She could almost hear the soft bristle of the brush, the quiet creak of the stool, the way her mother would hum under her breath—half lullaby, half prayer.

Flynn didn't say anything; they just gave her the space to take it in. Heather pressed a hand to her chest to steady the ache beneath her ribs.

It would be easy to stay. To curl up in this house, in this history, in the warmth Flynn had built for her here.

But what would staying mean? Would she feel trapped between two worlds —Millhaven and here —never fully belonging to either? She swallowed hard and turned back to Flynn. "Thank you," she said softly. "For everything."

His expression softened. "Ye dinnae have to thank me, *mo chridhe*."

She stepped closer, tilting her head up to meet his gaze. "Maybe I just want to," she said.

Flynn exhaled sharply, as if she'd knocked the breath out of him. She closed the distance between them and kissed him— slow this time, unhurried. A promise, not a demand. Heather sighed into it, letting herself sink—just for now.

Then, just as suddenly, he pulled back and smirked. "C'mon, lass. We've got furniture to move."

Chapter 31

Moving the rest of the furniture back into Glenoran was an exercise in controlled disaster. "You didn't even measure the doorway before dragging this thing upstairs?" Heather accused, hands on her hips, watching Flynn grunt as he wedged the heavy dresser at an awkward angle.

"Aye, well, I thought it would fit."

"You thought?" She echoed, lifting a brow like he'd personally offended her ancestors.

"Would ye rather I leave it downstairs?"

Heather huffed, stepping in to push alongside him. The dresser inched forward, but not without consequences—Flynn's hand slipped, catching her waist, and suddenly, they were too close in the tight hallway.

His breath fanned against her cheek.

Heather swallowed. "You're in my space."

"Aye," he murmured, his eyes darkening. "And I like it that way."

Her stomach flipped. "Are we moving furniture here or making out against it?"

"Why cannae it be both?"

Heather gave him a playful shove, but he caught her wrists, pinning them gently above her head, his body flush with hers. "Still want that dresser moved?" he whispered—then kissed her, hard and quick, like he couldn't help himself.

Her breath hitched.

Then, as if nothing had happened, he let go and went back to maneuvering the dresser—like they hadn't just gotten hot in that hallway.

By the time they finished, the house felt different—fuller. No longer just an abandoned estate, but a home. Heather stood in the center of the sitting room, hands on her hips, surveying their work. "Not bad, Duncan."

Standing behind her, Flynn wrapped his arms around her waist and rested his chin on her shoulder. "Aye, well. Would've been faster if someone hadnae kept distracting me."

She snorted. "Oh, please. You were the one doing the cornering."

"Deny it all you want, lass. But I saw the way ye looked at me lifting that sofa. Ye were practically swooning."

Heather let out a very undignified laugh, but then Flynn turned her in his arms, brushing a thumb across her cheek.

His expression softened. "Ye know, *mo chridhe...* it's okay to want this. All of it."

Heather's breath caught.

This.

This house. This place. This man.

Her heart ached with its weight. She knew what he meant. He wasn't talking about Glenoran.

He was talking about *them.*

She hesitated; the words stuck in her throat.

Flynn's blue eyes searched hers. He wasn't asking her to decide now; he was asking her to see it—to see this as a choice she could make.

Heather exhaled and pressed a slow, lingering kiss on his lips. The rest could wait. But this?

This, she was holding onto with both hands.

Chapter 32

The house was quiet.

For the first time since Heather had arrived in Glenoran, it was just her and the lingering echoes of the past. No workers hammering away at repairs, no piles of dust-covered boxes to sort through. Just her, Byrdie, and the hum of possibility.

She set her bags down in the entryway and exhaled slowly. This was it.

Byrdie jumped onto the window seat in the foyer with a soft chirp, her tail flicking as she surveyed her new domain. The cat stretched luxuriously, then promptly curled up in a warm patch of sunlight. Heather smiled. At least one of them was settling in effortlessly.

She walked through the house, fingers trailing over the newly refinished banister. The house looked and felt different now. The raw edges of its neglect had been smoothed away, its bones polished and strengthened, yet it still carried the same weight and history.

It wasn't just a project anymore.

It was hers.

Heather inhaled deeply, catching the lingering scent of fresh paint mixed with something older—wood smoke from the last fire, the faint trace of lavender and rosemary that always seemed woven into the very walls of Glenoran. The house had found its rhythm again.

She wondered if she had been wrong. If she had spent so much time convincing herself she didn't belong here that, she never considered the possibility that she did.

Her phone buzzed on the kitchen counter, pulling her out of her thoughts.

It was Flynn.

Settled in yet?

Heather smirked and tapped out a response.

More like staring at the walls and hoping I don't regret this decision.

His reply was quick:

That sounds about right. Need a distraction?

Before she could answer, another text popped up.

I'll be there in 10.

She rolled her eyes, but a small smile tugged at her lips.

Of course, he was coming over.

Flynn didn't knock. He just stepped inside, a bag of tools and paint supplies slung over one shoulder. His hair was damp from the summer rain, and his flannel rolled up to his elbows, revealing muscular, work-roughened forearms. He set the bag down with a thud.

"Getting awfully comfortable just walking in here, aren't you?" Heather remarked, leaning against the kitchen counter.

Flynn smirked, unbothered. "Figured you wouldn't mind."

He glanced around. "House looks great. Existential crisis penciled in for later?"

Heather groaned. "Shut up."

Flynn chuckled, nudging the bag toward her. "Thought you might need a second opinion on the library. You were still second-guessing that green, weren't you?"

Heather crossed her arms. "I was confident about it until you walked in here with backup supplies."

Flynn grinned. "Just covering my bases."

Heather sighed but led him toward the library anyway. The deep green walls looked rich and warm in the afternoon light, giving the space a cozy, old-world feel. But standing here now, she wasn't sure.

"I don't know," She chewed her lip, glancing at the far wall. 'I don't know... Is it too much?"

Flynn tilted his head, studying it. "Nah. It suits the place." He shot her a sideways glance. "You just have commitment issues."

Heather gave him a light shove. "Excuse me?"

Flynn only grinned wider. "Ye repainted the sitting room twice. And I recall a full-on spiral over the kitchen tile."

Heather groaned. "Why do you remember everything?"

"Because I like giving you a hard time," he said. Then, softer, "But also because I've spent months watching ye build this place back up."

Heather swallowed, his words hitting a little too close.

Flynn was observing her, but he didn't push. Instead, he turned toward the paint cans. "Alright, let's settle this. If we repaint, I pick the color."

Heather narrowed her eyes. "That's not how this works."

"It is if I win." Flynn reached for one of the paint rollers, giving her a devilish grin. "We could always do a test run. See what happens."

Heather recognized the challenge in his expression, which was too late.

He struck first, dragging a line of green across her bare arm. Heather gasped. "Flynn!"

"Whoops," he said, grinning like the devil himself.

Heather snatched up a paintbrush, launching a counterattack. The next thing she knew, they were in an all-out paint war—laughing, dodging, and smearing green streaks across each other like a pair of children.

Paint dripped from her brush, breathless laughter still on her lips—until Flynn caught her wrist mid-swipe, freezing her in place.

Heather's breath hitched.

They were close now—too close. His fingers were still curled around her wrist, his other hand resting lightly on her waist. There was paint on his cheek and a smudge on his jaw, yet he was looking at her like she was the only thing in the room.

The laughter between them faded into something quieter.

Heather swallowed hard, her pulse suddenly thrumming in her ears. His breath was warm against her cheek, and she suddenly couldn't remember what they'd been arguing about.

Flynn didn't move, his eyes locked on hers. "Still doubting the green?"

Heather exhaled a shaky breath. "It's growing on me." It wasn't just the color. It was what it meant—fresh start, rootedness, growth. Something new, and hers.

Flynn's grin softened into something more thoughtful. "Yeah. Me too."

For a moment, neither of them moved.

Then, before the tension could settle too deep, Flynn released her wrist and cleared his throat, stepping back. "We should probably clean up before you get paint in your hair."

Heather blinked, trying to ground herself. "Bold of you to assume I haven't already."

Flynn laughed, but the charged moment lingered between them.

Later, Heather stood in the library, arms crossed, as she took in the freshly painted walls.

Flynn came up beside her. "You sure this is the one?"

Heather smiled softly.

For the first time in a long time, she was sure of something.

"Yeah," she said. "I think this is it."

Flynn nudged her shoulder. "About time."

Heather rolled her eyes, but there was a warmth in her chest she couldn't deny.

Maybe, just maybe, she was exactly where she was meant to be.

Chapter 33

The paintbrushes were abandoned.

Heather let out an exhausted sigh, swiping at the streak of deep green that had somehow ended up on her cheek. Standing beside her, Flynn looked just as wrecked—his shirt streaked with smudges of paint, his hands stained from where he'd rolled fresh coats over the library walls.

"You look like a Jackson Pollock painting," she teased—though she knew she wasn't any better. Flynn smirked, lifting a brow as he wiped a paint streak down his forearm. "Aye, and you don't?" Heather rolled her eyes, turning toward the sink to wash her hands, but Flynn's voice stopped her. "Y'know, there's a much better way to clean up."

She turned back, catching the way his gaze darkened ever so slightly. Her pulse kicked up a notch as she swallowed. "Are you suggesting—"

Flynn stepped closer, tilting his head, voice low and deliberate. "I'm suggestin' we stop wasting time scrubbing paint off in separate places when there's a perfectly good shower upstairs."

Heather blushed at his bold suggestion. He was giving her an out. He always did. If she wanted to laugh it off, if she wanted to step away, he'd let her. But she didn't want to step away. She wanted to step closer.

So she did.

Flynn didn't move at first; he just waited, his patience like gravity pulling her in without a single touch. Heather let out a slow breath, searching his face. "Alright," she murmured. "Let's get cleaned up."

The smirk he gave her was devastating. She barely had time to react before his fingers curled around her wrist, tugging her gently but insistently toward the stairs. The bathroom was filled with steam before they even stepped inside. The old pipes rattled slightly as warm, inviting water poured from the shower head. Heather stood by the sink, her heartbeat loud in her ears. She could feel Flynn behind her, his presence like heat against her skin. He peeled off his shirt in one smooth motion. Heather didn't mean to stare... but she did.

His muscles flexed with every movement at the broad span of his chest. His skin was streaked with paint—deep green across his collarbone and a smear along his ribs. She swallowed hard, fingers twitching at her sides. Flynn caught her staring. Of course, he did. A slow, knowing smirk curved his lips. "Your turn, lass." Heather's breath caught. She could back out. She could laugh it off. Or—

She reached for the hem of her shirt and pulled it over her head. The air between them thickened. Flynn's gaze dropped. Not in a way that felt greedy or rushed, but in a way that *devoured.* Like he wanted to memorize every inch of her—

every freckle, every curve.

For so long, Heather had hated what she saw in the mirror. She wasn't blind—she knew she had her mother's emerald eyes, her mother's delicate features, her mother's curls that always refused to be tamed. But where her mother had been ethereal, stunning—a fairy out of a dream—Heather had spent years feeling like a poor imitation.

A shadow.

A reflection, never quite good enough.

And yet—Flynn wasn't looking at a ghost of the past. He wasn't comparing. He was looking at *her*. And he saw something worth wanting. Heat crept up her neck, but for once, she didn't shrink away from it. She didn't fold into herself or try to disappear. Neither did he. They undressed in silence—slow, unhurried. Letting the moment stretch. Letting the tension build. It was like stepping into something inevitable when Heather stepped under the water. The warmth cascaded over her skin, washing away the paint, the exhaustion, the weight of everything. And then Flynn stepped in behind her. His hands found her waist first—a simple touch, grounding, steady. His thumbs brushed her damp skin, trailing slow circles along her hips. Heather inhaled sharply, eyes fluttering shut as he pressed closer, his body warm, solid, inescapable.

His lips brushed her shoulder, then traced a path to the hollow beneath her ear. She shivered, not from the water, but from him.

"Still with me?" Flynn murmured, his voice like smoke, his breath warm against her neck. Heather's fingers curled over his hands, gripping him as if he were the only thing keeping her standing. "Yes," she whispered. "I'm with you."

That was all it took.

Flynn turned her in his arms, capturing her mouth in a kiss that stole the air from her lungs. It was slow at first—a quiet unraveling, a deep pull, the kind of kiss that felt like a **q**uestion and an answer all at once. Heather melted into him and let herself want. The water rushed over them, their skin slick and warm, and nothing else mattered. Not Glenoran. Not the past. Not the fear.

Only this.

Only him.

Only them.

Heather stirred beneath the sheets, her body warm, aching in the best way. She kept her eyes closed, just feeling —the softness of the linen, the steady rise and fall of breath beside her.

Flynn.

The realization hit her all at once. Last night hadn't been some fleeting moment, some impulse driven by exhaustion or proximity. She had chosen this. Chosen *him.* And now, morning had come. She turned her head slightly, her heart thudding in her chest. Flynn was still asleep, his face relaxed, his dark lashes stark against his tanned skin. He looked different this way—softer, peaceful.

She wanted to trace the faint scruff along his jaw. To memorize his shape. She'd never experienced a morning like this—the raw intimacy of it all. Instead, she swallowed hard and exhaled. She had spent so much of her life running—from places, people, and *herself.* But this morning, for the first time in a long time... She didn't want to run.

She wanted to stay.

Heather shifted carefully, rolling onto her side, closing the distance between them. As if sensing her movement, Flynn stirred, his arm slipping around her waist, pulling her against him instinctively, even in sleep. A small smile tugged at Heather's lips. Maybe, just maybe, this was exactly where she was meant to be.

Heather lay still, listening to the slow, steady rhythm of Flynn's breathing. The weight of his arm draped over her waist, the warmth of his body pressed against hers, solid and grounding —it sent a quiet thrill through her. She wasn't used to this—the comfort of waking up next to someone, the intimacy of shared warmth beneath the covers. It felt foreign and familiar all at once.

Flynn shifted slightly, his nose brushing against her shoulder as he exhaled a sleepy sigh. His grip around her tightened, like even in sleep, he wasn't ready to let her go. She bit her lip, torn between letting him rest and the overwhelming urge to see his eyes—those deep, piercing blue eyes that always seemed to see straight through her. Before she could decide, Flynn murmured something under his breath, his voice rough with sleep. Then, his lips grazed her bare shoulder in a lazy, absentminded kiss.

Heather stilled, warmth blooming in her chest. His small, unconscious action sent a gentle ache through her—not heavy, not overwhelming, just something quiet and steady, settling deep in her bones. Flynn hummed softly, then blinked awake, his arm flexing around her. She felt it the moment he registered where he was, the slow awareness seeping into him as his fingers traced over the curve of her hip. His lips brushed against her skin again, deliberate this time.

"Morning, mo chridhe," He murmured against her shoulder, his voice thick with sleep. Heather swallowed, her heart fluttering at the sound—the warmth of it, laced with something steady and sure. Something that made her feel safe, even as it left her breathless. She turned her head, meeting his gaze. His blue eyes were soft, still heavy with sleep, but there was something else there, too. Something that made her chest feel tight.

Flynn studied her, his expression unreadable for a long moment. Then, slowly, a lazy, knowing smirk curved his lips. "Didn't bolt," he mused, voice teasing but gentle.

Heather rolled her eyes, but the warmth in her chest spread. "Shut up."

Flynn chuckled, his fingers brushing up her spine, sending a shiver down her spine. "I'm serious," he murmured, his voice quieter now. "I half expected to wake up alone." Heather hesitated, her throat tightening. "I thought about it," she admitted, her voice barely above a whisper.

Flynn's smirk faltered, replaced by something softer. "And what made you stay?" Heather swallowed, her fingers curling slightly against his chest. "I don't know," she said honestly. "I just... I didn't want to leave." Flynn searched her face, something unreadable flickering through his eyes. Then, instead of pushing for more, he exhaled, his forehead resting against hers. "Good," he murmured.

Heather closed her eyes for a moment, letting the quiet settle between them, allowing herself just to be here, in this moment. She didn't know what came next. Didn't know what this meant or where they were heading. But for now, she knew one thing.

She wasn't running.

Not this time.

Heather stretched beneath the covers, the warmth of Flynn's body lingering against her skin. She felt light, almost weightless, starkly contrasting the heavy uncertainty she had carried for weeks. The quiet hum of the morning filled the room—the distant rustle of trees outside, the faint creaks of Glenoran settling, and the rhythmic sound of Flynn's breathing beside her.

Just as she was about to close her eyes again, a familiar, indignant chirp broke the peace. Heather peeked over the edge of the covers just in time to see Byrdie perched on the nightstand, tail flicking impatiently, her green eyes fixed on Flynn with pure feline disapproval.

Heather smirked. "Uh oh. You've been caught." Flynn cracked one eye open, his brows furrowing as he slowly registered the cat staring him down. He let out a low groan. "Bloody hell."

Byrdie chirped again, louder this time, her little nose twitching in accusation. Heather turned fully onto her side, propping her head on her hand as she watched the silent standoff. "I think she's mad you took her spot."

Flynn exhaled through his nose, rubbing a hand down his face. "You mean the spot on the bed she lets you borrow?"

"Exactly. I'm just the tenant here." She grinned.

Byrdie made her point clear by hopping onto the bed and landing directly on Flynn's chest with surprising force for such a small creature. Flynn let out an exaggerated grunt. "Och, are ye serious?"

Byrdie, completely unbothered, circled twice before sitting squarely on his sternum, her fluffy tail curling around her paws. Her glare was unwavering as if assessing whether or not he deserved to stay. Heather laughed as Flynn sighed in defeat, dropping his head back against the pillow. "This is it, isn't it? I've lost."

"I hate to break it to you, but she outranks you," Heather teased, reaching out to scratch behind Byrdie's ear. Byrdie purred a deep, smug rumble but didn't move from her perch.

"Traitorous wee beastie." Flynn opened one eye, shooting Heather a look. "Let me get this straight. I've had to work for *your* trust for weeks, and the cat's already got a throne?"

Heather shrugged. "She's been here longer." Flynn exhaled dramatically, giving Byrdie a pointed look. "Fine, lass. We'll negotiate terms."

Byrdie blinked slowly as if considering the offer, then stretched luxuriously before hopping off Flynn's chest and onto the empty pillow beside Heather, nestling into it as though she had allowed this arrangement to continue.

Flynn groaned. "So I'm allowed to stay, then?" Heather smirked. "Seems like it. Consider yourself lucky." Flynn rolled onto his side, propping himself up on his elbow. "Aye, I do." His voice had softened, and her stomach flipped when Heather met his gaze.

He wasn't just talking about Byrdie anymore.

Heather swallowed, her fingers grazing absently over the edge of the blanket. There was something about this moment—the warmth, the ease of it—that made her chest ache in a way that had nothing to do with fear. Flynn reached out, tucking a stray curl behind her ear before trailing his fingers lightly down her arm. "I like waking up with you," he admitted, quiet and unguarded.

Heather's breath caught. She wanted to say something, but the words tangled in her throat. Byrdie chose that moment to roll onto her back, stretching luxuriously before letting out a tiny snore.

Heather huffed out a laugh, breaking the tension. "Looks like you're stuck with both of us."

Flynn grinned, his hand still resting against her arm. "Aye, seems like I've got my work cut out for me."

Heather tilted her head. "You sure you're up for it?"

His fingers slid down to her hand, lacing them together. "I've never been more sure of anything in my life, lass."

Heather's heart stuttered, but she didn't pull away this time. She squeezed his hand back, and for once didn't feel so lost.

Chapter 34

She wasn't ready to make a decision—but she wasn't prepared to leave either. So, she settled in. For now.

Mornings at Glenoran started slow, with Byrdie curling up at the foot of her new king-sized bed as if she belonged there, her snores filling the quiet room. The primary suite was something out of a dream, a space Flynn had built with his hands. Expansive bay windows overlooked the misty moors, and the whirlpool tub—that glorious whirlpool tub— quickly became her sanctuary. But it wasn't just the suite that felt different. The entire house had changed.

When she first arrived, Glenoran had felt like a tomb— hollow, haunted by time and loss, its grand rooms filled with shadows and whispers of the past. The walls had creaked beneath the weight of history, and every darkened hallway had felt like a reminder of all the things she'd lost. She had tiptoed through its halls like a stranger, like she didn't belong, like she was just passing through.

Now, warmth had seeped into the very bones of the place.

The once-drafty corridors no longer felt cavernous but cozy, touched by the scent of fresh wood and the soft glow of light filtering through restored windows. The hearth in the sitting room crackled each evening, filling the space with golden light—not a relic of the past, but a steady, welcoming presence. The kitchen—where she had once stood feeling out of place—had become a second home, a place where she and Flynn made tea in the evenings, where Byrdie perched on the counter like a queen overseeing her domain.

Heather had never lived anywhere quite like this. Evenings were spent unpacking—truly unpacking, not just living out of suitcases, not just existing in a place, but making it her own.

She found little ways to claim the space: a vase of fresh wildflowers on the windowsill, a stack of well-loved books beside the bed, one of her mother's old sweaters draped over the chair in the corner. There was a candle on the nightstand that smelled like cedar and rain, a fuzzy throw blanket on the couch, and boots left by the front door—not because she was visiting but because she belonged here. Glenoran had been lost and forgotten once. So had she.

But now, both of them had been **restored.**

Flynn had stopped raising his brows when he found her curled up on the massive bed, wrapped in blankets, Byrdie tucked beside her. He smirked, muttered something about her "settlin' in nicely," and kissed her before heading downstairs. Heather ignored how her heart twisted whenever he said things like that. She wasn't staying. And she wasn't going either.

She sat on the edge of the bed, the soft morning light spilling through the bay windows. Byrdie stretched beside her, flicking her tail lazily, but Heather barely noticed. Her phone was in her hand. Ivy's name was on the screen. For a long time, she just stared at it.

Ivy had called her months ago, voice dripping with regret, with nostalgia, with all the little hooks that made Heather believe—just for a second—that maybe, maybe they could go back to the way things were. But now? After everything? She wasn't that girl anymore. Heather took a deep breath and hit call. Ivy answered on the second ring, her voice bright, effortless.

"Well, well. Look who finally remembered I exist."

Heather ignored the jab. "I've been busy."

"I bet." Ivy let out a little sigh. "Living in your Highland castle with your hunky contractor, I assume? I saw the pictures you posted. You're basically in a damn fairy tale."

Heather's stomach tightened. She hadn't expected this Ivy. The teasing Ivy. The charming Ivy. The Ivy who made her feel like they were just two best friends catching up, like nothing had ever happened. Like she hadn't betrayed her.

"I need to talk to you about something," Heather said, cutting straight to the point.

"Oh, God. You sound serious." Ivy's laugh was light but tinged with something sharper. "Are you dying? Did you elope with a sexy Scotsman? Are you role-playing *Outlander* with Sam Heughan? Please tell me it's something good!"

Her fingers clenched the bedsheets. "I think we need to stop this."

Silence.

Then, Ivy scoffed. "Stop what?"

Heather exhaled slowly. "This. Us. Pretending like we can just go back to how things were."

Ivy's voice lost its playful lilt. "Oh, for fuck's sake, Heather.

Are we really doing this again?"

Heather swallowed. "I forgave you."

"Then why the hell are we having this conversation?"

Heather hesitated. "Because I'm not the same person I was."

Ivy let out a dry laugh. "Oh, so what, you found yourself in the Highlands? Is this your *Eat, Pray, Love* moment?"

Heather ignored the jab. "I used to think I needed you." Her voice was quiet, but steady. "That I wouldn't survive without you in my life. But Ivy... I don't need you anymore."

Ivy went silent again. This time, the silence was dangerous. When she finally spoke, her voice was softer, but laced with something cold. "So that's it? You're just...*done* with me?"

Heather swallowed hard. She had imagined this moment so many times—breaking away. But she hadn't expected it to feel like this. Like mourning.

Like losing something she had spent her whole life holding onto. But she wasn't losing Ivy. She was letting her go.

"I love you, Ivy," she admitted. "And I always will. But I can't keep making excuses for you. I can't keep pretending that what you did didn't hurt me."

"I *apologized*—"

Heather cut her off. "You manipulated me."

Ivy let out a frustrated noise. "Holy shit, Heather. It wasn't that deep."

Heather's chest tightened, but she kept her voice even. "It was to me."

Ivy exhaled sharply. "I can't believe you're doing this. After everything."

Heather's throat ached. "I know."

Ivy was quiet for a long time. When she spoke again, her

voice was detached. "Fine. If that's what you want."

Heather closed her eyes, forcing herself to breathe. "It is."

Another pause. And then, in a voice too sweet, too practiced, too Ivy, she said, "You know, whoever this *guy* is— he won't stick around forever. They never do."

Heather's stomach twisted.

"You're a runner, babe," Ivy continued, her voice light and sharp as a blade. "You always have been. And maybe you're playing house now, but sooner or later, you'll get scared, and you'll leave. And when that happens? Don't come crawling back to me."

Heather's fingers tightened around the phone. "Goodbye, Ivy."

She hung up before Ivy could say another word. Her hands were shaking. Byrdie let out a quiet chirp, rubbing against her arm. Heather reached for her, burying her fingers in the soft fur, grounding herself. She had done it. She had cut the tether that had kept her bound for so many years. It should have felt freeing.

Instead, it just felt quiet. But maybe... maybe that was okay. Maybe peace was supposed to feel like this. Heather exhaled slowly, setting her phone aside as the weight of it all settled in. The air in the room felt still, like the moment after a storm when the world is holding its breath.

Ivy had been in her life for so long, woven into the fabric of her memories. Every late-night phone call, every inside joke, every whispered secret between them—it was all still there. But that history wasn't enough anymore.

Heather wasn't that girl anymore. She pulled the blankets tighter around herself, curling into their warmth as exhaustion crept in, heavier than before. Her body ached—not from physical strain but from the emotional toll of finally letting go.

Sleep didn't come easily, but when it did, it was deep. And when morning arrived, she was still wrapped in that strange, aching quiet.

The sun had barely risen when her phone rang.

Heather groaned, rolling over to fumble for it on the nightstand. Byrdie grumbled in protest and buried herself more deeply into the blankets. Heather rubbed her eyes and squinted at the screen.

Dr. Morrow.

A flicker of anticipation ran through her as she answered. "Hello?"

"Ms. Campbell," Dr. Morrow's voice came through, brimming with excitement. "I have news about your flag."

Heather stilled. She hadn't stopped thinking about that fragile piece of history since the day she'd found it tucked away in the attic, along with the torn scrap of Mackenzie tartan and that cryptic note:

April 16th.

"Go on," she urged, gripping the phone tighter.

Dr. Morrow chuckled softly. "You may want to sit down."

Her anxiety flared. "Just tell me."

"After deep research and consulting with a few experts on Jacobite artifacts, we've confirmed that the flag you found is a battle standard from Culloden."

Heather's stomach dropped. "Culloden? As in *the* Culloden?"

"The very same," Dr. Morrow confirmed. "The note, the tartan, and, most importantly, the flag's design all line up. It's been missing for over 270 years—presumed lost or destroyed after the battle."

Heather pressed a hand to her forehead. "Are you saying this—this relic—belonged to the Mackenzies at Culloden?"

"Not just the Mackenzies," Dr. Morrow said, his voice lowering. "To *your* Mackenzies. This could have been carried by one of your ancestors that day."

A lump formed in her throat. "But how did it end up at Glenoran?"

"We can only speculate," he admitted. "It's possible someone in your family smuggled it out after the battle, hidden away for generations. We know this is an astonishing discovery—not just for your family but for Scotland itself."

Heather turned toward the window, looking out over the snow-dusted hills. Glenoran had always felt like a place steeped in history, but this... This changed everything.

Dr. Morrow hesitated before adding, "Ms. Campbell, museums will want to see this. The Scottish National Museum is already interested in an official assessment."

She swallowed hard, heart pounding. "You're saying I should hand it over?"

"That's entirely up to you, dear." Dr. Morrow said gently. "But you have something extraordinary here. Something that deserves to be known."

Heather nodded absently, though he couldn't see her. The flag, tartan, and note weren't just remnants of the past. They were pieces of a story her family had safeguarded for centuries.

Now, she had to decide what to do with it.

She sat in Glenoran's grand old library, beautifully restored, thanks to Flynn and his crew. After picking up the relics from Dr. Morrow that afternoon, she carefully spread the flag on the massive oak table before her. Even after Dr. Morrow's call, she still couldn't believe what she was looking at. The fabric was faded and delicate, but the worn stitching of the St. Andrew's Cross was still strong. The scrap of Mackenzie tartan lay beside it, a silent witness to the history it carried.

This wasn't just some forgotten artifact. It was proof that someone—her ancestor—had been there at Culloden, standing for what they believed in. And somehow, through centuries of loss and change, wars and rebuilding, it survived.

A knock at the doorway made her turn. Flynn stood there, arms crossed over his chest, his blue eyes sharp as they swept over the table. "That's it, huh?" he said, stepping inside. "The flag?"

She nodded. "Dr. Morrow confirmed it. It hasn't been seen since the battle."

Flynn let out a low whistle. "Damn." He studied it, then glanced at her. "What are ye gonna do with it?"

Heather swallowed, tracing a finger lightly over the tartan scrap. "The museum wants it. Dr. Morrow thinks it belongs to Scotland—to history."

Flynn leaned a hip against the table. "And what do you think?"

She hesitated. "I don't know."

But that wasn't true. She did know. She just hadn't let herself say it yet. Her fingers hovered over the faded flag fabric, its texture rough beneath her touch. This history had been hidden in Glenoran for over two centuries, surviving war, time, and even the slow decay of forgotten things. It had belonged to her family, but it also belonged to Scotland.

The weight of that realization settled deep in her chest. She thought about all the people who had never gotten the chance to see it, to know that it had survived when so much had been lost at Culloden. It felt wrong to keep it locked away here, tucked into a private collection, or even just left within the walls of Glenoran. And more than that—it wasn't what her mother would have wanted.

Eilidh Mackenzie Campbell had spent her life chasing history, uncovering lost stories, and ensuring the past was preserved, not buried. She had dedicated herself to Jacobite research—to understanding the echoes of Culloden and the people who had fought there. If she had lived to see this, she would have given everything to make sure it was shared, protected, honored.

Heather exhaled slowly, her fingers tracing the edge of the flag. Her mother had kept so many secrets, but she had also left Heather with this. Maybe not as a burden—but as a choice. And now, Heather knew exactly what to do. She swallowed hard and looked up at Flynn.

"I'm giving it to the museum."

His brow lifted slightly like he'd expected her to wrestle with it longer. "Yeah?" She nodded, firmer this time. "This isn't just mine anymore. It belongs to something greater. It should be somewhere people can see it—where it can be remembered." Flynn studied her, then gave a slow nod. "That's a bonnie choice."

Heather exhaled and felt at peace for the first time since she had found the flag. She'd come here thinking she was closing a door—fixing up the house to leave it behind. But instead, Glenoran had given her something back. A piece of herself, a piece of her family's story, and now, the chance to do something that mattered. And she wasn't ready to walk away from that.

She turned to Flynn, who watched her with his quiet, steady gaze—the one that always made her feel like he saw more of her than she was ready to admit.

Heather ran a hand along the banister, feeling the smooth wood beneath her palm. This house had been a burden. A weight. A reminder of everything she'd lost. But it was also a beginning.

She exhaled, grounding herself, letting the truth settle deep in her bones.

"I'm staying."

Flynn stilled, just for a second. His lips twitched, but his eyes—his eyes softened, something flickering there she couldn't quite name. "Yeah," he said, like he'd been waiting for her to realize it. "I got that."

Heather narrowed her eyes. "What do you mean, you got that?"

Flynn shrugged, arms crossed over his broad chest. "You've been walking around here like ye own the place."

"I *do* own the place," she pointed out.

His smirk deepened. "You do now."

Heather rolled her eyes, but the warmth spread anyway,

curling in her chest and wrapping around her heart.

For months, she had been running from this. Convincing herself that Glenoran was a stop on the way to something else, a project to finish and leave behind. But now?

Now, she couldn't imagine leaving.

Not Glenoran.

Not Flynn.

The thought nearly stole the breath from her lungs.

She glanced around, taking in the space—the grand staircase, the sturdy beams, the soft light spilling in through the tall windows. The house didn't feel heavy anymore. It didn't feel haunted. It felt like it was at peace. She exhaled slowly, turning back to Flynn.

"And here I thought you'd finally be relieved to be done with this job."

Flynn let out a low chuckle. "Oh, don't get me wrong, I was looking forward to the day I didn't have to patch up another one of this place's ancient walls." He tapped a knuckle on the table. "But I guess it wouldn't have felt right, leaving Glenoran without you in it."

Her breath hitched. Something in her chest tightened, a slow, sweet ache blooming beneath her ribs.

She searched his face, trying to decide if he meant the house—the project—or something more. But the way he looked at her, quiet and steady, like he knew exactly how much this moment meant, made her think maybe it wasn't just Glenoran he wanted to stay. "You know," she mused, "if I'm staying, that means you're stuck with me."

Flynn tilted his head slightly, as if considering it. "Think I can handle that."

Heather arched a brow. "Oh? Even when I keep changing

my mind about paint colors?"

His grin was slow, lazy. "Wouldnae be the first time."

"And when I get in the way while you're working?"

He stepped closer, just enough that she had to tilt her head to look up at him. "I'll manage."

Heather swallowed, the air between them shifting, deepening. "And if I decide I need another project done?"

Flynn reached out, catching a curl between his fingers, rubbing it absently before letting it slip away. "Then I guess I'm exactly where I'm supposed to be." The warmth in his voice, the way his eyes searched hers, like he saw something in her she wasn't even sure she was ready to believe in, gave her a sense of peace. She finally let herself want this. Not just the house. Not just the history, but Flynn. She didn't move away. Didn't want to.

"Good," she murmured, her breath catching as his hand brushed her face. "Because I think I'd like that."

Flynn's smile softened, his thumb skimming lightly along her cheek. "Yeah," he said, his voice rough, steady. "Me too."

Glenoran had been lost.

So had she.

But not anymore.

Chapter 35

Heather stood at the massive stone entrance of the Scottish National Museum, the weight of history pressing against her chest. In her hands, she carried a carefully packed case that contained not just a fragile piece of cloth—but a piece of her family's past. The Jacobite battle flag, the scrap of Mackenzie tartan, and the parchment had already been authenticated. Now, it was time to decide their future.

She inhaled deeply, steadying herself. This was the right thing to do.

The doors swung open, and she stepped into the museum's grand hall. The air was thick with the scent of aged paper, polished wood, and the faint, metallic tang of preserved artifacts. The vaulted ceiling stretched high above her, and the towering walls were lined with relics of Scotland's past— armor from the Wars of Independence, faded battle maps, and weapons that had witnessed the rise and fall of kings.

She approached the reception desk, where a young woman

greeted her with a polite smile.

"I'm here for Dr. Henderson. She's expecting me."

The receptionist nodded and gestured toward an office behind the main exhibit halls. "Of course, right this way."

Heather followed her through the quiet corridors until they reached a modest but cozy office filled with books, historical sketches, and carefully labeled artifacts. Dr. Flora Henderson, a woman in her mid-fifties with sharp blue eyes and the kind of quiet intensity that made you sit straighter without realizing it.

"You must be Heather Campbell."

Dr. Henderson stood, offering a warm handshake. "I've been eager to meet you in person."

She returned the handshake, her grip firm despite the nerves swirling in her stomach. "I still can't believe everything you and your team have uncovered."

Dr. Henderson smiled. "It's truly remarkable." She gestured to the chair across from her desk. "Please, have a seat. Let's talk about what comes next."

Heather sat, carefully placing the case on the desk between them. With gentle precision, she unlatched it, lifting the lid to reveal the faded battle flag, its fabric worn but still striking, the St. Andrew's cross stitched into the cloth. The Mackenzie tartan lay beside it, frayed at the edges but still vibrant in its green and blue pattern. The same note she had found tucked away in Glenoran:

April 16, 1746.

Culloden.

Dr. Henderson let out a soft breath, reverence flickering in her expression.

"It's one thing to read about history," she murmured, "but

quite another to hold it in your hands." She looked up at Heather, her expression serious but kind. "The authentication process is complete. We've confirmed that the flag is an original battle standard from Culloden, likely smuggled away after the battle and hidden for generations. The tartan matches records of Mackenzie's regimental colors. And the parchment..." She exhaled. "It's an eyewitness account. A firsthand letter written by one of the men who fought that day."

Heather's breath caught. "Someone in my family?"

Dr. Henderson nodded, pulling out a document and sliding it toward her. "Yes. We traced the handwriting back to Harris Mackenzie—your direct ancestor. He was there at Culloden. He fought and survived."

Heather's fingers trembled as she reached for the letter—Harris's words, folded in time like a secret waiting for her. Faded but still legible, carrying the weight of a battlefield lost to time. A desperate plea to a loved one. A vow to return home. A promise never fulfilled.

What must it have been like for Harris, and how must it have felt to ultimately lose a fight he believed so strongly in? Yet his voice was reaching out from the shadows of history, bridging centuries with tales of valor and sacrifice.

She swallowed hard as the weight of history settled in her chest. The thought that she'd nearly left all of this behind—nearly gone back to Millhaven—felt impossible now. The thought now seemed unimaginable, as if this discovery was a calling she hadn't yet realized. Dr. Henderson watched her carefully.

"This is a significant piece of Scotland's past, Heather. The museum would be honored to house it, to ensure that it's preserved and shared with the world."

Heather nodded absently, still staring at the letter.

"You don't have to decide immediately," Dr. Henderson continued. "But given its historical value, we'd like to create an exhibit around it—around the flag, the tartan, and Harris Mackenzie's account."

Heather exhaled slowly. She'd come here thinking she was handing these things over. But now, as she sat there, holding the letter of an ancestor who had fought and bled for his beliefs, she realized she wasn't just giving away artifacts.

She was telling a story.

Not just Scotland's.

Not just history's.

Hers.

She looked up at Dr. Henderson. "I want that too," she said firmly. "I want people to see this, to know what happened. But I'd like to stay involved. To help tell the story."

Somewhere, her mother was smiling.

Dr. Henderson smiled. "I was hoping you'd say that."

A lightness settled in Heather's chest. She thought she was closing a chapter, but instead, she'd found a way to carry it forward.

"One more thing," Dr. Henderson added, reaching for another folder. "We've also been working on additional genealogical research into the Mackenzies of Glenoran."

Heather's heart pounded. "And?"

Dr. Henderson slid the folder toward her. "It seems your family's connection to Culloden and Scotland runs even deeper than we thought."

Heather stared at the folder, her hands steady now.

She had come here expecting to let go.

Instead, it felt like she was just beginning.

Chapter 36

Heather's fingers hovered over the folder, her pulse steady but fast. She had already uncovered so much—fragments of history that had survived for over two centuries, remnants of a past she hadn't known was hers. And yet, here she was, about to open another door.

She glanced up at Dr. Henderson. "What exactly did you find?"

Dr. Henderson leaned forward, hands clasped. "Your ancestor, Harris Mackenzie, wasn't just a soldier at Culloden. He was a courier—someone trusted to carry critical messages between Jacobite forces. He hadn't just been fighting for a cause—he was protecting secrets that could've changed the course of history."

Heather blinked, stunned. "What kind of information?"

Dr. Henderson opened the folder, pulling out a photocopy of another fragile document. "This," she said, pointing to the faded ink, "is a recovered record from a secret Jacobite network. It lists Harris Mackenzie as a key contact—one of the men responsible for moving intelligence between Bonnie Prince Charlie's forces and sympathizers across the Highlands."

Heather traced the name on the page, its weight pressing down on her. "So, he wasn't just a soldier. He was a messenger."

Dr. Henderson nodded. "And, based on this record, it appears he carried something of great importance on the day of the battle. Something that was never recovered."

Heather's breath caught. "Are you saying—?"

"We believe Harris was carrying intelligence about a hidden Jacobite treasure—gold smuggled in from France to fund the rebellion." Dr. Henderson's eyes shone with the thrill of discovery. "But he never got the chance to deliver it."

Heather exhaled slowly, sitting back in her chair. "So, what happened to it?"

Dr. Henderson sighed. "That's the mystery. Some historians believe the treasure was lost in the chaos of the battlefield. Others think it was hidden—maybe even buried somewhere near Glenoran." She tapped the parchment in the case. "Harris's letter might be the key to finding out what happened."

Heather's mind reeled. Could Glenoran hold more than just her family's history? Could it be part of an even bigger story?

There's no way.

She shook her head, trying to push the incredulous thought aside.

She swallowed, looking up at Dr. Henderson. "And you think there's still a chance the treasure exists?"

Dr. Henderson hesitated. "It's possible. If it was hidden rather than lost, and if Harris left clues in his letter, there's a chance it could still be out there."

Was she really about to embark on some crazy treasure hunt? The thought both excited and frightened her. But the allure of adventure was too strong. How long had she spent being a bystander to her own life, watching from the sidelines as the world moved around her? Heather leaned forward, determination igniting in her eyes.

She let the idea settle in her mind. The house had already given her so much—her past, roots, and connection to a history she had once ignored. But could it also hold the key to something even greater? Something people had been searching for, for generations?

Heather blinked. Once. Twice. Then, let out a sharp, disbelieving laugh.

"You're telling me that my ancestor wasn't just some soldier—he was a Jacobite spy? And that he might have hidden gold meant for Bonnie Prince Charlie?" She shook her head, leaning back in her chair. "That sounds like something from a historical novel, not my life."

Dr. Henderson gave a small, knowing smile. "That's what everyone says—until the evidence stacks up."

Heather looked down at the letter Harris Mackenzie had written, the faded ink like a whisper from the past. But what if it's true?

Her fingers traced the delicate parchment, reverent now in a way she hadn't been before.

She exhaled slowly. "Okay. Let's say this treasure is real... Where do I start?"

Dr. Henderson smiled knowingly. "That's up to you, Miss Campbell."

Heather drove back to Glenoran with the folder resting on the passenger seat beside her, the museum's offer still echoing in her mind. The weight of what she'd just learned pressed against her chest—not suffocating this time, but exhilarating.

She had thought she was settling into a home.

Now, she realized she might be unraveling a mystery.

As she pulled into the long gravel drive, Glenoran stood before her, bathed in the golden glow of the setting sun. The house—her house—looked more alive than ever. It had survived war, abandonment, and the passage of time itself. And if Harris had hidden something here, if secrets were still buried within these walls, she was determined to find them.

Byrdie meowed from the passenger seat, stretching lazily before hopping onto Heather's lap.

She chuckled, scratching behind the cat's ears. "Looks like we've got some digging to do."

Heather was still staring at the letter when a familiar knock sounded at the door.

She sighed, shaking her head. "You ever heard of texting before showing up?"

Flynn smirked as he stepped inside, his gaze immediately landing on the open folder on the table. "What's all this?"

Heather hesitated, then slid the documents toward him. "History."

Flynn's brow furrowed as he skimmed through the pages. "Is this what you took to the museum?"

She nodded. "Turns out my ancestor was a Jacobite courier.

And he might've hidden something people have searched for over two centuries."

Flynn let out a low whistle, setting the papers down. "You're telling me there's actual buried treasure on this property?"

Heather exhaled. "Maybe."

Flynn crossed his arms, looking at her with amusement. "So, let me get this straight. You were ready to sell this place and run back to the States, and now you're on a full-fledged treasure hunt?"

Heather groaned. "You make it sound ridiculous."

Flynn grinned. "Lass, that because it *is* completely ridiculous." He gestured around the room. "You were set on leaving and had the whole escape plan mapped out. Now, you're standing here with documents from a national museum and telling me you're about to uncover buried treasure."

Heather opened her mouth to protest, but Flynn held up a hand. "Not that I'm complaining. This is much more interesting than watching you pack up boxes."

She rolled her eyes. "So you're in?"

Flynn let out a slow, exaggerated sigh, then smirked. "Aye. But only because if you start digging without me, you'll end up buried in your own trench."

Heather hesitated before adding, "I don't need a babysitter, Flynn. I've got this."

Flynn chuckled. "So, you're planning to do all this investigating on your own?"

Heather opened her mouth to argue—of course, she was doing this alone. That was what she did. That was how she had always done things.

She had come here alone, sorting through her mother's

things alone. She had rebuilt her life without expecting anyone to step in.

And yet...

Flynn had been there, through every scraped knuckle, every late-night doubt, every moment when she thought she might walk away.

She swallowed, gripping the edge of the table. Maybe some things weren't meant to be done alone.

Flynn smirked. "This house tends to nearly collapse on you every time you so much as breathe near a weak floorboard."

Heather huffed. "Excuse you—it's structurally sound now, thank you very much."

Flynn leaned against the table, crossing his arms. "Fine. But if you think I'm letting you go digging around ancient ruins alone, you don't know me very well."

Heather gave him a look. "It's not a temple, it's a house."

Flynn grinned. "A house that might be sitting on lost Jacobite gold."

Heather sighed, but a smile tugged at her lips. "Alright, fine. But if you're going to help, you follow my lead."

Flynn pressed a hand to his chest. "Wouldn't dream of doing otherwise."

Heather rolled her eyes, but warmth spread through her chest.

Maybe, just maybe, she wasn't just uncovering history.

Perhaps she was writing a new one.

And she wasn't doing it alone.

Chapter 37

Heather stood at the edge of Glenoran's sprawling land, the setting sun casting the old stone walls in warm golds and deep blues. The wind carried the scent of damp earth and pine, rustling through the trees like a whisper of something long forgotten.

Flynn stood beside her, arms crossed, his gaze sweeping the land like he, too, could feel the weight of the past humming through the soil.

"So," he said, breaking the silence. "Where do we start?"

Heather exhaled, gripping the old missive in her hands—the last words of Harris Mackenzie, her ancestor, a Jacobite courier who once had a secret that might still be buried somewhere on this very land.

She'd spent so long trying to outrun Glenoran—her grief, her ghosts, the weight of inheritance. But now, she wasn't trapped anymore. She was choosing to stay.

For so long, she had seen this house as a burden, a weight she didn't ask for. But now, standing here with Flynn, the autumn wind tugging at her curls, she realized the truth. Her mother had left her a gift—not just a house, but a place to begin again. A place to heal.

Maybe it was never just about the history. Maybe it was always about finding her place inside it.

She turned to Flynn, a slow smile playing on her lips. "First, we get a proper map. And *no*, you're not allowed to ignore it because you 'have a good sense of direction.'"

Flynn chuckled. "And then?"

Heather let her gaze drift over the land—the rolling hills, the ancient trees, the stone ruins that had stood for centuries. She didn't know what they would find. Maybe nothing. Maybe everything. But for the first time in a long time, she wasn't afraid of what came next.

She met Flynn's eyes, the warmth of his presence steady beside her.

"And then," she said, slipping the parchment into her coat pocket, "we find the truth."

Flynn grinned, slinging an arm around her shoulders as they returned to the house. "Well, if nothing else," he said, voice light, "at least we won't be bored."

Heather laughed, shaking her head. "You have no idea what you've signed up for."

Flynn smirked. "I've got a feeling that's the fun of it."

Heather rolled her eyes, but before she could answer, Flynn reached down, threading his fingers through hers. His grip was steady, warm, and grounding.

She squeezed back, just once, before letting go.

As they walked back toward Glenoran, Byrdie trotted along at their heels, the house standing tall and proud in the fading light. Heather glanced up at the windows, catching the golden glow of the setting sun reflecting off the glass.

For a moment—just a breath—she could almost hear her mother's soft and warm voice whispering through the walls of the home she had left behind.

"Make it yours, love."

The words echoed like a promise. Heather exhaled, her grip tightening on the letter in her pocket.

Maybe, in a way, she already had.

Heather had once thought Glenoran was just a remnant of the past.

Now, she realized—it was her future.

And she was finally ready to embrace it.

Epilogue

Flynn

The first time Flynn set foot in Glenoran, it was just a job—stone and mortar, permits and plans. A structure to fix. Nothing more. Now, standing at the edge of the land, watching dusk spill across the heather-covered hills, he knew better.

Glenoran wasn't just a house.

It was hers—and somehow, it had become his, too.

The wind carried the scent of rain and earth, the crisp promise of an autumn storm rolling in from the west. Somewhere behind him, Heather was inside, curled up with Byrdie in one of the grand old chairs by the fire, a book in her lap. She'd said she was reading, but Flynn knew better. She was probably staring into the flames, lost in thought the way she so often was—half in the present, half tangled in the ghosts of her past.

And yet, she had chosen to stay.

He hadn't asked her to. He wouldn't have. It had to be her choice. But when she told him she wasn't leaving, that

Glenoran was where she belonged, something had settled inside him, quiet and sure—like a stone finally finding its place at the bottom of a river.

Flynn ran a hand over the rough stone of the outer wall, glancing to the old outbuildings beyond the garden. He'd have to take a look at them soon—Heather was convinced that the answer to the lost Jacobite gold was buried somewhere in Glenoran's past. And though he wasn't one for legends or ghosts, he'd follow her lead anywhere. If there was something to be found, he'd dig until they found it.

And if not? Well, he had already had everything he needed.

The sun dipped lower, casting Glenoran in dusk's soft, fading glow. With one last glance at the land stretching out before him, he turned back toward the house, toward the woman who had unknowingly changed everything.

Home, he realized, wasn't just a place.

It was a person.

And his had tumbling auburn curls and eyes the color of wild Scottish ferns.

Afterword

Historical Note

At its heart, *Of Heather and Thistle* is a story about finding where you belong—about uncovering truths buried beneath time and memory, and about love.

Not just romantic love, but the kind that ties us to a place, a legacy, and the people who help us become who we were always meant to be.

Scotland is a land of stories, and its landscapes endlessly inspire me—as do its people and its past. Though *Of Heather and Thistle* is a work of fiction, the Jacobite uprising, the Battle of Culloden, and the legends of lost treasures are very real.

Among the most defining moments in Scottish history was the Jacobite Rising of 1745, when Charles Edward Stuart—known to many as Bonnie Prince Charlie—led an ill-fated rebellion to restore the Stuart monarchy to the British throne.

It all ended in tragedy on April 16, 1746, at the Battle of Culloden. The Jacobite army, exhausted and ill-equipped, was brutally defeated by government forces led by the Duke of Cumberland.

In the aftermath, Highland culture was systematically dismantled. Tartan was banned. Clan leaders were stripped of power. Thousands of men were executed, imprisoned, or exiled. The way of life that had endured for centuries was nearly lost overnight.

And yet, stories remained.

For generations, rumors have persisted—of gold smuggled from France to fund the rebellion, of secret letters and hidden weapons buried deep in the Highlands. Whether truth or legend, these whispers remain part of Scotland's myth and mystery.

While *Of Heather and Thistle* is a novel, the echoes of history within it are very real. The resilience of the Scottish people, the enduring pull of home, and the stories passed down from one generation to the next continue to shape the country today.

If you're curious to learn more about the Jacobite era, Culloden, or Scotland's history, I encourage you to explore it. The past is never as far away as we think.

With gratitude for the stories that connect us all,

Erinn Maxwell

Bonus Chapter

Flynn's Introduction to Heather

The storm had been relentless the whole drive home.

Flynn gripped the steering wheel, watching the rain lash against the windshield as his truck rumbled down the long gravel road toward the cottage. The wipers barely kept up, the beams of his headlights swallowed by the sheets of water pouring from the sky.

By the time he reached the gate, the gravel had turned to mud, the wind howling through the valley. Through the streaked glass, he could just make out the hulking figure standing by the fence—unmoved by the storm, his thick, rust-colored coat drenched.

Angus.

Flynn huffed, shaking his head. "Ye daft beast, get inside somewhere," he muttered under his breath. But of course, the Highland cow only blinked at him through the rain, unbothered as ever. Never mind the perfectly good barn just yards away—Angus had apparently decided to weather the storm like some kind of battle-worn warhorse.

Flynn parked beside the cottage and made a run for it, ducking his head against the wind. The cold hit like a blade, slicing through his damp clothes as the rain soaked him instantly. By the time he reached the porch and shoved the key into the lock, his fingers were stiff with the chill.

Inside, the warmth was immediate, the familiar scent of woodsmoke and aged pine settling around him as he kicked the door shut behind him. The storm still rattled the cottage, the wind whistling through the eaves, but in here, at least, it was quiet.

He moved through the space on autopilot—tossing his soaked jacket over a chair, crouching by the hearth to get the fire going. The flames crackled to life, flickering against the stone walls, casting long shadows over the wooden beams. He let out a slow breath, rubbing a hand over his damp hair.

Long day. Cold night. And now, finally—some peace.

The thought barely settled before the knock came.

Sharp. Unexpected.

Flynn froze.

His brows pulled together as he turned toward the door.

Who the hell—?

No one showed up here unannounced. Not in weather like this.

Another knock, more insistent.

His muscles tensed on instinct, the quiet alertness of years on job sites shifting into place as he strode toward the door. He hesitated only a second before unlocking it and pulling it open.

And there she was.

The storm blurred behind her, but the rain had already done

its work, soaking through every inch of the stranger on his doorstep.

Her hair, bright red curls turned dark and wild with water, clung to her face and neck, stray tendrils dripping against her pale skin. And her eyes—emerald green, wide and uncertain— met his with a sharp jolt, something unspoken flickering between them.

Then, of course, there was the matter of what she was—or rather, wasn't—wearing.

Flynn's brain short-circuited.

The soaked white fabric clung to her in a way that left absolutely nothing to the imagination. Black lace peeked through—delicate and intricate, a sharp contrast to the soggy misery clinging to her.

His gaze barely flicked lower before he forced himself to look away so fast he nearly gave himself whiplash.

Gentleman, Duncan. Right now.

He cleared his throat, shifting his stance.

"Uh..." *Brilliant start, Flynn.* "Can I help ye?"

She blurted, "Hi." Her voice was breathless, the word rushed. "My car broke down. It's raining... obviously." She gestured vaguely to herself and the downpour.

Flynn blinked. *Aye.* He could see that.

She let out a half-hysterical huff, shaking her head. "And I stepped in cow poop. Twice. So if you could not judge me right now, and also not actually be a murderer, that'd be great."

The laugh caught him off guard. He barely managed to bite it back, grinning despite himself.

God help him, she was funny.

And entirely, devastatingly beautiful.

"Come in before ye catch yer death, lass," he said, stepping aside.

She didn't hesitate this time, darting past him into the warmth of the cottage. The moment she stopped, her eyes went wide with horror.

Flynn had already noticed. Between the rain, the mud, and, aye—the unmistakable earthy scent of Highland pasture—it was an...*aromatic* combination.

"Right, well... that's a smell."

The beautiful stranger closed her eyes tightly and balled her fists at her sides.

"I know! It's me... I'm the smell. I'm so sorry!"

Flynn bit the inside of his cheek to keep from laughing outright.

"Yer also drippin' all over my floor," he said instead, arms crossed in mock exasperation.

"Cool, cool. Add it to the list." She groaned louder, burying her face in her hands. "Oh, God. Do you have a towel—or a time machine, maybe?"

The exasperation in her voice sent another grin tugging at his mouth.

Flynn turned on his heel and opened an oak cabinet on the other side of the room, grabbing a small towel and tossing it to her.

She caught it, attempting—and failing—to pat herself dry. "Thank you."

"I'll put the kettle on," Flynn said, heading toward the kitchen. "Ye look like you could use some tea. Or maybe a dram."

"Tea would be great," she called out as he left her standing in the ever-growing puddle of dirty water in his living room.

He quickly poured her a cup of Yorkshire Tea, taking a wild

guess on her milk and sugar preferences.

When Flynn returned to the living room, he stifled a full-blown laugh when he saw her trying to cover her exposed, drenched figure behind the small hand towel he'd given her minutes before.

"Here," Flynn said, holding out the mug. "And, uh… if yer needin' somethin' to change into, I might have somethin' that'll fit."

His fingers brushed hers as he passed the steaming cup. The brief contact sent a pulse up his arm, and an unwelcome awareness curled through him.

"Thanks. Though, unless you happen to have a full set of dry clothes for a random stranger, I'll probably end up in, like, one of your t-shirts and—"

"—probably… uhh… safer? …than what ye've got on now," Flynn interrupted, his lips twitching with amusement.

The young woman groaned, burying her face once more in the now-soaked towel.

"This is officially the worst day of my life."

Flynn crossed his arms, amused. "Could've been worse."

She narrowed her eyes at him. "How?"

He pretended to think. "The cows could've chased ye."

The absolute horror that crossed her face nearly undid him. "That was an option?!"

Now outright laughing, Flynn shook his head. "Aye, since ye decided to traipse through the pasture. But dinnae fash, lass. Ye survived. And now ye've got a story to tell."

She sighed dramatically. "Yeah, a story about how I showed up half-naked and smelling like shit at some stranger's house," she muttered, taking a sip of tea. "Real inspirational."

"Och, at least I'm a friendly stranger," Flynn replied, winking at her this time.

She laughed.

And it was the most beautiful sound he had ever heard.

And just like that, something shifted.

Flynn didn't have a name for it—not yet.

But as he watched her, grinning despite everything, shaking out those wild curls, emerald eyes flickering with reluctant amusement— one look, one laugh... and that was it.

Flynn Duncan never stood a chance.

About the Author

Erinn Maxwell writes tender, atmospheric love stories rooted in legacy, longing, and the quiet kind of magic. When she isn't dreaming up sunshiny contractors and lost heirlooms, she's likely wandering old bookshops, sipping tea, or planning her next escape to the Scottish Highlands.

She believes in slow-burn romance, hidden history, and the kind of storytelling that stays with you like mist on the moor.

www.ingramcontent.com/pod-product-compliance
Lightning Source LLC
Chambersburg PA
CBHW040329020826
48978CB00013BC/973